These moments of my life

life

(Ces instants de ma vie)

Monique Dubois

Publication Data

These moments of my life (*Ces instants de ma vie*) © Monique Dubois, 2020

Book and cover design by Monique Dubois
ISBN: 978-1-940012-45-2

Other books by Monique Dubois
One day you will come back

Preface

This novel was inspired by the song, *Ces instants de ma vie, (These moments of my life)*, sung by Mireille Mathieu, released in 1983. Words and music by Didier Barbelivien, Pascal Auriet and Cyril Assous.

All characters in this work are fictional, any resemblance to people living or dead is purely coincidental. My apologies to the staff of the British High Commission in Nairobi for usurping their positions. My characters in the High Commission and the government of Kenya are purely fictional and in no way reflect upon actual government officials, staff or representatives who were in office at the time of this novel, or at any time before or since. The exceptions to this are references to actual heads of state, including Jomo Kenyatta and Idi Amin, who featured very much in this time. My apologies also to the warden of the Tsavo East National Park for usurping his position, the warden presented in this work is a fictional character.

Contents

I bury Ian

"We have entrusted Ian Hartley to God's mercy, and we now commit his body to the ground: earth to earth, ashes to ashes, dust to dust," the priest droned on while I looked down at the simple coffin deep in the hole dug in the black cotton soil and thought of my Ian, taken from me after such a short time by a stupid accident, if that is what it should be called. My mind wandered, and I wondered where the ashes to ashes came from, earth to earth I suppose I could understand as everything decomposed in time, dust to dust, that came from the Genesis part where God tells Adam that he came from dust and would return to dust, but ashes to ashes, where did that come from. Anyway, it was all very poetic, something that Ian was not, at least not in the literal sense, as he never wrote any poems or even simple doggerel, but he did write excellent prose, both in reports and letters. He had written to me in the past when we were separated by distance and his letters had been lyrical and a joy to read. He was a lovely man attuned to the environment where he lived, able to tell me about plants, animals and people, particularly in Africa, for African he was. He might have been white, but he was born and raised in Rhodesia, Zimbabwe as it is now known, and was a child of Africa in all but colour. He was fluent in MaShona, Ndebele, Swahili, and Portuguese, and understood cultural thinking, rites and rituals as well as most of the black Africans that he worked with. It was hard to focus on the reality that he was not coming back to me, that for the second time in my life, I had lost him, but, this time there would be no reconciliation, no happy reunion and no renewed romance, so my mind wandered, dealing in trivialities as they were the only things that seemed real at the moment.

I came back to the present and they were all looking at me, expecting me to throw in a handful of soil on top of the coffin. That I did, and that took me back to my daydreams and jumbled thoughts, thinking of Ian and his studies in anthropology. When we met he had been a graduate student pursuing his doctorate and had just returned from spending almost three years digging in the dirt looking for early human remains, so my throwing dirt on top of his coffin had meaning to me, one day in the far distant future, someone might dig up an ancient burial ground and speculate as to the identity and nature of the skeletal remains they might find and wonder what the person did and how they lived. It was not long after I met Ian, that I lost him for the first time. Ian had gone back to Tanzania to do some more studies, and through the intervention of an unpleasant third party and their interference with the mails, we had lost touch with each other for several years. I thought that I had lost him forever, until I went to Tanzania and investigated and heard the story about the third party. The upshot of that was that we found each other again and vowed never to lose communication again. So, was there a way to communicate from beyond the grave, or was this the end of an idyllic, but sadly all too short life together?

Maman, my mother, took my arm and brought me back again to the present.
"We should go Bébé," she said. "It's going to rain, so we should get back to the house."
"Thank you for coming, Maman," I said. "You've been a rock for me this week."
We walked back towards the car and I saw a familiar face, a face not from Nairobi. It was Tega, Tega from Arusha who had known Ian at the dig and who had provided me with the information that I needed to find Ian and renew our relationship. We talked in Swahili, because Tega's English was limited and Swahili was easier for him. He told me that he had heard of Ian's death, and had come to pay his respects. How he had heard, he never did say, but the African bush telegraph is amazing and information moves quickly and mysteriously. I invited Tega to the house and offered him shelter for the night, but he said no, he just wanted to see me and then go back to Arusha. I thanked him again for his kind words and watched him go, remembering how he had kept letters from myself and Ian that had been stolen by the third party, and how by saving them from the fire that he was supposed to have consigned them to, had saved the relationship between Ian and myself.

Maman took charge again and steered me to the car and she drove us back to our house, the house I would now have to vacate as it belonged to the British High Commission delegation in Nairobi, and Ian had been the accredited diplomat, not me. My brother James joined us there as did Charlize, his wife. Ian's sister, Irene, and her husband Tom were also there, my Dad was there with Felicity, Felicity the floozie to me, because of their relationship that had caused the breakup between Maman and Dad. The High Commissioner, Sir Walter Edgar, and others from the delegation were also there and a bevvy of other personages and friends and acquaintances of Ian and me, including a celebrity, Freya McIntosh, who under pen names of Mary Stuart and Edwina Campbell, was a well-known author who Ian and I had met when we stayed in her castle in Scotland. Maman and Portia, her partner, had organised the refreshments that were expected at funerals, but what I wanted was a stiff drink. I got myself a large brandy and steeled myself to mix and mingle and listen to the kind words, or were they just platitudes from people lost for words. We had to stay inside as the rain did come down, a typical tropical downpour, for about ten minutes, then the sun came out again briefly and the bougainvillea hedge glistened as the drops of water on the bracts and leaves reflected the sun. The clouds broke up more, leaving patches of blue and overcast, this may have been the last rains of the wet season, until late in the year when the small rains would come. I listened to all the kind words and nice things they said about Ian, but what were words, what I wanted was Ian back, after all, we had only been married a little under four years. We had got married in London in September of 1975, and we had come to Nairobi right after Christmas of that year so that Ian could take up his post as Third Secretary. So, count the years, a little bit of 1975, 1976, 1977, 1978 and now into 1979, so short a time, with so much in the way of new adventures and experiences, made particularly special because Ian was there to share it with me, adventures that were to be no more.

Hearing about the accident had been hard, I received a visit from the police, then from the High Commissioner telling me that the car in which Ian had been travelling had been hit side-on by a terrified Libyan, fleeing the war that was just ending between Uganda and Tanzania. The Tanzanians had moved after an incursion into their territory by Uganda in late 1978 and had pushed back the Ugandan army, plus its Libyan and PLO (Palestine Liberation Organization) allies, to the point that they were all running for cover, and it had meant the end of the Amin régime. What was still going on was the mopping up of resistance, and that looked as if it would take a few months yet. Ian had been close to the border with David, the new military attaché, to meet with an agent and had just been in the wrong place at the wrong time, which was small consolation to me. In the accident, Ian had been killed, as had the driver, but by some peculiar quirk of fate, probably because he was on the side of the car away from the oncoming lorry, David had survived. He had sustained injuries, but he would recover. I always knew that there was some risk to being in a diplomatic post, but Kenya was stable, there were no active wars between it or its neighbours, so the risk was minimal, just the mundane everyday things that could happen anywhere to anyone. It could just as easily have been me, crossing the road in London, hit by an errant tourist, unused to driving on the left, but it was not, it was Ian, gone forever, leaving a huge gaping hole in my life.

Finally, people started to say goodbye and take their leave, with the High Commissioner setting the example.

"Dr Hartley," he said, very formally, I think for the benefit of others present, because in private he was much less formal. "Please accept, again, my condolences and let us know if there is anything we may do for you."

"Thank you, Sir," I said. He had been kind and understanding after the accident and he had had one of the others in the High Commission work with me to arrange everything. Now, I think he was focused on replacing Ian earlier than had been planned and probably wondering how long it would be before I vacated the house, something that I quite understood. He had a mission to run and the business of the mission would continue, no matter what. After the Commissioner, Freya came to talk to me and to invite me to stay with her for as long as I liked. I told her that I had some things to sort out and some commitments to family, but that I would definitely go and spend some time with her.

Finally, all the guests left until only the family remained.

"How are you doing, Fi?" James asked.

"Terrible," I said. "I still can't believe that Ian's dead and gone. I know we just had the funeral and saw him planted in the ground, but, it just can't be him, he was so alive, we had so much we wanted to do, we were getting ready for his next posting to Italy, now all that has gone and I'm just left empty wondering what to do."

"Would you like to come and stay with us for a while?" he asked.

"I'll think about it," I said. "I've got some things to do here, then I'll be going back to London, I've got projects that need finishing for my clients. Then after that I've not made any plans, I've no idea what I'm going to do now, I may take a break from work and not take any new projects for a while. At this moment I just feel like shit, why did this have to happen?"

"Sorry, Fi," he said. "What can I do to help?"

"Nothing now," I said. "Perhaps tomorrow you can help me go through Ian's things."

"I'll do that," James promised.

"How are you, Irene?" I asked. For Irene, this was the third death in her family, first her, and Ian's, parents killed when their car hit a landmine in Zimbabwe, and now Ian, her younger brother, killed in another car-related event, just this time not as part of a war, at least not directly.

"I'm fine, Fi," she said. "If there's anything we can do, please don't wait or hesitate, just tell me."

"If you don't mind, Fi," James said. "Charlie and I are going to go back to the hotel, we'll be back here tomorrow morning around nine."

"Thanks, James," I said, grateful for his help. "How are you Charlize, do you still have morning sickness?"

"I seem to be fairly over that," she replied. "But I do have odd cravings for weird food."

"That's quite normal," Maman said. "When I was pregnant with Fiona, I had this craving for dark chocolate and pickles."

"Thank you for coming, Charlize," I said. "I can't imagine travelling is much fun for you at the moment."

"No man," she said. "I'm fine, I'm just dreading the day when my Ma decides that she has to come and help me through the last stages, she'll want to organise everything. I'll come tomorrow with James and make lunch while you sort out what you need to do."

"Thanks, Charlize," I said, grateful for her presence. Since she and James had married, I had grown to love her like a sister and enjoyed spending time at the vineyard they ran in France. Which was also convenient for me, as then I could go south and visit Maman and Portia at their villa on the Riviera.

5

"We'll go with you to the hotel," Irene said to James. "Fi, we're leaving Nairobi tomorrow, call me when you get back to London."

"I will," I promised. "Thank you both for coming."

"Fiona, if there's any help you need financially, please let me know," Dad said. "I'm so sorry for you, I know you loved Ian deeply and cannot begin to understand what it's like for you. We'll be on the same flight back to London with Irene and Tom, but if there is anything you need in London, please tell me."

"I will Dad," I promised. "Thank you both for coming."

"We'll say adieu for now then," he said. "But remember I'm only a phone call away."

After they had gone, it was just me, Maman and Portia. Portia did the sensible thing and poured us each a large glass of wine and handed them around.

"Ian," I said, raising my glass to them.

"Ian," they echoed. Now that everyone else had gone, we switched to French, which was the language Maman and I preferred to use when it was just the two of us, and Portia was equally comfortable in French or English, or for that matter Italian or Arabic, but relating everything in French and providing the translations would be tedious to say the least, so my tale will be in English.

"I miss him," I said miserably. "I miss his silly grin, I miss his touch, I miss his physical presence, I miss the sound of his voice, I miss the scent of his aftershave, if I could find the bloody Libyan who did this, I'd shoot the bastard."

"That may have already happened," Maman said. "I was talking to one of the Kenyan officials and he hinted that that had been done, as part of the chase that followed the accident."

"Well, serve the bugger right," I said. "What do I do now, Maman?"

"We sort things out here, then we go back to London and sort things out there while you finish up your projects, then come and stay with Portia and me for a week or two," she replied. "Will the people here pay to ship your belongings back to London?"

"They will," I confirmed. "And, there's a pittance of a pension from Ian, not that I need it, I make more than enough on my own, my biggest problem financially is keeping the bloody tax man away, we'll see if Thatcher's new government does something about the iniquitous rates that Callaghan and his gang put in. It's all so unfair, I was looking forward to Rome, I'd even started to teach Ian Italian, and I would have been closer to you both and to James and Charlize, now what?"

"I know it's a platitude, but things will get better in time, look how happy Tom and Irene are now, but I'm sure that when Tom's first wife died, he was devastated. Look back at the times you had with Ian and celebrate them," Maman said. "You should go to bed Bébé, you're falling off that chair."

"Yes, Maman," I said. I got up, a little shakily from the brandy and the wine, had a quick shower and collapsed into bed. Maman must have checked on me later, because in the morning, when I awoke my clothes were neatly folded, not strewn all over the floor as I had left them.

The aroma of coffee was strong, one of the nice things about Kenya was that coffee was grown and it was good. I got up and dressed and went through to the kitchen and found Maman and Portia already at the breakfast table.

"Good morning, Bébé," Maman said. "Coffee, breakfast?"

"Please," I said. "I shouldn't have had that wine last night, I feel rotten."

"Well, you'll recover," Maman promised. "James and Charlize will be here in about half an hour, so eat up."

"What is there?" I asked.

"Pawpaw, mango, croissants, smoked salmon," Portia replied. "What would you like?"

"I think a little of each, and I think I'll eat it outside," I said. Portia made a plate for me and brought it out to the terrace, then she and Maman brought coffee cups and fresh coffee. I sat and took in the sounds and sights of my back garden, soon not to be mine anymore.

"You know," I said. "I'm going to miss the jacaranda trees, the frangipani trees and the bougainvillaea. When we first came, I had no idea what they all were and Ian took me around the city one day for a botany tour. He also gave me a lesson in birds, so I know that that one is a pied crow, those are mousebirds and that one stalking across the bottom of the garden is a marabou stork. It was all part of our settling in here. It's one of those moments in your life that stays with you, it was all so new and different."

"That must have been fun," Portia said. "Tell us about it."

Settling in

"British Airways is pleased to announce the arrival of flight zero two five to Nairobi, the time here is eight o'clock in the morning, please take all your personal belongings with you and please take care descending the stairs," the stewardess said as we finally pulled up to a stop at the gate. I undid my seat belt and got up to collect my things. We had arrived, in Nairobi, early in the morning after our overnight flight from London, ready for a new adventure. We went to the door, while the stewardesses held back those from economy, there were some benefits for having first-class seats, and went down the stairs and walked across the tarmac under the brilliant clear sunny African sky, to the arrivals building. There was an immigration line for diplomats and such, so that is where we went.

"Welcome to Kenya," the officer said, stamping our passports and handing them back to us. An official stepped forward and greeted us and introduced himself as Daniel Bett from the Ministry of Foreign Affairs, he led us through to the luggage claim area.

"Is this your first time in Kenya?" he asked.

"No, I've been a few times on my way to Arusha to the digs at Olduvai," Ian said. "And my wife was here earlier this year on holiday."

"Well, we hope you will enjoy your time here," Daniel said. He waved over a porter and when our luggage arrived, he supervised its loading onto a trolley and then escorted us through customs.

"Thank you," Ian said. "I hope we will meet again soon."

"I hope so too, Mr Hartley, Dr Hartley, if I'm not mistaken this is your transport," he said, indicating a young man who came up to us.

"Thank you, Mr Bett," I said, then watched as he went back into the immigration area.

"They knew we were coming," Ian remarked.

"They knew. I'm sorry I was not at immigration to meet you," the young man said. "Trevor Whitmore, I'm from the High Commission. I'll drive you to the High Commission first to introduce you to everyone, then to your house.

We were driven into town and to the High Commission. There we were introduced to everyone and then whisked off to our house. As it turned out, going to the High Commission first made sense as it was between the airport and our house. The house was in a quiet neighbourhood in the Muthaiga area and was set back a little from the road, behind walls and a gate. Trevor helped us unload, handed us the keys to the house and the gate and then excused himself, telling us that some of the spouses would visit later in the day to see if we needed anything. I toured the house and was pleased to see that it was furnished, and that all we needed to do was add our own pieces, knickknacks and photographs to make it ours. There was a telephone on the hall table and when I picked up the handset, I heard a dial tone, so it obviously was connected. I wondered who paid the bill, whether we were expected to, or did the High Commission. I thought that I should ask about that as well as the electricity bill and if there was a water bill as well. I noted that the refrigerator had been stocked with basics, as had the pantry. Some kind person had been very thoughtful. There were also bed linens and towels set out on the beds, which meant that trips to the shops to buy essentials was not a priority. The house had a terrace at the back which opened out onto a lovely back garden, with some really nice trees.

"What are these trees?" I asked Ian.

"That one is a jacaranda, in October it will flower and you'll see masses of purple flowers, the one with the nice smelling yellow flowers is a frangipani, there's a lemon over there and an orange there, and the hedge with all the purple is bougainvillaea," he explained.

"I'm so glad we came," I said, taking his hand. "Are you happy?"

"Very," he said. "We're here, the sun is shining and there's lots to look forward to."

"Look, it's almost lunchtime, shall we find what there is in the house, or shall we see what we can find?" I asked.

"Let's explore a little and see what we can find," Ian suggested.

Our expedition was forestalled by the arrival of two ladies, who turned out to be spouses of two of the men we had met earlier at the High Commission. They pulled up to the gate and hooted. Ian went out to see who it was and opened the gate for them. I also went out to see who was calling on us.

"Hello," one said. "Welcome to Nairobi, I'm April and this is Valerie, we've been delegated to show you around and help you get settled."

"Thank you," I replied. "I'm Fiona and this is Ian. Should we thank you for stocking the pantry and the refrigerator?"

"That's quite all right," April said. "It's what we do for each other, we have to help each other where we can."

"Have you been here long?" I asked.

"I've been here three years and Val's been here six months," April replied.

"We were just thinking of going and finding some lunch," I said.

"We caught you in time then," Valerie said. "We've laid on a lunch with the other wives from the commission and hope you'll join us."

"We'd love to," I said.

"Jolly good," April said. "Shall we go?" Ian locked up the house and closed and locked the gate after we had pulled out of the drive.

We went to a house not too far distant from ours. It was a really nice house, larger than ours, more imposing and clearly for someone higher in the hierarchy than Ian. The house was set in beautiful grounds, well-manicured, with lawns and spectacular trees for shade. We were met at the gate by a uniformed security guard, who saluted April and let us in. April told us as we were pulling up to the front door, that this was the house of the High Commissioner, that explained the house and grounds, one has to keep up appearances.

"Welcome," a lady said, opening the door to us. "I'm Chloe, welcome to my home. Let me introduce you to the others. You've already met April and Valerie, so this is Geraldine, Janet and Heather, this is not all of us, there are quite a few more, but we didn't want to overwhelm you with people."

"I'm Fiona and this is Ian," I added. They all knew Ian's name as they had been advised of his arrival, but I could never quite work out if the advance notice briefing that included my name, had been shared with everyone.

"Did you have a nice flight?" Chloe asked.

"Thank you, yes," I said. "BA looked after us very nicely."

"Good," Chloe said. "We'd like to get to know you a little better, so, excuse us if we ask a lot of questions."

"That's quite all right," I assured her. Then the questioning started.

"Do you have any plans to work here?" Janet asked.

"Not really," I said. "I have a consulting business and most of my clients are UK-based, so I expect to be travelling back and forth for meetings."

"Oh, what do you do then?" Janet asked.

"I advise on economic matters," I explained. "I'm a mathematician and economist."

"Oh, so you have your degree in economics?" Geraldine asked.

"Well, I suppose so," I said. "I have a degree in mathematics and one in economics and doctorates in both."

"You have two PhDs?" Janet asked, looking at me in almost wide-eyed disbelief.

"I do," I said. "I got my first at Oxford and the second from LSE (London School of Economics)."

"Who are your clients?" Chloe asked.

"I've done work for a variety, from mining companies to vineyards to haute couture and budget fashions, and for the Treasury, I'm currently working on an interesting project looking at projected crop yields based on weather and other factors," I replied.

"She's actually hobnobbed with the Chancellor," Ian interjected. "Moves in circles that I may attain if I stay in the Service for forty years."

"You've done work in the fashion business, any designers that we might know?" Janet asked.

"My main client is Rachel Adams, but I've also done some for Vittoria Blengini," I replied.

"Did you get any of their designs?" Janet asked.

"A few," I said. "Rachel did my wedding clothes for me and Vittoria provided the lingerie items."

"Lucky you," Janet said. "I've always wanted a Rachel Adams dress."

"It's funny," I said. "The first dress I got from Rachel was not one of hers but an Yves Saint Laurent ensemble, I got it for a formal ball that Ian took me to."

"Very nice it was too," Ian said. "A little different from your typical ball gown, but very fetching all the same."

"Lucky you," Janet said. "I'd give anything for something by Saint Laurent, or from Rachel Adams for that matter."

"And you Ian?" April asked.

"I'm just a simple anthropologist," Ian grinning. "I spent a lot of time at Olduvai, digging up our ancestors."

"Are you from here?" Heather asked. "You've got an accent."

"Rhodesia, actually," Ian replied. "I was born and raised there and went to Oxford for my degree. That's where we met."

"What did you do in Rhodesia?" Chloe asked, probably for the benefit of the others, as I was sure that she had been fully briefed about both of us.

"My folks were tobacco farmers there who had gone out after the War, but they retained their British citizenship and passports," Ian replied. "I left to go to college and didn't have much to do with the tobacco farm."

"Are they still farming there with all the problems at the moment?" Chloe asked.

"No, they were killed in a landmine explosion," Ian said. "So, my sister and I sold the farm."

"I'm so sorry," Chloe said.

"Have you been to Africa before?" Janet asked me.

"I passed through Nairobi earlier this year on a safari with my mother, we went to Serengeti and the Ngorongoro Crater on our way to Arusha, then we stopped here again on our way to Johannesburg," I explained.

"Do you speak any Swahili?" Geraldine asked.

"I'm learning," I said. "Ian's been teaching me."

"You can speak it quite well then?" Chloe asked of Ian.

"I spent almost three years at Olduvai and probably used English five to ten per cent of the time, the rest was with the local staff, and was all Swahili," he replied.

"Is this your first posting?" Valerie asked.

"It is," Ian confirmed. "I was in London at the East Africa desk for a couple of years, and you?"

"First for me," Valerie said.

"Second for me," April added. "First was in Canberra."

"Third for me," Geraldine said. "First was Bangkok, then Brasilia."

"Third for me," Janet said. "First Karachi, then Mexico City."

"Second for me," Heather said. "First to Havana."

"Sixth for me," Chloe said. "First Ottawa, then Rabat, then Beijing, then Lima, then Helsinki."

"I feel so provincial," I said. "I've only ever lived in England."

"You'll move around soon enough," Chloe said. "It has its ups and downs, it's nice to have all the new experiences, but it's hard to make lifelong friends and we never really live anywhere long enough to consider it home. Do you have any children?"

"None," I said. "We've no plans for a family at the moment."

"But you must have travelled a bit," Janet said.

"I've been to France a lot, my mother lives there, I've been to Italy, Spain, Germany, Belgium, Luxembourg, Switzerland, apart from my trip here which was here, Tanzania and South Africa," I said.

"If your mother lives in France, do you speak French?" Chloe asked.

"I grew up speaking French and English," I said. "Maman is French, so she made sure we learned to speak the language fluently."

"Any other languages?" Chloe asked.

"Italian, Mandarin and now I'm learning Swahili," I replied.

"Ian?" Chloe asked.

"Portuguese, MaShona, Ndebele, Swahili and I'm learning French," he replied. "Fiona's hiding her light under a bushel, she actually speaks pretty good Swahili and she also has some Tahitian."

"Tahitian?" Heather asked.

"My grandmother is Tahitian," I explained. "My mother speaks the language quite well and I learned some when I spent holidays with my grandparents in Paris."

Chloe tried me out on some simple Mandarin and I was able to satisfy her that I did indeed speak the language, in fact, my impression was that her Mandarin was fairly rudimentary, while mine had been honed by deep philosophical discussions with my Chinese Tai Chi instructor at Oxford. I noted that she did not try any Swahili with Ian, or French with me, and nobody wanted to touch Tahitian. The situation was quite funny, all these ladies sitting around giving us the third degree, it felt almost like an interview with a panel of interviewers, and us as the luckless interviewees. Ian excelled in these situations, but I did not. My basic personality is very introverted and while I can happily converse on mathematics or economics with the best, my social skills were never the best, so general conversation and chitchat were never my strong suits. Geraldine did exchange a few phrases with Ian in Portuguese and even I could tell the accent and word differences between the Portuguese that Ian learned from the workers from Mozambique and the Brazilian Portuguese that Geraldine spoke, but for all the differences they could still communicate fairly well.

"Why don't we have lunch?" Chloe suggested. "We can still talk while we eat. I've set things up on the terrace, we'll put Ian and Fiona in the middle there, where we can all have a chance to talk to them."

"You're Fiona Barclay, aren't you?" Heather asked. "I finally put it together, I was sure that I knew you from somewhere. I remember you from Oxford, you had just come up and I was in my final year. I remember a lecture I went to where you took apart the prof and disproved just about everything he said, I was trying to finish my degree and my tutor had recommended the prof and his lecture on the economics of estate management, when I told my tutor about the lecture he laughed and said that he had expected it and that it was time that someone challenged the prof. I think for him it was really gratifying that it was someone who had just come up and who the prof never expected to be challenged by."

"I did that?" I laughed. "I didn't have much in the way of tact when I was fifteen, I made quite a few, if not real enemies, then close to. I've learned since then, particularly when I started dealing with people outside the college and being paid by them."

"You went up to Oxford when you were fifteen?" Janet asked.

"I was blessed with a flair for mathematics," I replied. "And lucky in my parents who encouraged me and helped me along the way."

"But you've managed other things too, like speaking five, no six, languages, don't tell me that you sing and dance as well?" Janet asked.

"Sing, no, that is something you don't want to hear," I said. "I did have my mother teach me the basics of ballroom dancing, so can shuffle around the floor when I have to."

"She does rather put me in the shade," Ian added. "But we manage and I've been teaching her about the other things in life."

"I'll bet you have," Chloe said, dryly.

It struck me watching the interactions between the women that there was a pecking order among the spouses. Clearly, the High Commissioner's wife, Chloe, would be at the top, but after that, it seemed to me that it was Geraldine, April, Janet, Heather and at the bottom, Valerie, the newcomer. I suppose that socially Valerie would now move up and I would be at the bottom as the newest member of the cabal. But, perhaps not, if things were based on status, then Ian was number four in the delegation, so that might put me between April and

14

the others, but if things were based on personality, or length of time on station, I would probably stay at the bottom, overshadowed by the forceful personalities of the others.

Over lunch, which I have to say was excellent, conversation ranged from which market to buy fruit and vegetables and where to get one's hair cut, to local leave taken in the national parks of Kenya, to the problems of boarding schools. The latter was of academic interest to me, but no real practical interest. I did have a lively interest in markets and where to buy food and Valerie promised to take me around the town the next day and show me her favourite places. I got a little more of an insight into the others, Chloe was a graduate of Edinburgh University, with a degree in French, she had met her husband, Walter, now Sir Walter Edgar, there and had trailed around after him ever since. She delighted in the social aspects of the life and was happy to host parties, receptions and other gatherings, I do not think she really approved of us newcomers having our own careers and being so independent. Geraldine came from old money. She was one of those women who would be the "girl in pearls", or as it was often less charitably styled, "dog of the week", featured as the frontispiece of Country Life Magazine, she came from a titled family that had large country estates in England and Scotland. She had met her husband, Vincent, also of a titled family, at Ascot when she had won an appreciable sum on a horse, and he had lost an almost similar amount. April was a graduate of Bedford College and had a degree in English, which she told me did nothing for her employment chances, except that she did have a part-time job teaching English at one of the high schools in town. She was an organiser, and it was thanks to her that our refrigerator and pantry were stocked and that there were bed linens. Apparently, she had a move-out, move-in, checklist and had taken over the management of the transitions. She was likely to leave in about a year when her husband, Henry, was reassigned. Janet was a botanist, now employed by the Ministry of Agriculture in Nairobi. She had taken her degree at Bristol University and had met her husband, Peter, there. Heather, as I now knew, had studied at Oxford and had one of those portmanteau degrees, philosophy, politics and economics. She had met her husband, Edward, in Harrods when they had literally bumped into one another. Now she volunteered at a local school, doing some teaching. Valerie, the youngest and newest one of the group, had been in the Metropolitan Police in Chelsea and had met Trevor, her husband, when she had booked him for speeding. Quite how that had led to romance and marriage was a longer tale, that eventually we would get to hear. Valerie was not working, but she told us that she was actively looking for something, perhaps in the tourism business.

"So how did you two meet?" Chloe asked.

"It was at a college dinner," I said. "I finally had broken down and gone to one and Ian was there. We talked afterwards, met for coffee the next day, and things progressed from there."

"That's it?" Janet asked.

"Well, there were a couple of complications along the way," Ian laughed. "But, we managed, and here we are."

"What was the most romantic thing you did?" Janet asked. I looked at Ian and he shrugged his shoulders and grinned at me.

"I think when we went for a boat ride and a picnic and he fell asleep on me," I said. "I just fell for him then."

"He fell asleep on your date?" Janet laughed.

"Well, in my defence, I'd been working long hours and after a couple of glasses of wine, some lunch and a nice sunny day, I just faded out. Fi let me sleep for a couple of hours before waking me and telling me that we needed to get back to return the boat to its owners," Ian explained.

"And you Ian, what's your version of the most romantic thing you did?" Heather asked.

"I think when she kissed me after she'd shot a possible in a college shooting event," he said.

"You shoot?" Geraldine asked.

"We both do," Ian said. "There's always an argument as to who's the better shot, but I have to admit that Fi's hard to beat."

"What do you shoot?" Geraldine asked.

"Small bore pistol and rifle, large bore pistol and rifle and shotgun," Ian enumerated.

"Have you ever been on any grouse or pheasant shoots?" Geraldine asked.

"No," he said. "Most of my bird hunting was in Rhodesia when I was growing up and was for geese, guinea fowl, francolins and the like."

"I did go on a couple of pheasant shoots when we lived in Henley," I added.

16

"We have an active rifle club here in Nairobi," Geraldine said. "If you like I'll take you one day."

"That would be fun," I said.

"Do you ride?" Geraldine asked.

"I have," I said. "I've done a bit of jumping as well, but not for a few years now."

"And you Ian?" she asked.

"I did some when I was younger," Ian said. "But, I preferred motorbikes and cars, a little less temperamental, not a lot, but a little."

"You're right, horses can be temperamental," Geraldine laughed.

"You said you lived in Henley?" April said. "I know Henley pretty well, where?"

"We had an estate on the Oxford Road," I replied.

"Not that big one with the massive walls and gates?" she asked.

"That was it," I said. "My grandfather had picked it up during the Depression and my dad inherited it. It was sold off a couple of years ago to an American company who wanted a place to conduct training and education."

"I'll bet it fetched a pretty penny," April said.

"It did," I confirmed. "I was sorry to see it go; I'd spent a wonderful childhood there."

"Where were you living before you came out here?" Valerie asked.

"I have a flat in London," I said. "I've kept it as a base for those times I go back on business. Ian moved in with me after we got married, I think my flat was nicer than his place in Notting Hill."

"The FCO (Foreign and Commonwealth Office) doesn't pay a lot," Ian laughed. "Even with London weighting I couldn't afford much, and Fi's place is really nice."

Conversation lagged a little as we all concentrated more on eating than talking, until Chloe asked if we wanted coffee. Coffee all around was requested so she went off to the kitchen to make some.

"It's Kenya coffee," she called out. "I hope you're fine with that?"

"Fine," I replied. I had tried Kenya coffee a few times and liked it. It had a nice flavour, rich and satisfying.

"Trevor has been working with the Kenya Coffee Board to improve exports to Britain," Valerie said. "It's a good export for Kenya and they get good prices for green beans. Luckily for us, enough stays here to be roasted and sold locally, but I wonder if the best grades aren't all sold on the export market."

"Trevor is the commercial attaché at the High Commission," Ian told me. "He's also been delegated to help us get settled in, setting up bank accounts, buying a car if we want, all the little things we have to do."

"What do we do about driving licences?" I asked.

"It's simple," Valerie said. "Take your British licence to the licensing office and they'll issue you with a Kenyan one, you'll need a picture, and a few shillings, but, it's straightforward, it took me no time at all, I'll take you there if you like."

"Thank you," I said. "I've heard a lot about house servants, do any of you have them?"

"We do," Chloe confirmed. "We have to be careful because of who we are and the possible risks, but we have a network and if you want to find someone, we can help."

"Thank you," I said. "I'll see how I manage."

"Do you need to buy a car?" Chloe asked.

"I would like one," Ian said. "I was looking for something simple and utilitarian like a Beetle."

"I know of a 65 Beetle that's for sale," Heather said. "If you like I could introduce you to the owner."

"Thanks, that would be super," Ian said.

"Fiona, you don't want a car?" Chloe asked.

"I bought one before we came, it's on its way and should be here any day," I explained. "I will need guidance with the registration and such."

"I can help you with that," Valerie promised. "I met this Kenyan chap at the police college at Hendon and he's here in Nairobi and he helps me with all that kind of stuff."

"Thank you," I said, grateful that I did not have to navigate officialdom by myself. "If you'll excuse us, the overnight flight is catching up on me and I'll fall asleep at the table here before long."

"Of course," April said. "Let me run you back to your house quickly."

"Before you go, we're having a New Year's Eve party here, and you'll be expected," Chloe added

"Do we need to bring anything?" I asked.

"Not at all, it's an official function, there'll be others here not from the High Commission," Chloe said. "We'll see on Wednesday at about seven?"

"We'll be here," I promised.

April dropped us off at our house and went back to join the others, probably to analyse and dissect us, Ian thought. Apparently, Trevor was collecting us in the morning to set up bank accounts and get a post office box. We also had insurance to think about, for our belongings and for the cars. The house was owned by the High Commission, so they carried the policy on it. I looked around the house again and thought that perhaps we should unpack our bags and put things away. There were three bedrooms, and we picked one as ours. There was a built-in wardrobe that had plenty of shelves, more than enough for all our clothes. We unpacked quickly then decided it was time to have a bath and go to bed and see if we could catch up on our lost sleep from the night before. I ran a bath and I was pleased to see that the bath was big enough for two. Ian and I got in and mutual washing quickly turned to other things.

We finally made it into bed and just dropped off to sleep, the flight the night before had been comfortable enough, but not conducive to sleep, sleeping in a seat is not quite the same as sleeping lying down. Gone were the days of the Pan Am China Clipper and the sleeping berths, but it would be hard to imagine what that would cost today, so perhaps that was as well, otherwise air travel would be out of the reach of most people. When I awoke, Ian was already up and I could hear him in the kitchen, banging around with pots and pans. I grabbed some clothes and went to see what he was doing.
"Morning my love," he said. "Can I get you tea, coffee, omelette?"
"I think tea this morning and an omelette would be super," I replied. "What were you doing making all that noise?"
"I dropped a frying pan, then a saucepan," he said. "Sorry to wake you, I was going to bring you breakfast in bed."
"What about breakfast on the terrace?" I suggested.
"Great idea," he said. "Make yourself comfortable, tea will be ready in a minute and then I'll start on breakfast." He was as good as his word and tea followed quickly, then he came out with two plates and rather good-looking cheese and tomato omelettes.
"When is Trevor supposed to be here?" I asked.

"Chloe said around ten," Ian replied. "I thought that this morning we could open bank accounts, get a post office box and perhaps do some more shopping. April did us well with the basics, but I wouldn't mind a beer or two in the house and some wine."

"Good idea," I agreed. "What's your impression of the ladies we met yesterday?"

"I like them," he said. "Chloe's a bit of a grande dame, but then she's the High Commissioner's wife, so I suppose it's logical, I get the sense that when she talks about the High Commissioner it's more along the lines of the "High Commissioner", in case you don't understand who he is and therefore who she is, I can see less respectful people creating a song rather like the Gilbert and Sullivan Lord High Executioner, but with words suited to Lord High Commissioner. I think Janet could be bossy, as could April. Geraldine's got enough money that it really doesn't matter to her what others think and Heather and Valerie are finding their way in the world."

"And where do I fit in?" I asked.

"That we'll have to see," he thought. "I doubt that any of them know really how to relate to you, you've clearly had a good education, you can speak a few languages, you have friends in different industries, you can ride and shoot, so you can probably relate to all of them in different ways. The main thing you will face is them being intimated by you, you're so bright that you pick up things really quickly and then you have a hard time understanding why others can't see what to you is obvious."

"I've been trying to work on that," I said. "I know that in the past I was really intolerant of others' shortcomings, but I'm trying to be nice."

"You don't have to try too hard," he laughed. "These women have all seen a lot, so don't think that you have to tread gently around them, be polite, but don't think you have to be nice just to be nice."

"I'll try," I promised. "Perhaps I should put on better clothes if we're going to the bank and the post office?"

"That might be a good idea," he agreed. "They're pretty conservative here."

"How many other embassies are there here?" I asked.

"I believe that at last count, there are fifty embassies and commissions here in Nairobi and there are another seven ambassadors who cover Kenya but actually live in Addis and another five who live in Dar," he said. "It's one of the sought-after postings, the climate is good, it's relatively peaceful, and the people themselves are nice."

"Who has the largest number of people in their legations?" I asked.

"We have a total of thirty-two and the Yanks have twenty-four," he replied. "We, us and the Yanks are the largest contingents."

"Will we meet any of the other legation people?" I asked.

"Probably," he thought. "It's a small enough place and the embassy staffs tend to know each other, so we could well get to know some others."

Trevor arrived at the appointed hour and took us into town and to the bank. We both had opted for Barclays, because we both had accounts with Barclays in England and I did all my business banking with them as well. The process of opening accounts was simple enough, we opened a joint account for general living and another account that I could use for business purposes. Then we tackled the Post Office. Trevor knew his way around the bureaucracy, and helped us get a box in record time. That done, we decided that there was time enough to get driving licences, and we had taken the precaution of getting photographs of the right size before we came, so we visited the office and walked out a few minutes later with Kenyan Driving Licences. Now the last task was insurance. We decided that that could wait until we had cars to insure. Mine had just arrived at the docks in Mombasa and would be on its way to Nairobi after the New Year, and Ian had yet to buy his. Heather had promised to contact the owner of the 65 Beetle, so all Ian needed for that was money. We decided to move some money from our account in London to Nairobi, so that could be taken care of.

Trevor then suggested lunch, which sounded like a splendid idea, so he took us to the Norfolk Hotel. I had stayed there earlier in the year when I had stopped briefly on my way to Johannesburg.

"Trevor," I started. "Apart from coffee, what else does Kenya export?"

"Tea, pyrethrum, flowers and soda ash," he replied. "Tea is growing as is the flower sector, and soda ash is a steady business, there are some smaller amounts of fluorite, talc and gold, but they don't contribute that much to the economy, we don't have the mineral base that Zambia does, so it's a relatively minor part of the economy."

"And imports?" I asked.

"All sorts of things," he said. "Oil, cars, machinery of all kinds, consumer goods, luxury goods, even some foodstuff. Imports outweigh exports, and probably always will. In the sixties, Mboya and Kibaki said that Kenya should avoid Western Capitalism and Eastern Communism, and instead focus on African Socialism. I'm not sure that that's working out as well as they would have liked, governments love to spend money and that has to come from somewhere and if people aren't earning obvious wages and companies are not showing profits, it's hard to tax things enough to pay for everything. Still, there's opportunity in knock down car kits and local assembly, other agricultural products and maybe they'll even find their own version of the Williamson Diamond Mines one day. Not, likely, I grant you, but that doesn't stop people from looking. Then, there's always tourism, Kenya does have nice parks, maybe not as good as those in Tanzania, but the Kenyans are better set up to use what they have. The Tanzanians haven't grasped yet that you need to encourage people to come and spend their money, so are not as organised as they should be, so Tanzania tends to be an adjunct to a Kenya trip. Still, it does generate revenue for both countries and brings in hard currency."

"It sounds as if you're busy," I commented.

"There's always something," he said. "Look, can I run you back to your house, I need to get back to the office?"

"No, no need," Ian said. "We'll either take a taxi back, or we'll walk back."

"You're sure?" Trevor asked.

"Sure, really, Trevor, we'll be fine," Ian assured him. "I've been to Nairobi a few times before and can find my way around."

"As long as you're sure, I'll see you both at the party?" Trevor asked.

"We'll be there," I promised.

After Trevor had left, we ordered more coffee, took it out on the terrace and just sat and took in the sights and sounds of the Norfolk. Ian started to point out birds to me, he pointed to a bird that looked to me like a crow, but it was black and white. He said that it was a pied crow, quite common in Central and Southern Africa, a bird that was very intelligent and that was made a pet of at times and taught to talk. Certainly, the one we were looking at seemed intelligent enough, it came quite close to us and looked at us speculatively, as if it were sizing us up for something, as though he were debating if we were good for an offering of food. Perhaps that was applying too much in the way of human characteristics, but I could have easily believed it of it. In time he stalked away, very sure of himself, or perhaps herself, as far as I could tell there was no obvious way to discern the sex, so am presuming here.

I looked about more and in the bushes were a number of small birds that were behaving almost like mice, they were scrambling about the bushes, not very elegantly, clambering around or hopping between branches and crashing into them, chirping to one another as they did. They had little crests, almost like topknots, and long tails.
"What are those?" I asked Ian.
"Mousebirds, particularly speckled mousebirds," he replied. "They're odd in that their outer toes on either side are reversible, the technical term for it is *semi-pamprodactyl*, it's a trait of mousebirds in general and some swifts, they bring the outer toe forward if they have to hang onto something, like a cliff, or upside down under a branch."
"How do you know so much about birds?" I asked him.
"I was interested growing up, so studied them and got to know most of them and their calls," he said.
"Anything else I should know about them?" I asked.
"Probably not," he laughed. "There are several species of mousebird, but the most common here is the speckled, it's adapted to urban living quite well."

"And that bird stalking across the grass there, that's a marabou stork, isn't it?" I asked.
"It is," he confirmed. "They're often found in the company of vultures around carcasses, you see the lack of feathers on the face and neck, that's common among the scavenger birds that clean up. They also eat fish, frogs, snakes and rats."
"So, handy to have around?" I asked.
"I think so," he said. "I quite like marabous, most people think they're ugly, but they serve a purpose. So, what's that bird circling above us?"
"Some kind of bird of prey," I said, looking at its shape as it soared above us, only very rarely flapping its wings.
"Right," he confirmed. "It's a black kite, you'll see quite a few of them above the city, riding the thermals, looking for insects, mice and voles, perhaps even something dead and for a change in diet, palm-nut husks."
"So, something of an omnivore," I said.

23

"A little," he agreed. "But, the major part of its diet is insects and small mammals."

"It's nice here, isn't it?" I asked him.

"It is," he agreed. "You won't have to worry about snow and ice here, if you want snow you'll have to go to the high mountains. Are you finished with your coffee?"

"I am, shall we go?" I suggested.

We discovered that Trevor had paid for lunch, so there was no account to settle, so we started out on our walk home. Ian estimated that the walk be a little over two miles, so not too arduous. As we walked, he pointed out trees to me. I was surprised at the number and variety of trees and shrubs that had been planted in the city. There were jacarandas, that I remembered from our own house, Kei apples, wattle trees, hibiscus hedges, palm trees, acacia trees, Nandi Flame trees and even a poinciana, that Ian told me was unusual because normally they were found at lower altitudes where it was warmer. The colours were amazing, from the reds of the flowers of the hibiscus hedges, to the purples of the bougainvillea bracts and the greens of the leaves. I was also intrigued by the leaves of some of the trees. These were not the simple leaves of the beeches and oaks I was familiar with, these were compound leaves, with tiny leaflets arranged on stalks sprouting out from a central stalk. Ian showed me how even they differed, depending on whether or not the end of the compound leaf was a single stalk of leaflets, or two stalks of leaflets. He also pointed out to me that the bright purple of the bougainvillaea was not from the flowers, which were little white blossoms, but the bracts that surrounded the flowers, something I would not have guessed. The time went by quickly and although it took us nearly three hours to meander our way home, it did not seem so long and it was a fascinating walk.

"Which tree was the Flame Tree of Thika?" I asked Ian, recalling the book by Elspeth Huxley that I had read before coming to Kenya.

"She wasn't very clear in her book," Ian said. "But, I had a first edition and the cover was of a flower from the Nandi Flame, taxonomic, *spathodea campanulata*. We saw one or two today on our way back."

"Did you study anthropology or botany?" I asked jokingly.

"I was interested in the bush when I grew up, so first identified all the trees and birds around the house and in the towns, then I looked at all the native species in the bush. A lot of the ornamentals in the towns are introduced, like the jacaranda, which is basically a Brazilian tree, but which does do well here in Africa and is pretty when it flowers."

"I feel so ignorant," I said. "I feel like I know nothing about the place we have come to, nothing about its people, its plants and animals, even about its geology."

"You will learn," he promised. "You will learn quicker than I did, you have an innate curiosity and you're a lot smarter than I am."

"I don't feel smarter," I complained.

"Don't confuse knowledge with intelligence," he said. "Knowledge can be gleaned, intelligence is innate, intelligence is recognising things that can be learned or worked out. So many people think that someone is intelligent just because they can cite facts and figures, but that is only what they have learned. Intelligence is deeper than that, and you are far more intelligent than me."

"But," I protested.

"No buts," he said. "It's true, why else do you think I married you, apart from your good looks?"

"You think I'm pretty?" I asked.

"No," he said. "You're not pretty, you're beautiful!"

"I love you too," I said. "Here we are back home, tea?"

"Tea would be nice," he said.

Ian opened the gate and let us in, then closed and locked it behind us, then we went into the house and I made for the kitchen to make tea. We took our tea outside on the terrace, just enjoying the sights of our garden and the sounds of the birds, and beyond that the background noise of the city as people went about their business. I shall never forget that afternoon, it was one of those moments in one's life when everything seemed just right. I was with the man I adored, we had just spent a fascinating afternoon walking about the city, with me learning about trees and birds and now we were sitting in a beautiful garden, surrounded by exotic trees, just taking in the afternoon air, with no cares in the world, just being together. I took his hand and held it, wanting the moment to last as long as possible.

The New Year's Eve party was an event. When we arrived, it was clear that this was going to be quite an occasion, the guard at the gate asked to see an invitation and Ian had to explain that he was part of the High Commission staff. The guard consulted a list and marked us off and then requested that we park to the side of the house on the grass, leaving the better parking for more honoured guests. Chloe saw us arrive and waved us in, giving us instructions for the evening. We were to mix and mingle, not engage in political discussions, talk up the relationship between HMG (Her Majesty's Government) and Kenya and generally be charming. That was easy for Ian, but was going to be a tall order for me, being charming was not one of my best attributes, but I would try. Guests, real guests, started to arrive and we would get a nod from Chloe as to which she wanted paid attention. I was saddled with the head of the university who asked me about my academics and once he learned that I had not one, but two doctorates, wanted to monopolise my time for the evening. He was interested in my researches and I gave him a general idea of my client base and the kinds of economic models I created for them. I was finally rescued by Ian who whisked me away to meet others. I met business people, lawyers, doctors and even an anthropologist or two. There was one who irritated me, he was an old-time colonial who called me dear lady and was about as condescending as one could be. I may have been just off the plane, but I was not a complete idiot. He seemed to think that he was God's gift to women and I was happy to excuse myself as I saw people who I recognised. When I had come out to Kenya earlier in the year, we had engaged a guide, Henry Conway and his wife Julia, and they were there. I found Ian and took him over to meet them.

"Henry, Julia, this is Ian," I said, introducing him, and for the benefit of Ian I explained who they were.

"Ah, so you're the one she was pining after," Julia said.

"She was pining?" Ian asked, jokingly.

"Pining isn't the word for it," Julia said. "She was hopeless."

"Fiona, hopeless, that's hard to believe," Ian said.

"So, what brings you here?" Henry asked.

"Ian is Third Secretary at the High Commission," I told them.

"So, a diplomat in the making," Henry said. "Have you been here long?"

"A couple of days," Ian replied. "We're just getting settled in."

"Well, as we promised Fiona, if you ever want to take a safari, just let us know and we'll see what we can arrange," Henry said.

"How are your mother and Portia?" Julia asked.

"They're fine," I said. "They're enjoying life on the Riviera. How's business with you?"

"It could be better," Henry said. "The UK economy is playing hell with our bookings, but we'll manage."

"Fiona told us that you were at the digs at Olduvai?" Julia asked.

"I spent almost three years there," Ian confirmed. "It was fascinating, a little hot and dusty at times, but I did get to learn Swahili while I was there."

"And you found Fiona," Henry commented.

"She found me," Ian said. "I thought I had lost her for good, but she found me and we've been making up for lost time ever since."

"Do you know any of these people?" I asked Julia.

"Most," she said. "Is there anyone you'd like to meet?"

"Who grows coffee?" I asked. Julia looked around the room and then said, "Robert Blake, over there, he has one of the larger plantations near Thika. Would you like to meet him?"

"I would," I said. "Ian?" I asked.

"No, go ahead," he said. "I'll just stay and chat to Henry for a while."

Julia led the way and we threaded our way through the people until we came to Robert Blake. He was chatting to another man, so we hovered and waited until a suitable lull in the conversation, then Julia introduced me.

"Robert, this is Fiona Hartley, she's just moved here as part of the Brit High Commission," she said.

"Nice to meet you," he said. "I didn't know we were getting a woman diplomat."

"I'm not," I said. "My husband, Ian, is the diplomat, I'm just the hanger-on."

"So, have you plans to work while you're here?" he asked.

"Probably not here, but I will work," I said. "I have a consulting practice in economics that is doing well, so will continue that."

"What will you do, fly to London every once in a while?" he asked.

"Probably at least once a month," I said.

"So, what kind of economics?" he asked.

"I've done work for the mining industry, for fashion, for the Treasury, and I currently have a project in agriculture," I explained.

"Oh, what kind of ag?" he asked.

"Tobacco and other crops," I replied. "And I have another project in wine, my sister-in-law and brother run a vineyard in France."

"No coffee?" he asked.

"Not yet," I said. "I've never seen a coffee plantation; would it be possible to come out one day and visit?"

"Of course," he said. "Why not next Wednesday, we're picking at the moment, and we've got a lot drying, so you'll see most of the process."

"How do you sell your coffee?" I asked.

"I take my green beans to the coffee exchange," he said.

"Do you roast any of it yourself?" I asked.

"I do some," he said. "I can show you that as well, Julia, you haven't been out in a while, are you off on a trip soon, or do you want to come out as well?"

"That's sounds like fun," Julia said. "We'll be there, Fiona, give me your address and I'll pick you up at seven on Wednesday next and we'll drive out to Thika."

"Thank you," I said. That was an outing I was looking forward to. I had wondered how different a coffee plantation was to a vineyard. Another man came to claim Robert's attention, so we said our goodbyes and went back to join Ian and Henry.

"Julia and I are going on a coffee tour next Wednesday," I told them.

"That sounds interesting," Ian said. "Let me see what we're doing and perhaps I'll join you."

"You should if you could," Henry said. "It's worth the visit and Robert does serve good coffee."

"Bring some older clothes, shoes you don't mind getting dirty, and a hat," Julia said. "We might spend some time in the fields, something I've never done, for as many times as I've been out there."

"So, what were you two plotting?" I asked Ian.

"Oh, we were just comparing notes about trips to the bush," Henry said. "We've a lot in common."

"You grew up in Rhodesia, right?" Julia asked.

"I did," Ian confirmed. "My folks grew tobacco there, but they were victims of the bush war, so my sister and I sold the farm and went our own ways."

"So, now it's Kenya," Julia said. "What's it like to work at the High Commission?"

"I'll tell you when I've been there a while," Ian laughed. "We're just off the plane, so new here, just settling in."

"If you need anything, just let us know," Julia offered. "Now, looking at the clock, I think we should get drinks and be ready for 1976."

The countdown to the New Year started, and I stood by Ian to give him a kiss to start the New Year properly. At the stroke of midnight, 1976 began and I kissed Ian, happy to be with him. This was the first New Year we had actually spent together. After we started dating, Ian had gone back to Tanzania just after Christmas, and then we had lost touch. We got back together and then got married and now, here we were in Kenya on our first New Year together. What a memorable New Year!

Ian's things

"It must have been very exciting then when everything was so new and different," Portia said as I came back to the present.

"It was," I confirmed. "I think made so special because of Ian. So, when can we expect James and Charlize?"

"If I'm not mistaken, I think that's them at the gate now," Maman said. "I'll go and let them in."

"Thank you, Maman," I said, grateful for her presence since Ian's death, but also reminded that she had not come alone and that I should acknowledge that. "Portia, I haven't thanked you for coming."

"I'm glad we were able to come," she replied. "Brigitte and I would not have let you go through this alone."

"So, Fi, how are you today?" James asked, when he and Charlize were ushered out onto the terrace by Maman.

"I'm doing better today, thanks James," I told him. "I was just reliving the first day or so we lived here and how different everything was back then, everything was new, strange and exotic, it was so exciting."

"I know what you mean," he said. "When I first went to France to live with Charlie, it was all different, now it's hard to imagine what it was like before I went. So, what do you want me to do today?"

"If you could help me go through Ian's clothes and things," I said. "I have no need of them, and I've already put aside the things I really want to keep, things that will remind me of the good times we had. Charlize, how are you this morning?"

"*Ag*, man, I'm fine," she replied. "I'm beginning to gain weight now; see I'm beginning to show now."

"You are," I agreed. "Is everything going well?"

"The doctor tells me that everything is normal and Brigitte and my Ma have both compared notes with me and tell me that all is as it should be," Charlize replied. "Now, you go and do what you have to do and we'll take care of lunch."

"What are you going to do with these clothes, Fi?" James asked.

"I've made arrangements with a local church," I told him. "They'll take whatever I can give them, clothes, shoes, the lot."

"Okay," James said. "We fold everything up and put it in these boxes?"

"That's the idea," I told him. "Make sure you go through all the pockets first; I don't want to throw anything out that I shouldn't."

"So, will you come and spend some time with us?" James asked as he folded up shirts and stacked them in a box.

"I'm going to finish up the projects I have first, then I'm going to spend a week or two with Maman and Portia, after that, maybe I'll come and see you and Charlize," I told him.

"We'd be happy if you did," he said. "I worry about you Fi."

"Thanks, James, but you needn't worry, I'm doing fine," I told him.

"So you say," he said. "But, I can't imagine what I'd do if I lost Charlie, it would take me a while just to accept that she was gone."

"I know," I said. "I still wake up expecting Ian to walk back in the door and tell me he's home."

"What do you want me to do about these hats?" James asked, indicating the bush hat and others that Ian had had.

"Put them with the other clothes," I told him. "Unfortunately, his hats won't fit me, so unless you want one and they fit you, we'll send them off with the other stuff. Just make sure that he hadn't tucked anything inside first. How are things at the vineyard?"

"We're doing well," James replied. "You know when you first came out here that we were looking at buying more property, well that has turned out very well. We had to add more vats and more bottling capacity. We've also had good grape yields, which has really made a difference. We're looking at the States now, trying to decide where it might be smart to buy. I know most people think of California, but I'm wondering if we might not do better in New Mexico. Land and vineyards are cheaper there, and the climate is still good for growing grapes."

"New Mexico?" I asked.

"New Mexico," he confirmed. "Biggish state, climate varies from the high mountains in the north to the deserts in the south and west. Not too many people, and many of them are in and around Albuquerque and there's also some in Las Cruces, as I said, big state, few people, my kind of place."

"What about water?" I asked.

"There are some rivers," he said. "The Rio Grande, the Pecos, the Canadian and some smaller ones, rainfall is pretty sparse, but they do get some, snow in the north in the mountains, you could even go skiing there."

31

"I'd like to try that one day," I mused. "Ian and I had talked about taking lessons when we moved to Italy. We thought we could take some time in the Italian Alps and learn to ski."

"Well, if you came and stayed with us, we could take you to the French Alps and you could learn there," James suggested.

"That might be fun," I thought. We were interrupted by Maman who called to us the coffee was ready and that we should take a break.

"Coffee, éclairs?" Charlize asked when we joined them on the terrace.

"Where did you get the éclairs?" I asked.

"She just made them," Maman said. "Try one, then you'll want another."

"These are good," I said, between mouthfuls. "I'll balloon up if I eat too many of these."

"How's it going?" Charlize asked.

"It's going," I said. "It's mainly just packing up clothes and such, then at some point I'll pack up all my things and have them shipped back to London. Fortunately, there isn't much in the way of furniture that was ours, so there's little in the way of bulky items to pack up."

"When are you leaving?" Charlize asked.

"On Friday," I said. "I'll be sorry to go, but have to leave this house as I'm sure the High Commission will want to move in someone else fairly soon."

"I'm sorry we can't stay longer," Charlize said. "But we have to get back to the vineyards and winemaking."

"Of course," I told her. "Maman and Portia are staying with me until I leave, then after I've finished up my current projects I'll take a break and after a week or two with them on the Riviera, I thought I might come and spend some time with you, would that be okay?"

"No man, that'll be only *lekker*" Charlize said, using the peculiar South African expression and sentence structure that actually said that it was fine with them.

"Fi was telling us what it was like when they first arrived and the impact it made on her," Maman commented.

"Was there anything else in that first few months that you remember?" James asked.

"There was the visit I made to the coffee plantation," I thought. "I got really grubby that day picking coffee."

"Tell us about that," Charlize asked. "I've wondered how coffee was picked and processed, is it like grapes?"

"Not really," I said. "With grapes, you pick the whole bunch, with coffee you pick only the ripe red cherries, which makes it perhaps even more labour intensive than running a vineyard. It was an interesting day, one of those days that stays with you as a memory. I met a coffee grower at the first New Year's party we went to here, so I took him up on his invitation and Julia and I went out there."

"Who's Julia?" Charlize asked.

"She and her husband run the safari company that Maman, Portia and I used when we took our trip before your wedding," I explained. "She was at the party as well and introduced me to the coffee grower."

"So, tell us about the visit," Charlize said.

Coffee

Julia was at our gate at seven as she had promised. She had a Land Rover that was similar to mine, a short wheelbase, with a petrol engine, but hers was a light green, whereas mine was a cream colour, called Limestone by Land Rover. She had on a pair of khaki trousers and a green shirt and light boots, so I felt that I had dressed appropriately in my trousers and shirt. I grabbed my bag with spare older clothes that I did not mind getting dirty, and said goodbye to Ian, who had been unable to join us, some pressing matter had come up, and he had been delegated to resolve it. Julia told him that we would be back late that afternoon. We drove out of Nairobi to Thika, only about twenty-five miles, so just about forty minutes. I thought about the time I had read *The Flame Trees of Thika*, and how it had taken them a couple of days to do the same distance, but also how the country had changed, this was no longer wild wide open spaces, now there were villages all along the route that had cropped up over time and the road was now surfaced, not the dusty path that Elspeth Huxley described in her book. Julia pointed things out to me as we went, places, companies, people, birds, animals, I was amazed at what she saw just driving along, she would point out birds to me that I had to really look to just see, let alone try and identify what species of bird it actually was. She saw animals and told me what they were, when all I saw was perhaps a backside or a tail disappearing into the long grass. She pointed out women to me who were married and unmarried and tried to explain to me the traditions that governed dress and ornamentation that were the clues to marital status. She pointed out the charcoal vendors who were selling charcoal that would be used in houses for cooking. It was a fascinating ride, and I just hoped that I would remember just a fraction of what Julia told me.

When we came into the Thika area, we passed the main town then we crossed a river and Julia told me that that was the Chania, then she pointed out the Blue Post Hotel, again mentioned in *The Flame Trees of Thika*, then we crossed another river, this one the Thika, then we turned off the road to the right.

"Is that coffee?" I asked, pointing to the rows and rows of spiky-looking green plants, thinking that it did not look much like coffee to me.

"No, those are pineapples," Julia said. "Right after independence the business got started, Del Monte from the US came in to help. Coffee is a back a little on the other side of the main road."

"Can we stop and take a look?" I asked.

"Of course," Julia said. "That's why I came this far, I wanted you to see this." We pulled off to the side of the road and both got out. Julia showed me a pineapple growing out of one of the spiky plants I had seen. "They're grown from the tops of other pineapples, or from suckers," she explained. "So, when this lot goes to the cannery, then the tops are taken and come back here to be replanted."

"Nothing from seed?" I asked.

"As far as I know, no," Julia said. "I've only ever heard of pineapples being grown from the tops, which begs the question of how the first one grew. Don't ask me too many details, like how long they take to grow and yields per acre and all that sort of thing, I just don't know the answers."

"I wonder how you know if these pineapples are ripe?" I asked.

"I'm not sure," Julia said. "If you would like, I'm sure we could arrange a visit and get all the details."

"That sounds interesting," I said. "Would you do that; do you know anyone at the pineapple place?"

"I know the farm manager," Julia said. "I'll call him and see what we can arrange."

"Thank you," I said. Then I poked and prodded at the spiky plants with the pineapples growing out of their tops. They were obviously too small to be picked just yet, but they were pineapples and on closer inspection even smelled like pineapples. It was fascinating, my experience with pineapples until then had been limited to opening tins of either chunks or rings, I had never actually seen a whole pineapple.

My curiosity satisfied, at least for the moment, we went back to the car and turned around and went back past the Blue Post Hotel, then past the town of Thika, then we turned off to the right and went up into some low hills.

"That's coffee," she said, pointing to rows of dark green-leafed bushes.

"Does coffee grow from seed?" I asked.

"It does," she confirmed. "Take a coffee bean, that hasn't been dried and roasted, and plant it and it will grow."

"What's all the red?" I asked.

"Those are coffee cherries," she said. "When they're red, they're ripe and ready to be picked. We're almost there, I'll let Robert give the full story."

We pulled up to a stone house and Robert, who had been sitting on the veranda drinking, tea or coffee, I never found out which, saw us and waved.

"Morning," he said. "How's things today?"

"We just took a short detour to look at pineapples," Julia said.

"Ah," he said. "Well, come, what can I get you? Tea, coffee, beer?"

"Coffee would be nice, thank you," I said.

"Coffee," Julia echoed. Robert disappeared into the house for a few minutes and came back with a French Press and two cups, plus milk and sugar. "Where's Ann?" Julia asked.

"She's looking into some land around the Nyanza area," he said. "We might buy some and expand our operation. Thika's going to be difficult as Nairobi creeps out this way and there's pressure to switch ag land to land for housing."

"How many acres do you have here?" I asked.

"We've 700 acres, with 500 under active coffee," he said.

"I picked up odd things from my sister-in-law, so how many trees per acre?" I asked.

"About 650," he replied.

"And what does that yield?" I asked.

"About 2,500 lbs per acre, at about 85 cents US per pound for green beans," Robert replied. "We've worked hard to get a good yielding variety that doesn't deplete the soils too quickly. Yields per acre vary a lot from less than 400 lbs to our 2,500 lbs."

"How much is yield affected by pests, diseases and parasites?" I asked.

"That can vary," he said. "Depending on farming practices and whether or not you're willing to use chemicals to control some things."

"What kind of pests are there?" I asked.

"Well, there's coffee berry borer, white coffee stem borer, green scale, coffee root mealybugs and your ever-present nematodes," he replied. "Any one of those could be just a nuisance or a disaster, as I said, some control can be gained with good farming practices."

"Are there diseases as well?" I asked.

"Plenty," he laughed. "You could have leaf rust, coffee berry disease and a few others."

"I suppose it's like any other farming," I commented. "There's always issues with rain, soils, bugs, diseases and even theft."

"True, but, as yet, we don't have too many enterprising souls coming and picking coffee for themselves," he said. "I gather in some places where they pick and leave to be collected there have been thefts of the cherries."

"How do you market the beans?" I asked.

"There is a coffee exchange in town and buyers come for grades of coffee, which is essentially a size sort, the more uniform the size, the more uniform the roast," he explained. "And there is an overall agreement, the International Coffee Agreement that was set up in 1961, and modified in 1968, that sets quotas by country. Compared to Brazil, we're still small, Brazil probably produces a third of the world's coffee."

"Who buys our coffee?' I asked.

"Nestlé, Lyons and General Foods, Maxwell House, from the UK and some others from France," he replied.

"85 cents a pound doesn't seem like much," I said. "Given the retail prices of the roasted coffee, who makes all the margin?"

"The rest of the supply chain," Robert said. "Nestlé and the rest, plus the grocery stores, that's where most of the margin is."

"For coffee shops here, do you supply directly?" I asked.

"We're working on that," Robert said. "But coffee is really a luxury item, it's not a diet staple, so the demand is driven by disposable income, after all the necessities have been met. We don't have that large a population with that much disposable income, so the home market will be small. The big markets are Western Europe and the US. How's the coffee?"

"It's really good," I said.

"That was roasted yesterday and ground this morning, so it hasn't had time to go stale," Robert said.

"So, there is a shelf life?" I asked.

"Coffee will never really spoil," Robert said. "But it will lose flavour over time and the longer between roasting and drinking, the more the flavour loss will be until it goes really flat. Are you ready for the tour?"

"That would be super," I said. "Can I change clothes first?"

"Of course," Robert said. "Let me show you where."

Julia and I both changed into our other older clothes and went back out to see Robert ready with an old Jeep. Where he acquired it, I have no idea, it looked as if it were a World War II relic. We hopped in and he drove off, first to a nursery where there were seedlings sprouting. The nursery was covered with a cloth that let light in, but reduced the intensity of the sun. He told us that when the seedlings got to be a suitable size, then they would be exposed to more sun, until they were ready to be planted out in the fields. I wondered how much had changed from the days when the Grants planted coffee in the Flame Trees of Thika, perhaps nothing, perhaps a lot. From the nursery, we went to an actual field of yielding coffee bushes. We got out of the Jeep and went to inspect the trees.

"The coffee bushes flower, and then about seven months later, the cherries are ripe enough to pick," Robert explained.

"So, the coffee bean is inside the cherry?" I asked.

"Two beans in each cherry," he said. "On rare occasions, there is only one, but generally two, see here." He picked a cherry and squeezed it so that the two beans popped out, which he dropped into my hand.

"They don't look much like coffee, or smell like coffee," I thought as I rolled them around in my hand thinking that they were sticky and slimy.

"No, that all comes later," he said. "First we ferment to get rid of this slimy stuff, the mucilage, then we dry, then we de-hull to get rid of the parchment and the silverskin that surrounds the bean, then we sell the green beans, or roast them."

"Whoever discovered coffee?" I asked, touching a bean to my tongue to see what it tasted like. "Looking at these cherries, even the beans just out of the cherry, it doesn't taste like coffee, in fact, it's quite sweet."

"There's a lot of sugars in the pulp," Robert agreed. "That's what makes it ferment so well. Probably be able to make wine out of the pulp. No, the flavour and smell comes after roasting when all the chemical changes occur. As to who discovered coffee as a drink, well, that's a story to be told over lunch."

"Who does your picking?" I asked.

"We hire local labour," he said. "They get paid by the tin of cherries picked, see over there, there are some pickers." We walked over to some other trees and there were four women all busy picking away. They had small baskets hung from their necks that they dropped the cherries into, and I saw one go to a bin and drop the contents of her basket into it.

"What happens when those big bins are full?" I asked.

"We take them to our processing station, then they're emptied out onto a sort tray, then any leaves and obviously unripe cherries are picked out, then the tray is emptied into a weigh bin, so we know what we're getting. We pay the ladies four shillings a tin," he explained. "Shall we go and see?" He drove us to the processing area and we saw some of the tins being emptied, then the sort process, then the weighing. The cherries were then poured into a hopper and run through a machine, out of which came beans down one chute and all the pulp down another chute. Then he showed us the beans being dumped into the large vats and water being added.

"In there, the beans will ferment for a while," Robert said. "There are some that float and our policy is to skim those off as unsuitable. I think if you just wanted to make weight with green beans, you might leave them, but I think it affects the quality of the coffee after roasting."

"After fermenting, then drying?" I asked.

"Indeed," he confirmed. He walked us to the drying racks, where there were tons of light brown beans sitting in the sun. He picked up one and crunched it between his fingers. "Not dry enough yet," he said. "The parchment comes off a lot easier if the moisture content is ten to twelve per cent, right now I'd put this at about twenty per cent, but we have more scientific methods for checking, so will check again later."

"Then after drying?" I asked.

"De-hulling," he replied. "We've a machine that removes the parchment and polishes up the green beans. The chaff goes as a mulch. The process is very similar to rice de-hulling, we also de-hull for other farms and for smallholders, on a toll rate."

"Then that's it, the green beans can be sold?" I asked.

"They can be," he confirmed. "But we all like to grade the beans first and the sell price is by grade, so we have a series of sizing sieves over here. The more uniform the size of beans, the more uniform the roast, too many small beans and they essentially turn to carbon before the bigger beans are ready, and they spoil the flavour of the brewed coffee." I looked on as bins of green coffee beans were emptied over the sieves and shaken, falling through to the different size racks, then they were bagged up into hessian bags with the name of the farm printed on them.

"So, how many pounds of cherries can a picker pick in a day?" I asked.

"That depends," Robert said. "A really good picker can pick up to 200 lbs in a day, but for most, it's between 100 and 150. Would you like to give it a try?"

"May I?" I asked.

"Of course," he said. "Julia?"

"Well, if Fiona will, then I will," she replied. Robert took us back to the field where we had seen the ladies picking. He talked to one of them, then he looked at me and asked how my Swahili was. I owned to some knowledge. So, he told me that Martha would show us what to do and help if we needed and that our pickings should be divided among the bins of the four ladies.

"I'll be back at noon to collect you," he said. "Got your hat and some water? Good, 'til noon then."

After he had driven off, Martha took us in hand and explained and showed us what to pick and how to pick. She then assigned us each some trees and watched as we started. Obviously, we passed muster, because she went back to her own picking. I quickly saw why Julia had suggested old clothes, it was quite a messy business. The cherries were sticky and quite soon my hands were blackening from the dust that they picked up that stuck to the sugars. The growth was interesting, there were clusters of beans along the branches, occasionally almost filling the whole branch. Sometimes there would be some yellow and green along the branch as well as the red, so we left those for a later picking. The other women were chattering away, but not in Swahili, I think they were speaking Kikuyu. I had picked up a word or two, but was completely lost when they spoke. So, I just concentrated on picking and soon had to go and empty my basket into one of the bins. Then, I was back for more. The time passed pleasantly, it was warm out, but not overly hot, there was a cool breeze and there was some shade from larger trees that were dotted about the field. I picked, emptied my basket, picked, emptied my basket, with a seemingly never-ending supply of red cherries, it seemed that just when I thought I had cleared a tree, there were more cherries to be picked. I heard birds in the trees, I heard monkeys chattering somewhere, and watched as a whole covey of francolins went scurrying through the trees. I had no idea which species of francolin they were, for that I would need Ian. I saw shadows on the ground and looked up to see black kites circling around, looking for something to eat and wondered if francolins were on the menu. I even saw a snake, a cobra, I say I saw, that was only true because the other pickers had seen it and were throwing rocks at it to get it to move away. I suppose the indignity of being pelted with rocks caused it to rethink its path, because it slithered away quickly down the slope and away from the coffee bushes.

"So, ready for lunch," I heard Robert say. I had been so engrossed in my task that I had not even heard him drive up. I thanked Martha for the opportunity and the instruction. She told me that I was welcome back to pick at any time, I think mainly because my labour was free and she and the others benefitted. Julia was also happy to take a break. She had had trees some distance from me, so conversation had been difficult.

"That was fun," I said. "But, I'm not sure that I would want it as a full-time occupation. It's a bit messy, isn't it?"

"Now you know why I suggested old clothes," Julia said. "If we'd gone picking pineapples, I would have suggested even more clothes, a suit of armour if you had it, as you saw, those things are spiky, really spiky."

"Are those ladies day labour or employed on a regular basis?" I asked Robert.

"They're day labour, they do the picking to make some extra money, some planters have full-time employees that do all the picking, but there are plusses and minuses to that, mainly because picking, although year round to some extent, tends to have peaks and valleys and it's hard to staff correctly, you either land up with too few or too many. So, I presume you'd like to wash your hands and change before we go to lunch?"

"Yes, please," I said, a sentiment echoed by Julia. We drove back to the house, and washed our hands and faces and changed back into our other clothes and rejoined Robert on the terrace.

"So, ready for lunch?" he asked.

"Absolutely," Julia said for both of us. We got back into his ancient Jeep and started back towards the main road.

"We'll go the Blue Posts," Robert said. "So, how do you two meet?"

"I went on a safari with my mother last year," I explained. "And Henry and Julia were our guides."

"I hope they did a good job," Robert said.

"They did," I confirmed. "Now that I'm here, I plan to take some more trips, when Ian gets time off."

"Well, there's plenty to see, where did you go before?" Robert asked.

"We started in Maasai Mara, then went across the border to Serengeti then to the Ngorongoro crater, and finished up in Arusha," I replied. "Then we went on to South Africa, my brother was getting married there."

"Why there?" Robert asked.

"His wife is from the Cape," I explained. "Her family has the Cillie winery, and she and James run the French vineyard they bought. And you, what brought you to Kenya?"

"My parents moved here just before World War I, and started the coffee farm, they were just part of the whole group that came out then to make their fortunes," Robert explained. "I was born here and took over the farm when my folks retired, they live in a small cottage on the farm."

"Fiona is a mathematics whiz," Julia said. "She's hired by people to create economic models for them."

"Really?" Robert said. "Could you do one for me?"

"I would need to check my agreement with one of my clients to see that there is no conflict," I temporised. "But, as far as I know, they don't have a coffee operation, so probably. What would you be looking for, some idea of how price elasticity would affect your earnings?"

"I think a basic model of the farm with some way to put in new investments and then see what the bottom line would look like," he said.

"That would be simple enough," I said. "I would need to understand fully the various process steps, from planting to harvesting, then access to data to test the model when it's done. I've done a similar one for my sister-in-law that models their vineyard."

"I'll give you a flow chart that describes the process after harvesting," he promised. "And, I have another that goes from seed to tree in the field."

"That should be enough," I thought. "I would need to know things like the number of pounds a picker might be expected to pick in a day and when the harvest occurs. Then prices of things like tins, baskets, pulping machines, fermenting tanks, sorting sieves, drying racks and de-hulling machines, and baggers and the breakpoints at which you would add capacity, just from a volume point of view, not necessarily an economic point of view."

"I think I have all that from previous purchases," he said. "I'll put it all together and let you have it when you return."

"You don't happen to have a UK entity?" I asked.

"I do, as it happens," he said. "We've an outlet in the UK that we use for odd things, why?"

"It would be easier for me to contract with the UK entity, then I don't have to worry about work permits in Kenya," I explained.

"We can do that," he said. "Do you have a form of contract?"

"I do," I said. "I'll bring you one that I used for the vineyard and you can have your solicitor take a look at it. Perhaps I should look at getting a work permit for Kenya to make life easier."

"Useful," he agreed.

"I know who you need to talk to," Julia said. "And, if you do get one, then maybe we'll talk to you about a model for the safari business."

"I doubt that she's cheap," Robert commented.

"I'm not," I laughed. "But I'll see what I can do."

We arrived at the Blue Posts, which I imagined was much changed from the days when Elspeth Huxley was there as a child. Over lunch we went back to the story of coffee, how it got discovered and how it spread throughout the Middle East, then Europe.

"So, where did coffee come from?" I asked.

"There are a couple of stories," Robert said. "The romantic one is that a 9th-century Ethiopian goat herder, by the name of Kaldi, noticed that when his goats ate the red berries of a particular bush, they were really active. He then took some of the berries to a local monastery, where a monk was less than impressed and threw the berries into a fire. Well, obviously they roasted and other monks came to investigate the aroma. They are supposed to have raked the beans from the ashes and ground them up and dissolved them in water, making coffee."

"You say romantic?" I asked.

"Well, I see a couple of problems with the story," Robert said. "First, un-roasted coffee doesn't have the free caffeine, which is what is supposed to have affected the goats, and why would you rake beans from the ashes, then grind them up and why add water?"

"So, what's the other story?" I asked.

"Well, another story is that a Moroccan Sufi was travelling in Ethiopia and he saw birds that had unusual activity. He tried the berries and got the same effect. A more likely story is that the disciple of the same Sufi was once exiled to a cave and got hungry. He tried some red berries, but the insides weren't very nice, so he tried roasting them to improve the flavour. But then they were too hard, so he boiled them to soften them, which essentially gave him coffee," Robert said.

"So, it's pretty certain that coffee came from Ethiopia?" I asked.

"Almost certainly," Robert confirmed. "Some of the tribes there used it to stave off hunger when on hunting trips. Coffee was imported from Ethiopia to Yemen, particularly the town of Mocha, which was the centre of the trade. Then it spread throughout the Middle East, by the 15th century. From the Middle East, it went to Italy in the 16th century and the rest of Europe and the Dutch shipped coffee plants to the East Indies and the Americas."

"How did coffee come to Kenya?" I asked.

"There's a couple of stories there as well," he said. "The generally accepted one is that coffee trees were introduced by French missionaries, either from Brazil or Réunion in 1893. Others claim that the Brits brought it in in 1900, take your pick."

"So, coffee has been around a while," I said.

"It has indeed, it's probably the most traded commodity after oil," Robert said.

"I noticed that in some of the fields, there were large trees that were not coffee bushes?" I said.

"The coffee seems to do better with shade, and not so much direct sun," Robert said. "And why not keep as many of the old trees as possible?"

"You pick by hand, can you do it mechanically?" I asked.

"There are plusses and minuses to the idea," Robert said. "On the one hand, it would be less labour intensive, on the other hand, you'd get a real mix of cherries, ripe and unripe, so there would be sorting to do after the fact, or the finished product would probably not be as good."

"Are there different varieties of coffee, like there are with grapes?" I asked.

"There are a couple of main varieties, *robusta* and *arabica*, and then there are varietals of those," Robert explained.

"Which is better?" I asked.

"Probably *arabica* has the overall better taste, but *robusta* has better yields, so for instant coffee, *robusta* is good enough, for fancy coffee houses serving coffee by the cup from French Presses and such, *arabica* may be the better choice," he elaborated. "I've got mainly *robusta* and most of my sales go to Nestlé and Lyons. I'm thinking that longer term I should switch to *arabica* as people begin to patronise coffee shops more."

"If Nestlé and Maxwell House are big buyers, how do they make instant coffee?" I asked.

"Essentially you brew coffee, but it's done in a series of columns, each with ground coffee in them, some at above atmospheric pressure and with high temperatures, until the liquid contains about 20 - 30% solids. Then it's filtered and then dried, either by spray drying or freeze drying, then you add back the aromatics, so that it smells nice when you make the coffee," he explained.

"Who invented the process?" I asked.

"The first instant coffee was developed by a Brit in 1771," Robert said. "Then there were American developments in the 1800's, then in 1901 a Japanese chap used the same process that he used for making instant tea, to make instant coffee. In 1906 another Brit in Guatemala, with the unlikely name of George Washington, developed the first commercially successful product that he called Red E Coffee, that was pretty much the standard from 1910 to 1940. Meanwhile, the Brazilians were working on things and Nestlé was as well, and Nestlé came out with Nescafé in 1938. Maxwell House came out with freeze-dried coffee in 1963, and it's become really popular."

"So, quite a long history of development," I thought. "I wonder what instant tea is like?"

"Never tried it," Robert said. "Not even sure where you'd get it, if you even can."

"What's your outlook for this harvest?" I asked.

"This year looks about average," he said. "But next year we're probably going to see higher prices for our beans."

"Why?" I asked. "Has demand gone up that much?"

"It's gone up a little," he said. "But the big factor is frost, frost in Brazil last August that has really played havoc with their output, so the supply will be down and we're looking to see where the world prices will go."

"So, coffee truly is a worldwide commodity?" I asked.

"Truly," he said. "Supplies come from Brazil and other South American countries, Indonesia and our neighbours, demand is from Europe and the US for the most part."

"You'll be happy to get higher prices, I'm sure," I commented.

"I will," he agreed. "But I'm concerned that some idiot in parliament will decide that we're going to get a windfall and add some extra tax. What they don't understand is that this will be a short-term blip, in the longer run, Brazil will still drive prices and when their harvest comes right again, price pressure will be on again and prices will go down. The other issue that some will face is madly expanding based on higher prices, which are not sustainable, so some will take on debt from expenditures on capital goods that they won't be able to manage, others will madly plant more trees, and then in the longer term, our prices may see an effect from that as the supply goes up, depending on whether or not the demand stays the same or goes up."

"So, all the more reason for an economic model of the enterprise," I suggested.

"Right," he agreed. "But one that will look out into the future and let me play with projected prices to see what might happen."

"I'll talk to my client and see what I can do," I promised.

"Thanks," he said. "That really would be helpful."

"This has been fascinating," I said. "I got a taste for the complexities of the ag business when my sister-in-law took me around her vineyard and explained about grape varietals, yields, soils and all that. Thank you for the time, the tour and the information, I really do appreciate it."

"Any time," he said. "It's always good to talk to someone who has an interest."

"I'm glad I came out," Julia said. "You know I've been out to your place many times, but I never got into the details of what you do, like Fiona has done. I can blather on to tourists now about coffee when we're sitting around the campfire talking."

"I can't see you blathering on," I said to Julia.

"Oh, I could," she said. "Should we be getting back to Nairobi?"

"I suppose so," I said.

"We'll run back to the house and you can get your car," Robert said. "Thanks for coming out, it was nice to have visitors."

We drove back to the farm and retrieved our car and each left with a pound bag of roasted coffee beans. On the way home, Julia was chatting about her experiences picking the coffee, which I gathered was a first

46

time for her. We both agreed, that while it was nice to do for part of the morning, we would rather not have to rely on it as a sole source of income. It was messy and tiring work and the pickers earned every penny they got. Julia dropped me at my house and the first thing I did was take a shower and clean off all the dust and dirt from the fields. When Ian came home, I was ready to tell him my story.

"So, how was your day?" he asked.

"Fascinating," I told him. "We got a tour of the farm; we saw all the process steps and we picked coffee."

"You picked coffee?" he asked.

"I picked coffee," I confirmed. "I got well and truly messy doing it, but it was fun, fun I think because it was only the morning and I don't have to rely on it as my source of income."

"So, how much did you pick?" he asked.

"I'm not sure of the exact amount, but I would guess about fifty pounds of ripe red cherries," I replied.

"I thought you were picking coffee, not cherries," he said.

"The red berries that contain the coffee beans are called cherries," I explained.

"So, fifty pounds of cherries, what does that give you for roasted coffee ready to use?" he asked.

"Just over seven pounds," I said. "Apparently the rule of thumb is seven pounds of cherries gives you about a pound of roasted beans. There are all kinds of losses along the way, mostly water, then there's different layers around the bean that get stripped off, plus there's a certain amount of loss because the beans are no good."

"So, what does a coffee farm look like?" he asked.

"Lines of bushes with dark green leaves," I said. "And on the branches, these clusters of coffee cherries, those that are ripe are this beautiful red and from there it goes back to green, which are definitely not ripe. There were even some flowers on a few bushes."

"What are the flowers like?" he asked.

"Delicate white flowers, with a really nice scent," I recalled. "I could smell them from a distance, and they attract bees by the ton."

"Are the bushes in regimented lines?" he asked.

"Somewhat," I said. "They seemed to be planted following contours more than just straight no matter what the terrain, and there weren't miles and miles of just coffee bushes, they seemed to be grouped in orchards with larger shade trees around."

47

"They left other trees?" he asked.

"Robert said that coffee bushes like shade, so they left a lot of taller trees to provide shade, and it means that they didn't take out all the original forest," I said.

"You said you wouldn't like to pick coffee for a living, but what was it actually like?" he asked.

"It was nice being outside in the fresh air, it was nice doing something constructive and being able to see the result with a full basket and it was interesting listening to the other ladies who were picking, chattering away in Kikuyu," I explained.

"What do you do, fill a basket them what?" he asked.

"The baskets get emptied into larger tins," I explained. "The expectation is for a good picker to fill three tins in a day, or if it's casual labour then they get paid four shillings per tin."

"Who else grows coffee?' he asked.

"Robert told us that the really big player is Brazil, who typically supply about a third of the world's coffee, but he also intimated that coffee prices will go up because Brazil had frost this year and it messed up the harvest," I replied.

"So, who else?" Ian asked.

"Colombia, Costa Rica, Sumatra, Ethiopia," I said.

"None in Europe?" he asked."

"The climate is not right for coffee there," I replied. "They drink a lot of it, as do the Americans, but it all gets imported."

"So, a good day?" he asked. "You learned a lot?"

"I did, and it was a good day," I confirmed.

"You said that the picking ladies were using Kikuyu," he commented. "I've been wondering if we should take some Kikuyu classes."

"Does someone offer them?" I asked.

"Yes, there's a prof from the university who will," he said. "Would you be interested?"

"I would," I said. "I'm sure it'll be really different from English or French. What's the prof's name?"

"Chalo Gatimu," Ian replied.

"So, what did you do today?" I asked Ian.

"Bailed out of a couple of stupid visitors who were trying to run *dagga*," he said.

"*Dagga?*" I asked.

"Marijuana, known here as *bhang* or *bhangi*," he explained. "I don't know what the hell they were thinking, but they had a whole load of it and were caught with it. They got picked up at the airport and taken off to the central police station. They asked for consular help, so I got to go and talk to them."

"Who were they?" I asked.

"A chap by the name of Jeremy North and his girlfriend, Norma Jones, I got the impression that neither of them was too bright and had been asked by this chap to take a couple of packages to England for him," Ian replied.

"They didn't ask what was in the packages?" I asked.

"Apparently not, if you believe what they say," he said. "Personally, I think that North knew damn well what was in the packages and had probably arranged a cut for himself when they got into London."

"So, what happens now?" I asked.

"That all depends on whether the judge believes their story about being unwitting shills," he said. "We'll see. If he doesn't buy their story, they could do time, or he could just throw them out of the country, fine them whatever money they have on them, and tell them never to come back."

"And, your bet?" I asked.

"We'll intercede and bleat and whine about poor unsuspecting tourists just wanting to help another human being out, then we'll promise to confiscate their passports and see them on their way," he said. "But it will depend on the judge. If it's Iregi, then they'll do time, then get thrown out of the country, if it's Kibet they may be lucky and just get booted out."

"Where did the *dagga*, that's right isn't it, *dagga*, come from?" I asked.

"It's been grown here for aeons," he said. "The Colonial Government banned it in 1914, but as with everything banned, there's always a way."

"Doesn't it have medicinal value?" I asked.

"I believe it can do," he said. "I've heard of it being used particularly by cancer patients undergoing chemotherapy. Apparently, it helps with the nausea caused by the chemo."

"So, why ban it?" I asked.

"Because it can also make you high as a kite, and do you really want someone who's high driving a car, or even worse a train?" he explained. "I saw *ouks* in the bush in Rhodesia who had been using it, and they had no fear and were really scary."

"I knew some chaps at Oxford who used to smoke it, and all I saw was that they got very mellow and stupid," I said.

"That can also happen," he agreed.

"So, nothing else of great import, no momentous items, just grubby drug runners?" I asked.

"Well, I did meet with the Kenyans to talk about security along their borders," he said. "When you think about it, they've got a long border and neighbours who could be friendly, but who could just as easily be a pain."

"Who's likely to be the biggest problem?" I asked.

"Difficult to say," he temporised. "You have political ambitions of Amin, philosophical differences with Nyerere, both supposed to be partners in the East African Community, then you've got the Marxist regimes of Somalia and Ethiopia, of which I think Somalia could be the bigger problem, because there are a lot of ethnic Somalis living in the north Eastern Province, and lastly the Sudanese, who, at least for now, have their own problems, mainly to the north."

"I thought this was supposed to be a nice quiet neighbourhood?" I asked.

"Supposed to be," he agreed. "But people are people and ambitions are always there, so who knows what they will actually do?"

"What's the Kenyan army like, are they any good?" I asked.

"Good enough," he replied. "But the borders are long and the conditions, especially in the north and east, are harsh, plus the Kenyan air force doesn't have much in the way of modern aircraft to defend the skies."

"Are we in any danger?" I asked.

"No," he said. "This was just a meeting to talk about borders, border security, what neighbours might or might not do and what assistance HMG might or might not offer in case of problems."

"We do live in exciting times," I commented.

"Changing the subject a minute," he said. "It looks like you caught the sun a bit today, did you put anything on it?"

"Not yet," I admitted. "But I did use some sunscreen when I went coffee picking."

"Let's see what the damage is," he suggested. I took off my shirt and the sun line was quite visible. "Should you put something on that?" he asked.

"I have some aloe," I said. "That should be fine."

"Where is it?" he asked.

"It's in the bathroom," I said. "Let's bath first then you can put it on for me." We ran a bath and climbed in together and he inspected me closely. "Not too bad," he said. "We'll put some aloe on you when you've dried yourself." I got out of the bath, dried myself and sat on the bed. Ian brought the aloe over sat on the bed in front of me and squeezed some onto his hands and gently applied it to my neck and upper chest.

"That's cold," I complained.

"Sissy," he teased.

The application of aloe led to more and we made love, not once but three times that night. It was the perfect end to a great day in the sun with new experiences.

Ian did arrange things with Chalo Gatimu and we started evening classes. I had been right; Kikuyu was a challenge. I struggled with the pronunciation and was jealous of Ian who seemed to manage much better than I did. There were sounds that I just had difficulty with, the way that Ian had problems with French, there were words he could never get quite right, and I was the same with Kikuyu. One thing Chalo did warn us of, was that the president was suspicious of foreigners who spoke Kikuyu, he seemed to think that they would be CIA or MI5. In his view, why else would anyone learn the language. We made progress, Ian faster than me, which was annoying, but as Ian pointed out, he already knew two other African languages that had similar ancient roots, so there were carryovers and similarities that he could use to make things easier. There was actually quite a lot of written material in Kikuyu and we were started on the easiest texts. I managed those quicker than Ian did, but it still rankled that he did better with the spoken language. Chalo alternated between structured grammar lessons and conversational lessons. Ian shone at those, whereas I did better with the grammar. We quickly learned how to introduce ourselves and go through all the routine greetings, then we advanced to more general conversation.

In a bookshop, I found a book published by the White Fathers, a Catholic missionary order who seemed to have been everywhere in Africa and mastered a hundred and one different languages. That added to the materials that Chalo had given us gave me all the published works I needed for study. The White Fathers' book was a little dated and there were differences between the Kikuyu of Chalo and their Kikuyu, but not enough to be a problem. I did wonder a couple of times if it was presumptuous of us to pick Kikuyu and not one of the other sixty-odd languages that were spoken around the country. I asked Chola about it, and he told me that Kikuyu was the language of the central part of Kenya where we lived and so the most useful, but that if at any time I wanted more of a challenge, he himself spoke five of the other languages and could put me in touch with speakers of all the others. I shrank from that possibility, and concluded that, for now at least, Kikuyu was challenge enough. Chalo also helped me improve my Swahili and pointed out the subtle differences between the coastal Swahili and the highlands Swahili. One thing was certain, it kept me busy and my brain active. I had to discipline myself to focus on my projects and not spend all my time on the languages.

I decided to try my hand at Kikuyu one day and went back out to Robert's coffee farm. I told him that I had been studying Kikuyu and wanted to see if I had any grasp on it at all. He took me out to the fields where the pickers were busy and we found the same ladies that I had met before. I introduced myself in Kikuyu and then had to quickly remember how to say slow down as they launched off into a torrent of Kikuyu. We reached an accommodation and I spent the day picking coffee and probably frustrated my fellow pickers with my slow grasp of what they were saying to me. I think they took it in good part and were very patient with me. We talked about the picking, we talked about family and I had to endure a whole litany of questions about why I had no children, we talked about houses and I had to describe what our house looked like, we talked about England the weather there, the people and the government. All this was very challenging and at times I struggled for words, at times throwing in a Swahili or English word, because I had no idea what the Kikuyu might be. It turned out that there were some words for which there just were no Kikuyu words, so they had borrowed the English word as an easier solution than trying to invent one.

By the end of the day, I have to say that I thought I had done quite well, and they all were full of praise for my efforts. I was tired when I got home, both from the physical work I had been doing and from the mental gymnastics my brain had been going through. I told Ian about my day and he was fascinated by the questions that had been put to me. I think he saw it as a measure of how the average Kenyan saw the British, not through the eyes of their government, but as ordinary people. I suppose that made sense, but, for me, it was just a day out in the sun talking to other women and it had been delightful, a day to remember, one of those that you treasure.

More sorting out

"Did coffee prices go up" James asked.

"They did," I confirmed. "The 75, 76 harvest went for 1,134 shillings per ton, whereas the 76, 77 harvest went for 2,020 per ton."

"And 77, 78?" James asked.

"Still up, but not quite as high as 76, 77, it only really declined this year," I explained. "But the Brazilians have had another frost, not as bad as the 75 frost, but still a frost, so it remains to be seen where prices will go.

"And did the government have a windfall tax?" Charlize asked.

"No, they discussed and debated it, but in the end left well alone, so the farmers did well for the short term, but, prices soon went back down and things returned to the status quo, sadly some of the farmers went off the deep end and invested and expanded when they shouldn't have, so now they are in trouble," I replied.

"Did you get to visit the pineapple plantation?" Charlize asked.

"We did," I confirmed. "Ian went with me that time as well as Julia and Henry. We were taken around the fields and shown planting of the tops and of suckers, offshoots from other plants, then we saw harvesting, so many people wading through the spiky plants, twisting off the pineapples and putting them on conveyors that took them to a harvesting lorry. Then we went to the factory where we saw the tops being taken off to go back to the fields for replanting, then the whole process of peeling, slicing and canning."

"What about whole pineapples that you buy in the shops?" James asked.

"They set those aside," I said. "Obviously the more whole you sell, the less tops there are, so the more suckers you need to plant."

"How do they know if the pineapples are ripe?" James asked.

"Apparently there's a measure for that, it's called the Brix number and it's a measure of the sugar content, but an experienced farm manager can also tell by taste," I recalled.

"What about your Kikuyu?" James asked.

"I got fairly proficient," I said. "Not as fluent as Ian, but good enough that I could haggle in the marketplace."

"It sounds like you had a really interesting first month or so in Kenya," James said. "Was it always so busy?"

"Not always so busy, but interesting," I replied. "It was all so new that there was always something cropping up that might have been normal to those who have always lived here, but to me it was different."

"How are you doing with sorting out Ian's things?" Maman asked.

"We've got a lot folded and boxed up," I said. "Now it's only a few things of his, and the rest is mine that will need to be packed to ship back."

"How much of the furniture is yours?" Charlize asked.

"Only a few pieces," I said. "The house came furnished, so we could settle right in. We've picked up books along the way, so I should probably look through them as well and decide what I want to keep and what can go. God, I hate this, going through Ian's stuff and giving it away, I want him to walk back through the door, grinning at me."

"It must be really hard for you," James sympathised. "I liked Ian a lot, but you were married to him, I can't imagine what it's like to lose someone that close. What else do we have to sort out and clear up for you?"

"There's the pictures around the house, those wooden animals and those woven baskets and the drums," I said, pointing out the items that were ours, now mine, and that did not come as part of the house.

"Shall I wrap them and put them all in these crates?" James asked.

"If you would," I said. "That will get shipped back to London."

"When do the shippers arrive?" Portia asked.

"The day after tomorrow," I replied. "But, there's no desperate rush, there's not that much to pack for shipping."

"How long before your things arrive in London?" Portia asked.

"I would guess anywhere from two weeks to a month," I thought. "The crates go from here to Mombasa to meet a ship, that should be in a about a week from now. Then, I'm not sure if the ship goes back to Southampton via the Suez or via Cape Town. If it's via Suez, then less than a week's sailing, if it's via Cape Town, then ten days there, a few more days in port, then another twelve to fourteen days back up to Southampton."

"And your crates will be safe that whole time?" Portia asked.

"I've no idea," I admitted. "But I have a very good record of what's in them, and photographs, and I'm fully insured, so if anything goes missing, I'll get the monetary value. But it would be sad to lose the things we got here; they have the memories. Things of real value I'm taking back with me on the plane."

"If there's anything you need us to take, just let us know," Maman said.

"Thanks, I might do that," I said.

"Do you have room in your flat for everything?" James asked.

"I think so," I said. "If not, I'm sure I can store things somewhere, or I might even get a bigger place."

"Are you going to change one of the rooms in your flat to an office?" James asked.

"I don't think so," I said. "I'd rather have my office away from my flat, especially if I meet clients there. They've no reason to know where I live."

"Do you need to work?" Charlize asked.

"Probably not, if I'm careful," I admitted. "But I enjoy what I do, so will keep at it for a while. I might take a short break when I clean up what I have on my plate right now, but if I gave up working I would need to develop something else to do, or I'd go crazy."

"That makes sense," Charlize agreed. "I suppose in the broader sense the family could always sell the vineyards and the wineries, and then live off the proceeds. But we enjoy making wine, so it's as much a labour of love as it is a money maker."

"Have you had offers?" I asked.

"Quite a few," she replied. "The last one was enough to sit back and really think about it, but, if we did sell, it would probably be only the South African operations, we'd keep France and New Mexico if we get started there."

"So, what else exciting happened the first year you were here?" James asked.

"Well, there was the threat of war between Kenya and Uganda," I replied.

"War between here and Uganda. I never heard anything about that," James said.

"There were newspaper articles here," I said. "There were also speeches made by Amin and Kenyatta, but it didn't really make the international press."

"I must have missed that," James said.

"We were never sure what Amin was thinking, but he made claims about lands transferred from Uganda to Kenya, long before independence. He had some of the story, but not all of it."

"So, what actually happened?" James asked.

"Well, I think it all started as a ploy by Amin to distract the people from problems domestically," I started. "Then it got a life of its own and things could have got out of hand. Kenyatta was having nothing of Amin's claims, but we, or should I say HMG and the High Commission here wanted to have all the information they could. So, Ian got the assignment to check on the history."

War?

"When are you leaving, Fi?" Ian asked me as I started to get ready for a trip to London to meet with several of my clients. This was going to be my first trip back from Nairobi since we had moved out and I was going to miss him.

"I'm going to take the flight on Saturday," I told him. "That way I'll have most of Sunday to sleep and get ready for my first meeting on Monday."

"Okay," he said. "And you're coming back on the Thursday after that?"

"Unless something comes up," I said. "I can't see anything getting in the way of coming home, but you never know."

"I wish I was coming with you," he said. "I don't like to be away from you."

"I know," I said. "That time when we lost touch with one another had to be the worst time of my life. I don't want that to happen again. I'll call you when I get to London and I'll book a call each evening, so we can talk," I promised.

"Won't that cost a bit?" he asked.

"I'm charging enough that I can readily afford it," I assured him. "What will be the best time to call you?"

"Let's make it eight here, so seven with you," he suggested. "Do you think you'll be done for the days by then?"

"I can't see why not," I said. "I'll call you at seven no matter what," I promised.

"Are you ready for your meetings?" he asked.

"As ready as I'll ever be," I said. "It's a pity that there really isn't easy access to a computer here, that would make life so much simpler, I could run simulations without having to go and buy time on a machine in England. I'll be spending much of Monday running jobs, and that probably really means de-bugging the programs I have written and then waiting for the jobs to be run again."

"Who are you buying time from?" he asked.

"Imperial College," I told him. "They have had a computing centre since 1964 and they do have quite a fast machine. I've become quite adept at programming and have been toying with the idea of writing up some of my concepts for publication."

"Do I sense another doctorate in the wind?" he laughed.

"I'm not specifically looking for one," I told him. "But they've made the offer, with a little more work, I'll have done enough."

"I love you," he said. "I just can't get over how you do all this stuff and how I was lucky enough to marry you."

"I thought I was the lucky one," I said. "You make me happy; you make me laugh, you look after me, and you're not so bad in bed either."

"Ha, is that an invitation or a challenge?" he asked.

"Maybe a bit of both," I said. "Can anyone see into the garden?"

"No," he said quite categorically. "We're on a slight rise here, and we look down on our neighbours and you'd have to be standing on a ladder right by the wall to see over. I did a check for security reasons, I don't want someone taking potshots at us, either with a camera or a rifle. When I was in the Rhodesian Army, I got to be quite expert at fields of fire and dead ground, so know what to look for."

"So, it's dark now, why don't we go outside and take advantage of the nice evening, bring some wine and glasses and we'll see where things might go," I suggested.

I went outside onto the terrace, where it was still quite warm from the day, which had been above average, almost in the 80s, warm enough that when I shed my clothes, I was still comfortable. I was sitting on a chair when Ian came out with the glasses and a bottle of wine. He looked at me, then looked again and laughed. I have to give him credit, he poured the wine and handed me a glass before he shed his clothes. I took my glass and spun around relishing the feel of the cool night air on me. It was very liberating to be without clothes, especially as the expectation was that one be conservatively dressed for trips into town. Ian just watched me and I was happy to get up and pirouette for him and I even did some Tahitian dance moves for him that swung the hips in a provocative way, guaranteed to excite him. I danced up close to him and brushed up against him and was rewarded with stirrings.

"I see we have *homo erectus* with us," I laughed.

"Are you surprised," he said. "Come and sit with me."

"No, come with me on the grass," I suggested. He followed me out, off the warmth of the bricks of the terrace to the cool of the grass and then looked at me for guidance. I knelt down onto the grass and he joined me. From there it was just a matter of time before I was in his lap and we were as one, moving enough that even as the night began to cool, we did not notice. We came together which was magical, then just sat for a while holding each other, until I thought he was ready to go again, then I pushed him down onto the grass and straddled him, gently moving until I felt his response. I was gratified that he was able to be ready so soon after our first lovemaking and took my time with him, just enjoying his body and all the sensations it created in me. I knew that things were coming to a head when his hips started to move under me.

"Oh, Fi," he said, pushing up with his body and holding me by the waist so that he could control how deep he went and how quickly he moved. "That's so good."

"It's good for me too," I told him. "I love you, Ian, I'm going to miss this when I'm in London, so we'll have to make a plan to make up for lost time and opportunities when I get back."

"Fi, Fi," he whispered, and with a few final upward strokes I felt his climax, and then let myself go as well. "That was wonderful," he said, grinning at me. "Maybe we should go in and have a bath and try again?"

"I'm ready if you are," I told him.

We gathered up our clothes and went inside, closing up the house after us. I ran a bath and Ian joined me in it. We washed quickly then repaired to the bedroom, where I lay back on the bed and invited him in. I loved the feel of his body against mine, the lingering scent of the aftershave he used, and the sensations of his penetration. I locked my legs around his back to pull him in and hold him in me. It took him longer this time to reach a climax, but when he did it was spectacular, and I just delighted in the moment. I thanked my lucky stars again that I had found him, he suited me, I know he loved me as I adored him and I was just so happy to be with him in this exotic place. Life was good. Sleep was quick to come and we drifted off in one another's arms.

For the next three days, I took every chance I could get to make love to Ian. We made love in the bath, in the garden, on the settee, in a chair, in the kitchen with me sitting on the counter and even in the bed. When Saturday came, I was quite sated and was prepared for a few days of celibacy. Ian took me to the airport and saw me off on the plane. I was travelling first class; I had divided the travel costs between four clients so it would not be a hardship for any one of them. The flight was quiet, and uneventful, which in my book was a good thing, and I had no seatmate, which was another good thing. I liked flying with Ian, but was uneasy about others in the seat next to me, I might have to make polite conversation. As we flew, I started thinking about taking flying lessons. It was in Kenya that Beryl Markham had perfected her flying skills before undertaking her epic flight across the Atlantic, so why should I not also learn to fly. I decided that when I got home, I would go to the Aero Club of East Africa and find myself an instructor. That then led to the question, to hire a plane when I wanted one, or to buy one. I had enough money that I could buy one easily enough, but what to buy. I thought that when I got to London, I would buy a couple of magazines, the type that were for private pilots. I would also find some books on the subject and read a little before going off to get lessons. My musings were interrupted by the stewardess who wanted to serve dinner. I paid attention to the menu and selected what I wanted, BA did actually do its passengers, at least its first-class passengers, proud, so it would be easy to overindulge with both food and alcohol. After dinner, I tried to make myself as comfortable as I could and get some sleep. I knew that I had no meetings the next day, but hated losing sleep.

When I arrived in London it was a dreary winter's day, with some sleet and rain and some cutting unpleasant wind. Fortunately, my flat had central heating and Dad had been by and made sure that it was turned on, so when I got there it was at least warm and welcoming, he had also put milk in the refrigerator and a few other perishable groceries. There was a stack of mail, Dad had also been by the service I used for mail and messages, and he had collected everything and arranged it on my kitchen table. I quickly scanned through it and consigned perhaps half to the bin then sorted the rest into those that I needed to address quickly and those items that could be put off to a later date. I made myself some lunch and stood at the window with a soup bowl looking out at the drear and thinking how lucky I was that I could go back to Nairobi soon and to the sun.

Lunch over I called the operator and booked a call for Nairobi for seven that night and then settled down to answer my letters. That took the better part of the afternoon and the sun was well down when I was finished, not that that was particularly late, as the sun goes down at about five in the afternoon in February. At seven I got my call from the operator who then put me through to Nairobi.

"Hello," I heard Ian say.

"Hello yourself," I said. "How are you, how was your day?"

"It rained a little," he replied. "Otherwise, I'm fine. I had to go into the office today to bail out some tourists who had got themselves into a spot of bother, but I think we have it all sorted out. How was your flight, how was your day, how are you Fi?"

"The flight was fine, it's dreary here, makes me long for Nairobi and the sun, and I spent the afternoon answering letters," I told him. We talked for our three minutes, then the operator broke in to tell us that our time was up. I told him that I loved him and that I would see him soon. I wondered after I hung up how long it would be before there was a decent connection to Nairobi that would not require an operator to complete the call. I supposed that high-volume traffic would get priority, so the United States, Canada, Australia and New Zealand and even South Africa was to get better service long before Kenya did.

I went to bed early, missing Ian, missing the warmth of his body, missing the scent of his aftershave, missing hearing his breathing, missing feeling him near me, and missing his touch, a touch that often led to more intimate moments. I might have been sated sexually for the immediate, but I still wanted him there, I wanted to be able to feel his body up against mine, I wanted to feel his hands on me and wonder how long it would be before he initiated something, or I did, but the separation was only for a few days and I would be back with him soon enough. In the days when I had been going out with Ian, before we slept together, I used to fantasise about him and I had a full-sized poster of him on my wall, and a vibrator that Maman had given me. It got a lot of use before I had the real thing, but that night I resorted to it as I thought about him.

In the morning I breakfasted, booked my call to Nairobi for that evening and went early to Imperial and started on my jobs immediately. My first two runs went without hitch and I got my printouts quickly, but the third job had problems. I got a whole series of notes back about syntax errors and it took me a little while to work out what I had done wrong. Finally, I lit upon the solution and submitted the job again, with much better results. The next run time I could get was after lunch so I called Dad and asked him if was doing anything particular at lunchtime. He was not, so we agreed upon a time and place.

"Hello, Fi," he said, as I joined him at his table at the Ritz. I was never quite sure why Dad liked the Ritz, but he did and had taken me there before. "How are you settling in?"

"I like Nairobi," I told him. "If nothing else the weather's a damn sight better there than here. Ian's busy and I'm thinking of taking flying lessons," I told him.

"Let me know if you ever want to buy your own plane," he said. "I can get you one at a good price."

"Thanks, Dad," I said. "I'll let you know, how's Felicity?"

"Well," he said. "She's busy at the moment doing some fabric designs for Liberty's."

"I didn't know she was interested in that," I said.

"Neither did I," he said wryly. "But she seems to have taken to it and has sold quite a few design patterns to them. So, what else is going on?"

"I'm a little concerned about the rampant inflation that seems to have overtaken this country," I told him. "It's not the best for my bank balance."

"I know," he said. "Lending rates are stupid these days, I'm hoping that Thatcher will win the next election and try and get us back to sanity. I was even approached by the Treasury to help them set up some loans to try and cover the excesses in spending."

"I think I've covered myself fairly well," I said. "I was only kidding about my bank balance, I've taken steps to protect myself and am actually doing pretty well, despite the inflation, what I need now is another Poseidon Nickel to boost my holdings, that was my first real killing."

"Good to know," Dad said. "So, what about your business, how is it working out doing it from a distance?"

"It's actually going quite well," I said. "My only wish would be to have better access to computers, but Kenya is lagging in that, so I have to grab time here when I can, so expect at least monthly trips back, just to get the time."

"Have you got many projects on right now?" he asked.

"A few and several of them are clamouring for their economic models," I told him. "I really do wish I had better access to a good computer, so that I could run more simulations. I use the Imperial machine, I even signed up as a post-grad so that I could get better rates."

"Smart move," Dad said. "What shall we eat?"

"As I recall, they do do a rather nice Dover Sole," I replied.

"Good idea, and with it what about something to drink with it?" he asked.

"Nothing too heavy," I said. "I have to do some thinking this afternoon." Dad looked over the wine list and looked over at me and asked, "What about a Les Charmes Meursault?"

"That sounds nice," I said, not actually sure what we were going to get. I was not familiar with the particular vineyard, so had to rely on his judgement. He called over a waiter and we ordered food and wine, then talked about the economy in general until the food arrived. In between mouthfuls, Dad told me about a couple of his latest ventures, he had invested in a manufacturing company that made systems for aircraft and it was doing really well, he had also invested in a clothing retailer, and that was not doing so well, but he thought that when the rampant inflation was brought a little under control, then personal spending habits would change a little and the retailer would do better. He had set himself a series of benchmarks and if those were not achieved, he would walk away from that venture. As I said before, my own fortunes were actually quite rosy, my investments were still paying off, even in the poor economy and I was positioning myself to take advantage of what I saw as an upturn in the years ahead. 1976 was probably going to go down in history as one of the worst for Britain as far as economics went. After we finished lunch, I excused myself and scurried back to my computing and was gratified to see that my last program had run successfully and that I had now had yards of printed output to review. I took that and went home to look over the results at leisure and see what I could glean from them.

At home I delved into the numbers, looking for patterns and trends and finally began to see something emerge. My thesis had been correct and the simulation numbers were proving it. This was really good news as now I had a workable model for my client and could let them know the next day that I had good news. It might not be the best news financially, but at least they would now have a view to the future and some idea of what to expect in the coming months and years. I was so engrossed in the data that when the telephone rang, I was quite startled. It was the operator with my call to Nairobi. I listened to the telephone ringing and then it was answered, but not by Ian,

"Hello Fiona, this is Trevor," he said.

"What's wrong Trevor, where's Ian, has something happened?" I asked in a mad panic, thinking the worst had happened and that one of the neighbours had lost their minds and had attacked Kenya, or that Ian had been injured or killed in a traffic accident.

"He's fine," Trevor said. "He's on his way to the airport, he's arriving at Heathrow at 6:55 tomorrow morning."

"Why, what's wrong?" I asked.

"Nothing," Trevor assured me. "Ian will explain when he gets there, he has to research something and get back here pronto."

"That's a relief," I said. "How are you and Valerie?" I asked Trevor.

"We're fine," he said. "I just wanted to be here when you called, so that you wouldn't panic and wonder why Ian was not answering the phone."

"Thanks, Trevor," I said. "I really appreciate this, what can I bring you from London?"

"Just some Quality Street," Trevor said, referring to the popular brand of chocolates made by Cadbury.

"I'll do that," I promised. "I should let you get back to Valerie."

"That's quite all right," he said. "I'll see you when you get back."

So, Ian was on his way, I had time in the morning so could go out to Heathrow to meet the plane. I did wonder what was going on that Ian would make a literal and figurative flying visit to London. Still, I was going to see him sooner than I had hoped, so whatever the issue was, it was like a cloud that truly had a silver lining. I made myself some dinner, called to book a taxi for the morning, then went to bed early setting my alarm for five the next morning. It was pitch black when I awoke and it was drizzling, but even that failed to dampen my spirits. The taxi was waiting for me, and was happy for the fare out to Heathrow so early in the morning. Getting a fare back was probably going to be fairly easy as there were a number of arrivals early in the morning. I was at the airport by six-thirty, which was as well, because the flight from Nairobi was thirty minutes early, so had just landed. I was surprised how quickly Ian came through, I suppose he must have used his diplomatic passport and he only had a small piece of hand luggage with him, so would clear everything quickly.

"Fi," he said when he saw me. "Thanks for coming to get me."

"What's up?" I asked him.

"I'll tell you when we get home," he promised. "I have some research to do then I must get back to Nairobi quickly, so I'll be on the same flight as you on Thursday. I should have all I need by then. How did you get here?"

"I took a taxi," I replied. "Shall we go and get one back into London?"

"Good idea," he said. "It's great to be here with you, I know it's only been a day, but I missed you."

"I missed you too," I told him. "I was really surprised when Trevor answered the phone, I had moments of sheer panic, wondering if something had gone wrong, or if Kenya was at war with Uganda, Tanzania or Somalia, but then Trevor told me that you were on your way here, so that was a relief."

We hailed a taxi and on the way into London, talked about the weather and other general things, I noticed that Ian was saying nothing at all about why he was there. I wondered if he was even supposed to tell me, or whether or not it was secret and not to be discussed. At our flat, I made tea for us and then Ian told me what the flap was all about.

"We've heard from an agent in Kampala that Amin is casting covetous eyes at Kenyan territory," he said. "Apparently he's finally worked out that back in the colonial administration days that the administration of territory was moved quite a bit and chunks of what was the old Buganda Kingdom landed up in Sudan and Kenya. I'm supposed to research everything and have all the background information so that we can feed it to the Kenyan Foreign Ministry, our friend, Mr Bett."

"Where will you find all that?" I asked.

"Probably the National Archives, the Parliamentary Papers and records," he said. "There may also be some in the files at the FCO, I'll have to dig and look."

"If I can help at all, just let me know," I told him.

"I think I'll be fine," he said. "What about you, how are your projects?"

"Actually, I've made significant progress," I replied. "I spent a good part of yesterday running computer simulations and got that data back, that's all that stuff on the table there. I've got a meeting with one client at ten this morning and two more tomorrow, one in the morning at ten and one in the afternoon at two, so will be busy all day. Should I cook dinner for us tonight, or will you be working late?"

"I don't know," he said. "Will you be here this afternoon?"

"I should be, no later than three I would think," I said.

"I'll call you then and give you some idea of when I'll be back," he said. "I'd better get started, the sooner I can find files and dig, the sooner I can get done today. So, see you later, Fi, love you."

"Love you," I said and walked with him to the door and kissed him goodbye. Then I organised myself and got ready for my first meeting.

My client was happy with my researches, but not the implications of the results, they indicated troubled times ahead for them, but, as they said, forewarned was forearmed so they could take actions before crises set in.

I then went back to Imperial to test out some theories using different programming languages. I had been using FORTRAN and COBOL, but also wanted to try some ideas out in BASIC and LISP. LISP presented a difficulty because it ran best on a machine designed for it and they were not commonly available. I finally gave it up for the day at about six and went back to my flat. Ian was already there, busy at the dining table making notes from piles of paper.

"Fi," he said. "How was your day?"

"Interesting," I replied. "And yours?"

"The same," he laughed. "I found some of what I was looking for and discovered that I have to go back a little more into history for the full story."

"Will you have it all done by Thursday?" I asked.

"I think so," he said. "We have an appointment with Daniel Bett at one of Friday, he needs to be prepared to brief his government on the situation."

"Would you like some dinner?" I asked.

"I need to take a break, why don't we just go down to the bistro?" he suggested.

"Good idea," I said.

The next day, Ian left early to continue his delving into the arcane history of the colonies and I got ready for my meetings. Those went well and I also picked up what looked like a new contract in the car business. It was actually quite exciting and I had been asked to go to Paris in two weeks for a meeting with the client, who was a French company, to finalise a contract. I was curious to know how they had selected me to do the work and learned from the service I used to screen calls, mail and enquiries, that the client had had dealings with another of my clients and they had been singing my praises. From there the French had done their own checking and had also learned that I was fluent in French as well as economics, so were comfortable with their selection. They had called my service and arranged a luncheon date to meet me and discuss the project and possible terms. I met with three men from the client and they outlined in general terms what they wanted. We conducted all our business in French which was good for me as since we moved to Nairobi, I had not had the chance to use my French much. The three were trying to understand the debacle that had been British Leyland that had led to its nationalisation by the government. What should have been a profitable enterprise had turned sour, so my new client wanted to understand the niceties of the economics of the company that had led to its collapse. The project sounded really interesting and I was looking forward to it. I did need to gather information, so after lunch called Dad and told him what I needed in terms of annual reports and reports that might be available but not usually widely distributed, I also asked him to get for me all the information on the government hearings that had preceded the actually nationalisation. He promised to get what he could for by the next day and the rest he would forward to Nairobi. I was going to become a forensic accountant, delving into the dark mysteries of poorly led and managed companies. I already had some economic models that I thought might be applicable, and all I needed was data in order to test the models. From there I could refine the models and see what they suggested.

I then met with another of my clients, with whom I had a contract to develop a model to correlate and predict agricultural yields with rainfall. My meeting was with Adam Hill, with whom I had first worked on a model for the mining industry. Adam now ran his company's non-mining interests and that included agriculture. By a strict reading of my agreement with Adam, I was not permitted to take on another project for an agricultural enterprise, but I was going to test the waters and see if he would bend a little. I had made some real progress with his project and now had a complex model that fed off weather forecasting data and developed crop yields as a product. What Robert Blake wanted was a simple economic model of his own coffee farm, and that was not in the same league as the model I was doing for Adam. I went to their office and was greeted by Andrea, his secretary and now my friend.

"Fiona, lovely to see you, how's Nairobi?" she asked.

"So far, it's been delightful," I said. "We're just about settled in, and there's lots going on. How are you?"

"I'm fine, no better than fine," she said. "I'm having a great time, I met this really nice chap, he's a *bwana* with BA, so maybe I can get some cheap travel, Adam's waiting for you."

"Thanks, Andrea, I'll get more information when we're done," I said. I went into Adam's office and he was there with two others.

"Dr Hartley," he said. "How is Nairobi?"

"Warmer than here," I said. "How are you, Mr Hill?"

"I'm feeling the cold," he said. "There are days when I wonder if I shouldn't just retire and move somewhere warmer. Anyway, let me introduce Gregory Chalmers, he's one of our financial experts, and Bill Winter, he's one of our operations managers for our farming unit."

"Good morning gentlemen," I said, and after the usual polite chit-chat about the weather in England and in Kenya, we got down to business. "This morning, I will run through the models I have created and also have some output data to show you based upon input assumptions, that are listed here." I handed around the sheet of assumptions, then started in on my presentation of the models I had created. I talked for the next hour or so, stopping at times to show them diagrams, graphs and screeds of output data.

"This is way over my head," Gregory said. "I understand the basics of the financial side of things, but the other mathematics is beyond me."

"I think perhaps focus on the output," I suggested. "Adam gave me some historical data and I went back to the weather forecast data for the same period and ran a test of the model, perhaps you have some comments about how the output matches your experience for that period?"

"It's not perfect, but it's damned close to our results," Bill said. "It's close enough that I could have made decisions from it. If I had this, I may not make all the right decisions, or things may not work out exactly as this model suggests, but it'd be a damn sight better than what we do now."

"I have some refinements that I am thinking of making," I said. "But, to test those will take a little time, it's all driven by when I can get time on a computer to run the models."

"We've just acquired a new larger computer," Gregory said. "Perhaps we could give you some time on that. I'll take a look and see what the scheduling is. How long do these models take to run?"

"Unfortunately, they are quite complex models with a lot of iterations, so the run time is usually in the hours," I said. "I typically try and get them run overnight."

"Let me check," Gregory said. "Can anyone input the data?"

"Yes," I confirmed. "I have some changes to make to the model itself, but after that, anyone can enter the data."

"When do you go back?" Gregory asked.

"On Thursday night," I said.

"I'll have an answer for you before then," Gregory said. "We have a phone number for you?"

"You do," I confirmed.

"Well, thank you, Dr Hartley," Adam said. "Greg, Bill, anything else?"

"No, just where were you ten years ago?" Bill said. "I could have used this then."

"Sadly, ten years ago I had just started college," I laughed. "Annoying my professors with endless questions."

"Well, come and see one of our farms one day," Bill said. "Adam, I need to go to another meeting, anything else we need to do now?"

"No, I'll call you later," Adam said. With that Bill left and Gregory followed soon after.

"This looks like it will be very useful," Adam said. "Thank you for that. I think Gregory and Bill were just a little intimidated."

"They shouldn't be," I said. "What they should focus on is validating the model against experience."

"We'll do that," he said. "So, what else, I know you want to ask me for something."

"Well," I said. "I met this coffee grower and he's looking for a simple economic model to use to make investment decisions, it would be very similar to the one I did for my sister-in-law and her vineyard. I know that our agreement precludes working for other agricultural enterprises, but I wondered if I might get your permission to vary from the agreement."

"Well, we don't have any coffee," Adam said. "And, unless we buy an existing farm, I don't see us getting into the business. Would you give us a copy of the same model?"

"I think I could do that, without the specific data of course," I said. "The process steps for coffee are fairly standard across the industry, so I wouldn't be giving away any trade secrets. The model would have no actual input as to trees per acre and all that kind of thing, but if your own farmers wanted to use the model they could, they would just have to modify the process steps and then input their own data."

"I think we can do that," Adam said. "Who's the farmer?"

"Robert Blake," I replied. "He has about 500 acres under coffee near Thika," Adam called Andrea in and asked her to type up a simple addendum to the contract that agreed to me providing Robert Blake with economic models. She was back within five minutes with two copies, we each signed and each took a copy.

"Thank you," I said. "When next I come, I'll bring some coffee with me."

"I look forward to that, enjoy your flight home," Adam said. "We'll see you next month."

I went home and got myself some wine and thought about the day. All in all, it had been successful. When Ian came back to our flat that evening, I was eager to tell him about my new project for the car company, and apparently, he was just as eager to tell me about his researches. So, we compromised and tossed a coin to see who would go first. Ian won, so he went first, as I put together a light snack that we could eat as we talked.

"I've gone back as far as 1902 when part of the Uganda Protectorate was transferred to British East Africa, Kenya," he said. "Since then there were changes in 1910, when there was a minor change around the Mount Elgon area when territory was transferred to BEA, then in 1912 part of Sudan was transferred to Uganda, then in 1914 the border between

Sudan and Uganda was redrawn and a chunk of land went to Sudan, and, then in 1926 there was another swathe of territory moved from Uganda to BEA, that was up in the north up to Lake Rudolf, and in the same year there was a further change to the border with Sudan, in Sudan's favour."

"So, what does that mean now?" I asked.

"Actually, it's probably all academic because Uganda and Kenya and Sudan were all signatories to the Cairo resolution of the OAU (Organization for African Unity), in July of 1964, which agreed to leave the colonial borders as they were. I think they all agreed that once they started messing with the borders it would be chaos and might even lead to wars."

"So, what's Amin's problem?" I wondered.

"I'm not quite sure," Ian said. "Amin seems to me to be coming more irrational as the days go on. Maybe this is some kind of ploy to divert attention from a domestic problem."

"If Amin comes out and talks about the movements of territory what will be HMG's position?" I asked.

"That the Cairo resolution holds and that there is no claim to territory, but even if there was, it's an issue between Uganda and Kenya," he said.

"So, what will you tell Bett on Friday?" I asked.

"I'll give him a more detailed version of what I've just told you, with all the Orders in Council references and copies of the documents," Ian said. "After that, it's up to them."

"What will Kenya do if Amin raises a stink?" I asked.

"I can't see Kenyatta backing away from anything," Ian said. "I suspect that they'll tell Amin to fly a kite and then beef up border security."

"Will Amin go to war over this?" I asked.

"I doubt it," Ian said. "I don't think he's in a good position to go to war."

"Wait a minute," I said. "Isn't Amin the current chair of the OAU?"

"He is," Ian confirmed.

"So much for African Unity," I thought. "I don't much fancy the idea of Kenya being in a war with Uganda, it's not that far from Nairobi to the Uganda border."

"Even closer if you look at the territory that was transferred in 1902," Ian said. "If the 1902 territory was moved back to Uganda the border would be about fifty miles from Nairobi."

"So, a little too close for comfort," I commented.

"A little," he agreed. "But, as I said, I don't see Kenyatta giving anything away."

"I hope it doesn't come to war," I said. "I didn't imagine when we came here that we'd be involved in a war.

"Nor did I, but I doubt if it will come to that, but you never know, it all depends on how far off the deep end Amin's gone," he said. "If things get at all risky, we'll fly you out, but I see that as a last resort."

"I don't want to be separated from you again," I said. "War won't be good for anyone; you could be killed!"

"I managed to stay safe in the Rhodesian war," he said. "I think I could manage here, but I don't see war as even a low probability, even as a distant possibility. So, what about you, what's your news?"

"I may have a new client," I told him. "A French car company that wants to fully understand the debacle of British Leyland and the events and economics that led up to nationalisation."

"Sounds interesting," he said.

"It does, doesn't it?" I said. "I have been asked to be in Paris in two weeks' time to negotiate a contract and settle on a scope of work. I'd fly to Heathrow then take a plane over to Paris."

"You'll be leaving me again?" he said. "We'll have to make sure we make up for things when you get back."

"What did you have in mind?" I asked, knowing full well where this conversation was going.

"I think I should demonstrate," he said. "If you'll just come with me." He led the way to the bedroom where he proceeded to undress me, with a little help from me, I might add. Then he picked me up and laid me down on the bed and stripped off. After that it was predictable, we made love, then had a bath, then made love again. I revelled in it, it was such a nice way to end the day. Life with Ian was magical, and the only dark cloud on the horizon was the possibility of war with Uganda.

Thursday was another day full of meetings and sessions at the computer centre and I made considerable progress. The professor who was working with me as my ostensible supervisor for a doctorate admitted that he was getting out of his depth and asked if he could bring in another advisor who was more familiar with the concepts that I was using. I was happy with that, I was looking forward to learning more, and another advisor who had more experience would be useful. I stopped at Dad's office and he already had a pile of reports for me, both public and internal to British Leyland. Where those had come from I did not ask, but he promised more and said that they would be on their way to Nairobi within the week using a courier service that went by the airlines, so would be on a BA flight, not wandering around in the morass that was the postal system. Dad also promised that he would stop at my flat the next day and empty the refrigerator, so that nothing went bad while I was away. I told him that I would be back in two weeks, but only in transit to Paris for my meeting. I picked up some Quality Street for Trevor, then I found the books that I thought I would need for a pilot's licence, there were a few of them, covering everything from basic aviation, meteorology, radiotelephony, and navigation to human factors and performance, all in all, plenty to read and absorb. Then, I went back to the flat briefly before leaving for the airport and made sure that everything was secure. I took a taxi out to the airport and was checking in when Ian arrived, driven out to the airport by an official government driver. He had a thick briefcase with him, which I supposed contained the product of his researches. We were able to get seats together and then went through the immigration checkpoint, which was very much a formality.

On the flight home to Nairobi, I talked about my idea of taking flying lessons with Ian.

"I think that would be super," he said. "Just stay away from the Uganda border."

"I doubt that any instructor would take me near there," I said. "But I'll check to be sure. Dad actually said that he'd help me buy a plane if and when I get a licence."

"What does he want in return?" Ian asked. "You're Dad's a banker, I doubt that he does too much out of the goodness of his heart."

"You're right, but this time I think he's just offering to help me with the best contacts, so that I can get a good price," I said.

"Have you any ideas about what you might like?" Ian asked.

"I haven't even taken a lesson yet," I laughed. "But when I do and decide on a plane nothing as big as this."

"Probably best," he agreed. "The fuel bill alone must be astronomical."

"Maybe, something like this," I said, pointing to an advertisement in a pilot's magazine that I had picked up earlier.

"What's that, a Cessna?" he asked.

"A Cessna 172 Skyhawk," I read out. "Four passengers, including the pilot, maybe that or this one, Cessna 206, Stationair, six passengers, including the pilot, then I can take you and me, James and Charlize and even Maman and Portia."

"How much?" he asked.

"Enough," I said, covering up the prices, I did not want him to die of a heart attack, as the prices were more than he was paid in a year. "I can afford it, either one, I wonder how they get them to Kenya?"

"Probably crated and shipped by sea," he thought. "I would think that delivering by air has its risks."

Further conversation was interrupted by a stewardess who came to offer dinner. They did do us proud and I probably ate and drank far too much. But I did manage to make myself comfortable enough that I fell asleep and only awoke with Ian prodding me and asking if I wanted breakfast. I thought that might be a good idea, but needed to visit the loo first. When I went back to my seat the meal was there along with tea and a happy-looking husband who was grinning at me.

"What?" I asked him.

"I just love you," he said. "But perhaps you should find a hairbrush somewhere and tame that mop." I had a small mirror in my bag, so took a look, and I did indeed look like I had been dragged through a hedge backwards, so scratched around in my bag and found a small brush and put some order into my hair. I kept my hair short, but it still needed a brush once in a while.

"Better?" I asked him.

"Lovely," he said. "You would look lovely no matter what."

"You're just saying that to get out of trouble," I accused him.

"I am," he agreed. "I'll make it up to you tonight."

"Oh, you will, will you?" I asked. "We'll see about that, are you sure you're up to the challenge?"

"I'll try," he said, grinning again. My retort was cut off when the steward came by and asked if we wanted more tea. The breakfast things were then cleared away and we started our descent into Nairobi. We were met at the airport by Trevor who took Ian to the High Commission, then dropped me off at home. I gave Trevor his chocolates and he was thrilled, I think he missed them, not that we could not get them in Nairobi, but I had to agree with him, they were not always on the shelves, so one could not guarantee to find them.

I was busy for the rest of the day and Ian finally came home at about seven that night.

"Long day," I said to him.

"Long day," he agreed. "I spent the morning with the high commish, then we both went and met Daniel Bett and briefed him on what I had found. It was no real surprise to him, but he did tell us that Kenyatta has no intention of giving up an inch to Amin, so when the shouting starts, look for troop movements to the border."

"Are they prepared to go to war?" I asked.

"They are," he confirmed. "I doubt it will come to that, but they're making preparations."

"Should I be worried?" I asked.

"No," he said. "If, and it is a big if, actual fighting breaks out then we'll think about whether or not you should go to London, but I really don't think it will come to that. Amin is a bully and if someone stands up to him, I doubt that he will follow through. There will be lots of noise and hand waving and sabre rattling, but real shooting, probably not."

"I just don't like the idea of a war breaking out, Maman told me about her experiences in Paris during the War and the German occupation of Paris and all the people that were killed in the fighting, and Dad told me about the D-Day landings and the fighting that took place up to the liberation of Paris, after which he was out of the fighting. I'm sure that war between Uganda and Kenya would be brutal, look at the Congo and what happened there, think about what's going on in Rhodesia now, with all the landmines and shootings," I said.

"I'm sure it won't come to that," he said. "But I will keep a very close eye on things, and if think there is any danger to you, I will let you know and we will take appropriate steps for your safety."

"I never thought that something like this would happen in Kenya," I said. "But I suppose once you start getting coups in different countries, who knows what's going to happen?"

"True," he agreed. "If you look back since most of the old colonial territories got independence, there have been lots of coups, in 1966

76

alone there were six, in more recent times, there were the Ghana and Dahomey coups of 72, Rwanda in 73, Niger and Ethiopia in 74 and Chad and Nigeria last year."

"Lots going on, should we have a gun in the house?" I asked.

"I don't think so," he said. "If it ever gets to shooting in Nairobi, you will have been evacuated to London, and we might even close the commission for the duration."

"Okay," I said. "I'll try not to worry about it, but I need to know what's going on, so tell me everything, even if it's not good."

"I will," he promised. "If we have to ship you out, just take what you can't replace, we've both got enough clothes and stuff in London, so no need for big suitcases."

"Good," I said. "Now, on the plane you were promising things, are you ready for your penance for making rude comments about my hair?"

"Yes, Dear," he said, trying to look meek and mild.

"Well, come on then," I told him. "Bath and bed."

"What nothing to eat or drink?" he said.

"Afterwards," I promised

Later, sated and content, we sat and munched on a snack and drank some wine, happy to be together.

"Do you have to work tomorrow?" I asked Ian.

"Unfortunately, my duty turn," he replied.

"I thought I might drive out to the gun club and get some practice," I said.

"You don't have to worry Fi," he said. "We're not going to have any shooting in Nairobi."

"I know," I told him. "But I'm rusty and need to brush up on a few things, so will spend an hour or two with Geraldine. She's good, but not that good and she's asked for some advice, so I'll help her. Then I thought in the next couple of weeks I might stop at one or two of the flight schools and investigate lessons and rates."

"I can see you'll have a licence before I can turn around," he laughed. "The instructors are going to have to stay on their toes."

"I bought a book in London on aircraft navigation and the maths look pretty simple," I said.

"Simple to you, maybe," he said. "But then as I recall you can also do celestial navigation calculations already."

"I find it interesting," I said. "I like the ideas of planet movements and the apparent position of the stars with time, so doing survey calculations to fix a point on the ground from star shots is a simple enough task."

"As I said, simple for you," Ian said.

"So, are you ready to navigate your way to the gates of heaven?" I asked him, jokingly.

"That I can manage," he laughed.

Amin duly made his announcement on February 15th, claiming that he had a letter written by the then Colonial Secretary, Herbert Asquith, plus a map, describing territory to be transferred from Uganda to Kenya in 1914 and 1926. As Ian had told me before, Asquith was never the Colonial Secretary and Amin had missed the really big chunk that was moved in 1902. Predictably, Kenyatta came out a few days later with a strong speech in which he said that Kenya would never cede an inch of territory. By the 24th of February Amin had climbed down and said that he never had any designs upon Kenyan territory. Nevertheless, Kenya moved troops to the border, in case Amin threw caution to the wind and did something really reckless, like invade Kenya.

So, war never came, at least not to Kenya and not then. But Amin's problems did not go away and he kept bringing up issues with all his neighbours, it was as though the man was desperately trying to divert attention away from domestic affairs. I was thankful that war did not come, I had been dreading a possible separation from Ian for however long the war might have gone on. I was wedded to him body and soul and the notion of an enforced separation was anathema to me. It seemed to me the Kenyatta read it right, face down Amin with strong words and obvious resolution and he would back down. Chances of war were then likely to be miscalculation on the part of some local commander who did something stupid.

My plane

"It sounds like it was an interesting time," Maman said.

"It was," I agreed. "I have to admit I was concerned for a while, but Ian was keeping a close eye on things and he would have shipped me off if there had been real trouble, my real concern was that if war did break out and I left, that Ian would stay behind, and I didn't want him to be in another shooting war. It's another of those moments in your life that you remember."

"I could have done without the details of your sex life with Ian," James said.

"Sorry," I said. "I didn't think, but, it's a normal human interaction, don't you ever talk about it?"

"With Charlie," he said. "But, no one else. Don't tell me that you do?"

"Maman, Portia and I have had long conversations about things," I said. "And, when I first went out with Ian it was most helpful."

"Even so," James protested. "I don't think I could ever talk about it the way you just did."

"Not everyone can," Portia said. "Fiona is probably one of the very few women I know that will actually talk about sex with us without getting red in the face and embarrassed, and I don't know any men who would, apart from the boasting that goes on with some men, most of which I think can be discounted."

"What are going to do with your plane?" Charlize asked, discretely changing the subject, away from sex to the more mundane.

"I've sold it already," I replied. "I had toyed with the idea of flying it back, but couldn't work out a route that didn't have too many risks, so I decided to sell it and I had four buyers all clamouring for it. I've ordered a new one, a bigger one, the Cessna 206, Stationair, to be delivered in England when I get back."

"Where will you keep that one in England?" James asked.

"Probably somewhere like White Waltham," I said. "Or perhaps the Biggin Hill airfield, then it's a shorter hop across the Channel. What's the closest general aviation field to you?"

"Probably the field that's near Cosne," James thought. "It's not like here where every little outlying town and farm has its own strip. The Cosne-sur-Loire strip I think is tarred, so no dirt, and it's not too far from us."

"And Maman?" I asked.

"The Cannes airport, there just aren't many airports of any kind on the coast, certainly not little strips like you have here," she replied. "They have a pretty big general aviation business at the Cannes airport, so it would be a good place to fly into, and it's not that long a drive to our house from there."

"Do you still enjoy flying?" Charlize asked.

"A lot," I said. "It's a great way to see Kenya and the Stationair that I'm buying has enough room for people and luggage, and it's got enough range to go to most places and back without having to worry about getting fuel."

"So, you could fly from London to Cannes?" James asked.

"Easily," I said. "I'm guessing that Biggin Hill to Cannes must be about 550 nautical miles, and the Stationair has a range of 730 nautical miles, the only issue is the time, it would be well over three hours, almost four, so make sure you go to the loo before you leave!"

"Are you going to keep your Land Rover?" James asked.

"Yes," I said. "I like it and there's plenty of miles left in it, so I'll just ship it back and keep it in London. Irene told me that she knows a garage close to my flat where I can keep it off the road, for a reasonable rate per month. I asked her to book the space for me, and I'll just pay for the space until it gets there. The Land Rover distributor here is working with the people they ship with to take it back for me. I've already taken lots of photographs of it and the shipping company rep has been over it and we've agreed on its condition, so if it arrives with any new damage, they pay, or give me a new one."

"Back to your plane for a minute, tell us about your flying lessons," Charlize said.

Flying lessons

When Beryl Markham got her Class A Pilot's Licence in 1931, there was probably a lot less rigmarole than now, so I had prepared myself to face bureaucracy at its best. I went out one day to the Wilson Airfield and found the Aviation Club of East Africa, dressed in khaki trousers, a khaki shirt, plimsoles and my best aviator sunglasses, and enquired after the process for getting a Private Pilot Licence and for instructors to teach me the basics of flying. I was directed to a middle-aged man, by the name of Brian Green, who allowed as he could teach me to fly and guide me through the ground course work that would be required. He named a fee and I haggled a little, but not too much, and we agreed upon a price. The next step, he told me, was to get a medical clearance certificate and there were designated physicians who were authorised to issue those. He gave me a list, and most usefully, added comments on each. Apparently, I had already passed two of the requirements, I was over seventeen and, in all probability, far exceeded the minimum education requirements laid down by statute. He then offered to take me for a quick spin and even let me try my hand at the controls, to see if this was something that I really wanted to pursue.

We walked out onto the tarmac and went to a small aircraft. It was one of those I had shown Ian on the plane from London, a Cessna 172, Skyhawk. He walked around and fiddled with different things and poked and prodded and peered at the plane, doing his walk-around inspection. Apparently, all was in order, because he then opened the passenger door for me and showed me where to step to climb in. I settled in the seat and thought that I should probably keep my feet off the pedals that were in front of me, and keep my hands off the yoke that was also in front of me. Brian got in his side and told me to put on the seat harness, this was not just the simple seat belt that I was used to, but over both shoulders and across the waist, all ending in a fancy buckle. He then told me to put on the headset that was hanging by the seat, so that I could always hear him above the noise of the engine. He then quickly ran his hands over various switches, buttons and levers, muttering a kind of mantra as he did so, all part of his pre-startup checklist. Then he started the engine and ran it up a little and then settled it back down. I noted that he moved the yoke and at the same time looked back at the wings to see if things actually moved. Finally, he waved to one of the workers who had been waiting for us and the man pulled the chocks away from the wheels. Then he started chatting on the radio, and I learned that we were Delta Tango Zulu. The tower gave us clearance and instructions and we started off down the taxiway. At the end of the runway, we waited and when told to go, he pushed the throttle forward, let go of the brakes, and we were off. It seemed to me that we were in the air in a very short time on our climb out. We were given instructions as to altitude and heading, then we were off into the wide blue yonder. It was lovely up there. It was quite unlike flying in a big commercial jet, we were low enough that we could see everything on the ground, even our own shadow as we flew along.

Brian explained the various controls to me, then told me to put my feet on the pedals, the rudder pedals, then my hands on the yoke, then he told me that it was all mine. I experimented by pulling back on the yoke and climbing up a little, then pushing forward and descending, then I tried turns, to the left, to the right, and saw how the plane banked as we turned, and Brian explained to me how to coordinate the rudder movements with the ailerons as we turned. It was fun. It was so much fun, I could understand what Saint-Exupéry had meant when he talked about the witchery of flying. We flew around, doing turns, ups and downs and more turns, until Brian told me that we should go back to the airport. He directed me on when and where to turn while he talked to the tower people. Then I realised he was going to have me land the plane. I did not panic, but my heart rate did go up, more than a little. I glanced over and noted that he had his hands lightly on his yoke, so that if things went awry, he could take over immediately. We reduced speed and lost altitude and I lined us up on the runway. There was a slight cross breeze, but Brian told me how to correct for that and he talked me down to the ground, until we touched down, without a bounce I might add, and ran down the runway until he told me to apply the brakes and slow down enough that we could turn off. I had done it! I had managed to land the plane, it was such a thrill, so satisfying and so rewarding to achieve that. I was hooked, I was going to definitely sign up for lessons

Brian took over and parked the plane where he wanted it and then shut things down.

"Well, how was it?" he asked.

"Super," I said. "I'll be back for lessons, when can I start?"

"Get your medical cert," he said. "Then we can start right away, we'll do ground book work as well as flights, what does your schedule look like?"

"I can manage most days," I told him. "But I do need to go to London and Paris for a few days at the end of the month and thereafter there will be odd trips to Paris and London."

"What takes you to London and Paris?" he asked.

"I have some clients there," I said. "I do mathematical models for them."

"So, the mathematics part of the ground exam should be fairly simple for you then?" he asked.

"I imagine so," I said. "I can do celestial navigation calculations using star shots, so simple navigation calculations should be much easier."

"Much," he agreed. "Okay then, come back and see me with the Class II medical cert and we'll get started."

"Thank you," I said. "And, thank you for the ride, it was fun."

My next stop was the office of one of the doctors on the list who was authorised to issue Class II Medical Certificates. As it turned out he had time that afternoon, so all I had to do was go away for an hour or so, then go back and all would be done. I wondered what Ian might be doing so stopped by the High Commission. He was actually not that busy, so we went to lunch.

"I went to check out flying lessons today," I told him.

"And?" he asked.

"It was fun," I said. "I'm going to take lessons, first I need to get a medical clearance and then I can start, oh, and I landed a plane today."

"You what?" he asked.

"The flight instructor took me for a spin," I explained. "And, he let me take the controls, and he even talked me down so that I landed the plane."

"And you enjoyed yourself?" he asked.

"I did," I confirmed. "It was lovely up there, I went up, I went down, I turned right, I turned left, I went in a circle, I went in a circle going up,

I went in a circle going down, I was able to look at the ground and see things, I think I'm going to really enjoy this."

"What's involved with the lessons?" he asked.

"There's groundwork, which is classroom lessons, principals of flight, navigation, weather, law and some other stuff, then there's the flying lessons themselves," I explained. "The same instructor will do both."

"What does the medical entail?" he asked.

"I think mainly that I'm breathing and in reasonable health, an eye exam and a colour blindness test," I replied.

"Well, you're in better health than most people I know," he said.

"I'm sure they'll check my blood pressure, pulse rate and all that kind of thing," I said. "I have an appointment this afternoon with a Dr Blake."

"Blake, Blake," he mused. "I've heard of him, not all good, make sure that the nurse stays in the room with you."

"One of those, is he?" I said. "Well, I'll make sure the nurse stays and if I think anything untoward is going to happen, I'll warn him, then I'll hit him, he may regret the day he met me, but then again he might be really nice and professional."

"Just watch yourself," Ian cautioned.

"I will, now what shall we have for lunch?" I asked.

I went to my appointment with Dr Blake, who was a fussy man, in his mid-forties, balding and generally going to seed. He had the requisite forms at hand and motioned to me to hop up onto the examination table. He looked at the nurse who had shown me to the room, and she made as if to leave.

"The nurse stays," I said.

"That's preposterous," Blake said.

"Not at all," I said. "I had an unfortunate experience with a doctor in England, so, I'm protecting you and your reputation."

Blake agreed, I think a little reluctantly and the nurse, Jane Benson, stayed. The whole examination did not take long, there was a quick eye test, a colour blindness test, then weight, height, blood pressure and listen to the heart and lungs.

"You're in remarkable shape," Blake said. "Do you exercise much?"

"I do," I confirmed. "I run, often ten kilometres or more, I also do karate and tai chi."

"It shows," he said. "Well, you won't need another medical for a couple of years, but if you just keep doing what you're doing, I can't see any issues with that."

"Thank you, Dr Blake," I said.

"I see here it says that you're Dr Hartley," he said. "Doctor of what?"

"I have doctorates in mathematics and economics," I explained.

"Oh," he said. "Well, nice to have met you Dr Hartley." With that, he scuttled off to another patient and left me with Nurse Benson.

"Thank you for staying," I told her. "As I said before, I had had a poor experience in London with a doctor."

"How did you resolve it?" she asked.

"I broke his nose," I said. "He tried to bring an assault charge, but I counter-sued with a sexual assault charge and complained to the BMA (British Medical Association). I won and he was struck off and lost his licence, I think because it had happened before, so he was known. What annoyed me was that the BMA had done nothing really after the first three complaints, so they knew they had a problem child and chose not to do anything."

"They do rather look after each other," Nurse Benson agreed. "Next time you need a flight medical go and see Dr Barrett, he's very nice and you'll have no complaints about him."

"Thank you," I said. "There are no women doctors on this list?"

Jane looked it over quickly, then handed it back to me, "None," she said. "Maybe one day, but for now it's pretty much a bastion of male ego and chauvinism. Don't you find the same thing with mathematics and economics?"

"I do," I confirmed. "I happen to be rather good at what I do, so have a reputation and clients come to me, and I have the luxury of being able to turn away those that I don't like."

"You must be well set to be able to do that," Jane commented.

"I was fortunate with the first major assignment that I had," I explained. "Since then word has gone out and I've not had any problem getting work, rather the opposite, I'm turning away jobs. I know I need to be careful about that, so that if things dry up for me, I haven't burnt too many bridges. But, for now, it works."

"Well, good for you," Jane said. "Doesn't your husband work at the Brit High Commission?"

"He does," I confirmed. "We arrived right at the end of last year."

"Well, I hope you enjoy your time here," Jane said. "I know you folks tend to come and go, but I suppose that all part of the diplomatic service, you go where they send you."

"That does appear to be the size of it," I agreed. "I've no idea where they might send us next."

"I should get back to work," Jane said. "It was really nice to meet you, Doctor Hartley, I hope we meet again."

"So do I," I echoed. "Thank you for your time and understanding."

I went home and waited for Ian to come so that I could tell him about my afternoon and relate my experiences with Dr Blake. He was not at all surprised that Dr Blake was less than thrilled by my insistence that the nurse stay and said that none of the High Commission staff would go to him. Perhaps with men, it was different, but as far as I was concerned, he was not to be trusted.

"So," Ian said. "What's next with the flying lessons?"

"I'll go out tomorrow with my medical certificate and arrange for the flight lessons and the classroom time," I said.

"How long do you think it will be before you can get a licence?" he asked.

"I suppose that depends on how frequent the lessons are and how much effort I put into the ground classes," I thought. "I understand that the requirement for flying time is forty-five hours of which ten has to be solo, so, if I go out two or three times a week for one to one and a half hours at a time, and I add in some extra time for my trips to London and Paris, I could be done in three or four months, or I could just go mad and do five to six hours a day until I get it done."

"Can you take lessons in England or France while you're there?" he asked.

"I'm sure I could," I said. "But I'd talk to my instructor before I did that to get his agreement and his suggestions."

"If you did, you'd get some experience in lousy weather," he said. "Let's face it, the weather in England and France is not like it is here."

"That's true," I agreed. "I wonder how much longer it would take in England, just because of weather delays?"

"Who knows," he said.

"Anyway, what would you like for dinner?" I asked.

"I'll cook," he said. "There's a Moroccan chicken dish I heard about today that I'd like to try. Why don't you just set the table and let me get on with the cooking?"

Dinner was very good, the Moroccan-style chicken dish had lots of cumin and other spices, and couscous to go with it. Ian told me about his day which seemed to have been mostly writing reports. There were assessments due of the economic and political state of the State, so he had been tasked to write about the state of play with respect to local politics and relations with the neighbouring countries. Others in the staff had been commissioned to provide the economic and defence portions of the report, but as he explained, the political situation could not be divorced from the realities of the economy and the state of readiness of the armed forces, particularly in light of the recent events with Idi Amin. It was fascinating and I was, as ever, impressed by Ian's ability to see through things and quickly note the points of major interest and concern. I then told him about my own adventures with the French and their project to understand the debacle that was British Leyland. Why governments thought that nationalisation was the answer to anything had always escaped me. I could see for the mineral-rich countries that taking full ownership of mineral rights was important, but that did not mean that they had to run the mines, only intelligently price the royalties. Pricing the royalties was a challenge, too low and one might just as well give the stuff away with no benefit to the country, too high and one then ran the risk of competition from other sources making one's minerals less attractive, but the royalties had to be high enough that the government received something for their value, because once extracted they were gone forever and that asset was depleted. There were, of course, additional taxes to be levied on income and company profits, but how did that work if the enterprise was a government entity that would then, in effect, be taxing itself. For industries like the car business, national ownership might be a way to inject capital, but was that in and of itself a good idea. The British Leyland combination was a disaster and they were headed for troubled times. One would have thought that the Soviet Union would have taught some people lessons in how not to run an economy. Theirs was a classic example of centrally planned economies just not delivering the desired results. But I suppose every successive socialist regime felt that it could be better than the last, and the current British government was no different.

The next day I went back to the flight club, medical certificate in hand, and started on my lessons. The first thing I was given was a pilot's log book, in which each flight I took would be recorded, even as a student, and there would be notes on what I actually did. So, the first entry was something like, straight and level flight, turns, climb, descent, landing, and the instructor signed off on each flight. We also did some classroom work, starting with meteorology. Weather was after all a really big factor in whether or not it was safe to fly. I learned about clouds, winds, rain, density altitude, fog, icing and a variety of other things. When I drove home that day, I took a new look at the clouds that were in the sky. What I saw was generally clement weather with no storms brewing. I listened to the weather forecast that night and heard, to my satisfaction, that the weather service people also said that there were no storms brewing. Ian wanted to know about my day, so I related to him my experiences, from the ground walk around of the plane, looking for things amiss, to the pre-flight checks, to the radio procedures asking for clearance to taxi and take off, then the flight itself. He suggested that I ask the instructor to find a plane that did have problems and then see if I could spot them. I thought that a splendid suggestion. Looking at something that has no issues gives you no indication of what bad looks like. I had some classroom homework and had Ian grill me on the questions that were included with the book. Then, I realised that I had been monopolising the time and asked him, a little shamefaced, about his day. He told me that nothing of note had transpired that day, just routine items, mostly paperwork and reports needing to be submitted so that the FCO was abreast of happenings.

I kept up with regular flying lessons, going out three times a week for two hours at a time. I confess that for the first few lessons, I was tired after the two hours, but as my skills improved the lessons seemed shorter and shorter, even though the actual time stayed the same. I did discuss with Brian finding an aircraft that was less than perfect and he took me one day to a hangar and asked me to do a walk around of the plane there. Well, of the fifteen or so issues, I am pleased to say that I picked up on twelve of them, and Brian then pointed out the other items. We did that once a week on different aircraft until I finally picked up something that he had not spotted immediately. He was very nice about it and congratulated me on my observation. Ian had been right, looking over a well-maintained plane was nice, but far more instructive was to look over one that had problems. All those we did look over and find problems with were all in for maintenance as the owners knew of the problems, so we were not discovering anything new and momentous, only new to me.

On one of my trips to London, I met with an aviation broker and agreed upon the purchase of a Cessna 172, Skyhawk, to be ferried to Nairobi. It transpired that most deliveries were by ferry pilot and crating and shipping was rare. I had ordered the factory option of long-range tanks and wondered if they would also add bladder fuel tanks to make sure that there was enough to make the crossing from the United States to England, but then I learned that the plane would actually be built in France by the affiliate of Cessna in Reims. So, all the ferry pilot had to worry about was the trip over the Mediterranean and on down through Africa. I hoped that the pilot would be able to make the journey down from Egypt across the Sudan with the minimum of problems, but that was Cessna's problem not mine, as the contact was for delivery to Nairobi. The biggest issue was what colour should the plane be and what type of seats and what colour should the seats be. I chose basic white for the plane, but with some light blue striping, and for the seats I chose fabric seat covers that were tan in colour. The broker tried to sell me on the idea of leather seats, but leather in the tropics. I had enough troubles with the black seats in my Land Rover. I know they were not leather, but some kind of vinyl, but the same principle held, I wanted seat covers that breathed. I bought the best seat harnesses I could and also the best avionics that were available at the time and the best radio and headsets. I knew that in time new avionic systems would probably come out, so would upgrade when that happened.

On another trip to London, I took time off and went out to Biggin Hill for a flying lesson. I had found a school there, that seemed to have been there forever, since 1947 in fact. I had talked to Brian and he had given me the name of one of the instructors at the school, so I called and booked dual time. The plane was a tiny Cessna 150, a two-seater plane. It was quite different flying in England. The weather was fair, winds light and variable, but visibility was not the same as in Kenya, no vistas that seemed to stretch to infinity, but the ride was less bouncy as the thermals caused by the heat of Kenya were just not present in Southern England, at least not in early spring. The radio traffic was much more intense. In Kenya there was an occasional chat on the radio between the tower at Nairobi and some aircraft, in England, it seemed like a constant stream of chatter, but then the sheer number of aircraft flying overhead in and out of Heathrow and Gatwick meant that things would be busy. I am pleased to say that I did not make an idiot of myself and the instructor signed off my log book and told me that I was ready to solo. He also said that he would be reporting back to Brian on my lesson. That was fine with me, I had learned when I first took up shooting that the instructors were not all doom and gloom and did have advice to offer and that criticism was often useful, providing it was offered in a constructive way.

One other thing I did while I was in England once, was spend some time in a simulator. That was really useful because I was able to learn how to respond to all kinds of scenarios, some of which led to me crashing the plane, without actually crashing the plane. Those times that I crashed I repeated the exercise until I got it right. It cost me a little for the simulator time, but I thought that it was money well spent. When I returned after that trip, Brian said that I was ready to solo, so heart in hand I went out one day to the Aero Club and he sent me on my way. I confess to some apprehension, but routine set in and I followed all the procedures that Brian had drilled me on and my first solo was a success. He even congratulated me on my landing, telling me that it was as perfect as it could be. That was high praise indeed. The next lesson I just did circuits and bumps, which meant that I flew around the airport, came into land, just bumped the ground, then took off again for another circuit. I learned from Brian that the Americans called this touch and go, which I think for us was a little confusing as we were used to touch and go meaning something chancy. Brian also drilled me on what to do if the engine failed as I was taking off. As the plane had only one engine, the best thing that could happen is that it would restart quickly, if not then it was how good a glider was it, and where could I turn to, to put it down on the ground. We also practised aborted take-offs and aborted landings, what are known in the business as a go-around. That happened when there was some reason why I could not land safely, so had to climb back out, go around the airport and try again. It struck me that most of the training had to do with what to do if something went wrong, rather like a contract that often had one page of what I was going to do and one hundred pages of what happened if either I, or the client, did not meet the terms of the contract. So, we practised engine out procedures, stalls, spins and all manner of untoward events.

We went looking for likely places where we could land in the event of an engine failure, and several times Brian had me drive us to that place, so that we could see what it looked like on the ground, which was often quite different from the view from the air. I learned to look for agricultural impacts, like furrows and irrigation ditches, I also learned about trees and bushes and which were likely to give way to an aircraft and which would likely cause real damage. Brian also had me study weather charts a lot and wanted me to discuss the weather patterns and what different winds meant in terms of likely rain and other bad weather. The little planes we were flying did not fly high enough to clear much of potential bad weather, unlike commercial aircraft that often flew above the clouds, and only occasionally encountered high thunderheads and poor conditions. I got pretty good at predicting the weather, based on temperatures, wind speeds and direction and barometric pressure. Brian also took me through a fairly intensive course on field repairs. It was always possible in Kenya that one might have to put down in a remote area and try and effect repairs oneself. So, I learned about the engine, the flight controls and the instruments. I even had a go, on a plane in for maintenance, at stripping down various engine parts and fixing them. It was quite a departure for me from my usual mathematical models, but there was logic to it and I quite enjoyed my odd stint as a field mechanic. Ian joked that he should buy me a set of overalls and a toolbox. I took him up on that, at least for the toolbox and he presented me with a nice toolbox that had all the right sizes of spanners and such to fit the engine nuts and bolts and other systems on the Cessna. Although it did weigh a bit, I stowed it in the plane, so that it would always be there in the event of an emergency.

I was invited to visit the factory in Reims at any time I happened to be in France, to see my aircraft being built. So, on one of my trips to Paris, I took a side trip and took a train to Reims and visited the factory there. I was met at the station by a representative from the factory and driven out to the factory. We made a tour of the factory floor and saw all kinds of aircraft in various stages of construction and found mine, just a fuselage awaiting to have its wings installed. I looked it over, inspected it, eyed it up, walked around it, tapped on it, patted it and had to admit that it looked good. The workers were making some remarks about the aircraft and me, thinking that because I was from Kenya that I probably did not speak French. I quickly disabused them of that notion and asked them some questions about the design and manufacturing processes. They could answer most of my questions about the manufacturing processes, but for the design issues, they referred me back to their engineering office.

The company man asked if I would like to test fly an equivalent plane, so, of course, I said yes and produced my logbook. The company had an instructor pilot and I was introduced to him and went out with him to a plane on the tarmac of the field adjacent to the factory. We were fortunate with the weather, it was clear and cool and there was a watery sun, so quite nice weather for a short take-off and clear enough to fly by visual flight rules. I did a walk around and poked and prodded, waggled things and asked the instructor what to look for in the immediate and over time as the plane aged. He was very helpful and pointed out areas that might be of concern in time and what to look for and how to detect early things that might become more of an issue. Then we climbed aboard the plane and took a ride around the area for the next hour. He let me fly it all the way, keeping his hands lightly on the controls until he was satisfied that I was not going to fly us into the ground. Then he sat back and relaxed and just chatted about things, while managing the radio contacts with the local controllers. He wanted to know about Kenya and how it was to fly there. He also wanted to know why I had taken up flying. He gave me hints and tips about flying and told me to go back at any time, even after I had received my plane. After the flight, he signed off my log book and made an entry in French, that I translated and had him initial as an accurate translation.

While I was busy with flying lessons, Ian was busy with issues at the High Commission. There were tourists to bail out of trouble, there were reports to complete and submit, there were meetings with various Kenyan ministries to attend and there were even social events to promote relations between HMG and Kenya. After the debacle with Uganda earlier in the year there were also frequent assessments of the neighbours and what their politics might be and how their relations with Kenya might change over time. Ian once told me that he could see more issues with Uganda and eventually some with Tanzania. He foresaw real issues in time with Somalia and Sudan as more radical Islam took hold in those countries, that would lead to border conflicts. But, for the moment things were relatively quiet and we could just enjoy our posting to Nairobi. There had been problems with Somalis in the past, when armed gangs would prey upon the Kenyans, but it had not yet become a real problem. However, Ian saw it as a long-term issue that would not be readily resolved, in fact, he saw Somalia as a powder keg of issues that would explode into terrorism, piracy and all manner of criminal activity. He saw the government there as collapsing in time and had advised the Kenyans on several occasions to step up their surveillance of the border. Somalia was a desperately poor country that was mostly desert and had little in the way of minerals, industry or infrastructure, so the quickest and easiest way to acquire wealth and possessions was to take them from someone who already had them.

My plane arrived a month before I received my licence. I had been told of its departure from France and when we might expect it in Nairobi. So, Ian and I went out on the appointed day and waited. We heard the pilot contact the tower and watched as it landed. Various and sundry officials were on hand for customs and immigration procedures and we waited until they were done before introducing ourselves. The pilot wanted to hand everything over to Ian, but Ian set him straight and I got the package of documents that I would need to register the plane in Kenya. We tied the plane down then took the pilot to the Norfolk and told him that we would join him later for dinner. Over dinner, the pilot regaled us with his tales of his flight down over Africa. I gathered that the main problems had to do with bureaucracy in Egypt and Sudan. He hinted that bribes were expected and paid, but that he had been prepared for that and had come well-equipped. I had wondered if he would have any other problems, but it seemed that once in the air, his trip had been uneventful, just long and tedious. His route had taken him from Cairo to Wadi Halfa, then to Khartoum, then Juba and finally on into Nairobi. I am glad someone else made that trip, it did not strike me as particularly glamorous, and it had its element of risk. The pilot laughed off the perils of the flight and said that he had delivered planes on worse routes. The next day I took him back to the airport and, with Brian and one of the certified mechanics, we went through the plane carefully until I was satisfied that all was in good order. Then I signed for the plane and it was now mine. The ferry pilot then just wanted dropping at the airport to catch the overnight BA flight back to London. I dropped him off, far too early for the flight, but he was happy enough writing up reports, then I went to the ministry that dealt with aircraft registrations. Fortunately, I had been to see them before and they knew that I would be coming. I had also reserved a registration number, 5Y-FTF, 5Y for Kenya and for me FTF, foxtrot tango foxtrot, all dance steps. They knew the procedure for changing registrations from another country, it was not the first time they had done this. The paperwork was completed in record time and I went away with the new papers and the new number. I had made arrangements with a sign writer to come out to the airport and put the new number on for me, so called him and told him that he could attend to that at any time.

Lessons continued, with Brian setting me specific things to do and on occasion he would go with me and deliberately mess things up to see how I would respond. I began to look upon those trips as challenges to see how quickly I could analyse the situation and come up with the best solution. We even started on the requirements for an instrument rating, so he would put this weird hood thing on my head that would allow me to see the instruments but not look outside. He made me do stalls and recoveries from various unusual attitudes, all just using the instruments. It was instructive and very useful. He also set cross-country routes for me to fly, so that I could prove that I could navigate as well as fly. I did a number of those to far-flung places. My final solo cross-country flight was interesting, he had me go from Nairobi to Isiolo, around Mount Kenya, and then to Nyahururu, avoiding the Laikipia air base at

Nanyuki, and thence back to Nairobi. Flying around Mount Kenya was interesting, first, the views were terrific, and the winds were generally fairly light, but around the mountain, there were local effects that I had to adjust for. I rather think that was why he sent me on the particular triangular course, to see if I would handle the navigation challenges brought about by the odd winds. The upshot of that flight was that he passed me on all my requirements for the licence and I was now a bona fide private pilot.

After I had gained my licence I took Ian up for a spin, not literally, I had no desire to do aerobatics, so stayed staid and sober for the whole flight. He was very good about the flight, he did not hang on as if for dear life, but he was quite relaxed the whole flight, which I took as a vote of confidence in my abilities. After we had landed, I then broached the really big issue, what were we going to call the plane?
"Have you any suggestions?" he asked.
"Not at the moment," I said. "I was waiting to talk to you about it."
"What about Function X?" he suggested.
"Function X?" I asked.
"Function X," he confirmed. "Maybe not, a bit too mathematical."
"What was your favourite bird when you were growing up?" I asked.
"Martial eagle," he said.
"Then, why don't we just call it Martial?" I suggested.
"That sounds nice," he agreed.
"I'll have the chap who did the number for us add the name," I said. So, a couple of days later, we had a name on the plane and a small martial eagle to boot. I must say that it looked very nice and added something to the plane. There were times I felt a little guilty. I was having the time of my life. I could pick and choose clients, I had just learned to fly, I now had my own plane and poor Ian was stuck with consular duties, including some weekends when he was the duty officer. But he assured me that he was enjoying life, even when he had to work his weekend stints at the commission. I did promise to take him away for a weekend, so we made a date and checked, re-checked, and double-checked to make sure that he would be free.

We decided to go out to Maasai Mara for our jaunt. I talked to Julia and got a recommendation for a camp that had its own landing strip, I talked to their booking agent in town and made arrangements to go and to be met at the strip. I gave them an approximate arrival time and said that we would call in when we were fifteen minutes out. On the appointed day I collected Ian when he had finished for the day at the High Commission and brought him a change of clothes. I had decided on shorts, a khaki shirt and my best Ray Ban aviator sunglasses for myself. We went out to the Wilson Airfield, where we kept our plane and stowed our small overnight bags. I did my walk around then had Ian read out the various checklists, for start, taxi and take off. The flight took us just under an hour, flying almost straight west. I had been close to the camp when I had taken my trip to Kenya before with Maman and Portia, but then it took us hours and hours by road to get there. Flying certainly reduced the travel time, providing that there was someone there at the other end to pick you up. When we were about fifteen minutes, I called the camp and told them when we would land. As we approached, I flew down over the strip to ensure there was nothing on it and then came back into land. The camp people were there with a Land Rover to meet us and they took our bags for us while I saw to the plane. I had checked the weather and although there were no high winds expected, it paid to be cautious, so we tied the plane down. I told Ian what I wanted and he busily hammered away at pins, four to a star, of which there were three, one under each wind and one behind the tail. The pins were angled in so would not pull out with the effects of any winds. The drive to the camp was short, only a few minutes and we were there, a tented camp, just what you might expect to see in a Hollywood version of an African Safari. Our hosts were Jack and Emily Blake. They had been running the camp for some years and were beginning to broaden their client base to the States as well as England. Apparently, they had an agent in Chicago who was particularly keen and was getting them all kinds of bookings.

There were six others at the camp, all Americans apparently getting their first taste of Africa. They were out on a game drive when we arrived, so we would have the pleasure of their company over dinner. Our tent was nicely set up, similar to the one that I had used a year earlier when I had taken the safari with Maman and Portia. Was it only a year ago. It was, in fact, less than a year ago. We had gone in July of the previous year, and it was now only May. So much had happened in that time. We had been to Arusha and discovered the truth about the missing letters sent by both myself and Ian, we had seen James and Charlize married, I had found Ian again and we had been married soon after. Now, here we were in Maasai Mara, a place that Ian had wanted to take me. We dropped our bags by the beds and went back out to enjoy the afternoon and have a sundowner when the sun did finally go down. I recalled the first African sunset I had seen the previous year and the terrible sense of loss, because Ian had not been there to enjoy it with me. But this time things were different. We were together and could enjoy the sunset together. Emily saw us wandering out to the *boma* area, where they had a lounge, dining area and bar, and offered us something to drink. I was not flying us back until Sunday afternoon, so opted for wine. Ian went with a beer, a Tusker, the standard beer of Kenya since the 1920s. The camp had a clear view of the sunset, so we sat and watched as the sun fell lower in the sky, waiting for the actual sunset.

"Glad we came?" I asked Ian.

"Oh, yes," he replied. "I really wanted to show you Africa, this is not quite how I expected things to turn out, but what a way to see it. We flew out in our own plane; we can come and go pretty much as we like. I can't get over how fortunate we are, you're here, we both have jobs we like, it's the middle of Africa, the day is beautiful and the sunset promises to be spectacular, what else could I wish for?"

"Well, Ian Hartley, here's to us," I toasted.

"To us," he echoed. "Which bed shall we sleep in tonight?"

"We'll pick one when we go back," I said. "It's been a while since we've both slept in a single bed. What's that over there?"

"Grant's gazelle," he replied. "And, over there, wildebeest, zebra, and even a black rhino hiding in the middle of the wildebeest."

"And the bird that's flitting around above us?" I asked.

"Lilac-breasted roller, and over there a secretary bird and by the edge of that water hole, a saddle-billed stork, a couple of hadedas and a wagtail," he enumerated.

"You know your birds," Emily said as she came over to where we were seated.

"I grew up in the bush in Rhodesia," Ian explained. "I also spent almost three years at Olduvai, and had to do something other than dig in the dirt."

"Where in Rhodesia?" Emily asked.

"Close to Mount Darwin," he replied. "My folks had a tobacco farm there."

"And you, Fiona, you didn't grow up in Africa?" Emily asked.

"No," I confirmed. "I was raised in England, near Henley, I met Ian at Oxford when he came back from Olduvai."

"And now you're here, with your own plane, how did you manage that?" Emily asked.

"I've been fortunate with a consulting business," I explained.

"Must have been really fortunate," Emily commented.

"Fiona is a mathematician and economist," Ian explained. "She creates models for people to predict economic outcomes and help people plan their business strategies."

"Julia told me that you're with the Brit High Commission," Emily said to Ian.

"I am," he confirmed. "I'm the Third Secretary, which I think means that I'm the dogsbody that does all the running around. I do most of the consular affairs, so if a Brit loses their passport, or gets thrown in gaol, I'm the one who has to sort it all out."

"A little different from archaeology," Emily laughed.

"A little," he agreed. "So, tell us about the other guests."

"They're all from the States," she replied. "I gather they're all business bigwigs of some sort and the women are spouses, partners or latest flings, I didn't ask too many questions, the women are all so much younger than the men. Jack has them out on a game drive right now, they'll be back after the sun goes down."

"What are they like?" I asked.

"Nice enough," Emily said. "A little on the privileged side, expect people to jump at their every command or whim, particularly the women. But we're managing. Money doesn't seem to be a problem with them."

"I'm surprised they didn't buy out the camp," Ian said. "Perhaps they won't like interlopers."

"They know you're coming," Emily said. "We've just told them that you're from Nairobi and that you were flying out in your own plane for the weekend. So, they probably think you're rich landowners or something."

"Not penniless government servants?" Ian laughed.

"No," Emily agreed. "If you'll excuse me, I'll just see to drinks and snacks for them when they get back."

The sun was finally going down and I was reminded of the words of the song that had prompted me to go searching for Ian after we had lost touch with one another, *Quand le soleil va se perdre à l'horizon, Tous nos souvenirs me font souffrir encore*. Well, the sun was sinking below the horizon and those memories that would make me suffer were now replaced by the more recent better memories of the past months now that Ian and I were together again, this time for good. I held his hand and we watched as the sun literally dropped below the horizon, something that had not yet ceased to amaze me, how quickly that happened in the tropics. One could almost take a camera and shoot picture after picture and see the difference in each shot. For Ian, that was what he had known until he went to Oxford to university, so for him, the long drawn-out setting sun and the extended twilight of the high latitudes had been new and unusual.

"I love you," he said, quite out of the blue.

"I love you," I told him. I really did love him; he was everything to me and imagining life without him was difficult if not nigh on impossible.

"There are the others coming back," he said, pointing to pinpricks of light that were the headlights of the camp Land Rover. "They'll be here in about twenty minutes."

Ian was right, to the minute and we watched as the Land Rover pulled up and the other guests got out. They all went scurrying off, probably to use loos and perhaps wash their hands and faces before coming for a drink before dinner. Jack came over and introduced himself and he and Ian quickly found out that they had mutual acquaintances. The first of the guests to show was Tom Skaff, followed almost immediately by his wife, Amanda. Emily was right, the age difference was striking and one could not help but wonder whether this was a first marriage for both. We had barely introduced ourselves when the others arrived, so went through the introductions again.

"Jack told us that you're from Nairobi?" Amanda asked of Ian.

"We are," Ian confirmed. "We flew out this afternoon for the weekend."

"What kind of plane do you have?" one of the men, Bob Lesnewski, asked.

"We've a Cessna 172," Ian replied.

"We do most of the avionics for that," Tom said. "When did you get it?"

"Only recently," Ian explained. "It was delivered about a month ago."

"What do you do that you can have your own plane?" Tom asked.

"It's really Fiona's plane," Ian explained. "She consults on economic matters for big companies and for the British government at times."

"You are an economist?" Amanda asked me.

"I have degrees in mathematics and economics," I admitted

"Not just degrees, doctorates in both," Ian added.

"Must be lucrative contracts if you can afford a plane," another man, who I identified as Richard Harris, said.

"I've done quite well," I agreed. "But we've also done fairly well in the stock markets."

"What's your plane?" Amanda asked of Richard.

"Cessna Citation," Richard replied. "A little faster than the 172, but also a damn sight more expensive, both to buy and operate."

"I do like flying in it when we go on a trip with Richard and Jane," Amanda told us. "It's so nice to be able to come and go as you like and not have to worry about airline reservations and messing about in the airports."

"Richard runs a large construction company," Jane, explained. "We're always off to look at some project or other, and there are some away from major airports, so it's handy to have your own plane so that you can get to the smaller towns quickly."

"Business is good right now," Richard said. "There's a coal mining boom going in the States, and we've got quite a few contracts, both to build infrastructure and in one case to do the actual mining."

"Have you done anything with metals mines?" I asked.

"In the past, why have you done work for them?" he asked.

"I created some models that looked at reserves," I explained. "I worked for a consortium of companies that were looking to get a better grasp of proven, probable and possible reserves, that they could defend against the tax authorities."

"Who else have you worked for?" Paul, the third man of the Americans, asked.

"I've done some tax models for the government, some models for the fashion industry, some road and traffic pattern models, I'm working with a French car company at the moment and I've done a vineyard model," I replied.

"We run a retail clothing chain," Victoria, Paul's wife, added. "Who have you worked with in the fashion industry?"

"My main client has been Rachel Adams and I've also done some for Vittoria Blengini," I replied.

"I'd love to get their lines," Victoria said. "If you have any pull with them, put in a good word for us."

"Dinner is served," one of the staff announced, interrupting the flow of conversation.

Over dinner, I was bombarded with questions by Victoria, who only stopped when Paul told her that she needed to let me eat. Richard asked Ian what he did and Ian explained that he was attached to the British diplomatic mission in Nairobi. I felt embarrassed and guilty, all the chat before dinner had centred around what I did, and I was afraid that poor Ian had been left in the shade. Dinner was good, excellent in fact and after dinner, Ian and I excused ourselves saying that we both had been at work all day, and were looking to retire early. I really did not want to sit around the fire and relive the day with the Americans, I wanted Ian in bed, or in the shower, or anywhere else that we could manage.

In our tent, I apologised to Ian for monopolising the conversation before dinner.

"Nothing to apologise for," he grinned. "I'm proud of you and what you've done, they may have their young floozies, but you're with me and you put all of them in the shade."

"Which bed do you want me to ravish you on?" I asked.

"What about this one?" he said, grinning even more.

"Is there water in the bucket for a shower?" I asked.

"There is," he confirmed. "I had asked Emily to have it filled when we were partway through dinner."

"Let's see if we can both get wet at the same time," I suggested. I shed clothes and went and stood under the shower bucket and Ian quickly joined me. I put my arms around his neck and he hoisted me up so that I could impale myself upon him. He turned on the shower and we made love with water running down over us. I thought that one day I might like a house that had a shower big enough for two. I thought that it was probably as well that I was fairly small and light, otherwise it might have been a trial for Ian to hold me up for that long. When the water was done, so were we, so we disengaged, dried off and went to bed for the second round. We both sat on the cot, then decided that that was not the best move, so we pushed the cots to the edges of the tent and pulled all the bedclothes onto the floor and slept there, after our second round. Later, when the camp was quiet, we lay listening to the night noises, the hyæna in the distance, the lions calling and a leopard cough. There were also the noises of a myriad of insects. Ian identified things for me and I lay snuggled up close to him, relishing every moment of the night and thinking how lucky I was to be having this experience. I had experienced the night noise in the bush before when I had taken the safari with Maman and Portia, but this was different, this was listening in the arms of the man I loved. Truly a moment in life to remember.

The following morning, we were awakened by the staff, who announced that coffee and tea was ready. We got up and dressed and went over to the *boma* area and helped ourselves, me to coffee, Ian to tea. There was also a light breakfast, which we availed ourselves of. The rest of the guests drifted over and conversation was centred around what to do that day. It turned out that they were leaving at noon for the long drive back to Nairobi, so Jack suggested a last game drive. That was acceptable to everyone, so breakfast done we gathered cameras, binoculars, water and hats and joined Jack by his Land Rover. We let the others climb aboard and sit where they wanted, and then just took the two empty seats at the very back. That actually was quite nice, because it put us a little higher than the rest and we could see further. There was no roof or canopy to restrict viewing, but that also meant that hats were a must. Jack drove off and started pointing out things as we went. He was good, I have to say, almost as good as Ian, who from time to time would nudge me and point to something, often a few seconds before Jack pointed out the same thing. But then Jack was driving, so he had to pay some attention to where we were going. The Americans to a man had fancy cameras with huge telephoto lenses, making mine look rather pathetic. Jack pointed out birds as we went, but the interest was mainly in the mammals. There was great excitement when we came across a rhino and some elephants at the same water hole, so we spent a little time there just watching them. I gathered from comments made that the "Big Five" were very important to the other guests, so Jack had been trying very hard to find them all, and this was their first sighting of a rhino.

"That's great," Paul said. "That's the Big Five done now, I'm glad we got to see them all on this trip, it made it really worthwhile."

We wandered around a little more then made our way back to camp, so that the rest could shower, pack and get ready for the trek back to Nairobi. Emily had put together lunch packages for them, and helped them load all their luggage, of which it seemed to me that they had a mountain, into the closed-in Land Rover that would take them back to Nairobi. That would be a long drive. I remember coming out this way with Maman and Portia and the drive out from Nairobi had been hours. I much preferred our new mode of travel with the plane. It did mean a limited amount of luggage, but what could we possibly want just for a weekend?

"Lunch?" Emily asked, after the other guests had departed.

"That would be great," I replied.

"Jack will be with us shortly," Emily said. "He's just fixing an issue with the water supply. Did you enjoy your drive this morning?"

"It was wonderful," I said. "I just enjoy going out, it doesn't matter to me what we see, I don't have a list of must sees."

"I know that Jack was getting agitated because the Yanks had all said that they had to see the Big Five, and we hadn't found a rhino for them," Emily commented.

"There was one wandering around over there with a herd of wildebeest last night," Ian said, pointing out to the savanna.

"Don't tell Jack," Emily laughed.

"Don't tell me what?" Jack said as he joined us at the table.

"Ian and Fiona saw a rhino with that herd of wildebeest that often passes here," Emily explained.

"Ha, and I spent hours traipsing around trying to find one of the bloody things," Jack said. "Well, that's the bush for you. Emily told me that you grew up in Rhodesia Ian, did you spend much time in the bush?"

"I did," Ian confirmed. "I had to work on the tobacco farm, but I tried to get away as much as I could when I was growing up. Then when I went back for the parent's funeral I got called up and spent some time in the bush, before I said to hell with it and went AWOL."

"I'll bet they didn't like that," Jack commented.

"Probably not, I can't go back, but I see it as a war they can't win, so I left," Ian said.

"And you, Fiona, I gather from Julia that you came out this way last year, how was that?" Jack asked.

"It was wonderful," I said. "I came with my mother and her partner and we came through here, then went down through Serengeti to Arusha, I was on a mission then."

"Julia told us," Emily said. "I'm glad it worked out for you."

"So, this afternoon, what do you want to do?" Jack asked.

"Perhaps another game drive?" I asked.

"Of course," Jack said. "It'll be a little more relaxed, unless you have something you really want to see?"

"No, we'll take things as they come," I said.

"Great," Jack said. "So, after lunch, quiet time until three, then we'll grab some tea, then be off to see what we can find."

We set out on the afternoon game drive with me in the seat next to Jack and Ian right behind me. We saw impala, gazelles, wildebeest, buffalo, topi, warthogs by the score, giraffe, zebra, a leopard, a whole pride of lions, just lazing under a tree, several cheetah, the same herd of elephants we had seen that morning and not one, but three rhinos.

"Isn't that the bloody way?" Jack laughed. "All week, we've been driving around trying to find rhino and because we're not really looking, there they are."

"There's been people here," Ian commented. "There's tracks over there."

"Damn, you're right," Jack said. "I wonder who? Let's take a look." He and Ian got out of the Land Rover and examined the tracks.

"Two days," Ian said. "Headed towards the border, four of them."

"Two days?" Jack mused. "So probably over the border by now, so why don't we backtrack and see where they came from?" He turned the Land Rover around and followed the tracks back. We had driven about half an hour when he stopped and pointed.

"Camp there," he said. "Let's take a look." He and Ian got out of the Land Rover again and walked over to some trees.

"Camped here for about three to four days," Ian said. "They'd been hunting, look there's remains that the hyæna and jackals haven't cleaned

104

up yet. There's a cartridge case here, nine three, heavy gun for a poacher, must be after ivory or rhino horn."

"They're not just looking for meat to eat?" I asked.

"Could be," Ian admitted. "But, unlikely, too much gun just to shoot for the pot, expensive gun too, so someone financed this and is looking for a return."

"I wonder how much farther we can backtrack them?" Jack said.

"I'll try," Ian said. "Follow me." He set off at a quick walk following the tracks while we trailed along behind. At times I could no longer see the tracks clearly, but Ian seemed to be able to either see them, or guess which way they would go, because I would eventually see what he was following. We finally came to a track and it was clear that a vehicle had stopped there.

"They debussed here," Ian said. "Looks like a Bedford truck based on the wheelbase and tyre types. It turned around over there and headed back towards Nairobi."

"They'll probably come back here after their trip to get a ride back to town," Jack said. "I'll let the game chaps know and they can keep an eye on the road. Your tracking's pretty good Ian."

"When I got called up, it was either get good or die," Ian said, shrugging his shoulders. "I was lucky I had spent so much time in the bush as a kid, the only difference was that I was tracking people, not animals."

"Well, we should get back if we don't want to drive too long in the dark," Jack said.

When we got back to the camp, Jack used his radio to report what they had found, while Ian and I took a shower and cleaned ourselves up. We then joined Emily for a sundowner.

"So, Jack tells me that you back-tracked some people," she said. "I hope that doesn't mean we're going to see poaching again."

"You've had problems before?" Ian asked.

"We went through a spell, then the game chaps came and cleaned things up for a while, now perhaps it's starting again," she lamented.

"If they're after ivory, where does it get sold?" I asked.

"They're plenty of people in Nairobi who will take it," Ian said. "Then, it goes to Japan or Singapore, no questions asked."

"Can't it be stopped?" I asked.

"You can bet that somewhere there's a crooked businessman or politician who will smooth the way," Ian said. "Money talks."

"Is it lucrative?" I asked.

"For the four we tracked, enough, not real money to you and I, but to them more than enough to feed their families for a while," he explained.

"It's a perennial problem," Emily added. "The immediate cash for the ivory is more than earnings over time working as a guide, so getting people to think in the longer term is always hard."

"The game chaps had suspected a gang operating near here, but had had no real leads until now," Jack said as he joined us. "So, now they're going to pay close attention to that track, and they may be lucky enough to nab them with some ivory."

"So, for dinner tonight we have warthog, is that okay?" Emily asked.

"Sounds wonderful," I said. "It's so nice to be able to dine on what we in England would think of as exotic dishes."

After dinner, Ian and I spent a little time talking to Emily and Jack and then excused ourselves to go off to bed. There was a bucket shower waiting for us, so we both stripped off and I watched while Ian showered, then took my turn.

"I see we have *homo erectus* with us again," I commented to Ian.

"What do you expect?" he said. "I only have to look at you."

"Well, are you going to just stand there and look, or do you plan to do something?" I teased.

"Lean up against the wall," he suggested. I did that and felt him come up behind me and cup my boobs in his hands and then I felt him between my legs and reached down to guide him in. This was new and exciting; we'd never actually done it like that before. Ian trailed his hands down me and reached around to find me and helped me reach a climax. God, it was good! We finally pulled apart and repaired to the bedclothes on the floor where I pushed Ian down and climbed on top of him. It did not take long for me to get him erect and ready again and I rode him to another successful climax for both of us.

"Will it always be this good?" he asked.

"As long as there's bush in Kenya and we're able, I imagine so," I said.

"I love you Fi," he said.

"I love you," I replied.

"So, did you have a nice day?" he asked.

106

"It was wonderful," I rhapsodised "What could be better, a great day for game drives and I get to fuck you at the end of it."

"I've never heard you say that before," he said.

"No," I agreed. "This is a whole new me, in good old Anglo-Saxon terms, I've just fucked you and expect you to fuck me, what about it?"

"I can do that," he said. I reached out to him with my arms and spread my legs in wanton invitation and invited him in. I helped him back into erection then he reached down and picked me up and found his way in. It was so good feeling him there and he began to slowly make love to me. I think the wanton had come upon me because we were in the bush and I felt the primitive in me and wanted to abandon all vestiges of polite society. I did not want it to end, the whole experience was magical, the sounds of the bush outside, the smell of the earth and the sheer naughtiness of it all, making passionate love within earshot of the others in the camp. I felt myself nearing a climax and started to writhe in rhythm with him. He slowly speeded up his strokes and we both climaxed together gasping for breath. I wondered about myself, was I becoming a nymphomaniac. I thought about it and decided that no, I was not abnormal in any way, I was just a healthy young woman with a normal sexual appetite who was lucky enough to have a husband who enjoyed her, her company, her presence and her body. I do not think I could have been happier, I was with my husband, my lover and my friend and we had just capped the most wonderful day in such a glorious way, that was a day to remember.

Did you ever?

"Is that all you two ever did?" James asked.

"What?" I asked.

"You seemed to spend a lot of time in bed, or if not in bed rolling in the hay," he commented, I think more than a little embarrassed at my recounting of the finale to the day.

"I suppose, those are times I remember and relish," I said. "He was good to be with."

"What about the rest of your weekend?" Portia asked.

"It was fun," I recalled. "We did the game drive Saturday morning with the Americans, then we lazed around after lunch until we went on the game drive in the afternoon, then we took another game drive on Sunday morning."

"And the Americans?" Portia asked. "You said that they left early?"

"They left at noon on Saturday, so it was only us for the afternoon game drive and just Jack and Emily with us on Saturday night for dinner," I explained.

"So, you had an eventful drive on Saturday afternoon?" James asked.

"It was," I agreed. "I'd never seen Ian in action like that before. He was able to follow those tracks even when I had no idea where they were and couldn't see them. Then on the Sunday morning game drive, Ian and Jack got into one of those male things, who could spot the most birds, I think in the end it was a draw, but Jack did comment that he'd never had a guest who was as a good a birder as he was."

"Did you ever go back?" Portia asked.

"We did," I replied. "We went back there three times, twice just for a weekend and once for a week, having the plane meant that we could get out here in less than an hour, driving would have been four to five hours, so not really practical for just a weekend. We also went out with Julia and Henry twice, and that was fun. When we went with them, it was just us, so we had the chance to get to know them better and to spend as much time as we wanted if we saw something interesting."

"Did they ever catch the poachers?" Maman asked.

"They did," I said. "Apparently they staked out what they thought was the rendezvous point and caught them red-handed. They all did time, but even better they sold out the go-between and he's doing time."

"Is the safari industry going to grow?" James asked.

"It will," I said. "As disposable income in the developed countries grows, then more will look to adventurous holidays, and what could appeal more than an African safari?"

"I suppose that's true," James commented. "What does it do for the local population?"

"I suppose each operator has to have camp staff, guides, drivers, cooks and bottle washers and such, so apart from the park fees, there are the hotel stays usually at the beginning and end of a trip, then there is a distribution of wealth to an extent among the staff. Undoubtedly the operators take their cut, which has to be pretty good, else why do it?" I replied.

"Did you and Ian ever think about running a camp?" Charlize asked.

"We talked about it from time to time, I had done a model for Julia and Henry, so we knew what the economics would be and it was doable, but it always came down to the fact that we'd have to deal with people, and that's hardly my strong suit," I replied. "So, we usually shelved the idea until our next bush trip."

"So, not long after you got your pilot's licence, wasn't that when the Israelis raided Entebbe?" Charlize asked, changing the subject.

"It was," I confirmed. "It was a busy time for Ian, and he told me that he would prefer it if I grounded my plane for a little while, and certainly not to stray anywhere near the Uganda border."

"We heard what was said on the news," Maman said. "But, what did you hear?"

Hijacking

"Have you heard the news?" Ian asked me when he got home from the High Commission.

"Yes, an Air France plane was hijacked after it left Athens," I replied. "I'm not sure where it is now."

"It's in Benghazi," Ian said. "It landed there a few hours ago and the hijackers let one woman go, she's a Brit and she's pregnant, so I suppose even the hijackers are not looking for too much adverse publicity."

"Who are they?" I asked.

"Our information is that it's a mixed group," Ian said. "Four got on the plane in Athens, security there is not the greatest and they also have a strike by airport employees going on at the moment. The four, three men and a woman all claim to be the Che Guevara cell of the Haifa section of the Popular Front for the Liberation of Palestine. The PLFP office in Beirut denies that they have anything to do with it."

"Do you know who the hijackers are?" I asked.

"We do," he said. "But, keep this between us for the moment. The leader is a German, Wilfried Bose, he's quite well known to security services. Then there's Gabriele Krocher-Tiedemann, another German, she was part of a swap for Peter Lorenz in Berlin. The other two are Palestinians, their identities tentatively known, but not yet confirmed."

"So, what happens now?" I asked.

"We wait," Ian said. "We wait to see where they will finally go and what their demands are."

"So, should I worry about flying to London such a lot?" I asked.

"I don't think so," he said. "This flight was an Air France from Tel Aviv to Paris, stop in Athens. So, probably a lot of Israelis on board, plus maybe a fairly large Jewish contingent, so a target for the Palestinian-Israeli conflict."

"So, if I get offered any kind of contract with Israel, what do I do?" I asked.

"I think decline, at least for the moment," he said. "I don't want you to be at any risk."

"And Paris?" I asked.

"I think continue to fly to London direct from here, then hop over the Channel to France," he suggested. "If you're not happy about flying into Paris, you could always take a ferry over and then the train from Calais."

"Haven't there been a few hijackings this year?" I asked.

"Six so far this year, not counting the one today," he replied. "Three of those were in the Philippines, two in Colombia and one in France."

"The France one bothers me," I commented.

"That was a Turkish Airlines plane and it was a Turk who had been expelled from France and he didn't want to go back to Istanbul, so he hijacked the plane and wanted to go to Lyon or Marseille, the plane went back to Orly after Lyon and Marseille turned off their runway lights and couldn't land, and he surrendered after a couple of hours," Ian explained.

"Do you know how he hijacked the plane?" I asked.

"No," he said.

"I wonder if Charles de Gaul is a better bet than Orly?" I said.

"I don't suppose there's much difference," he said. "I think that that case was an outlier, it wasn't politically motivated, he didn't want release of hostages or anything like that, he just didn't want to leave France and go back to Turkey."

"I just don't fancy the idea of being hijacked," I said.

"Nor do I," he said. "I would be in a mad panic if I heard that a plane you were on had been grabbed."

"Wasn't there a BA plane hijacked last year?" I asked.

"There was," Ian confirmed. "Some joker with a toy gun and fake dynamite hijacked a plane between Manchester and Heathrow. The passengers all got off at Heathrow and the hijacker wanted to be flown to Paris. Instead, they flew to Stansted and the man was arrested."

"When will the world's governments get together and improve airport security so that these things don't happen?" I wondered.

"I think when economics forces them to do something," he said. "Let's face it, it's going to cost money to beef up security so people can't board with guns, knives or other things, and there are some airports where terrorists can just go out onto the tarmac and storm the plane. So, it's going to be loss of revenue, either because people won't go there, or they have to pay out for lawsuits, or loss of trade because countries won't do business with you, that will drive the decisions, that plus being worldwide pariahs because you're seen as complicit with hijackers."

"So, do I go to London tomorrow?" I asked.

"I think so," he said. "I don't see any particular risk."

"What a world?" I thought.

"What a world indeed?" he agreed. "Anyway, do you want me to cook dinner?"

"No, I have it ready," I said.

We were awakened early in the morning by a telephone call, it was from the High Commission and Ian was called in to go and man the fort. He told me before he left that the hijacked plane had left Benghazi and was now in Entebbe, where it had been met with more members of the hijack group and by the Ugandan military, who were apparently aiding and abetting.

"So, do I leave tonight?" I asked.

"I think so," he said. "I'd be happier with you in London."

"But, what about you?" I asked. "I don't like being away from you, and when something like this comes along, I like it even less."

"I don't see any reason for this to spill over into Kenya," he said. "So, go and I'll talk to you tomorrow."

"Okay," I agreed. "I'll stop at the High Commission on my way to the airport, and then I'll call you when I arrive in London. I'll go straight to the flat and call from there."

"What were you planning to do today?" he asked.

"Nothing particular," I said. "I have some mathematics to work out on one of the models I'm creating, but that shouldn't take too long."

"Wait, shouldn't you hear about your computing science doctorate?" he asked.

"Any day now," I confirmed. "Now that they've accepted the thesis, it will be orals."

"Well, don't do too much, and, I know it's easy to say, but don't fret too much about the Air France plane," he cautioned.

"I'll try not to," I promised.

I moped around the house, did my mathematics, then went out to the gun club we belonged to. I took my own gun and shot off quite a few

112

rounds. I was pleased with the results, and wondered a few times whether I was not just doing this to cover my nervousness about flying. Ian was right, of course, statistically the odds of my flight being hijacked were long, but that did not remove the unease. As I had promised Ian, I stopped at the High Commission on my way to the airport that afternoon, and he gave me a private update.

"So, here's what we know," he started. "The plane is an Airbus A300 with 12 crew and 247 passengers. It took off from Athens at 11:55 yesterday morning. Soon after takeoff it was taken over by the four. They flew to Benghazi where it sat for nine hours, during which time they let the pregnant woman go. Then they left Benghazi and flew to Entebbe, a flight of about five hours, which would have put them in there in the middle of the night. It seems that the passengers were held on the plane for about six hours and now they're in an old building that was the terminal building at one time."

"So, what do they want?" I asked.

"We're waiting to hear," he said. "Apparently Amin has been to see them and said that he knew that the hostages were innocent, and that he looked for early release of the hostages if Israel met the demands of the hijackers."

"So, I suppose we now have to wait and see what those demands are?" I asked.

"We do," he agreed. "Given that the hijackers include Palestinians, it's my guess that they'll want people in exchange for the hostages."

"So, do I go?" I asked.

"Yes, go," he confirmed. "I've talked to the people at the airport, and they're not taking any chances today, so expect a little extra scrutiny."

"I don't mind that," I said. "Promise me you'll be careful."

"I will," he said. "I don't see any involvement from here, but you never know."

I went out to the airport and the BA staff there greeted me as a regular customer. They told me that they were looking at everyone a little more carefully, but that they knew me and trusted me. I did note that a couple of men were getting the once over, both by the BA people and by the Kenya Police who were there at the airport, and they were not even trying to be subtle about it. The flight to London was uneventful and we landed at some unearthly hour of the morning, but at least it was light.

The longest day had just come and gone, so the days were still long, much longer than the daylight hours in Nairobi. I took a taxi into London and went to our flat. I dropped my bags then called the operator to get a line to Nairobi. She managed that in record time and I called the High Commission. As we were being connected, I heard the operator respond to another call and heard the clicks as she dropped off the line. Ian had taught me what to listen for to tell if the operator was still on the line. Trevor answered the phone and he got Ian for me.

"You're there already?" he asked.

"The flight was on time leaving and early in," I told him. "Plus, the taxi ride in was fast, I think the driver must have had a hot date, because he didn't mess around at all. Anything new?"

"No, we're still waiting to hear what the demands are," he said. "We do know that the French have sent a special envoy out and that our people at the Kampala High Commission have gone to Entebbe as well. What's on your agenda today?"

"I have some meetings scheduled at Imperial, and a client meeting at two," I told him. "I'm also having lunch with Rachel; she's got some new fashions she wants to show me."

"Well, enjoy your day, call me tonight, try here first, and if I'm not here, call me at home," he said.

"I will," I promised. "I miss you already, I love you."

"I love you *chérie*," he replied.

When I called Ian that evening, he had news for me.

"They've communicated their demands to the Israeli ambassador in Paris. They want people released from prison in Israel, West Germany, Switzerland, France and here," he explained.

"In Kenya?" I asked.

"Here," he confirmed. "They claim that the Kenyans have five detainees who were seized in January after the Israelis had warned of a PFLP attack against El Al planes in Nairobi. Our contacts here tell us that there are no prisoners here. What happened to them, I don't know. The rest is a mixed bag of various people all held for bombings, assassinations, attempted murders, explosives crimes, you name it."

"When do they say that want these people released?" I asked.

"By, the 1st of July at noon, GMT," he replied.

"Or else what?" I asked.

114

"The exact words they used are that the hostages would suffer strict and severe punishment," he quoted.

"How many Brits on the plane?" I asked.

"We're getting the list from Air France," he said. "My guess is that it's a mix of Brits and Brit cum Israelis."

"So, what will the Israelis do?" I asked.

"I'm not sure," he said. "It will be interesting to see, on the one hand, Israel will want all its people freed, but on the other hand, they have a policy of non-negotiation with those they call terrorists. So, we wait and see."

"I predict they'll do something dramatic," I said.

"Such as?" he asked.

"I don't know, kidnap Amin, grab all the OPEC heads of state, I've no idea, but there will be something that they'll do, that most of the world will condemn," I predicted. "Oh, something else, I've been asked to go to the Chancellor's office tomorrow morning and talk about updating my taxation model."

"I wonder if the Chancellor will stay more than five minutes, or if he'll just hand you off to his minions?" Ian commented.

"I'll let you know tomorrow," I promised. "I also heard from the college; my orals are scheduled for the day after tomorrow."

"Well, I know you'll knock 'em dead," he laughed. "I'm not sure who will be examining who."

"I love you," I said.

"I love you," he replied. "Look after yourself and I'll see you later in the week."

I hung up the telephone and wondered about the plight of those passengers on the Air France plane, what was it like to be huddled into an old airport building, under guard, could they use the loos, were there even any loos to use. Amin had really stuck his neck out on this one. He was reported to have gone out to see the prisoners, then why, did he not just release them all, he had the army, the people were not on the plane with the hijackers, there was nothing to stop him from overpowering the few hijackers that there were and releasing all the hostages, unless he was in league with them. That had to be the only explanation for why he had not done the right thing. So, now Amin was allied with the Palestinians against his old ally the Israelis, who until 1972 had been assisting him in all kinds of ways. I wondered what had brought about that change of heart. I could come up with no explanation, so had to accept things as status quo for now.

I ate at the bistro that I frequented when in London, and wondered what, if anything, the hijack victims were getting to eat. The following day I presented myself at the Chancellor's office and a list was consulted and I was admitted. The Chancellor himself was there, and he stayed for the whole meeting that lasted over an hour. They wanted me to update the taxation model I had created for them a couple of years ago and add some new sources of income. That was a pseudonym for new taxes, so I was sworn to secrecy, no point in things leaking out before the budget had been presented to the people. I offered to provide a new computer model that would allow them to vary tax rates, so that they could see what the revenue streams would be from the various and sundry taxes on anything from income to the classic sin taxes on alcohol and cigarettes. What the government would do if the country went tea-total or gave up smoking altogether, did not bear thinking about. I wondered what the American government had lost in tax revenues during the ill-fated era of prohibition. I received a deadline from them, then came the moment of truth, how much were they going to pay me.

The Chancellor excused himself at that point, as did most of the others, leaving me with the Permanent Secretary and his hanger-on. I named my price and they both sat back and looked at me as though I had dropped from the moon. The hanger-on commented that that was as much as they paid Gerald Hopkins, and Hopkins was an esteemed full professor at Cambridge. I failed to see why that was significant, but it slowly leaked out that as a mere woman, I could not possibly command the same rates as Hopkins, who was a man, a respected professor at a prestigious university and recognised in the field. My own view of Hopkins was that he was adequate but not particularly brilliant and that his economic models tended to be pedestrian and simplistic. On, that note I told them to take it or leave it and that I was going. They were in a turmoil and wanted me to sign an agreement that I would not disclose what I had heard. I told them that they should have made that request before they told me anything, but that the very fact that they were

116

asking me to sign something told me more about their own likely behaviour, but I did assure them that there would be no leaks from me, I had better things to do in my life than leak government secrets. We parted politely enough, but they were clearly irritated, and probably wondering how they would tell the Chancellor that I had walked out on them, but I was also sure that they already had an alternate ready in the wings to do the work, perhaps even Hopkins. They had come to me because of the previous work I had done for them, but there were others in the field who would probably rate the same as me, at least in their view. The rate they were proposing to pay me was ludicrous, it was far less than I had been paid the first time I did work for them, I wondered who had thought that I would drop my rates and why. I was not about to do any work for anyone at that rate, unless I felt that it was something that I was really interested in, like Robert's coffee business, and quite frankly, taxes and tax revenues were just not that interesting, except where it might impact me, which, sadly they did, as I was in the highest income bracket.

My meetings at Imperial were short, they were essentially preparatory meetings for the orals scheduled the next day. I was as ready as I would ever be, so the orals held no fears for me. I knew my stuff and knew that they knew that I knew and that I knew that they knew that I knew, if that is enough convoluted knews. So, I was able to depart quickly and go on to lunch with Rachel which was much more fun. Rachel knew her stuff, but constantly worried about her markets, because her fashions were definitely discretionary spending, and not the run-of-the-mill ready-to-wear. With high tax rates, it took a high income to be able to have enough disposable income to afford her creations, so the market was smaller than it could have been under a different taxing regime. Still, she still had a thriving business and she used the tax system to her best advantage, by expensing all kinds of odd expenditures against her income, to reduce the net taxable. I had noticed many companies doing that, as it was not really attractive to offer higher and higher salaries, without pushing people into the really high tax brackets. Perquisites were coming in, and chauffeur-driven cars, in-town accommodations, fancy dining rooms were the order of the day. The tax people had yet to work out how to assess value of these perquisites and treat them as imputed income. In time they would, and the ever-existing war of the people versus the tax man would continue, rather like the Spy versus Spy cartoon in Mad Magazine.

My client meeting after lunch was rather more successful than my meeting with the Exchequer. My client, a major retailer of sporting goods had never cavilled at my fees and were happy to pay me. They had made offers a few times for discounted goods from their stores, but the only things I really wanted were a new shotgun and possibly a new handgun. I did not express my desire for those items, I did not want to put them in any kind of awkward situation of providing me with firearms. They were somewhat in the same situation as Rachel, much of their merchandise could be classed as that purchased with discretionary funds, so their markets were largely limited to the mass purchases associated with football, cricket and to a lesser extent rugby, and the other more esoteric sports were struggling because, like Rachel, there was a limited customer base. They wanted to talk about the Air France hijacking and I told them that I knew no more than they did, which what had been broadcast on the radio and television. There was concern about me travelling back to Nairobi, it was a little too close to Entebbe for them. I assured them that I would be fine and told them of my observations at the Nairobi airport of the very unsubtle scrutiny of a few passengers. I promised to send them a message when I did go back to Nairobi to let them know that I had arrived safely.

When I called Ian that evening, he did not have much more to tell me about the fate of the Air France plane, or was unwilling to in case our conversation was overheard.
"We'll maybe have something to tell you when you get back," he said. "How was your day?"
"Not so successful to start with," I told him. "The Chancellor's office cavilled at paying me the same as a man, so I left."
"Who was the man, as a matter of interest?" Ian asked.
"Hopkins, from Cambridge," I replied.
"You've mentioned him before, as I recall in less than flattering terms," he said.
"He's adequate," I said. "But, a little pedestrian, and he has no real idea of how to take his models and write computer programs to actually use

them, he has to get someone else to do that for him. So, the process takes a lot longer with him, because he has a difficult time translating the models into something programmers can grasp and use."

"So, what about the rest of your day?" Ian asked.

"Lunch with Rachel was fun," I said. "And my sporting goods people just wanted to know if I would be safe flying home."

"You'll be safe," he assured me. "At least for the moment everyone is a little more aware and cautious, when things settle down a little and time passes, complacency will set in again, until the next time. What about your orals?"

"I'm confident," I told him. "I know my stuff and they know it. It will be interesting tomorrow."

"Well, good luck, not that you need it, I'm not sure who will be examining who, I actually feel a little sorry for them," he laughed.

"I should get some sleep, if I'm going to be awake and on top form tomorrow," I said. "I love you."

"I love you *chérie*," he replied.

My orals the next day went very well. Whatever questions they had I answered and even got them into areas where they had to admit little familiarity. It was all over well before lunch and I was then invited to join them for lunch. The college dining facilities were not quite as plush as those at Oxford, but then they had not had the time, or money, to acquire the facilities and amenities that many of the Oxford colleges had. I was congratulated and was informed that they were going to confer a doctorate upon me and asked if I would consider being a visiting professor from time to time. That worked for me, as long as it fit with my travels to and from Nairobi. The lunchtime discussion also touched upon the Air France plane and the fate of the passengers and crew. The opinion around the table was split on what was the best course of action. Two were for some kind of military action and two were for the Israelis making arrangements to get all the demands met, even if that meant letting convicted killers free. That led to a long discussion about the ethics of such a move, and would the Swiss and others cooperate. I was asked if Kenya had in fact any Palestinians in custody, and I was able to answer truthfully, that I did not know. They were still wrangling when I excused myself and told them that I needed to make my way to the airport to get my flight back to Nairobi.

I stopped at our flat first and changed out of my business attire and donned some much lighter clothes for travelling. I had the afternoon to kill, so I called the White Waltham aerodrome and made arrangements with the West London Aero Club to rent a plane for a couple of hours, and book an instructor as they had planes of a type that I had not flown before. White Waltham was a better choice than Biggin Hill, it was just west of Heathrow, so much easier to get to and also to get back to Heathrow when I was done. I splurged and took a taxi out there and showed my new pilot's licence before signing out the plane and meeting my instructor, Andrew. Flying out of there was much more complicated than out of Wilson field. The proximity to Heathrow meant that you spent a lot of time on the radio. But it was a grass strip, which made it interesting. Andrew ran through the controls and instruments with me, then handed me the various pre-start, start and taxi and take-off checklists. We went through them and when we were ready and had clearance from the local air traffic controllers, I took off and went west over the Thames Valley and the Chilterns, staying low enough to be well away from any inbound Heathrow traffic. I had decided to follow the River Thames as far as I could, and had filed a flight plan declaring that, so we flew a crazy wiggly route.

Over Henley, I circled and looked at the house where I had grown up, now an education centre for an American company. It looked as if something was in session as I counted twenty cars parked in and around the driveway. I wished I had brought a camera with me. I could have handed the controls off to the instructor for a few minutes while I took pictures. From Henley, I followed the river through all its twists and turns to Oxford, circled the college briefly, and then on to Godstow and the Trout Inn, where Ian and I had enjoyed a couple of dates and nights together. I went a farther upriver, past Lechlade, then, upriver a little way from Lechlade, had a difficult time discerning which was the river and which were just streams joining the Thames, so turned around and went back the way we had come, this time not circling any buildings. It was fun. I had not seen our old house from the air, so it was a good opportunity to take in the size of the estate and appreciate just what a desirable property it really was. Landing back at White Waltham was simple enough, just a lot of radio work, which was good for me as we got little in Kenya. I thanked my instructor and he signed off my log book for me, as being checked out on the Piper Arrow. I have to say I liked my Cessna better. I liked the high wing, the view of the ground was better. But the Arrow did have retractable gear, which was new to me.

I got the people at the aerodrome to get me a taxi to Heathrow and arrived there several hours before my flight was due to leave. They did let me check in, and as I had no luggage to send, it was simple enough. I whiled away the time at the airport, mainly watching people, trying to speculate on why they were there and where were they going. I had bought myself a new book on the psychology of military incompetence. It was a fascinating look at British military blunders in Crimea, the Boer War and the two major world wars. It was interesting how much of it rang true with Ian's descriptions of the military hierarchy of Rhodesia, and how, in his view at least, they were doomed to failure. I wondered if any of it applied to Amin and his current escapades. Amin was certainly an interesting character, what I knew about him was that he had started out in the King's African Rifles, and served in Kenya of all places. He had risen through the noncommissioned ranks and returned to Uganda in the early 60's and was then commissioned as a lieutenant. From there he rose steadily in the officer ranks until he was the commander of the army under Obote. Clearly, he and Obote fell out at some point, because while Obote was out of the country in 1971, Amin seized power and then quickly named himself president. By all accounts, he was something of an athlete, but there were questions about his basic intellect. One rather facetious comment was that things had to be explained to him in words of one syllable.

When the flight boarded for Nairobi, it was full, there was not an empty seat to be seen. I had a woman sitting next to me who wanted to talk, oh, did she want to talk. She was an author, whom I had never heard of, but that meant little as my knowledge of the arts and literature was lacking. She was going to Kenya to research a new book; I was not sure I caught the genre. I would have put her in her mid-forties, a little above average height, raven hair, slightly built, broad Scots accent and, if her stories were to be believed, had a castle in Scotland, on one of the smaller islands. She was clever enough not to interrogate me directly, but kept circling around trying to get me to open up and talk about myself. I gave her the briefest résumé that I could, I was a boring mathematician who made her living developing economic models, I lived in Kenya with my husband. On the mention of husband, my life was waved aside, for a long diatribe about husbands and their perfidy. I gathered that her husband of ten years had abandoned her for someone younger. She was rather put out by that and I suspect that if it had been feasible then the husband and the lover would have been victims in a murder mystery. I will say that after dinner she announced that she would try and sleep, and thus be quiet. Well, sleep she did, but she must have been agitated by something, because it looked as if she just could not get comfortable.

When we landed in Nairobi, we made our way to the arrivals area and lined up for immigration, with my seat companion chatting all the way. I was rescued by one of the immigration agents that I knew, he was manning the diplomatic desk and waved me over, so I was through quickly and as I had no luggage to collect walked straight out of the airport. Ian was waiting for me outside the terminal building.

"Drive," I commanded when I got into his car.

"What's up?" he asked.

"There was this lady on the plane," I explained. "She said she was an author and she just wanted to talk and talk."

"Poor you," he sympathised. "Who was she?"

"Somebody by the name of Freya McIntosh," I told him.

"Really?" he said. "I heard somewhere that Freya McIntosh writes under the pen name Mary Stuart and she must have written a ton of books, worth a penny or two."

"She's not someone I've ever read," I said. "Should I?"

"That depends on your taste," he said. "If you like who-dunnits and bodice rippers, then yes."

"Bodice rippers?" I asked.

"You know, when the hero rips the clothes off the heroine, who's usually dressed up in some period costume and does little to complain about her clothes being summarily removed," he explained.

"Well, I don't see myself rushing out to buy any of your bodice rippers just yet, what about those poor people in Entebbe, how are they doing, are there any new developments?" I asked.

"Amin has been back to the airport," Ian said. "Forty-seven of the hostages were released and all but one went to Paris, the last one is in hospital in Kampala, then they divided up the rest into Israelis and those who had joint Israeli citizenship, and the rest, all those with no particular affiliation with Israel."

"I suppose that's a good sign," I thought.

"There's more," Ian said. "Israeli was supposed to make good on the demands today, but they've bought some time by saying that it's a complicated situation, Yaakobi, their transport chief said that they'd decided to negotiate the release of the prisoners, so today another 101 hostages have been released into the hands of the French, and the hijackers agreed to extend the deadline."

"Are the Israelis just stalling for time?" I asked.

"My bet, yes," Ian said. "There are 98 passengers left, plus all 12 of the crew, who declined the opportunity to leave with the others and said that they would stay with the remaining passengers."

"That's either very brave or very stupid," I thought.

"I gather the French captain sees it as his duty as the captain of the plane to be there, and the rest of the crew are with him," Ian explained.

"So, what's the new deadline?" I asked.

"July the 4th," Ian said. "But, there's another wrinkle, GCHQ has been intercepting telephone calls by Amin to Bar-Lev in Israel. Baruch Bar-Lev is a retired colonel who had been in charge of the Israeli military mission to Uganda until 1972. Amin regards Bar-Lev as a personal friend, so there's a back channel of communication going on there."

"So, what are the Israelis going to do?" I asked.

"They're coming to get the rest of their people," Ian predicted. "They know what the old airport looks like, they'll be interviewing people in Paris who have been released, getting a sense of how many hijackers and how many Ugandan soldiers and how the airport has changed since they left. They've got about two days to come up with a plan. Our intel is also telling us that there are Ugandans opposed to Amin who are passing on information about the airport. Israel may well have the prisoners lined up ready to be released in case they can't get things done in time, but my guess is that that is really a backup plan, to be used only in case their first plan doesn't work. So, tell me about your week?"

"I told you that the Chancellor's people were cheap, didn't I," I said.

"You did," he confirmed.

"I was annoyed by their attitude, I should come cheap because I'm not some reclusive man in Cambridge living off my reputation from long ago," I complained.

"It'll be a while before people like them treat you as an equal, if they ever do," he commented.

"I know," I agreed. "But that doesn't make it any more palatable."

"What else did you do, what about your orals?" he asked.

"I flattened them," I said, rather smugly. "I lost them, I overwhelmed them, I confused them, I obliterated them and they just had to admit defeat. It was rather fun actually. They told me that they were going to confer the degree of doctorate upon me, then they took me to lunch. That was nice enough, but not quite as plush as the lunches used to be in Oxford. They just haven't had the time and money to build up all that it takes to live high off the hog. Then to celebrate I rented a plane and went for a flight up the Thames."

"Sounds like fun, how far do you go?" he asked.

"Above Lechlade," I said. "That's supposed to be the highest navigable point, beyond that it's hard to tell which is the river and which are just streams. I flew around our old house and around the college in Oxford. Unfortunately, I didn't take a camera, so no pictures."

"Could you have flown the plane and taken pictures?" he asked.

"I got an instructor with the plane," I explained. "So, I could have handed the controls over to him while I took pictures."

"What kind of plane did you hire?" he asked.

"It was a Piper, and I'd not flown one of them before. It was for the most part the same as ours, but different in that it's a low wing, not a high wing and it has retractable gear, so the wheels come up," I replied.

"Which do you prefer?" he asked.

"Ours, definitely," I said. "The high wing gives you a better view of the ground, so much better for game viewing. Anyway, thanks for picking me up, are you on duty today?"

"We all are until this issue in Entebbe is resolved," he said. "May I just drop you at home?"

"Of course," I said. "When will you be home tonight?"

"I'm not sure," he said. "I'll call you, why don't you come into town and get some lunch with me."

"Great idea," I agreed. "Would twelve-thirty be convenient?"

"Should be," he said. "If not, I'll call you before you set out."

"So, when do you have to be in the office this morning?" I asked.

"About ten," he said. "Why?"

"I have designs on you," I said. "I've missed you this week, so I was thinking we could start making up for lost time."

"I like the sound of that," he said. "Here we are, if you'll get the gate, we can be in the house quicker."

At ten, I was having coffee, sated for the moment, and thinking about Ian and how much I loved him, loved him for who he was as well as his lovely body, which I could not get enough of. I sent him to work with a big grin on his face and I was sure that it would be obvious to all and sundry at the commission what he had been doing that morning. Well, that was too bad, I had wanted him, wanted to feel him close to me, wanted to put my arms around him and have his arms around me. He had been happy to oblige and we had made love in the shower, and on the bed, there might have been another tryst had he not had to go to work and do his part to monitor the situation in Entebbe. I sat on the patio, drinking my coffee and wondered if the remaining hostages in Entebbe were being fed and watered. I doubted that they were getting coffee as nice as the brew I was drinking, but presumed that someone in Uganda had made arrangements to provide food and water. With the Israeli announcement that they were ready to negotiate, I was even more convinced that they were working on a plan. It would be interesting to see what that plan turned out to be.

Ian and I had lunch, but not alone, we were joined by Trevor and Edward.

"So, we hear congratulations are in order," Trevor commented. "What do we call you now, Doctor, Doctor, Doctor Hartley?"

"Fiona will do just fine," I laughed. "And, how are you, Trevor?"

"Busy," he said. "But my business rather pales in light of the Air France plane."

"What do you think will happen, Edward?" I asked.

"My guess is that the Israelis will come and get the rest of the hostages," Edward replied.

"How would you do it?" I asked.

"Fly in, there's no other way with the short time frame, I'd land at some ungodly hour of the morning, shoot the shit out of anyone carrying a gun, then leave," he explained.

"What if some hostages get killed in the crossfire?" I asked.

"My guess is that they've got the hostages all on the ground anyway, so they'll be at the most seated, I don't see anyone standing, so providing you keep your fire at chest height, the chances of hitting a hostage are low, it may happen, shit happens in ops like that, oh sorry, didn't mean to offend," he said.

"Don't the Ugandans have some fighter planes that might scramble to intercept incoming planes, or chase them afterwards?" I asked.

"They do," Edward confirmed. "They've got MiG 21 and MiG 17 fighters, some of them at Entebbe."

"Would the Israelis bring fighter cover if they do stage a rescue?" I asked.

"No, too far," Edward replied. "If they were to think about fighter cover, they have to have tankers for refuelling, then the whole operation gets much more complicated, plus that's a lot of flying for fighter pilots, it would be about six and a half to seven hours each way, plus a loiter over Entebbe, unless they land and swap pilots, but if they land why bring them, they would supposedly be for air cover."

"What would they use to fly people in?" I asked.

"They've got C-130 transports," Edward replied. "They've got the range for the outbound, I'm not sure what they would plan to do for the return, my guess is look for a friendly nation not too far away and refuel before going back."

"Won't people see them coming?" I asked.

"If I were them, as soon as I took off, I'd turn off the transponders on the planes, then it would need an active search radar to pick them up and that is usually military," he explained. "So, I'd fly over the Red Sea, I'd fly low under any search radar that the Egyptians or Saudis might have going, then I'd down over Sudan, the attempted coup today against Nimeiry may help them, because I'll bet that most of their military systems are down at the moment, and if they're not, they're too busy to worry about any planes overflying."

"So, it's possible?" I asked.

"I suppose it could be possible," he confirmed. "Just barely possible, very risky, all kinds of things would have to go right, and you'd have to hope that you weren't spotted and challenged on the way down. There's all kinds of other things that could go wrong, but with a determined group, just possible, we'll have to wait and see if that's what they do, the Israelis have a history of doing the impossible, so we'll see if they've managed to work out a plan for this one."

"What's the position of HMG regarding the hijacking?" I asked. Ian and Edward looked at each other and it was obvious that they were debating as to who should answer that question, Ian won or lost, depending on how you saw the situation.

"Officially HMG wishes to see that resolution of the situation with the minimum loss of life or risk to the hostages," he said. "Privately, I'll bet that in Parliament that there's a split between those who'd like to see the hijackers taken out and those who just want to negotiate."

"When's the deadline?" I asked.

"Day after tomorrow," Ian said.

"How many hijackers are there?" I asked.

"Our information is that there's the original 4 plus another 6 Palestinians and that there's about 80 Ugandans there as well," Edward replied. "To me that smacks of complicity on Idi Amin's part, because if 80 Ugandans can't take out 10 hijackers, what good are they? That's an unofficial comment."

"What's Kenya's position?" I asked.

"They're not the best friends of Amin," Ian said. "They've denied that they have any Palestinians in gaol, I think they're waiting to see what happens in the next few days."

"We should get back," Edward interrupted. "Briefing at one."

"Sorry, Fi, must go," Ian said. "See you tonight."

I watched them go and wondered if the remaining hostages would see the light of day, or would be quietly dumped in a mass grave somewhere in Uganda. I wondered, not for the first time, when the international community was going to get tired of all these hijackings and agree on something that would not give any potential hijackers the confidence that they would see a welcome mat anywhere. I supposed that politics would play a large part in that and each country would be looking at how it would best benefit by either outlawing hijackings and arresting any perpetrators that landed in their country, or by playing along to embarrass someone else, or extract something from them. I went home and pulled out some of the work I had to do for my sporting goods client and started to review it. Several hours later I was still at it when Ian came home.

"What are you doing sitting here in the near dark?" he asked.

"Oh, I got engrossed and time seemed to just flash by," I replied. "I'm sorry I haven't thought about dinner yet, give me a few minutes and I'll think of something."

"No need," he said. "I stopped by the Desai place and picked up some samosas."

"Samosas, that sounds wonderful," I said. "What do you fancy to drink with them?"

"I think a beer," he said.

"Beer it is," I said and went to the kitchen to get two. Ian had bought a lot of samosas, probably more than we could eat at one sitting, but they smelled so good I was willing to give it a try.

"Cheers," he said.

"Cheers," I echoed. "Promise me something."

"What?" he asked.

"Don't ever get hijacked," I said. "I couldn't stand the idea of you sitting there under someone's gun, I'd be sick with fear."

"I'd be the same way," he said. "I think I'd be looking for a way to get wherever you were to mount a one-man rescue operation."

"Who is the most acceptable country to just about everyone?" I asked.

"I'm not sure, maybe Singapore, it probably depends on who you're talking about, why?" he asked.

"I was wondering if your people could fake us up a couple of passports so that if we ever got hijacked, then we wouldn't be Brits, but someone innocuous," I explained.

"So, you fancy being James, or maybe Jane, Bond?" he asked.

"I was just thinking," I said.

"So, if you're going to be Jane Bond does that make me a Bond boy?" he laughed.

"Maybe," I said. "I'll have to see how you fare in the romantic scenes."

"I'm willing to give it a try," he said.

The next day I listened to the news, but there was nothing new about the situation in Entebbe. However, that afternoon, when Ian came home, he was excited and I could tell that he was eager to tell me what he had heard.

"We've an agent in Israel," he started. "And he reported that six planes just left Sharm el-Sheikh, all heavily laden and all lying low, 4 C-130 transports and two 707's. The Israelis have apparently decided to go for it."

"Do the Ugandans know that they're on their way?" I asked.

"We're not telling them," Ian said. "GCHQ has stepped up its listening, but the reports so far are that there's no unusual chatter."

"If we know, what are the chances that others know, like the Russians or the Americans?" I asked. "I wouldn't trust the Russians not to tell the Palestinians, and the American secret services seem to leak like sieves."

"We don't know," he admitted. "But there doesn't seem to be any increase in the chatter we're monitoring, so perhaps they got away without being seen by anyone else."

"So, now what?" I asked.

"Well, Edward's best guess, is that they'll be at Entebbe close to midnight, so we wait and see," Ian said.

"How many people can all those planes carry?" I asked.

"Edward told me that the agent reported that one plane has a Mercedes aboard and a couple of Land Rovers, we know that Amin likes to ride around in a Mercedes, usually with a couple of Land Rovers as escorts, so our guess is that they're going to try and confuse the Ugandan army chaps into thinking that it's Amin flying in. The other planes have troops, other military vehicles, probably to protect the perimeter in case the Ugandans try and reinforce," Ian explained.

"And the 707s?" I asked.

"We're not sure," Ian admitted. "But Edward thinks that one may be for medical issues, should there be real casualties, either with the hostages or the Israeli military, he thinks the other is for command and control, someone has to manage the whole operation."

"That's a lot of guesswork, based on one sighting," I said.

"It is," Ian agreed. "But, Edward's pretty good, and he said that that's the most likely scenario that he had come up with to fit the information we have."

"So, will you be involved in anything?" I asked.

"I'll probably go to the commission before midnight and then just listen in to whatever we can pick up. I'm sure our commission people in Kampala have been alerted and are trying to decide what they should do," he replied. "Edward's all excited, I'm sure if he could he'd go to Entebbe just to watch and see how everything unfolds."

I went to bed that night when Ian went off to the High Commission. He was back at about five in the morning. I had been awake because I was sure I had heard a number of large planes fly overhead, obviously headed to the Nairobi airport, and I had wondered if they had anything to do with the Israeli operation.

"You're back already," I said. "What happened?"

"Well, first one of the Israeli planes landed here, it was one of the 707's and the airport staff told me that it was fitted out to be an ambulance plane. Then just after one an Israeli C-130 showed up, then another three, then the other 707. They all just wanted fuel, and a couple of people were transferred to the hospital plane, then they left, in fact, the last one left just after four. They're on their way back to Israel now," he told me.

"I heard the planes. Was the operation a success?" I asked.

"I gather it was," he said. "Edward called it fairly well. They got all the hostages, bar one, a lady who is in the Kampala hospital. The story we got was that the first plane landed just before midnight, the Mercedes and the Land Rovers were unloaded and they went to the terminal building, then some minutes later the other three C-130s also landed. At some point, the shooting started and seven of the hijackers were killed, plus about twenty Ugandans, one Israeli commando and three hostages. There were also quite a few Ugandans injured and a few Israelis injured. Those numbers may change as we get more definitive information. We heard that they also destroyed a bunch of the MiG fighters that Uganda had there. So, all in all, a very successful job, which took less than an hour on the ground. People are going to be talking about this for a while. Because the planes were refuelled here, expect Amin to make noise."

"Will he attack us?" I asked.

"I doubt it," Ian said. "This raid rather destroyed the invincible image that Amin has tried to cultivate. Some countries will praise the Israelis for doing this, and a whole lot will condemn them as violating the sovereignty of Uganda. They should have negotiated and exchanged prisoners for hostages, blah, blah, blah."

"What do you think?" I asked.

"I think they did the right thing," he said. "Amin was clearly in cahoots with the hijackers, so he asked for it."

"What's the position of HMG?" I asked.

"We're waiting to hear from the FCO, so that we can comment," he said.

"What about the Kenyans?" I asked.

"My guess, they're going to stay quiet about this, if anything they'll say that they did the humanitarian thing by providing fuel for the planes so that they could get medical attention to the released hostages as soon as possible, but beyond that, they're going to stay mum," he thought. "But I'm sure that they'll move some army units closer to the Uganda border in case Amin does something stupid."

"I never thought that I'd be this close to any hijacking," I said. "It's not something I will forget in a hurry."

Aftermath

"I remember when all that happened," Portia said. "And I remember the resolutions that were put forward at the UN to condemn Israel, and to outlaw hijacking internationally, but as I recall neither went anywhere."

"That's right," I confirmed. "Uganda was pissed off at Kenya for letting the planes land and refuel, they even accused Kenya of being complicit in the raid. There was an ugly note though, the Brit who had been in the hospital was murdered by Amin's people in retaliation and the body buried somewhere. Relations between HMG and Uganda went downhill after that, and they hadn't been rosy for a while. Eventually HMG broke off diplomatic relations with Uganda, which was a first for a Commonwealth country."

"I thought they'd severed relations with the Rhodesians?" James asked.

"No, Ian told me that the Rhodesians did the severing, not HMG," I explained.

"What about relations between Uganda and Kenya?" Charlize asked.

"They went from bad to worse," I said. "Amin started killing people left, right and centre, Kenya would only allow goods to Uganda if they paid for them at the border with Kenya Shillings, there were stories of mutinies in the Ugandan army, mainly because they hadn't been paid, both sides beefed up military presence, Uganda got new planes from Libya to replace the ones lost in the Israeli raid. It was all happening. Amin even made a fatuous comment that Kenyatta's residence was within bombing range of his aircraft. Then Amin started to be more conciliatory and things settled down for a while."

"Did you fly at all while this was going on?" James asked.

"I did, but generally away from Uganda," I said.

"How did things go between Uganda and Kenya?" Charlize asked.

"It got nasty," I said. "Both sides accused the other of all manner of crimes and there were killings on both sides."

"We only heard a little of that in France," Maman said. "Didn't it bother you here?"

"It did," I admitted. "When we came here, I was expecting a nice quiet posting with friendly neighbours and no real chance of war, but there always seemed to be something."

"I suppose with the egos of Amin and Kenyatta involved, there was probably going to be at least a clash of personalities, if not direct warfare," James suggested.

"It did all seem to come down to government and leadership," I agreed. "It looked to me as if Amin was trying to bolster his support at home by blaming all the ills of Uganda on the nasty neighbours who wouldn't play nicely."

"So, how did things get worse between Kenya and Uganda?" Portia asked.

"There was a lot or arm waving and sabre rattling, but nothing really happened," I said. "There was one other thing that did happen, I got a call from the Chancellor's office asking me to go to the High Commission and use their secure line. It turned out that they were not happy with the proposal from Hopkins, so wanted me to do the work for them, at the rates I had quoted. I was almost tempted to raise my fees, but decided that that was being petty. So, I went back a week or so later and signed a contract with them and did the work. I suppose it was vindication of a sort."

"And, between Kenya and Uganda, I don't recall any actual fighting, so things must have quietened down," Maman remarked. "Did you venture near the border at all?"

"I was quite concerned there for a while, but we did manage to take a quick trip to the coast to see another part of Kenya, that was a fascinating trip and I saw a completely different side of Kenya," I replied.

"Tell us about that," Maman requested.

A trip to the beach

"I thought this was supposed to be a nice quiet place," I commented to Ian over dinner a few days after the Israeli raid on Entebbe. "It seems that we've been at the point of war with Uganda and now they're shouting about support for the Israelis."

"All the Kenyans did was fuel some planes," he said. "We haven't heard anything that would suggest that they had prior knowledge of this operation."

"But, you knew, or guessed," I said.

"That's only because we had someone there who saw the planes take off," he said. "We didn't share that information with anyone."

"So, the Ugandans are just looking for someone to blame?" I asked.

"That's my guess," he said. "When you get caught flat-footed like they were, you've got to have some excuse, and why not blame your next door neighbour?"

"So, what's next?" I asked.

"That all rather depends on what Amin will do," he said. "I know that the Kenyans are moving more troops to the border."

"Are we safe here?" I asked.

"Yes," he assured me. "And, if anything looks as if it will become too much of a risk, we have a plan to evacuate families to London."

"And would you come too?" I asked.

"Only at the last minute," he said.

"I don't like that idea," I complained. "Why can't I stay with you?"

"If it comes to a shooting war, and if that war reaches Nairobi, then you definitely wouldn't want to be here," he told me. "Conflicts in Africa have a habit of becoming very brutal, so a Ugandan occupation of Nairobi would not be pleasant for anyone. Think about what happened in the Congo, it was ugly, really ugly."

"I know," I said. "But I worry about you, you're all I have."

"I'll be fine," he assured me. "If I had to, I'd take to the bush, and there I'd rank my chances as very high, I learned a lot in Rhodesia, apart from what I already knew from growing up. Anyway, to change the subject, when's your next trip to London or Paris?"

"Two weeks from now," I said. "I have a meeting in London and one in Paris, but I can do the Paris one as a day trip from London."

"Would you get some books for me when you're there?" he asked.

"Of course," I said. "What do you want?"

"I have a list," he said.

"So, how many?" I asked.

"Five," he said. "They're all about anthropology and the rise of humans."

"So, are you still thinking about your doctorate?" I asked.

"It rankles," he admitted. "I was so sure that I was on the right track, I was really thrown when my advisor threw so much cold water on my ideas. In retrospect, I think he may have done the dirty on me and published as if my ideas were his."

"The bastard," I said. "You're sure?"

"Pretty sure, but that's why I need the books, I need to see things in writing to compare against my own notes," he said.

"Did you keep your notes when you left the dig?" I asked.

"I posted them to myself," he explained. "I sent them care of a friend in London, and he kept them for me."

"If he did plagiarise your work, is there anything you can do?" I asked.

"Probably not," he said. "Ambrose is the one with the reputation and the standing, rather like Hopkins is to you."

"I knew that academia was not very nice," I said. "But I confess I was pretty naive; I didn't expect outright theft of work."

"It's not always theft," Ian explained. "Sometimes it's a matter of a name on a paper. Say, I write a paper and my thesis advisor suggests that it will be better received if his name is also on the paper, so, I agree, and then his name goes first as the lead researcher and I trail along as an add-on, so he gets most if not all of the credit, and I'm just there as an also ran."

"And, they do that?" I asked.

"They do, more than you would think," he said. "Remember it's publish or perish, and what better way to build your reputation than get your grad students to do all the work, then you claim credit and allow them to add their names to the paper, knowing that almost no one will look at all the authors."

"I'm so sorry if that happened to you," I said.

"I'll find out," he said. "Then, I'll have to decide what, if anything, I can or should do."

"Apart from books are there any publications or journals that papers may have appeared in?" I asked.

"Try, *Man*, it's the journal of the Royal Anthropological Institute," he suggested.

"I'll get some back issues for you," I promised. "Anything else?"

"I don't think so," he said. "What I'm really after is the references and citations, that will probably tell me as much as any article itself."

"I'll see what I can get you," I promised.

Ian came home from the commission the next day and told me that they had picked up a Ugandan broadcast claiming that some thirty enemy aircraft, either Israeli or American were approaching Uganda from Kenya. Well, Kenya said that that was ridiculous, as it was, how these planes were supposed to have got to Kenya was never mentioned.

"Where did Amin get an idea like that?" I asked Ian.

"Who knows," he replied. "The man's losing it and is conjuring up foes and enemies at every turn."

"Does he still have the support of his army?" I asked.

"So far," Ian said. "They seem to be going along with whatever he says, for now. How long that will last, who knows? What is a little more disturbing are reports we are getting of killings of Kenyans in Uganda. Most of the people who were on duty at the Entebbe airport when the Israelis hit the place have disappeared, probably dead."

"I presume that Amin had something to do with that," I commented.

"It seems probable," Ian agreed.

"What does HMG say about that?" I asked.

"Very little," he said. "We need confirmation on the deaths, and then it will be our mission in Kampala who make the representations to the Amin government."

"I never thought that there would be so much going on," I said. "I thought we were coming to a quiet out of the way place, where you could gain some experience with the Foreign Service, and then perhaps move on to a posting with more activity, it seems now that almost anywhere we may go will have less happening than here."

"I don't want to alarm you in any way, but Uganda claims that Gaddafi has started sending Mirage fighters to replace the MiGs that the Israelis destroyed," Ian said.

"What does Kenya have, are the Mirages any good?" I asked.

"Kenya has some old Hunters that they got from the RAF and some Strikefighters, but neither would outmatch a Mirage in a straight fight, but in reality, it would all come down to how good the pilots were and how well they had been trained," he said. "But that all supposes that

Gaddafi is in fact sending Mirages to Uganda, personally I doubt it, better to stick with the MiGs that they have and replace those that were destroyed. Adding a new plane to the inventory would mean more pilot training on a different system, different spare parts, different weapons systems, altogether, too much complication."

"What a world we live in," I thought. "Well, what do you fancy to drink, we've got beer, wine, something stronger?"

"Just a beer, thanks," he said. "You know Fi, I had no idea when we came here that things would be so active. All we need now is the Tanzanians to get Bolshy."

"That may happen yet," I said. "I've been looking at East African Airways and the East African Railways and Harbours, and things are not all rosy there. It's difficult to sort through the accounting, but it looks as if Tanzania hasn't been paying its way to support the headquarters of East African Airways, so look for trouble there, the whole arrangement may come apart over who is paying for what."

"That's all we need," he said. "I'll tell Trevor to keep an eye on things."

"Anyway, here's to us," I said raising my glass to him. "I hope that you can find what you're looking for with your doctoral work, and, who knows, they may actually agree with you."

"To us," he said. "Fancy another trip to the bush?"

"Any time," I said. "When can you get a free weekend?"

"I'm not on duty this weekend, where shall we go?" he asked.

"How about the coast?" I suggested. "We could fly down to Lamu, Valerie was telling me about an old fort near the village of Shela, which is right by Lamu."

"Sounds like fun," Ian said. "Do we fly into Lamu?"

"We fly into the Manda airstrip, which is over a strip of water from Lamu, but Valerie told me that there are ferries going back and forth and the whole place is full of boats," I explained.

"Okay," he said. "How long to get there?"

"Just under two hours," I said. "I'll make sure we have enough fuel on board to get back as I'm pretty sure they don't have any there. Maybe you could check at the commission to see where Trevor and Val stayed when they went there."

"I'll do that," Ian promised.

Ian made arrangements at a hotel, with the unlikely name of Peponi. I gathered that Trevor and Valerie had stayed there and had enjoyed it. The other thing that they told us was that there were no cars, or even bicycles, in Lamu. There were boats in abundance in the surrounding waterways, but, on land, it was shanks' pony, or local donkeys, of which there were many. Well, that was fine, we were not planning to go too far. I was excited to go. We had not been down to the coast and it promised to be different to the highlands where we lived. One note of caution that Valerie had passed on to me was that most of the people who lived in and around Lamu were Islamic, so I should take care not to offend dress standards by going too brazen. I think that just meant no shorts and a top with sleeves and a head covering of some sort, either a scarf or a hat. Well, I could manage that, I had some light trousers and matching shirts, and I did not cavil at wearing a hat in the tropics. It rankled that those same caveats over dress standards did not apply to men, but we were the guests, so better to respect local custom. It would be worse if we went to Tanzania where the fashion police went after miniskirts, bell bottom trousers and wigs. As far as we knew those who had fallen victim to the Tanzanian fashion police had all been local girls, and we had had no reports of tourists being similarly harassed.

I took the time that week to go back to the flying club and get my instrument rating. I had been training for it and had been up with Brian a lot when he used the hood to force me to use instruments only. Sometimes you were fighting against yourself, because your body was trying to tell you something about the attitude of the plane that was just not borne out by the instruments. I learned to trust the instruments and fly by them. We actually went out a few times when it was cloudy and the ground was not visible, I must say that I preferred to see the ground, but I managed to fly us in the right direction and at the right altitude on each occasion. Flying with instruments also meant relying on the air traffic controllers, such as there were, to warn us of other traffic, otherwise we broadcast our altitude and heading regularly in case someone else was out there that we could not see. My instrument rating also included night flights, which I actually rather enjoyed, particularly if it was clear and the stars were visible. I could navigate by the stars, so that was a check on my own dead reckoning.

By Friday I was ready for our trip, I had spent the week diligently working on economic models and writing reports, so was ready for a real change. Ian came home just after lunch, packed a small bag, and we were off. At the Wilson airport, I did my pre-flight checks, made sure we had enough fuel to get there and back and then we were actually off. Our flight took us a little south of east and at first the ground climbed up towards us, then it quickly fell away as we descended from the highlands to the coastal plains. There was little in the way of real landmarks, so navigation was by compass heading. We saw the sea long before we actually got to the coast and we started our descent.

"What are we looking for?" Ian asked.

"There's a strip on the Manda Island, which is the next island to Lamu," I told him.

"Would that be them?" Ian asked pointing ahead to a couple of islands.

"It is," I confirmed. "Let's see if we can raise anyone on the ground at the airstrip." I tried but there was no reply. We took a spin around Lamu and Manda and saw no other aircraft on the runway or in the approaches, so we did a quick flyover of the runway to check the wind sock, which showed us that the wind was out of the south, then made another circuit to get lined up for upwind landing.

"Nicely done," Ian commented as we touched down, and I have to say it was a rather nice landing, no bouncing or bumps, just a smooth touch down. We taxied over to an area where there two other small planes parked. A chap with a hand cart came over to us.

"You are for Peponi?" he asked.

"We are," Ian confirmed. We both got down from the plane and Ian chocked the wheels while I dug around in one of the compartments and got the tie down straps and pegs and my hammer. Hammering in the pegs I left to Ian, then I actually tied the plane down so that it would stay in place if the wind picked up. I noted that the other two planes on the ground had also been tied down, so saw no particular risk from them moving and hitting my plane. I put in place a windshield cover we had devised that reflected the sun and stopped the interior of the plane heating up too much, and last, I covered the pitot tubes, so that insects did not get adventurous and crawl up into them. All set for the weekend I then got our bags and locked the plane. Another chap came scurrying over and we gathered that he was the airstrip manager and he had come out to meet a scheduled flight. What he wanted was landing fees, and I paid as they were small enough, but did get an official receipt. I imagined that the possibility for dishonest dealings could be rife in such an out of the place.

The chap with the hand cart took our bags, small as they were and led the way to the landing dock where a boat was waiting. He chattered away in Swahili and I did note that there were accent and word differences to the Swahili we spoke, but not enough that understanding was difficult. Our hand cart chap helped us onto the boat, then he went back to the airstrip to also greet the Air Kenya flight we saw coming in. I supposed that was one of the regular flights from Mombasa and Malindi. Our boat was a dhow with the classic lateen sail, and our boatman's name was Ahmed. The wind was against us as we went down the channel, so Ahmed used a small outboard motor, we scudded along, dodging other boats and marvelling at the view of Lamu town. This was not the Kenya of plains, giraffes, elephants and zebras, this was the Kenya of ocean, of the coastal Swahili people, of Islam and of ancient Arab trading, made possible by the predictable trade winds that blew in set patterns at different times of the year, so traders could come south in December and go north in June. This was also the Kenya of sandy beaches, palm trees, tiger prawns, turtles, lobsters, octopi, and all manner of fish from the ocean. As we went down the channel, we could see the town of Lamu, clustered along the waterfront. The buildings tended to be square, some with flat roofs, some with red tiled roofs, most painted white and Valerie had been right, there were boats everywhere. We even saw the old Lamu fort, now a prison according to Ahmed. The fort I gathered was over two hundred years old and was from the Omani period.

"Look," Ian said, pointing ahead.

"Oh, I see," I said, enthralled and entranced by the dolphins that were going ahead of the boat and surfacing to breathe just in front of the bows. Ahmed told us that this was not uncommon, but not as common as it had been, he blamed the decline on the sightings on engines, outboard engines that powered many of the boats, a somewhat ironic statement in that we had just come down the channel using an outboard.

"That's a first for me," I commented to Ian. "I've never seen dolphins before, you?"

140

"A couple of times when I was a child and we went on holidays to Beira," he replied. "But, never this close."

"Peponi Hotel," Ahmed announced, pointing to a collection of buildings right on the waterfront. He skillfully beached us so that we could step ashore without wading and I heard Ian negotiating for a trip the next day to take us all around the archipelago. There were islands, coral reefs, mangrove swamps and beaches in abundance, so it promised to be an interesting day. The Peponi staff came out to meet us and I think were a little surprised at the small amount of luggage that we had, only a small rucksack each.

Our room looked out east onto the channel, so would get the sunrise, it was very nice and I gathered that it was a superior room, to be distinguished from the more mundane standard rooms, I think the real difference was size, ours was a little bigger than a standard room. The hotel was quite new, only ten years old and it was fairly small, only twenty-eight rooms, as I recall, and my quick review of the register showed it to be actually quite full, mainly with Brits, a couple of French and four Americans. I gathered from the manager that most guests were there for snorkelling along the reefs that protected the island from the ocean, or for ocean fishing. Listening to the conversations later in the bar, it seemed that the reefs were worth seeing and spectacular in their own way, but that this was not the best time of year for that. The winds were out of the south and tended to stir up the ocean and reduce the water clarity. At least for us it was well away from the Uganda border, so safe from any ill-conceived notions that Amin might have. I was not to know, but years in the future Lamu would have its own problems with raids from Somalia by groups of Islamic extremists, but that was to be many years hence. Peponi's seemed to be the place to go for locals, at least white and wealthier black locals, for drinks on a Friday night. The bar was well stocked and well patronised and did a thriving business. Ian got us each a beer and we went and sat out on the terrace and looked out at the channel in front of us.

"So, what's the plan tomorrow?" I asked him.

"We'll take a trip around the islands and have lunch somewhere," he replied. "I've engaged the boatman we had today to pick us up in the morning at nine."

"And tonight?" I asked.

"Dinner here," he said. "The manager suggested a sea food meal, with things caught today, so probably crabs, lobsters, prawns, maybe even a fish or two."

"Ian, Ian, is that you," a woman's voice said. He looked up and I saw recognition in his eyes as well as real disquiet.

"Rosalind," he said, guardedly. "What brings you here?"

"I'm on my honeymoon," she said. "Honey, this is Ian Hartley, he was one of those who worked for me at Olduvai."

"Pleased to meet you," the man said. "Name's Bob, Bob Bannon."

"My wife, Fiona," Ian said, completing the introductions in the coldest manner I had ever seen him use, and completely ignoring the barefaced lie of him working for Rosalind. I saw reactions run across Rosalind's face, from surprise to amusement, and for myself I knew I had seen Bob before, but then he had not been calling himself Bob.

"So, Bob, what do you do in the States?" Ian asked.

"I work in DC, and you?" Bob asked.

"We're just on vacation from England, trying to work out what to do in life," Ian lied. "How did you two meet?"

"I was at a fund raiser dinner for the museum and Rosalind was there and we just hit it off," Bob explained. "Say, we've had a great trip to Kenya, love to come back someday, but got to get back, got projects to manage, things to do."

"When do you leave?" Ian asked.

"We've got an early charter to Nairobi in the morning, then home to Washington," Bob explained. "Say, we should leave you to your vacation, nice to meet to both." On that note he led Rosalind off and left us to our thoughts.

"Should I kill her or just beat her up?" I asked. "Did you see her look when you told her my name, you could see the calculation running through her mind and the amusement. Bitch, and since when was she in charge of the dig at Olduvai?"

"Just how were you planning to remove her from this world?" Ian asked.

"I noticed that too, I never thought of myself as working for her, but perhaps it sounds good to her husband, she the cracker of the whip."

"I was thinking of a snake to get rid of her, I'm sure there have to be venomous snakes around," I said.

"But, are you going to go out and catch one?" he asked.

"You're right, probably not," I said. "Have you any better ideas?"

"I'd forget about her," he said. "We both know what she is, and maybe we should have some sympathy for Bob, who may yet find out what she is."

"What are the chances that we'd run into her here?" I thought.

"Slim," he said. "If you meet her on your own later tonight, please don't inflict too much harm, we need to know that they will leave tomorrow."

"Okay," I grudgingly agreed, although deep down I still longed to just beat the living daylights out of her. "Oh, by the way, I seen Bob before, only then he wasn't Bob but Norris Olander, he was at a presentation I was giving in late 1973 to a client in the oil business," I added. "He was part of an American contingent that the oil company was wooing to get money from to invest in a new field in the Gulf of Mexico."

"Was he now?" Ian said. "That's interesting. He gave no indication that he had seen you before."

"He didn't did he," I said. "And he could have hardly missed me as I was the one giving the presentation."

"Interesting, do you think he knew that you'd recognised him?" Ian asked.

"I don't know," I admitted. "He maybe thought that I wouldn't recall seeing him, there were twenty-one people there that day, so perhaps he thought he was lost in the crowd, and even if I did, I probably wouldn't know his name, there were no introductions or name tags, I just happened to overhear an introduction to someone else."

"Interesting, I fancy another beer, one for you?" Ian asked.

"Please," I said. So, now I had met the infamous Rosalind, the cause of my temporary loss of Ian. I suppose she was beautiful in her own way, a sort of Natalie Wood look alike, and if Ian was not getting any communication from me, I could see where she might hold attractions. But the fact that she had intercepted all our mail and withheld it still rankled and I was tempted to accost her and ask her what the hell she thought she had been doing.

Our paths did cross, Rosalind's and mine, later that evening, we had both been to the loo and met on our way back to the dining room.

"So, you're Fiona," she said with a smirk on her face. "No hard feelings?"

"Look, bitch," I said. "If ever I meet you in an out of the way place, you'll learn just what hard feelings are."

"Are you threatening me?" she asked, a little less confident now.

143

"No, just telling you how it is," I told her. "Perhaps I should give Bob chapter and verse about your activities in Tanzania, and perhaps tell him that you were just the office girl and had nothing really to do with the dig?"

"You wouldn't do that," she said, even less confident now.

"You're right," I said. "Because, unlike you, I'm not by nature a conniving bitch, enjoy your trip back to the States, I hope Bob finds a better person in you than the one I've heard of." I went back to the dinner table and Ian immediately sensed that something had occurred.

"What happened?" he asked.

"The bitch asked me to have no hard feelings," I said.

"And?" he asked.

"I told her that if I ever met her in an out of the way place, she'd learn just what hard feelings were," I said. "I'm sorry, it just came out, she stood there smirking at me and said, so, you're Fiona, in such a smarmy way, I could have belted her right then and there."

"Well, they should be gone tomorrow," he said. "Just as well, it would have been beyond awkward if they had been staying longer."

"I'll say," I agreed.

We did not meet Rosalind and Bob the next day, apparently, they had made their early flight and had left the hotel before breakfast. We ate our breakfast then went out to meet Ahmed for the day trip. He was there, as promised and helped us aboard. We went first down the channel to the ocean, then as we rounded the tip of Manda Island Ahmed shut off the motor and hoisted the sail, and we scudded along borne by the southerly winds. We rounded the northern tip of the island and went into Manda Bay, which was truly huge. Along the coast lines, it was either sandy beaches or mangrove swamps. The mangroves I knew were tremendously important to hold the soils together and protect the islands, they also filtered out all kinds of pollutants and rubbish from the water and they provided places to hide for fish, crabs, and other things found in the water. It was nice enough cruising along in our dhow, but convention meant that I had to stay clothed, when what I really wanted to do was strip off completely and feel the breeze and the sun against my skin. Perhaps if we did this again, we should hire a boat for ourselves and try our hand at sailing it. With that notion in mind I started to pay close attention to how Ahmed handled the boat and how he positioned the sail with respect to the wind direction and the direction we wanted to go and how he used the rudder. Tacking in the dhow to sail into the wind seemed out of the question, which was probably why he used the outboard motor, and why historically the Arab traders had come and gone at very specific times of the year, when the trade winds blew either from the north or the south. We saw fishermen in the water pushing a net in front of them, which when gathered up yielded tiger prawns, I suppose some of which might up end on the dining tables of the hotel that evening. Ahmed pointed out to the starboard of the boat and there we saw a group of dugong swimming along. Ahmed told us that they migrated through the area and that their numbers had been slowly declining since the sixties. He told us that they also saw turtles in the area, dolphins, some of which we had already seen, and off shore sometimes even whales. It was such a different Kenya to the uplands and the savanna with its myriad of animals. It was something that just was not imagined when Kenya was mentioned. I confess that it had not occurred to me that there was this whole other ecosystem, that was just as diverse as the land system, and which in many ways was more in danger of loss than the land system. The national parks protected the land animals, but there were no coastal national parks to protect the fish, turtles, dugongs and other species, so that future generations of Kenyans were unlikely to see what I was seeing.

We had lunch on a secluded beach, we dined on prawns and crabs, both caught by Ahmed. Over lunch Ahmed asked us about the hotel and the other guests, about whom we could actually say very little. He also was interested in why we had journeyed to Lamu. We told him that we just wanted to see something different and having never been to the coast of Kenya, it seemed an ideal spot to visit. After lunch we motored back through backwaters until we came back around the southern tip of Lamu Island and thus up the coast, past an old fort to Peponi's. It had been a delightful day and I had seen something completely new to me. We said farewell to Ahmed and went to our room.

"So, what did you think of the day?" Ian asked.

"It was marvellous," I told him. "But I think I would have preferred it had it been just us with no boatman. I wanted to talk to you about what we saw, I wanted to strip off and enjoy the sun and sea air, I wanted to swim naked in the ocean, but I'm afraid I didn't trust Ahmed."

"You were right to do that," Ian said. "He's a paid informant for the Kenya police."

"How do you know that?" I asked.

"I pieced it together," he said. "He wanted to know too much, he knew too much and I can spot an informant, I got good at it at Olduvai."

"They had people like that at Olduvai?" I asked in wonder.

"They had agents who visited from time to time to keep an eye on all the foreigners and their comings and goings, and they met with the local paid informants," he explained. "The Tanzanians are paranoid about someone upending their socialist regime and have a hearty mistrust of foreigners. They also want to be sure that discoveries are properly handled and that nothing disappears. For that, I can't blame them, archeology is rife with thefts and with artifacts disappearing into the hands of foreign museums or private collectors."

"Was Tega an informant?" I asked. Tega was a man I had met at Arusha who had worked in the office that managed the digs, and it was he who had been tasked to destroy all the letters from me and from Ian that Rosalind had intercepted. Fortunately for us Tega had not burned the letters as instructed but had hung on to them and had given them to me when I had gone to Arusha the year before.

"No, he was the one who first tipped me off to them," Ian said. "Tega liked me for some reason and he hinted around the true purpose of one of the local dig labour supervisors, he told me where he had seen him before and what he had been doing then, after that, I looked at all the local labour much more closely and worked out who the informants were."

"Did Ahmed know we were coming?" I asked.

"No," Ian said. "He probably just reports to the Kenya police as a matter of routine who comes and goes and what they do."

"Why?" I asked. "If you knew Ahmed was an informant why engage him as our boatman?"

"Last question first, better to have your possible adversary close so that you can manage the information he gets, and first question, this coast has always been sensitive," he said. "The main port is at Mombasa, but there are smuggling routes from the Arabian Peninsula and beyond that bring goods in and take ivory and rhino horns out, and this system of islands and bays is perfect for those operations."

"I think he spoke Italian," I said. "I said something, I forget what we were looking at, but the Italian just came to mind, and he reacted, then tried hard to cover his reaction."

"It's quite possible," Ian said. "Somalia used to be an Italian territory long ago, and there are still Italian speakers there, and my guess is that Ahmed may be Kenyan born, but his folks came from Somalia."

"So, is he a Kenyan spy or a Somali spy?" I asked.

"Ostensibly Kenyan," Ian said. "But he may sell information to both, I'm sure the Kenyans keep an eye on him."

"I never thought of these countries having spies," I said. "I thought that was something that happened in Europe and Russia and the US, all the stuff you read about in Le Carré novels."

"All countries have some form of security service, Bob, who we met last night is CIA," Ian said, dropping that last *bon mot* quite casually. "The Kenyans keep an active network in Uganda, just to keep an eye on what Amin is up to, and I'm sure that they've got people in Tanzania, Ethiopia, Sudan and Somalia, all the neighbours."

"How do you know Bob is CIA?" I asked, I knew he was probably not what he said he was, but the explanation could have been many things.

"Again, it all fits, particularly with what you told me last night," Ian told me. "Bob has probably been in country to assess what is going on with Uganda and to advise on what the US posture should be, particularly after the Israeli raid on Entebbe."

"Is Rosalind a spy?" I asked.

"I doubt it," Ian said. "Nothing about her rings true for an operative, but you never know, she may just be far better at maintaining her cover than Bob is. I'll be reporting on them when we get back to Nairobi. The folks in London will want to know that someone has been poking around in their sphere of influence. Talking about Le Carré, I knew a chap in London who had worked with Cornwell when he was in the service and before he started writing novels."

"So, that leads to the really big question, are you a spy?" I asked.

"Me, no," he said. "I'll report on what I see and hear, but I'm not part of the security services, I'm just a plodding diplomat."

"Plodding, I doubt," I said hotly. "You've got the measure of all the others at the commission and I think you're streets smarter than they are."

"You're biased," he said, leaning over and giving me a kiss. That kiss led to more and more.

"Do you remember the bush trip we took out to Jack and Emily's place?" I asked him.

"Vividly," he said. "Why?"

"I was thinking that it would be nice of you to make love to me like you did then," I said dreamily.

"Which time?" he asked.

"The third time," I said. "As I recall you performed well then." I lay back and held my arms out to him and opened my legs wide in invitation. He gave a sort of growl and then said, "God, but you are beautiful Fi."

"That's the lust talking," I laughed.

"No, I mean it," he said. "I keep thinking how lucky I am to be with you."

"Well, are you going to keep feeling lucky, or are you going to do something?" I asked. I guided him in and he slipped his hands under my backside and lifted me up towards him. I felt him go in as far as he could and revelled in the feeling. I lifted my legs up and put them around his back and pulled him even closer.

"Yes, Ian," I whispered. "Yes!"

"I love you Fi," he said. "Oh God, Fi, I can't hold on any longer."

"Let it go," I told him, then felt his climax as he came. "God, that was good," I told him. "How long before we can do that again?"

"Give me a few minutes," he said. I gave him his minutes and we made love again, this time more leisurely and with us both reaching climaxes together.

We had dinner that evening and I looked around the room at the other guests and tried to imagine if any of them were something other than simple holiday makers. I confess that I probably attributed more to them than was actually true and saw a den of a spies, counter spies, all along the lines of Mad Magazine, Spy versus Spy. In truth they were probably all what they appeared to be, just people on holiday. I wondered what people made of us, did they see Ian as a spy, even as a diplomat, or did that even cross their minds, and what did they make of me. While we were eating dinner, Ian was given a message by the manager.

"Is there anything wrong?" I asked Ian.

"No, but, if you don't mind, we've been asked to pick up a couple of people in Mombasa tomorrow and take them back with us to Nairobi," he explained.

148

"They can't just take one of the regular flights?" I asked.

"Apparently not," he said. "We've been asked to pick two up at the Bamburi Airport just this side of Mombasa."

"All very clandestine," I said. "I doubt that there's any fuel at Bamburi, so that may be an issue. Is this something we need to be concerned about?"

"I don't think so," he said. "Do we have enough fuel, or do we need to stop in Mombasa for fuel?"

"Let me see," I said. I recalled the amount of fuel we had left, then did the calculations quickly for the extra trip down to Mombasa, then on up to Nairobi, with the extra load of two more people. We had enough, barely, leaving us no margin for safety. It was a pity that the Manda strip did not have fuel, if they had one, I could have bought some and given myself a better margin for safety. "There's no way they'll meet us at the main Mombasa airport? We really don't have enough fuel for the extra trip."

"I gather that they would rather be discreet about their movements," he said.

"I doubt that's possible here," I said. "The bush telegraph seems to get information and send it quicker than the mail or even the telephone, so I doubt your two are going to get to Nairobi, even flying with us, without being noted."

"I'll tell Nairobi we don't have enough fuel, unless we stop at the Mombasa airport and get some, and ask them what they want to do," Ian said. He went off to use the hotel telephone and came back soon with the reply that I had hoped for, we need not stop in Mombasa and pick up these mysterious people.

"So, ready for bed?" I asked him.

"Always," he said. "Why?"

I leaned over and whispered in his ear and told him what I was going to do to him.

"What are we waiting for?" he said, grinning. We almost ran to our room, where we both ripped off clothes then stared hungrily at each other.

"I fancy being a lion," I told him, then knelt down onto the bed on all fours. He climbed up behind me and I felt him enter. I had needed no stimulation, neither had he. He moved back and forth, moving in and out, it was marvellous. As he grew more excited, he speeded up, but I slowed him down, I wanted this to last as long as possible. Finally, neither he nor I could wait any longer.

"Now, Ian," I said. "Now!"

"With pleasure," he said. He speeded up his thrusts and we both cried out as the climaxes hit us.

"That was spectacular," I said.

The next morning, we took a walk along the beach from the hotel. The beach ran on for what seemed like miles with no houses, no hotels, just sand dunes, with some scrub grass growing in among them. There were no people on the beach, and judging by the lack of tracks in the sand, there had not been any for a day or two. I was tempted to strip off and enjoy the sun, but as I got ready to do so, two men appeared with a string of donkeys, all of which had panniers on them filled with coral, probably for some construction project. We went back to the hotel for lunch, then arranged for a ride back to Manda and our plane. It was still there, undisturbed, which was a relief. Leaving our plane at bush camps was one thing, leaving it at such a busy place as the Manda airstrip was another thing. Ian pulled up all the pins we had used to stake the plane down, while I did my walk around then my pre-flight checks, then we stowed everything and climbed aboard to start the pre-flight checks. All in order, we taxied out and took off for the trip back to Nairobi. The southerly wind helped a little pushing us over the ground faster than we had been able to go when we came, putting us into Nairobi mid-afternoon. We closed the plane up, tied it down and went home, delighted with our trip.

Ian went off to the commission the next day and came back with all kinds of news. Things had heated up between Uganda and Kenya and accusations and recriminations were flying back and forth. Amin made a statement about the CIA being behind a plot to overthrow him and also accused the British and the Americans of pressuring Kenya to demand payment for cross border goods in Kenya Shillings. Uganda cut off power to Kenya, power that came from a hydroelectric station at Owen Falls, but had problems itself with power with the lack of fuel. This went on for a week or two and it reached a sort of climax when Amin fatuously remarked that it would not be difficult to destroy Kenyatta's

150

residence at Nakura from the air, and that their air force could reach Mombasa and back. Amin accused Kenya of working with the Zionists and the South Africans, but then he also went on to say that he would never attack Kenya. It was a very confusing time. It was hard to work out what actually was going on. Ian had also heard that some of the Ugandan army had mutinied because they had not been paid. That did not seem to be to be a good idea, if you want loyalty from the army, surely the first thing to do is pay them. Amin then changed tack and sent more conciliatory messages to Kenya, that fell on deaf ears. So, he went to the UN and the OAU, accusing the Kenyans of conspiring against him and asking for them to intervene or he might have to take desperate action. Quite what that meant, we were not quite sure, but Kenya did the logical thing and beefed up security at the border. While all this was going on, the British High Commission in Kampala was closed as Britain broke off diplomatic relations with Uganda, the first time they had broken with a Commonwealth country. That had all stemmed from the murder of Dora Bloch, one of the hostages from the Air France flight who had been in hospital when the Entebbe raid took place. Subsequent to the raid she disappeared and the only logical conclusion was that she had been murdered on the orders of Amin. That did not sit well with the British Government, and notes were exchanged, questions were asked, until it got so bad that diplomatic ties were severed. After the recall of the High Commission staff, all British interests were handled by the French Embassy.

I had not expected all this and the animosity that existed between Uganda and Kenya, or perhaps more properly, Amin and Kenyatta. I doubt that the average Ugandan or Kenyan was overly concerned with the niceties of cross border trade, but killings did rather bring it home that relations were poor to say the least. Eventually things settled down and Amin was all peace and love for a while. But there was still the issue of the dead Kenyan airport workers, so relations never really returned to normality. That was a shame, because I had had a notion to visit Uganda and see Murchison Falls. Clearly that was out for the foreseeable future, the notion that people from Kenya flying up in their own plane would be highly suspicious to the Ugandans and if we went we would be lucky to get out of there with our plane, perhaps even our lives, so Murchison Falls would have to wait for better times.

Ian also told me that he had passed on his suspicions about Bob Bannon, otherwise known as Norris Olander, being with the CIA and that information had been passed on to London, who had responded asking for more information, if he could get it, about where Bannon had been and who he had talked to. The UK and the US might be allies and have a special relationship, but that did not mean that the various security services really trusted one another. Ian also told me that the Americans had lost a lot of faith in the Brits after the Burgess and Maclean debacle and the subsequent defection of Philby and he also told me of two more confessions, not yet made public, those of Blunt and Cairncross. Ian's take on the matter was that there had been complacency in the intelligence service and that the problems could have been spotted earlier if there had been more scrutiny, but that was just not done with, as he put it, chaps like us.

Spies and informants aside, I had really enjoyed our trip to the coast. It was another Kenya, quite different to the game parks and animals of the highlands or the deserts of the north. We had watched the sun come up over the Indian Ocean, we had listened to the waves breaking on the roar, the subdued roar of the ocean, we had dabbled our toes in the warm water, we had dined on freshly caught prawns and crabs, we had sailed in a dhow, and walked along a long sandy beach, we had explored mangrove swamps, watched dolphins and dugongs, and explored Lamu town with its rich history of trade with the Arabian Peninsula, it had been a moment to remember.

Collapse of EAA

"So, you met Rosalind?" Maman asked.

"I did, she was a smarmy sort, I could image her being sweetness and light until things didn't go her way, then I could see her as being nasty and vindictive," I commented. "She was attractive enough, a little shorter than me, heavier, bigger boobs, longer hair and had this grating accent, I not sure where in the US from."

"So, you never got to beat her up?" Portia asked.

"No, Ian wanted me to leave her alone, so that she and her husband could go on their merry way and leave Kenya," I explained.

"So, was the husband with the CIA?" James asked.

"He was," I confirmed. "Ian reported things up the chain and got requests back, so he did the obvious thing, he contacted one of the people he knew at the American Embassy and had coffee with him. I gather that he managed to wangle out of his contact what Bob had been doing in the country, I never asked how. It turned out that Bob Bannon was his actual name and that Norris Olander had been a fictitious name. Ian was a very good poker player, he had this ability to read people, but could also make himself unreadable, so the few times I ever saw him play poker, he was the winner and took everyone's money."

"Did you go back to Lamu?" Charlize asked.

"We did," I said. "We flew back another time and rented a boat and sailed around. I enjoyed that a lot, I could strip off and dance naked on the beach, swim in the ocean and do all the things that you can't do when there's a third party there."

"Who were the two that they wanted you to pick up in Mombasa?" James asked.

"Some friend of the Commissioner," I told them. "We gathered that he wanted the bush plane experience before going back to London, they could have got that anywhere, but I think he was too bloody cheap to charter a plane, so was trying to hitch a ride for free and tick off the experience from his list of things to do. Why they wanted picking up at the Bamburi field I never found out, and why we just couldn't pick them up in Mombasa I also never found out, it was just too weird, maybe he thought it was a bush strip and not a tarmac runway."

"Perhaps he was smuggling some kind of contraband," Portia suggested.

"Maybe," I thought. "But if he was, how was he going to get it out of Kenya?"

"In the diplomatic bag?" Maman suggested.

"I doubt it," I said. "The commish didn't go in for that sort of thing. I did learn one thing though, each time we took a trip anywhere Ian would write a report with impressions of the place, the economy there, the political leanings of people we talked to, any military activity we saw and anything else that might be of interest to the intelligence gatherers."

"You said something about East African Airways, what happened there?" Charlize asked.

Escape from Arusha

It was early in 1977, Ian came home one day and suggested that we fly down to Arusha and drive out to see the Olduvai digs. I had found copies of books for him and academic papers that showed that his old thesis advisor, Professor Ambrose, had plagiarised, or stolen depending on your view point, a lot of Ian's work that he had done while working at the digs. Ambrose had been critical of Ian's thesis and had sent him back to Olduvai for more work. Meanwhile other researchers had unearthed remains that tended to prove Ian's ideas, so Ambrose had done something that I learned was all too common in the academic world and had used Ian's ideas and notes and published as if it were his work. He had given some minor credit in the end notes to Ian, but had hardly given him the credit that was due. Ian was annoyed, to say the least, but as he had pointed out to me before, Ambrose had the reputation and the following in the field, whereas he, Ian, was a newcomer and relatively unknown. There was probably little that could be done to amend the situation, so he had resigned himself to live with it for the moment. I think he was planning in the longer term to write up his findings himself and submit them for publishing in *Man,* Ambrose be damned.

I set up a trip, first I called the dig office in Arusha and talked to Alison Baker. I had met her when I had gone to Tanzania to unravel the mystery of not hearing from Ian after he had gone back there. She arranged things for us to be met at the Arusha airport, and then to be transported out to the site and housed for the few days we would be there, apparently one of the dig members was away for a week or two, so we could use the tent he normally had. Flying down to Arusha would take us about one hour and twenty minutes, so it would be a fairly short trip. I checked the weather, and there were some storms predicted, but nothing that would interfere with our trip. I had not flown across a border yet and checked on the regulations that governed. It seemed that all one really needed to do was check with customs and immigration at the port of entry. Well, that we could do, because there was a post at the Arusha airport. Things were in a turmoil again; East African Airways had just declared bankruptcy. I was not surprised, there was an attitude among the three country owners that government officials could travel gratis. That notion displayed an uncommon ignorance about how the economics of airlines work, or an arrogance. Lease payments for aircraft, fuel bills, wages for crews, maintenance costs and other expenses have to be paid, whether or not there is revenue. The idea that just because one is a member of the government that travel was free on the supposed national airline was idiotic to me, but obviously not to the officials and politicians who preempted seats and paid nothing. Small wonder that the airline was in trouble financially. The Kenyans blamed the Tanzanians for not paying their share, and they probably both had harsh words for Uganda the third member of the community. At any rate, at the end of January, East Africa Airlines ceased to operate. Along with the airline, the joint ferry and harbour system that operated on Lake Victoria had also ceased operations and the Kenyans had possession of all the ferries and boats. That was going to cause problems with Tanzania at least. It looked as if the whole notion of an East African Community was destined to failure, I think the basic issues was that of serious differences in politics and philosophy of government. Kenya was still something of a capitalist democracy, Uganda was under a dictator who was mercurial to say the least, and Tanzania under Nyerere was solidly socialist. I think therein lay the fundamental problem, the socialist ideals of Nyerere just did not fit well with the more freewheeling economies of Kenya and Uganda. It would be interesting to see in the longer term whether I was right or not.

Ian came home early on the Friday the week of our trip and we left for the airport. We had both packed bags the night before, so for Ian it was just a question of changing clothes and we were ready for the off. At the airport I did my walk around then the pre-flight checks, made sure we had enough fuel to get there and back, and we were off. Our route took us almost straight south, not quite straight south, but only five degrees off. We generally lost altitude as we went, but there was a high point near Kajido where we passed over a small hill. From there it was basically downhill until Arusha, except for a peak right at the border and then the slopes of Longido, then the slopes of Mt. Meru as we approached the Arusha airport. We were going to use the actual Arusha airport as opposed to the Mt. Kilimanjaro International Airport, which was not only more expensive in terms of landing fees, but altogether the wrong side of Arusha. As we landed and taxied into the hard stand, a customs and immigration official came bustling over to see us. We presented our passports and were stamped in as visitors. We had nothing to declare as all we were bringing was our personal clothes for the few days we would be there, and my camera. The official left and we tied down our plane and closed it up. We had just finished when a Land Rover pulled up and two men got out, one I recognised as Tega, Tega who I had met before in Arusha, Tega who had essentially saved my relationship with Ian by not following instructions from Rosalind.

"Tega, jambo, habari?" Ian said, greeting him and asking him how he was.

"Mzuri, Bwana," Tega replied, telling Ian that he was well. *"Bibi, habari?"* he said to me.

"Mzuri, Tega," I replied. Tega then went on to introduce Alan Edwards who was one of the researchers at the dig. He was going to drive us out there and show us around. Tega was not coming with us, but had wanted to meet us at the airport. It was good to see him again and I asked how his granddaughter was doing. The last time I had seen him he was trying to get the funding to send her off to university. Maman had helped a little. Tega told us that his granddaughter was doing well at university and that he was confident of great things to come. Alan took our bags and stowed them in the back of the Land Rover and we first dropped Tega back into town at the dig office and to say hello and thank you to Alison.

"Fiona," she said. "How nice to see you again, you must be Ian."

"I am," he admitted. "Thank you for arranging this for us, I've wanted to come back for a while, but it never seemed possible. Now that we live in Nairobi, it's just a quick trip down."

"So, everything worked out well?" she asked.

"It did," Ian and I said together. "Much of the credit goes to Tega and his keeping all the letters, without them it would have been much harder."

"If there's anything else you need while you're here, just let me know," Alison said. "I can arrange most things."

"Thank you," I said. "And, thank you again for arranging this."

We said our goodbyes and then we left for the drive out to Olduvai.

"I understand you were here before?" Alan asked Ian as we headed out of town towards the west.

"I was," Ian confirmed. "I spent three years here, then another few months before I was called away for a family emergency."

"The digging crew all remember you," Alan said. "I'm still trying to build a relationship with them, and improve my Swahili."

"Whose tent are we stealing?" Ian asked.

"Pete Bishop's" Alan replied. "Pete's away for a couple of weeks taking care of some things in London."

"Where are you from?" Ian asked.

"I'm at Cambridge," Alan replied. "King's actually. You were at Oxford?"

"We both were," Ian replied. "Fiona did her work in mathematics and later economics, while I stayed with anthropology."

"And now I gather you're in Nairobi?" Alan asked.

"I'm with the High Commission there," Ian replied.

"You have your own plane, wow," Alan said.

"Actually, it's really Fiona's," Ian said. "She makes all the money in the family; she consults on economic matters and her fees can be pretty steep."

"Who's the pilot?" Alan asked.

"I am," I replied. "I thought it might be fun to get a licence, so took lessons and got my licence. It's really convenient getting around Kenya, much quicker than driving. I'm thinking of teaching Ian to fly."

"Wouldn't that be rather like teaching your wife to drive, sounds good, but leads to arguments and unpleasantness?" Alan suggested.

"Could be," Ian laughed. "No, we were thinking of the same instructor who taught Fiona, he's a little abrupt and dour, but very thorough."

"The tent should be set up for you when we arrive, two cots I'm afraid, no doubles on the site," Alan said. "We should be there in about four hours, just in time for dinner. Then, I thought that tomorrow morning we could take a look around and talk about what you found and what we've found since."

"Sounds good," Ian said. "Fi?"

"Sounds good to me," I echoed.

We made the camp in the four hours and were shown to our tent, where we dropped our bags and went immediately to dinner. Introductions were made all around and we met Professor Arthur Ekstrom from the

158

US, three of his students, all post graduates, Jim Butcher, Emily Sharp and Monica Blake, then there was Doctor Henry Wilson and his students, again all post graduates, Amanda Thomas, Greta Thorn and Kimberley Stewart, again all from the US, then there was Alan, Doctor Janet White and Ann Cuthbert, all from King's and finally, Professor Robert Pence, Donald Mann, Vittoria Vitale and Sofia Romero, also all from the US. Alan introduced us simply as Ian and Fiona, telling the rest that we were guests of King's and just visiting for a couple of days. He did note that Ian had worked there a few years earlier. Ekstrom, who seemed to have appointed himself as the de-facto leader of the current expedition, asked Ian what he had done. Ian then gave a quick review of the time he had spent there and the things that he had found.

"Is it possible to get a copy of your thesis?" Ekstrom asked. Ekstrom struck me as one of those controlling men who think that they should know all that was involved and as a side note who also consider themselves God's gift to women, he was attractive enough, what a Brazilian friend of mine would call a magazine cover, he looked reasonably fit and projected this image of, I'm in charge here.

"I never completed it," Ian said.

"Oh, you did not get it approved, or was your work not original enough?" Ekstrom asked, rather rude of him, I thought.

"No, my time was cut short by the death of my parents," Ian said.

"Oh, so sorry, why could you not finish things after their funeral?" Pence asked.

"It was little more complicated than that," Ian said. "They were killed when their car hit a landmine, so I had to go back and bury them, then sell the farm and clean up loose ends."

"Oh, where did they live?" Pence asked.

"Rhodesia," Ian replied.

"What did they farm there?" White asked.

"Tobacco," Ian said. "It was not a business I wanted to go into, so I sold the farm, which took a little while and after that I had no inclination to go back to college, so I joined the British Civil Service."

"Pity," Ekstrom said. "We're doing important work here, delving into the past and continuing the work started by the Leakeys, we could use a competent digger and researcher, so many who come have no experience and we lose a lot due to ignorance."

"How long have you been here?" Ian asked, wondering at the level of assumed expertise that Ekstrom implied he had.

"Two years now," Ekstrom replied. "We have a grant that will fund us for another six years, so expect great things."

"Had you been to Africa before coming here?" Ian asked.

"No, first time to Tanzania, first time to Africa, they're doing marvellous things here in Tanzania, President Nyerere has really got things under control," Ekstrom expounded. "I know you old colonials despise these new guys, but you didn't do them any favours."

"Probably not," Ian said, very noncommittally.

Conversation then focused on the current finds at the dig and what they might mean. It was a discussion that at time got quite heated. I suppose that pet theories are pet theories and facts and data that may tend to call the theory into question are not really welcome. Ekstrom was the most vocal of the group and the most disparaging of any notion that did not conform with his view of things. I got the impression that he almost regarded the Olduvai Gorge as his private property and if he could he would evict the other teams. I had come across some of these petty jealousies before in the academic world, but Ekstrom seemed to carry it to an extreme. He was also a condescending git, and to top it all, he was also a chauvinist pig. His remarks to his female students and to Doctor White made me want to thump him. I suppose being a tenured professor, a fact that we were made aware of several times, at a well-known American university gave him airs and graces that he thought were due to him. Personally, I thought he was a braggart and as I said before, a real git. I wondered of the work that his graduate students were doing, how much would appear as papers with Ekstrom as the lead author. Ian and I finally excused ourselves and went off to bed, leaving the rest of them swigging brandy and arguing. The tent had the two cots that Alan had alluded to, so we pulled all the bedclothes off and arranged them on the floor between the beds. There was a shower nearby, with piped hot water. One of the camp staff had the job of keeping a forty-four gallon drum filled with water and with stoking the fire that was beneath it. So, there was always warm to hot water, depending on what had been the demands. I showered first and went to bed and dropped off immediately, only waking briefly when Ian came to bed after his shower.

In the morning we were up with the dawn and the birds and the smell of coffee. We were up and dressed quickly and piled the bedclothes back on the cots, then went to find coffee and breakfast. Ian saw a cook he knew and they chattered away in Swahili. Alan joined us and apologised for Ekstrom.

"You've nothing to apologise for," Ian said. "We had some Americans here working at the site when I was here, and two of them were really great, but one was a real *doës.*"

"A what?" Alan asked.

"Sorry, bad Afrikaans slang," Ian explained.

"Oh," Alan said. "What about Swahili slang?"

"There are quite a few words," Ian said. "Most of the time you'll hear words that sound just fine, but they usually have a deeper meaning. I'm sure the camp staff and the diggers have got some choice ones for your Professor Ekstrom. What's White like?"

"She's really nice," Alan said. "She's demanding, but she's fair. In my view, she actually knows a lot more than Ekstrom, but he's got the funding to be a prick and we just have to accept him being here."

"How long has King's had people here?" Ian asked.

"About five years now, we were here with some others, then all the Yanks showed up and told us that everything we were doing was wrong," Alan bemoaned. "Would you like a tour now?"

"That would be great," Ian said. "Let me just get some hats from our tent."

"Would you get my sunglasses for me?" I asked him.

"Sure, I'll bring some water too," he promised.

With Alan leading we set off for our tour of the dig site. Alan led us past the areas where the various teams were working and pointed out, in general terms, what they were doing. It seemed to me that archeology was a lot of grubbing in the dirt on one's hands and knees. It was hot, but not too dusty, there had been rain recently, so the dust had been dampened down. I watched as researchers and diggers, gently cut the soft strata from around objects they had seen, and then used brushes to clean them even more. Sometimes the objects were pebbles, but occasionally there was a cry of triumph as something of note was uncovered. It amazed me that the diggers could discern the difference between remains of bones and rocks. After all, the bones themselves had been turned into rock over the millennia, but Ian picked some pieces up and showed me the difference and how I could tell which was which. He identified a radius for me and a carpus and a metacarpus. With the carpal bones, I had no idea how he could tell what they were, to me they just looked like little pieces of roughly cylindrical rock. That, Ian explained was part of the recognition, rocks essentially did not occur like that, the pieces had to be something that had been fossilised. Alan was listening to all this very closely and I think he appreciated the lesson almost as much as I did.

We took a short break for lunch, and that seemed to be a haphazard affair, with people from the various teams coming and going and just grabbing something. I have to say this, they were all very dedicated to what they were doing. After lunch, we took a walk farther afield, away from the current trenches into the surrounding area. It was amazing to me that anything had been found, how had Leakey known where to dig, or was it just luck. Certainly, the formation of the gorge provided for a look back in time as various strata had been exposed. From items found in each layer, dates could be estimated. As Ian and Alan both explained what we were looking at went back over a span of two million years. It was hard to imagine what the area would have looked like that long ago, but because we were looking at sedimentary rocks, there must have been water and lots of it. So, the people would have lived, then the area would have been covered with water, so where did they go?

Over dinner that night, Ekstrom asked Ian what he thought about the digs. Ian was polite and expounded on all the possibilities of great discoveries, and there really were amazing things being unearthed. Then Ekstrom committed a real sin, he asked me what I thought, but he asked in such a condescending manner, as if he expected me to ooh and aah over his discoveries, without having any clue as to what they might mean.
"So, fair Fiona, what do you think?" he asked.
"It's very interesting," I said.
"It's more than interesting," he said. "It's ground breaking, but then I wouldn't expect such a pretty young thing to understand."

"Well, Arthur," I said. "I received a good explanation from Alan and my husband today, so have a better understanding."

"You should address me by my proper title, I'm Professor Ekstrom to you," he said haughtily. I felt Ian squeezing my knee, but I was not going to let that pass.

"In that case, Professor, do me the kindness of calling me by my title, Doctor Hartley," I responded archly.

"Doctor, doctor of what?" he said, dismissively.

"My first doctorate was in mathematics," I said.

"Mathematics, huh, any fool can do that, this is real science," he said.

"Wait a minute," Henry Wilson said. "You said your first doctorate, you have another?"

"Two more," I said. "One in economics and one in computer science."

"When did you get your first?" Henry asked.

"When I was twenty-one," I replied.

"Are you published?" Ekstrom asked.

"Most of my clients prefer that I do not publish the work I do for them," I said.

"Clients, what kind of clients?" Ekstrom demanded.

"The Chancellor of the Exchequer, various mining houses, vineyards, car companies, fashion houses, among others," I shot back at him.

"Do they pay well?" Henry asked.

"They are all happy to pay my fees," I said.

"Her fees must be pretty steep," Alan interjected. "She has her own plane."

"So, what else do you do?" Robert Pence asked, sensing that Ekstrom was going to go down in flames and wanting to being in at the kill. In the background I heard someone mutter, batter up.

"I speak a couple of languages," I admitted.

"Ha, English and Swahili, I know because I heard you today, it's a simple enough language to pick up," Ekstrom commented.

"English and Swahili, yes," I confirmed. "And, by the way, your Swahili is appalling, I also speak French, Italian, Mandarin and Tahitian." With the latter I was stretching the truth a little as my knowledge was limited to what I remembered from my grandmother and mother talking. "And you?" I challenged.

"What I speak is of no concern to you," he said huffily. In the background I heard a muttered, strike one to Hartley.

"So," Pence said. "We know you've got three doctorates, you can speak six languages, who flies the plane?"

"I do," I said.

"Do you have a pilot's licence Arthur?" Pence asked.

"Of course not," Ekstrom said. "I wouldn't waste my time." I heard a strike two.

"So, what else do you do?" Pence asked.

"Not a lot," I admitted.

"She's a crack shot," Ian said, throwing his piece into things. "Even outshot me once and I learned to shoot growing up in the bush in Rhodesia and was rated by the army as marksman."

"Can you shoot Arthur?" Pence asked. In the background I heard, strike three.

"Of course not," Ekstrom said angrily. "I got a deferment during Vietnam and missed my service there. Look, I can run a 10k in forty-five minutes, can you?"

"I just ran one in Nairobi," I replied. "My time was forty-four minutes and ten seconds." The background mutter this time was, yer out.

"So, Arthur, I think you owe Doctor Hartley an apology, you may have the title of Professor, but she has also earned her title and then some," Pence said.

"Don't be ridiculous," Ekstrom said. "Apologise to a slip of a girl, don't be silly."

"You know," Ian said. "Fiona once put three chaps in hospital because they were stupid enough to try and attack her."

"I'm not attacking anyone," Ekstrom said. "Is that a threat?"

"No, just a historical fact," Ian said. "You would do well to be polite to my wife, or I might take a dim view, or worse, she might."

"Look, Hartley, I have no beef with you," Ekstrom said.

"No, you're just a condescending git," Ian said. The Brits around the table all struggled to cover explosions of laughter, while most of the Americans were none the wiser, but sensed that that was a real insult.

"Oh, very well, I'm sorry I was less than polite, Doctor Hartley, it never occurred to me that you could have already earned a doctorate," he said in very smarmy tones. I could imagine what a bear he would be towards the rest of the camp after we had gone, but perhaps he had learned something, but my intuition said not. Men like him regard others as less than themselves and women are even further down. Dinner was finally served, breaking things up and we went to the table and seated ourselves.

Ian and I sat as far away from Ekstrom as we could, next to the Brit contingent.

"You're Fiona Barclay, aren't you?" Janet White asked.

"Was," I agreed. "Now Hartley."

"I went to a lecture you gave at Oxford; it was about statistical methods, I needed the statistics course for my degree," she explained.

"I hope it was useful," I said.

"Oh, very," she replied. "As I recall you were standing in for a prof who had taken a tumble from his bike."

"He had, broke a femur," I explained. "I was a last-minute substitute."

"The one thing I really remember is that you did the whole lecture with no notes," Janet said.

"I never needed them," I said. "I can remember things and the statistic course was just the basics."

"It was a great help to me," Janet said. "Would it be possible for you to spend a little time with me tomorrow talking about some ideas I have to apply some of those techniques here?"

"Of course," I said. "I'd be happy to."

"I'm glad you took Ekstrom down a peg or two," Janet said. "He's been a royal pain in the arse since he arrived, seems to think he owns the place, he's often conniving with the Tanzanians to get permits revoked or denied."

"That's one of the reasons I got out of academia," I said. "I couldn't stand the pettiness, the backbiting, the theft of others' work and the constant scrounging after funding. I was lucky, right after I got my first doctorate, I received a funded fellowship to do some work for the mining industry, that allowed me to establish myself, without having to worry too much about publishing."

"Academia does have its drawbacks," Janet admitted. "But, for all that, I enjoy it, it would just be a little better if Ekstrom and his posse left."

"So, what would you like me to look at?" I asked.

"I'll go and grab some stuff from my tent," Janet said. She left and was back in a few minutes with diagrams and sheets of data. "I'm trying to statistically predict what we might find where, but am having some issues," she said.

"We could use statistical models similar to those that the diamond miners use," I suggested. "But we would need to know how the fossils got here, were they just buried in situ, or were they washed here by water draining into a sea or a lake or something."

"So, we need a better understanding of the ancient geology?" Janet asked.

"I would think that would be the best place to start. If you map where each find has been made, we can probably model things to tell us if the burial was in situ or the items were washed to where they are now. The diamond people do this a lot," I commented. "I would think for that you'd need a pretty good estimate of ages, if you could reliably date a few hundred pieces, and if you could guess whether or not they came from the same skeleton, you could determine whether bone scatter was by predators or scavengers, or the elements, I know of a couple of studies that have been done on bone scatter due to predators and scavengers, so I could use their methods to determine what is what."

"Such a lot to think about," Janet said. "Thank you, could I call upon from time to time to test ideas?"

"Of course," I said. "This is our number in Nairobi."

"Brilliant," Janet said. "What's it like working in what I thought was truly a male dominated field?"

"It has its challenges," I admitted. "But I manage and have a reputation now, so people are coming to me."

"That must be nice," Janet said. "We have to, as you said, scrounge for funding and are very much the poor relations here."

I apologised to Ian after we had gone to bed. I had not meant to go after Ekstrom, but the call me Professor bit rankled. He really was the most unpleasant man. Ian told me that there was nothing to apologise for, Ekstrom had had it coming.

"So, who's the paid informant at the dig?" I asked.

"The cook, Abbas, is one, then there's Hassan the dig foreman and also Ismail one of the diggers," Ian said.

"You seemed to be very friendly with all of them?" I asked.

"Remember the axiom of the Godfather, keep your friends close and your enemies closer," he explained.

"Does that mean you consider them enemies?" I asked.

"No, I just like to know what they're up to. They've all been here a while, they were here when I first came here, and, they're still here," he said.

"So, what did you learn from them?" I asked.

166

"That Ekstrom is in fact trying his damnedest to get the place to himself and is obstructing others' permits as best he can," Ian told me.

"That seems rather poor spirited," I said.

"It's academia," Ian said. "If he can control who's here, he can control discoveries and have his name attached to them all and be the king of early hominids."

"What do we do tomorrow?" I asked.

"Unless you want to go exploring here, I think leave," he said. "Maybe we could rent a Land Rover in Arusha and go and visit the Ngorongoro Crater, I've had it with academia and all their bullshit."

"Fine with me," I said. "The atmosphere here is poisonous, I'm surprised there haven't been any deaths."

"Just wait," Ian laughed. "There's time yet."

We heard some activity and a vehicle arrive. It was late for anyone visiting so we were surprised when we heard Tega's voice at our tent.

"Bwana, I have a telegram for you," he said. Ian got up and put on some clothes and went out to talk to Tega. He read through the telegram, then poked his head back into the tent.

"We need to leave first thing in the morning," he said. "I've been ordered back, let's see what it says, *Imperative you return soonest, stop, London needs your attention to certain matters, stop, end.*"

"Very cryptic," I said. "Who drove Tega out?"

"Alison," Ian said. "I see her delivering mail to the people here and probably telling them that we've been summoned back."

"That will make Ekstrom happy," I said. "He'll probably be very glad to see the backs of us."

"Thanks, Tega," Ian said. Then Alison came over to see us.

"Sorry about that," she said. "I was planning to leave in the morning at about six, is that okay?"

"Fine," Ian said. "We'll be ready."

We were up before the dawn and away by six the following morning. Tega had procured coffee for all of us and something to eat. We gave Alison a chance to eat and drink by swapping places at the wheel.

"I wonder what's so damned important?" Ian thought aloud.

"Nothing," Alison said. "Tega picked up some information that he should tell you about." The conversation then switched to Swahili as Tega told his tale.

"I heard murmurings in the market place about a big movement of the paramilitary police," he started. "I listened and heard that today at noon we will close the border with Kenya, all the official border crossings, and that any Kenyan trucks, cars, trains or planes this side of the border will be impounded."

"What brought that about?" I asked.

"It is not clear," Tega said. "But the regular customs and immigration people are being pushed aside by the paramilitary. The time is set for noon today, because they have to move many people to the border."

"Tega came to me with this information yesterday at lunchtime," Alison said. "So, I called the number you have given me Fiona for emergencies and spoke to a Trevor, I told him that he should send a telegram to you telling you to return. That way there was a reason for you to cut short your visit and leave today."

"He didn't ask why?" I asked.

"No, he just said, fine," she said. "He may have had an inkling that something was going on, but he didn't say."

"Your phone isn't bugged is it?" I asked.

"Not as far as we know," she said. "The Yanks are pretty paranoid and Ekstrom even had someone come in and run some tests, and as of last week there were no taps and no bugs. So, I suppose it's possible that a tap has been put on our line, but why? We have no real contact with anyone from Kenya, the UK and the US, yes, but that's pretty much all academic stuff and pretty boring to a listener."

"Thank you Tega," I said. "Will we be away in time?"

"You should be," Alison said. "We should be back in Arusha by ten, and then how long will it take you to take off?"

"I'll file a flight plan as soon as we get to the airport, the plane's already fuelled up, so then it's just a question of pre-flight and then go, say half an hour at the most," I thought. "We'll tell the immigration chap that we've been summoned back and that we have to leave. We should be well over the border by noon. Tega, where's the closest air force base?"

"That would be the new one that the Chinese have just built," he said. "It's near Ngerengere, so two hundred and fifty miles or more away."

"So, even if they get a scramble order to stop us, it's a good half an hour away even in one of the MiG's," I thought. "By then we'd be well over the border. Any signs of military jets at Arusha or at Kilimanjaro?"

"We have heard nothing," Tega said. "We heard no planes landing at Arusha yesterday."

We were passing close to the turn off for the Ngorongoro crater when I saw a familiar lorry. I was driving, so pulled over and waved them down. It was Julia with her team and camping equipment.

"Fiona," she said. "How nice to see you, what are you doing here?"

"Just flew in for a quick trip," I said. "Look, Julia, we've just heard that the Tanzanians are going to close the border with Kenya at noon today, so you might want to think about getting out while you can or your lorry and Land Rover will be impounded, and we've no idea what they plan to do about your guests."

"Shit," she said. "Okay, I'll get hold of Henry and we'll see what we can do, thanks Fiona,"

"Good luck," I told her, then got back behind the wheel and drove off as quickly as I could. I saw in the mirror that Julia was consulting a map and then her saw her use her radio. Whether or not they would be able to avoid the border closure remained to be seen.

We pulled into the Arusha airport at nine thirty-five, we all had been had really been pushing it and luckily there were no traffic police out and other traffic had been really light. I went to the appropriate desk and filed my flight plan, simple enough, Arusha to Nairobi. Then Ian and I found the immigration officer and got our passports stamped for exit. Ian explained to him that we were really disappointed that we had to leave early and told him that we would try and be back the next month to visit the Ngorongoro Crater. Ian complained bitterly about the people in Nairobi sending him cursory summonses to return and even showed the telegram. The officer was sympathetic, and if he knew what was coming, he did not let on, but neither did he hold us up. I suppose in his mind, noon was noon, and anything that happened before noon was just fate. Alison and Tega came with us to the tarmac and watched as we untied the plane, then as I did my walk around and the pre-flight checks. We were thankful that no military jets had landed that morning, so there would be no interception once we were airborne. We said our goodbyes and I thanked Tega again for letting us know that we needed to leave. He waved it off and said that he was ever in our debt for the help we had provided for his granddaughter. Ian and I climbed aboard and started up the plane, I ran though the pre-flight checks then contacted the tower for clearance to take off. We had a few anxious moments as we waited for them to respond. We could see the tower and there was obviously a discussion going on, then one waved at the clock and then we heard the okay to go. We taxied out and again had a few anxious moments, wondering if we were going to have to just ignore an instruction to return to the hard stand. But we finally got our take off clearance and we were off. Once off the ground, the only way I would go back to land was if they actually sent a military plane to force us back, and that seemed highly unlikely. I had heard none in the sky, loitering, so unless some had flown into Kilimanjaro that morning and could scramble immediately, we were safe.

We cleared the end of the runway and I turned and headed north. We had about eighty miles to go to the border, so I took us up as fast as I could. Ian looked out the window and pointed.

"Down there," he said. "That's a military convoy, there's a couple of trucks headed to the Arusha airport, but most of them are going up the main road to the border crossing at Namanga."

"I'm glad we got away before they arrived," I said. "I'll bet that they would have stopped us. Better be good and let the ATC folks known where we are."

I radioed in our position as required, and was pleased to just hear a response from the Kilimanjaro traffic control people. I had been a little concerned that they might have told us to return, but if we had ignored them, what could they have done. Perhaps, bar us from future entries into Tanzania, or perhaps they might have scrambled a plane, but it was really too late for that, so they probably thought it easier to let us go on our way.

"So far, so good," I said to Ian. "Let's burn a little more fuel and pick up a little speed and get us over the border."

"How long before we're over?" Ian asked. "Can this plane go any faster?"

"Well, the never exceed is 158 knots, and we're doing over 140 now," I said. "I don't want to push things to the limit, unless our lives actually depend on it."

"So, how long to the border?" he asked.

"About twenty minutes," I said. "Can you see anything above or behind us?" Ian craned his neck around and looked through the rear window.

"As far as I can see, nothing," he said.

"I wish Cessna had designed this for a little faster flight," I said. "It would be nice now to have that little extra. Anything behind us?"

"Not that I can see," he said.

We flew on and I checked for landmarks that would tell me when we crossed the border. The best way to tell was to follow the road and then the crossing would be apparent on the ground. I saw the border crossing, we had gone around Longido and were coming up on Namanga, and I could see the buildings that housed the various customs and immigration people of both sides. There was a small queue of lorries waiting to cross north, that was going to get much longer after the paramilitary troops arrived. We flew over the town and when we were well on the Kenya side, I called into Kilimanjaro and told them where I was and said good-bye and then changed frequencies on the radio and called in our position to the traffic control people in Nairobi.

"So, what brought all that about?" I asked Ian, as we droned on, now at a better slower cruising speed, safe in Kenyan airspace.

"If I had to guess, it would be a fundamental difference in political philosophy between Tanzania and Kenya, and that the rapid growth of the Kenya economy and the slow growth of the Tanzanian economy, plus the recent collapse of East African Airways, just was too much, so Tanzania isolated itself from the perceived unwelcome influences of the quasi-capitalist Kenyans," he said.

"That sounds like a speech or a report," I laughed.

"It did a bit, didn't it?" he laughed as well. "I suppose I was mulling it over on the drive from Olduvai, and those were the thoughts that I came up, and probably what I'll say in my official report. Tanzania will in public blame the Kenyans for taking the planes and ferries of the defunct joint systems, and will claim that they had to close the border to get Kenya to at least hand over their share. The Kenyans will argue that the systems have not been profitable for a while and that Tanzania has not been paying its share so they had to take action."

"Will it lead to gunfire?" I asked.

"I doubt it," Ian said. "I think this will be a very gentlemanly squabble, with speeches and words, but no violence."

"If the border's closed and there are no flights, how are tourists going to get back to Nairobi for flights back to the UK?" I asked.

"I doubt that they've worked that out yet, but there will be some plan that eventually will be put in place," Ian thought. "The Tanzanians can't afford to upset everyone. Upsetting Kenya is one thing, but, Britain, France, Germany, the US, anywhere tourists might be from, they don't want all those countries hounding them to release their captive tourists."

"Captive tourists?" I asked.

"If the border is closed and there are no flights or buses, how are they supposed to leave, there are precious few flights to Dar and who would pay for a new booking on another airline?" he said. "So, in essence they are unwitting and hapless captives, stranded in a dispute between neighbours. Reality will hit after a day or two and they will want to expedite the departure of all the trapped tourists."

"Will you have to do anything about any tourists stranded in Tanzania?" I asked.

"No, the High Commission in Dar will have that problem," he said. "My guess is that they'll contact BA and see if they can lay on extra flights to Dar and Kilimanjaro and take out people directly, or they'll shuttle people to Nairobi and let them get their booked flights from there."

"So, it's going to be a mess for a while?" I suggested.

"For a while," he agreed. "I pity poor lorry drivers who are trying to bring loads north, they'll get stopped at the border and who knows when they may get through."

"Will Kenya allow stuff to go south?" I asked.

"My guess is that Kenya will not stop anything going south, but Tanzania will probably not let any through traffic to say, Zambia, pass and anything that goes south will not be allowed to return, so it would be a risk, unless you were just going home," Ian thought.

"What a mess?" I thought. "Well, there's Athi River, let's get ourselves set up to land," I called the air traffic controllers and got put into the landing pattern for the Wilson field. There were no problems, no delays, and no traffic in front of us, so we went straight in. Once on the ground, I attended to the plane while Ian went in and saw the customs and immigration chap. We knew him, he was stationed at the airfield, so we had often seen him in passing. This time though, we actually had business with him. We had just heard on the radio the first news about the border closure, so we went to the commission to report that we were back.

172

"Trevor, thanks for the telegram," Ian said when we arrived.

"Not at all," he said. "Alison is one of ours."

"Really?" Ian asked.

"Need to know and all that," Trevor said. "But this was one of those times when better to be safe than sorry."

"Well, I'm glad we got out," Ian said. "After we had taken off, we could see paramilitary going towards the border crossing and saw some headed to the Arusha airport that we had just left from. Fiona's biggest concern was that they might try and force us down."

"I don't think they'd go that far," Trevor said. "But you never know. So, what brought this all about?"

"Our guess is Kenya starting up Kenya Air with equipment from EAA was the final trigger," Ian said. "But we both think it's deeper than that. We think that the Tanzanians are concerned lest the Kenyan way of doing things, which is manifestly successful, contaminates their idea of socialism, so better to isolate yourself than let those ideas in."

"The HC wants a meeting at two to talk about this, why don't you run Fiona home and come back?" Trevor suggested.

"I'll be back," Ian promised. We drove home and Ian said that he would be back as soon as he could, he doubted whether there was a lot they could do, except wait and see what transpired and how many tourists might need rescuing.

Four days later, there was a hoot at the gate and I saw that it was Julia. I went and let her in, keen to know how they had evaded the paramilitary troops that had taken over the border.

"Fiona, thanks for the tip-off," she said. "Saved our bacon."

"What did you do?" I asked.

"I raised Henry on the radio and told him that I had a breakdown and needed help and to meet me at our campsite from three days earlier," she said. "I didn't want to get too specific in case anyone was listening. I met up with Henry and told him what was going on and we decided to take back roads and trails north, past Lake Natron and slip over the border to Lake Magadi. He had been too far from the Ngorongoro turn-off for us to have both made it to Namanga before noon, by the time we met up it was almost eleven, so we opted for the bush route."

"Did you see anyone?" I asked.

"We saw a couple of other tour groups from here, passed on the news and left them to work out what they would do," she said. "I think most didn't believe us. We saw a couple of Tanzanian game parks people, but they were more concerned with something else that we couldn't see, so they ignored us."

"Was the border patrolled?" I asked.

"It may have been," she said. "We tried to avoid actually meeting up with anyone once we'd got past Ngorongoro, it would have been obvious that we were headed for the border. We *bundu* bashed in a few places and kept going, even after dark, with no lights, which was slow until the moon came up at nine-thirty, we kept going until we came to a village and a road that led north. They told us that we were about four miles north of the border, so that was good news, and we camped there the night. I think our guests were relieved that they weren't going to have to wait it out in Tanzania. By the time we got back here, the closure was all over the news and there were lots of stories about stranded, even arrested tourists, so we were heroes. We managed to arrange a tour of the soda ash plant at Magadi and a couple of village trips, so less wild animals and more the rest of life. I don't think our guests were disappointed, so no calls for refunds."

"What about future bookings?" I asked.

"We're going to have to rethink those," she said. "Probably more Maasai Mara, Amboseli and probably Tsavo. We're sending out notices now to our next bookings, offering cancellations or replanning, my guess is that most will take an alternate itinerary. They won't want to cancel, for many it's a once in a lifetime trip."

"They won't opt to go straight to Tanzania?" I asked.

"The further out bookings might," she thought. "But, the closer in will look at the fact that some tourists were actually arrested and think fuck that and stay this side of the border."

I thought that Julia was right about that and wondered what had happened that some tourists had been arrested. I could see the Tanzanian authorities picking up Kenya tour operators and detaining them, but throwing tourists in jail just because they were with a Kenyan outfit was a little extreme.

"Would you like some lunch?" I asked Julia.

"Thanks, that would be super," she said. "You know, the border closure is going to be a real pain in the arse, most tourists want Serengeti, so for us it's probably going to mean some impact. But, I suppose, just one of the challenges of trying to run a business in Africa."

"Rather you than me," I said. "I wonder when the border will reopen?"

"Who knows?" Julia said. "So, what were you doing there?"

"Ian wanted to show me Olduvai," I explained. "So, we flew down to Arusha and the dig people arranged transport and a tent. It was really interesting, but some of the people there were a real pain."

"Why?" Julia asked.

"They're arrogant academic types, full of themselves, or at least one was, he was a real git," I said. "We had planned to cut short our visit and instead go to Ngorongoro when this all happened."

"How do you hear it was going to happen?" Julia asked.

"One of the Tanzanians who Ian knew when he worked at the dig, he heard murmurings in the marketplaces, and heard of troop movements and put two and two together," I explained.

"What was it like for you?" Julia asked. "We were just trying to avoid anyone, but to get your plane, you had to go to Arusha and deal with them."

"I had anxious moments," I said. "We were all ready to go and asked for take-off clearance and I could see a debate in the control room. In the end, I saw one chap wave at the clock, then they told us we could go. I would guess that they had set the closure for noon, and if anyone left before then, then that was fate. I have to tell you though, when we were climbing out, we saw a convoy of paramilitary types heading for the border and some also heading for the airport. I think if they had been there when we had tried to take off, then permission would have been denied and we would be worried now about our plane. It is a moment that I will not forget in a hurry."

What next?

"The border with Tanzania is still closed, isn't it?" Maman asked.

"It is," I confirmed. "Who knows when it will re-open. It's been difficult for the tourist industry because so many want to go to Serengeti, but, it's probably just as much a pain for the Tanzanians."

"What about the planes that were stuck there?" Portia asked.

"As far as I know, they're still there," I said. "That will mean problems for the owners as I'm sure they've had not maintenance or protection since they've been sitting there, and the insurance companies will scratch around to find arcane clauses to deny payments if the planes are scrapped."

"Well, they can't use act of war as an excuse," Maman said. "Kenya and Tanzania are not at war; I wonder what other excuse they could find."

"I'm sure they'll dig something up," I said. "But I wonder if one could pull the wings off and bring them back on a lorry, as far as I know, the proscription is actually flying over Tanzania?"

"I doubt the Tanzanians would fall for that one," Portia laughed. "After all, what they really want is leverage on the Kenyan government and if they hold planes of people with some money, they may be hoping that those people will try and pressure the government to come to an arrangement."

"Perhaps," I thought. "Anyway, I'm glad we got our plane out. I have to thank Tega for that, he had his ear to the ground and was nice enough to tip us off."

"You said that Trevor had said that Alison was, what was it, one of ours?" Maman commented. "What did he mean by that?"

"I think he meant that she worked for one of our security services," I explained. "Ian finally admitted to me that she was an agent. She's since been withdrawn and assigned somewhere else."

"Why do need spies in Tanzania?" James asked.

"I think just to keep an eye on things and provide the government with another assessment of the situation," I replied. "Tanzania is very socialist and has strong ties to China and we would do well to keep an eye on what the Chinese are doing and what their long-term plans really are. You don't think they built the Tanzam Railway out of the goodness of their hearts, they have a view to acquire the minerals that Zambia has to offer, so expect their influence to grow, even here."

"If you couldn't travel to Tanzania, did you go anywhere else?" James asked.

"We took a few trips, one up to Lake Turkana, used to be Rudolph, it's up near the border with Ethiopia," I replied.

"Isn't that where they've been finding all kinds of human fossils?" James asked.

"It is," I confirmed. "Richard Leakey has been leading digs up there for a few years now. Ian actually found a partial skeleton when we went there, he handed it over to the right people, and it would have probably helped him finish his doctorate."

"Did you go looking for fossils?" Maman asked.

"No, we had planned to just go for a weekend, but when we took a walk and found this little gorge where the strata were all exposed, and Ian started poking around and telling me what was what, then he saw it, I'd rarely seen him so excited," I replied.

"Where did you go?" Portia asked.

"We flew into Alia Bay, there's a strip there and a rest camp. On Saturday afternoon we took a walk and then we found it," I said.

"Tells us about that," Charlize asked.

Lake Turkana

After our abortive trip to Olduvai, we were looking for somewhere else to go, and one of the others at the commission suggested Lake Rudolf, I suppose he was still living in the recent past, because it had been renamed to Lake Turkana in 1975. Ian and I consulted a map and I did some calculations and decided that part of Lake Turkana was within the radius I had set myself for air trips, carrying enough fuel to go there and back. There was a Kenya Wildlife Service rest camp at a place called Alia Bay and there was a landing strip there. So, Ian went off to book us space at the rest camp and I set about preparing things to take. I found myself a local guidebook and looked up Lake Turkana. It was a salt lake, created by rivers running in, like the Omo from Ethiopia, but nothing running out, so the only control on depth was evaporation, and that probably happened a lot as it was hot up there. So, it was rather like the Great Salt Lake in the US and the Dead Sea between Jordan and Israel. I also gathered that it was the home to many crocodiles, fish and birds. The local people mainly fished for a living, and apparently wore little, if anything in the way of clothes. When Ian came home, I was ready with my list.

"So, *chérie*, how was your day?" he asked.

"Busy," I said. "I have a list of what we need to take to Turkana, do we have a place to stay?"

"I fixed that," he said. "It also dawned on me that it's the area where Richard Leakey has been doing a lot of work, they found a skull there not long ago that is old, really old. So, what do we need?"

"I'll fill the tanks on the plane, that'll give us enough to go there and back, there aren't really any places we could stop between here and there that have fuel," I told him. "The fuel will come to 325 lbs, then there's you and me, say another 300 lbs between us and clothes, then water, I gather the lake is brackish, so not good to drink too much of, so twenty gallons of water, another 200 lbs, food, another twenty, plus a tool kit of another thirty, what's that come to?"

"875 lbs," he said. "Can we carry that?"

"We can," I said. "It's just a longer take-off roll, but we're going out of Wilson, so we've got a nice long runway, we've got at least 4,800ft on the shorter runway, so plenty of room."

"What about coming back?" he asked.

"Well, the information I have says that the Alia Bay strip is only at about 1,200ft, so much lower than here, and we'll have used fuel to get there, drunk water and eaten food, so we'll be much lighter coming back," I explained.

"What are you going to put the water in?" he asked.

"Collapsible bladders," I said. "I don't want large containers of water that would allow the stuff to slosh around, I'd rather use bladders than we can squash down as we use the water. I've worked out where they'd go in the plane."

"Can I take a hammer?" he asked. "It only weighs five pounds."

"Of course," I said. "What do you know about the guest house?"

"I gather it's quite large, three bedrooms, but only one bathroom, it's set by the lake shore and has a view of the lake, the parks people told me that no one else will be there, except the caretaker who has his own place," Ian told me. "They also told me that it's about a mile from the strip to the house. So, we'll have to lug our stuff, unless the caretaker has transport and takes pity on us."

"We'll manage," I assured him.

"Okay, so we're set for three weeks from now, we're out of the rains, so will there be any weather problems?" he asked.

"I doubt it, but I'll keep an eye on the forecasts," I replied.

"Don't you have to be in Paris next week?" he asked.

"I hadn't forgotten," I assured him. "I'll leave on Saturday night for London, then hop over to Paris on Sunday, ready for a Monday morning meeting."

"Which client is this?" he asked.

"A major airline, they are looking at the economics of their system, which is pretty much all long-haul routes with feeder routes in certain areas and they want a model of their system," I explained.

"So, you're going to be the Dr Beeching of the airlines?" he laughed.

"Heaven forbid," I said. "Beeching faced enormous difficulties with British Rail, too many lines that didn't pay, but against which was the need for essential services and the public good, so he probably couldn't win no matter what he did. At least with an airline most people can't argue the common good, with alternate means of travel like the trains, air travel is more of a convenience than a necessity. I think for this client it would be more instructive to review the report by Sir Ronald Edwards, he was commissioned to do a study of British Air Transport in the Seventies, and the report came out in 1969, so not too out of date."

"I suppose air travel is kind of a luxury, unless you live in a place like Hawai'i, or Tahiti," he said. "With the decline of shipping, the only practical way to get there is by plane. The same is true of here, if there were no planes how would we get here?"

"True," I agreed. "I'll have to look at the client route structure and see how they service the out of the way places and how sensitive those routes are to price changes. It also strikes me that the customer base is going to be significant, am I looking at business travel or holiday makers?"

"What's the split here?" he asked. "If you took a typical BA flight to Nairobi, how many are business or some sort of official government travel and how many are holidaymakers?"

"Interesting question," I thought. "I should take a look when I go on Saturday and see if I can guess. I doubt that BA can tell me definitely, but probably most of the families will be holidaymakers, those on their own, like me, are more likely to be on business, so I'll take a look and see if I can come up with a split."

"So, are you cooking tonight, or shall I?" he asked.

"I've got something in the oven, it should be about done," I replied. "If you set the table then I'll finish in the kitchen."

We ate, washed up the dishes, then lounged around for a while until baser desires took hold. Then it was bath and lovemaking, then to bed and another tryst. I loved Ian, he was sensitive to my needs and desires and always happy to go along with whatever I suggested. I thanked my lucky stars again that I had met him, if not I would probably be some spinsterish academic in Oxford, becoming more and more like Ekstrom, perish the thought! Ian was still busy helping the odd tourist who had finally made it back from Tanzania, and who was now trying to get back to England. Ian could never work out why they just did not just go directly to the airlines, plead their case and negotiate a ride home. That is all Ian did, he would contact BA and make arrangements. Payment was always an issue, and several were repatriated with the expectation that they would refund the money upon return to England. The chaps in the High Commission in Dodoma and at the consulate in Dar es Salaam were quite busy for a while, sorting out issues for those who just wanted to go home and who had no interest in returning to Kenya. There were also briefing papers sent back to London with assessments of the state of affairs between Kenya and Tanzania. Ian gave me a history lesson one evening of the British and German interests that led to the colonisation of Kenya, Uganda and Tanzania and the squabbles that had gone on between the governors of Kenya and Tanzania, post the Great War, when whites had tried to settle an area in Tanzania, Tanganyika as it was then. He pointed out to me the biggest difference between Kenya and Tanganyika as one being a British-settled country and the other a territory administered under a mandate from the League of Nations, following the stripping of colonies from Germany post the Great War. The one great quotation he gave me, following a row between the governors of Kenya and Tanganyika, was from Sir Donald Cameron, then Governor of Tanganyika who said, "The trouble with your 'Great White Dominion' is that the gods saw fit to place a large and predominant proportion of Africans in these territories. We've no right to squeeze them out of here." It took a little while after that for the cooperation between colonial administrators to become the order of the day, but eventually, it did. So, the East African community idea came about and eventually, there were all kinds of East African ventures, now all falling apart.

I took myself off to fly to London and as I checked in for the flight, I asked the people there, who I by now knew quite well, if they had any estimate of the split between business travellers, like myself and holidaymakers. Their guess was eighty percent holidaymakers and then the rest. On board, I looked around the first-class cabin, and decided, rightly or wrongly, that four were travelling for pleasure and the rest of us were there for business. I had a seatmate, which I never really liked. He was from London and a representative of a pharmaceutical company. He had been in Kenya trying to get the government to buy his company's products for the hospitals. I did not like him a bit, he was very full of himself and even had the audacity to ask me out to dinner. I pointed out, in no uncertain terms, that I was married, and had absolutely no interest in him whatsoever. If I could have moved to another seat, I would have, but the plane was full, so contented myself by erecting a barrier of pillows and blankets. When we landed, I breezed through the immigration line, and being without luggage went straight on through customs. Dad and Felicity were there to meet me and took me back to their flat for lunch. They had been to my flat the day before and collected what mail there was and had also picked up the mail from the business service that I used. There were a few things of interest, but they could all wait until I was in Paris. Dad was full of news of his businesses and apparently, they were all doing quite well, despite the best efforts of Callaghan and crew to put obstacles in the way of success. The United Kingdom was still in the throes of dealing with the Labour Government that seemed to have managed to kill economic growth, introduce a degree of discontent all around, have iniquitous tax rates and yet still stay in power. I could see that the next election was going to be interesting. After lunch I told Dad not to bother taking me to the airport, I would take a taxi. Actually, I took the Tube to Hatton Cross and took a bus from there. The Tube line into the terminals was supposed to have been completed, but there had been a three-day week in 1974 and a strike in 1976 that had delayed the work, so completion was supposed to be late that year, 1977.

When I got to Paris, I went to Mémère Monique's house, what was the point of having a grandmother in Paris if you could not impose yourself upon her from time to time. She was delighted to see me and wanted to know all the news and what we had been doing since I saw her last. Her house, flat actually, was just off the Boulevard Saint-Germaine and was probably far too large for just one, but she liked it there and had no intention of leaving, for all James and Maman had offered her places to live. I think she liked Paris too much to leave and go off to the Riviera or Orléans. Mémère and I went out to dinner at a bistro that she favoured and she asked me what my visit to Paris was about this time. I told her about the airline and she surprised me with a very concise and insightful view of the airline. I knew that she was an intelligent woman, but there are times when one forgets and I was ashamed that it had come as a surprise to me that she knew so much about the company. I should have known better, she had flown them back and forth to Tahiti in recent years, so would know something about them, but her knowledge went beyond that, she knew about the ownership of the company even knew, personally, a couple of the family who owned the parent company. After dinner I called Ian and even made him speak French a little to Mémère, but not for too long, he was still learning French and it was limited and I knew that it was a struggle for him. After I hung up the phone, Mémère asked me about Ian, she asked me if we were getting on well, and, to my surprise, how was he in bed. I was able to tell her that he was really good in bed, or out of it and that we made love as often as we good. She seemed pleased by that and told me to be sure that we continued. She told me some stories about her early life when they first moved from Tahiti to Paris and how she longed for Pépère to come home, how she would greet him at their flat dressed only in a sarong and how that had nearly embarrassed them both one day when he brought a friend home with him. I began to understand where Maman got her liberal attitudes towards sex and discussing sex, it all stemmed from Mémère, who was as frank as Maman. It was really nice to be able to talk to my grandmother about sex in such a free and easy way. She gave me suggestions for ways to spice up our lives, as if they needed much spicing, but as I thought about it, some of her suggestions sounded like fun. We finally went to bed and I did something I had not done since I was a child, I slept with her. It was comforting to feel her presence and rejoice in the fact that I was descended from this wonderful person.

I met the next day with a Pierre Garnier and a Pascal Leclère. They had heard of me through the car company that I had done work for. They started by talking about the airline and its routes and they had data on passenger kilometres flown and tonne kilometres of cargo hauled. Their routes were interesting, they seemed to dance back and forth competing then cooperating with Air France and others. The French government had set spheres of influence and they, plus Air France and Air Inter were careful not to tread on each other's toes, but they were interested to see what would happen if the government relaxed the rules and wholesale competition broke out, how much could they gain and how much could they lose, and if there was a price war, what might it cost them?

"How much of your cost structure is variable?" I asked them.

"Some of the planes are leased," Pierre replied. "Then fuel, staff, spares, maintenance and repairs, tyres, brakes, are all variables. The fixed costs are those planes that we purchased outright and have yet to arrange a lease back on them, and some of the ground installations where we do our own maintenance."

"If we look at flying hours of the equipment, how many hours of the possible do you have to set aside for required mechanical checks?" I asked.

"By that you mean A, B, C and D checks?" Pascal asked.

"Right," I agreed, thankful that my own forays into flying had taught me the terminology of required maintenance checks on planes.

"Well, for each plane, we lose 10 hours every 600 hours, then 2 days every 8 months, then 2 weeks every 2 years, and finally 3 months every 10 years," Pascal explained.

"Could you give me that data in a chart?" I asked. "And, I presume you have good records of mechanical availability for each plane?"

"We do," Pascal agreed.

"That would be useful as well," I said. "Are there constraints on when you can fly, like airport curfews?"

"Some," Pascal said. "I can get you a list of destinations and local noise restrictions which are normally linked to curfews."

We went back and forth for a while, establishing all the costs that are associated with running an airline, then we talked about the revenue base.

"What proportion of the passengers are business?" I asked.

"We would guess about 10 percent," Pierre said. "We're not like the American airlines where much of their revenue is from business people. Much of ours is from people on vacation and going to warmer places. We do have some government employees travelling back and forth, but not too many."

"Do you have predictive models that help you know when to forward buy fuel supplies?" I asked.

"We have some tools," Pierre said. "But if you could come up with a better tool that would allow us to see out into the future, we would be in a better position to negotiate with Total for supplies."

"I could do that for you," I said. We then talked about staff levels and payment practices and other things and then came back to the idea of predictive models, this time for items that might fail. Their fleet size was not that large, and there was quite a mix of aircraft types, but all the long-haul planes had either three or four engines, so the numbers added up a little. I told them that with enough data I could probably give them some models that would predict time to failure, so that they could plan for replacements. That was of great interest to Pascal, who I gathered was the operations manager, whereas Pierre was the finance manager. We finally closed our meeting at one and they suggested lunch. I was hungry by then and was happy to agree. We went to a nearby restaurant that was new to me. Over lunch we talked more generalities and they were both

184

intrigued to learn that I had my pilot's licence and my own plane. Both being long term airline men they wholeheartedly approved. The airline had a wide network in Africa, but did not fly to Nairobi, I asked why.

"We think that most of the traffic will come out of London," Pierre said. "And there are already BA, EAA, and British Caledonian in the market, we don't think the current market will stand another, unless with the collapse of EAA that the new Air Kenya or Kenya Air, whatever they call it, does not continue the route."

"But you fly to Lusaka, as do BA and British Caledonian," I noted.

"That is true," Pierre agreed. "But we think there is enough traffic to justify the weekly flight to Lusaka."

"Have you read the Edwards report?" I asked, referring to a report issued in 1969 that dealt with British air transport in the seventies.

"I have not," Pierre admitted.

"I'll get you a copy," I promised. "It's worth reading. I may not agree with all the conclusions, but the logic of the study is worth a review." I had read it because Edwards was a professor at LSE, and having a been granted a doctorate by the same institution I was interested.

We finally finished lunch at three and went our separate ways, with my promise to have some models to them as soon as I could. They had no deadline, but did express a lively interest in getting a fuel price predictive model as soon as possible. I told them that I would do one for fuel, another for maintenance items and a more encompassing one for the airline itself. That would take me much longer, a few months at least, but they did not demur at the time, nor did they cavil at my fees, but they did ask if I had a bank account in France and could they pay the fees into that. I told them that I had an account and gave them the relevant details so that they could pay the money in. Pierre promised that my fees would be deposited within a day. That was refreshing, often the terms of payment might be payment upon presentation of invoice, but in actuality it was often thirty, sometimes ninety days before anything showed up. With two clients I had actually insisted on cash up front before I did any work. I had taken quick looks at their financial positions and had concluded that they were near to collapse, so I was not going to be saddled with an uncollectible receivable. In one case my analysis had saved them from collapse, in the other they were too far gone and my analysis showed that there was no chance of recovery. They had simply let things go too far for any hope of redemption. They bemoaned the fact that they had called me in too late, but blamed their board for dilly dallying and not making a more timely decision. I think for them to have had a chance they should have called me in a good year earlier, but I think the first approach to the board had been met with a reluctance to spend money on an outside consultant, so they paid the price for poor decision making.

I called Ian that evening and gave him a précis of the day, without disclosing any secrets of the company. Ian was a very ethical person and would not pass on to the British government information about my client that could be used by British Airways, but why put him in the position of even having to consider what was right. Ian told me that he had the weekend off after I got back, so we could make our trip to Lake Turkana. Mémère was interested in where that was, so we got an atlas and found Kenya, then the lake. The atlas was only a few years old, but it still showed the lake as Lake Rudolph, so I had to explain to Mémère why the name had been changed. We did not go out to dinner that night, but had a really nice meal at home that Mémère cooked. After dinner I called Dad and asked him to get a couple of copies of the Edwards report and send them to Pierre, I had to wait a minute or so until he found a pen and paper, then I gave him the address and asked him to include a note indicating that it was from me. I was at a loose end of much of the next day, until I had to get the plane back to Heathrow to connect with the Nairobi flight. Mémère suggested that we visit the *Musée de l'air et de l'espace*, the French air and space museum at the Le Bourget airport, I could go on from there direct to Charles De Gaulle and my flight to London. The museum was really interesting, it had been opened in1919, so was one of the older air museums. We wandered the halls and looked at exhibits and talked about all manner of things, most of the time quite unrelated to aerospace. Mémère saw me to the airport, and instructed me to relate to her all my exploits, both in work and at play with Ian, then took a taxi back to her flat. My flight, on BA, was on time and I made my transfer from Terminal 2 to Terminal 3 at Heathrow with time to spare.

The flight to Nairobi was full, full of holiday makers, all keen to see what Africa and Kenya had to offer. I had a seat mate, a woman this time, who was going out to take what she described as a private safari to Tsavo. She had booked a guide and a vehicle and seemed to be under the impression that the park would be hers for the week, or at least parts of it. Actually she may have partly correct for my understanding was that the warden of the Tsavo East park was very particular about granting permits for entry, trying his best to keep the park as pristine as he could, and she had booked out the whole of a tented camp, so there would be no other guests there while she was in residence. Tsavo, west or east, were parks we had not visited yet, but that were on our list. The woman introduced herself as Miranda Clements and I gathered that she had inherited a fortune from her uncle who had made his money in shoes, and who had no one else to leave it to. I put her at about thirty-five, a little above average height and thin as a rake. She told me that after the Kenya trip she was debating what to do with her life and new found fortune. She had a mind to start a travel business, so this trip was part pleasure and part exploration of the possibilities. I pointed out the difficulties at the moment with the border closure between Tanzania and Kenya, but she brushed that off, telling me that in her view relations would return to normal shortly. I was not that sanguine, but perhaps her crystal ball was better than mine.

When we landed, I said my good-byes to Miranda then passed easily and quickly through the immigration line and on out. I had driven myself to the airport, so collected my Land Rover and went home, stopping at the High Commission briefly to let Ian know that I was back safely. Once home, I sat down and thought through all the information I had been given by Pierre and Pascal and started creating the various models that I had promised them. The oil price one was the easiest, I already had the basis of a model I could use and just needed to refine it. I would be able to deliver it to Pierre within a month, I just needed to run some tests before I gave it to him. That meant a trip back to London so that I could get access to a computer, but I had other business to attend to, so that would not be a problem. The other models would take a little longer, but I was confident that I could create them. When Ian came home that evening, I told him about my trip to the museum and then asked him about his days since I had been gone. They seemed to be filled with the

187

usual travails of tourists and visitors who somehow had fallen afoul of the local laws and needed help. I wondered sometimes at the intelligence of people, they seemed to either leave their brains at home when they went away, or were either arrogant enough to think that they would not be caught with prohibited items, or just failed to read any of the warnings about contraband. It certainly kept Ian busy and some of the stories were actually quite hilarious. He got me laughing over dinner and it was hard to stop. The laughing led to teasing and that led to love making on the terrace, then in the bath and finally in bed. I had missed Ian for the few days I was gone and was making up for lost time.

By Friday of the week, I had my fuel model ready and a maintenance one well in the works, so felt that I had earned our excursion to Lake Turkana. I stopped work at lunchtime and went out to Wilson field to fuel the plane and load up the supplies and other items we had agreed upon, including a hammer for Ian. Ian left work a little early and met me at the airport. I had brought a change of clothes for him, so he changed while I untied the plane and did my pre-flight checks. We took off at three, which would put us into Alia Bay at about five-thirty that evening. We could not fly direct to Alia Bay because the Aberdares were in the way and flying over them would mean going up well over 10,000ft, so we took a detour to the west and went around the high ground. We passed over the town of Nakuru and I jokingly suggested to Ian that he keep his eyes open for the Equator when we crossed it. I think he must have been half asleep, because he actually looked out of the window before laughing at me. We flew over Lake Baringo, then watched the ground go by until we saw the bottom end of Lake Turkana. Alia Bay was actually quite a long way up on the eastern shore of the lake, easy to spot from the air, as was the airstrip, actually marked out with obvious markers, as was the hard stand. Landing was interesting, the wind was out of the southeast and blowing strongly, in fact it was accelerated by the local terrain, so it was typically twenty knots or better. Our landing was a little wobbly going in, but because of the wind we had a really short landing as our ground speed was well down by the time we actually touched down. We taxied to the hard stand and unloaded the plane, then set about tying it down. I had been told by some members of the aero club that overnight the winds could really pick up, so it was prudent to ensure that the plane was secure, so I also added a baffle on top of the wing to disrupt the airflow over the wing and reduce the possibility of it lifting off the ground. While we were busy doing that a Land Rover arrived. It was the caretaker; he had seen us land and had come to pick us up and take us back to the guest house. For that I was very grateful, lugging all our water would have meant a couple of trips.

"*Jambo*," Ian said. "*Habari?*"

"*Jambo*," the caretaker replied. "*Karibu.*"

We had a quick further conversation, going through the usual formalities of greeting, and learned that his name was Isaac. We introduced ourselves, but we had already assumed that he knew our names from the booking that Ian had made. He helped us load our luggage and supplies into his Land Rover then drove us the short distance to the guest house.

"Look, Ian," I said as we drove along. "Oryx, those are the first I've ever seen in the wild, what's oryx, *choroa?*"

"It is," he said. "First time for oryx for me too, we didn't get them in Olduvai."

"You were in Olduvai?" Isaac asked.

"For three years," Ian confirmed.

"There are many people digging to the north of here," Isaac said. "They have found really exciting things."

"I read about them," Ian said. "I would really like to find something."

"Try south of Alia Bay," Isaac suggested. "I walked down there once, about a mile and a half and I thought I saw something in one of the gullies."

"Thank you," Ian said. "We'll try that tomorrow. Is it safe to swim in the lake?"

"Watch out for crocodiles," Isaac laughed. "But, yes, the water is very salty, so don't drink too much, but the fish, birds and crocodiles thrive here, so enjoy your swim, the water should be warm. Here we are, this is the guest house, my cottage if you need anything is over there. The other buildings are those of the Kenya Wildlife Service Sibiloi National Park."

"Thank you," I said. We unloaded the Land Rover and Isaac gave us a tour of the house and pointed out the features and amenities. I was most interested in the loo, it had been a long flight up, so nature was calling.

We decided to try the lake before dinner, so changed and went down to the water. Isaac was right, it was quite salty and very warm, not quite bath water, but warm enough. I waded out and Ian followed and we swam around for a while, until Ian pointed at some crocodiles that seemed to be taking an interest in us. Even though Isaac had assured us that they would not attack it seemed prudent to go ashore. I was awed by the number of birds we saw out in the lake and along the shoreline, Ian was having a field day and reeling off to me all the names of the ones he saw. I saw some zebra walking towards us and behind them some gazelles. They ignored us, apart from a quick look at us to see what we were doing, and carried on walking, headed for some secret zebra spot that only they knew about. Dinner called, so we set about cooking and soon had a meal ready. We dined in style in our own dining room, then had a glass of wine outside, looking out over the lake. We heard hyæna in the distance and we also heard a lion, then another. It was truly a magical place. When the sun was well and truly down, the star viewing was terrific, there was no light pollution at all, so there were myriads of stars visible and I wondered if there were others out there looking back at us and wondering as I was, is there intelligent life out there?

In the morning Ian was up early and made breakfast, which we ate outside standing up looking out at the birds on the lake. I had read in the guide book that I had that there was an island just a little south of where we were and it had all kinds of volcanic craters, three of which were filled with water and each of which had its own bird and reptile life. I thought that when we left, we might just take a low flight over the island to see what we might spot. Ian was keen to take a walk south to the area where Isaac had said he had seen some possible fossil remains, so, we took hats and water and walked south along the lake shore. We came to an area where there were little gullies leading down to the lake and Ian picked one to explore. We walked up the gully, and Ian poked and prodded the exposed strata, finding the odd thing of interest, but no fossilised bones. So, we retraced our steps and picked another gully. Again, we walked up the gully looking at the beds, but no fossils there either. It was getting hot, so I sat down and drank some water and watched Ian poking around in the bank of the gully.
"How on earth did they first stumble onto things at Olduvai?" I asked him.

"I'm not sure," he said. "Just luck I suppose. The gorge has been cut through the sediments through the ages and exposed all kinds, so I suppose as good a place as any to at least start looking."

"Will you find anything here?" I asked.

"Who knows?" he laughed. "This may be the most boring day for you."

"While you poke away at the rocks?" I said. "No, it's fine, it's a beautiful day, there's nothing we need to do, we can just wander about and see what we can see."

"Shall we try another gully?" he asked.

"Why not?" I countered. "It's only nine, so there's plenty of time left in the day. What about that one over there?"

"Okay," he agreed. We walked to the next gully and started walking slowly up it. "Look," Ian said. "Look, that's part of a bone." He was pointing at what I now recognised as a fossil. It was long and the surface was quite polished.

"What is it?" I asked.

"Don't know yet," he said. "Need to expose more of it. Can you take a photograph of it before we start?" I did as he asked, then he got to work. He hammered gently away, then produced a brush from his small rucksack, and started brushing away the soils.

"I didn't see you load that onto the plane," I commented. "When did you slip that by me?"

"When you were doing your walk around," he confessed. "I thought about the weights you had added up and thought that we'd be fine with this."

"Hm," I said, a little miffed that he had not told me that he was smuggling extra things aboard. "So, what is it?"

"It's a leg bone, a femur," he said. "It's intact, this is amazing, imagine that all those years ago this person was walking around here."

"Are there any more bones?" I asked. "Is that a right or left femur?"

"Right," he said.

"How can you tell?" I asked.

"Well, by experience I know, but if you want the full technical explanation then the various bits of the bone give clues, the greater trochanter, that's this bit, should be on the lateral side of the bone, that will put it away from the middle of the body, the front side of a femur is smooth, and there are two other bits, the lesser trochanter and the condyles, that these bits here, they both project towards the back. So, with those two bits pointing back, then the head points to the hip joint, so left or right," he said.

"Oh," was about all I could think to say. I knew he had a pretty good knowledge of the skeleton and anatomy, but there were bits that I had never heard of, like a trochanter. Ian chipped more away and then brushed, while I took more photographs, then the bone came out. He got out a tape and some callipers and started measuring and recording. He produced a brown paper bag from his rucksack, bagged the bone and labelled the bag and then started prodding and poking anew.

"How old is this?" I asked.

"Based on the strata and what else is there, I would put that as about one and a half million years ago," he said. "That would need to be confirmed, but it's a good a guess as any right now."

"Are there any more bones?" I asked.

"There's another," he said.

"Big or small?" I asked.

"Smaller," he said. "You never know it might be a tibia or fibula, it's not a patella, I can tell without chipping further."

"So, are we going to find a whole leg?" I asked.

"I would doubt that," he said. "But you never know your luck."

"So, what's your bet?" I asked.

"Tibia by the look of it," he said. "The femur was lying as if the person had been on their back, so, if the body had not been disturbed by predators, scavengers or erosion, then the next logical find would be the tibia. Could you take a picture of this?" I did as asked, then took some of the gully and the surrounds and finally a couple of Ian busily chipping away at the stratum where the bones were. I had not seen him so excited in a while, this clearly was something really important to him.

"So, how tall was this person, and are we talking man or woman?" I asked.

"Can't tell sex definitively from these bones," he admitted. "We need the pelvis for that. But, based on the femur length, I would guess that this chap was about 160 cm tall, making it more likely that it's a he, a she would be shorter. What's really remarkable about this femur, is that it's intact, normally we find parts of a femur not that whole thing."

"So, what kind of human is he?" I asked.

"I would need confirmation," he said. "But my initial hypothesis is that this is *homo erectus* from about 1.5 million years ago."

"We've come across him before," I laughed.

"In the bedroom," he laughed. "But this is not you and I fooling around, this is the real *homo erectus*."

"Has anyone found the *homo erectus* here before?" I asked.

"I don't think so," he said. "A couple of years ago a chap by the name of Bernard Ngenyeo found remains of *homo habilis* not far from here, that would have dated from about 1.9 million years ago."

"So, people were here for at least half a million years?" I asked.

"Amazing, isn't it?" he confirmed.

"Do you have to tell people what you've found and where?" I asked.

"Absolutely," he said. "This needs to be properly excavated to see if there are more remains here."

"Do, you want to take a break for lunch?" I asked. "I need to get some more films for my camera, I've shot off over a hundred already, so would be happy to take a break, I should have put more spare films in my pocket when we came down here."

"Yes, and no," he said. "I could eat, but this is amazing and I don't want to stop."

"Why don't I go back to the house and make us some lunch and bring it here, and should I also tell Isaac?" I asked.

"That's a good idea," he said. "Then he can tell the chaps to the north that we found something, and we can show him where, so that he can lead people here when we're gone. If you'd leave your camera, I'll take pictures of anything that seems significant."

I left Ian to his digging and walked back to the house. I saw Isaac and told him that Ian had found something and asked him to notify the various entities that would need to know. We were probably breaking all kinds of rules because we were digging without a permit, but Isaac waved that off. To him this was not a dig, but a visitor who happened to see something interesting and unearthed it to see what it was. The permits and sanctioned digs could follow, now that there was something to follow up. He came with me back to where Ian was industriously scratching away at the rock.

"So, you did find something," Isaac said to Ian.

"Was this the place?" Ian asked. Isaac looked around and nodded.

"Yes, this was the place," he confirmed.

"Well, whenever this gets written up in the journals, we must make sure that you are credited as spotting the fossil," Ian said.

"But you are the one who dug it up," Isaac said.

"True, but I would not have come looking here if you had not told me that there was something to find," Ian said.

"Lunch?" I offered interrupting this exchange. "Isaac, I have enough for three?"

"What's the next step?" Ian asked Isaac.

"I'll go to the dig headquarters to the north and tell them," Isaac said. "I'm sure they'll send someone to look. May I see?"

"Of course," Ian said. He took the femur out of the paper bag and showed it to Isaac. "It's a femur, right femur," Ian explained. "There's also a tibia that I'm fishing out now."

"Does that mean that there's more?" Isaac asked.

"I don't know," Ian admitted. "It's going to take more digging. I've taken measurements and recorded where I found it, so can write a report for you so that you can submit it to the Parks people."

"Thank you," Isaac said. "Then I'm sure the Antiquities people will want to get involved. This is good for the park and for Lake Turkana."

"How big a find is this?" I asked.

"Big," Ian and Isaac said in unison.

"It's really big, Fi," Ian said. "*Homo habilis* was found north of here, but this is probably *homo erectus*, nearly half a million years younger, think about that, proto-humans living here for who knows how long. Then where did they go when this area flooded, and think about it, *homo habilis* was fossilised long before *homo erectus*, so this area must have been under water, then not, then under water again for all the sediments to fall and give us the strata we see today."

"How does this fit with the work you had done at Olduvai?" I asked.

"It actually goes a long way to showing that I was right and that Ambrose was wrong, or if not wrong, no, he was wrong," Ian said. "I think I'll quit here before I mess anything up. I have the femur and the tibia, I'll let the team from Koobi Fora do all the real work."

"If this chap is *homo erectus*, and to the north there was *homo habilis*, and given that there isn't much variation in elevation along the coast here, shouldn't there have been more sediment deposited over the half a million years?" I asked.

"Good question," Ian said. "We don't know much about the topography and climate back then, so we don't know what happened with erosion and deposition and subsequent geologic activity, so that deserves a lot of study."

"So, who will study that?" I asked.

"Not me," Ian said. "I'm just happy that I found something. I think this deserves a beer, what do think Isaac?"

"A beer sounds good," Isaac agreed. "But, only one, then I drive to Koobi Fora and tell them what we have found."

We walked back to the guest house, Ian clutching his precious paper bags with his femur and his tibia. I wondered who they had belonged to. Ian had said that based on size it was probably a man, was he a hunter, was he a fisherman, did he have a wife, or whatever the social construct of the time was, did he have children, how did he live, how old was he. Ian had also brought along a lot of stone pieces that he had dug up and he told me that they were all tools and that he would explain them over a beer. At the house, Ian arranged his finds on the dining table so that I could photograph them again, set against a ruler that he had brought with him, and he had me photograph all the stone tools that he had unearthed. I did wonder what else he had smuggled aboard the plane when I was not looking, so far there had been the brush, paper bags, now the ruler, what else. He then proceeded to tell me all about the bits of stone and how he knew that they were actually stone tools, how the stone tools had been shaped, how they were probably used and what for, then he talked about the bones, telling me as much as he could about each bone and what it told him. I had never really before taken that much interest, but it was very instructive to see what Ian deduced from the things he found, and what he inferred. He was careful to point out to me the difference between logical deductions and inferences. That, at least, I understood only too well, deducing things from data was something I was good at, making inferences I had often found to be fraught with risk, all too often an inference was proven later by data to be incorrect. Isaac listened to all the explanations, then excused himself and went off to let the people at Koobi Fora that we had found something of interest. While Isaac was gone, Ian measured, drew and recorded everything he could think of that would apply to the bones he had found. He had me take close up shots of the ends of the bones and even of some marks that were part of the way up the shaft of the femur. I had rarely seen him so excited; it was fun to watch; he was like a boy with a new toy.

195

Isaac was back in about an hour, with another Land Rover in tow. One of the people from Koobi Fora had come and wanted to see what Ian had unearthed and where. We were introduced to Barbara Green, a graduate student who was working on the dig to the north. Ian showed her what we had and then we all walked down to the gully where Ian had been digging. Isaac explained that he had thought he had seen something of interest, and that Ian had gone to investigate and had, indeed, found something. Ian showed her the place where he had been digging, now marked with a little cairn and a stick pointing up as a flag, and I told her that I had photographed the bone in situ and had other general photographs of the area and promised her copies when I had them developed. Barbara was very excited by the find and was happy to take custody of the bones and tools, after she had signed a receipt for them. Ian had had experience before of people stealing work, artifacts and theses, so he was taking no chances. With me and Isaac as witnesses, the items were handed over and signed for, and she went scurrying off to report on the find, and Isaac went back to his cottage to start filling out paperwork.

"You don't want to stay longer and get involved in this dig?" I asked Ian.

"No," he said. "Isaac pointed out to us where we might find something, and I found a femur and a tibia, I'm happy. All I need to hear is that my surmise that it's *homo erectus* is confirmed."

"So, a successful trip?" I asked.

"Absolutely," he said. "What is most exciting to me is vindication, I was right and Ambrose was wrong, it can't get much better than that."

"So, does this mean you'll complete your doctoral thesis?" I asked.

"With this, yes," he said. "You could write a whole thesis on these bones alone, so added to what I already had, it makes a much better thesis."

"If you write it up and submit it, who is going to look at it?" I asked.

"It'll be Farnsworth now," Ian said. "Ambrose is gone."

"How well do you know Farnsworth?" I asked.

"Pretty well," Ian said. "He was just in the position of a prof at college when I was a PG, then he moved up when Ambrose went. He was pretty supportive when I was arguing with Ambrose, but new enough in the post that he couldn't be too vocal. If you remember, I wrote to him a while ago and he agreed to take me on as a part time student, working towards the completion of my doctorate."

"When this chap you just dug up was alive, did zebras look like zebras?" I asked.

"Good question," Ian said. "It's thought today that the modern *equus* developed about 1.5 million years ago, so about the same time as our chap, there was certainly a zebra looking horsey chap about that time, whether or not he had stripes or if that was a later adaptation, I don't know. We do know that the horse family is really old and that in many ways the zebra is a remnant species of a prehistoric age, then we have the quagga that died out, probably hunted to extinction by man. There are three species of zebra today, Burchell's, Grévy's and mountain."

"And the one's we saw here, they are?" I asked.

"Those were Grévy's," Ian replied. "Their range is getter smaller and smaller, almost as small as the mountain. What most people see is the Burchell's or plains zebra."

"Are they good to eat?" I asked.

"You know, I've never actually eaten one," Ian said. "But I imagine it's very much like horse, probably pretty lean. They're grazers not browsers, so probably don't pick up much flavouring from the grasses."

"So, now that you've found your fossils, what do we do tomorrow?" I asked.

"Why don't we take a walk along the lake shore to the south and see what we can see?" he suggested.

"Do we take a packed lunch?" I asked.

"No, let's take a short walk, then come back for lunch, we need to leave tomorrow afternoon to go home," he said.

"How far away is that hill?" I asked, pointing to a hill that was off to the east of us.

"About six miles," he said. "We can go there if you like, but it will be hot and we need to be sure to take plenty of water."

"Why don't we scrap the lake walk and just go there tomorrow?" I suggested. "Six miles, say three hours there, including the hill climb, and two back, if we leave at seven, we can be back by lunchtime."

"Sounds like a plan," he said. "Take your camera and binoculars, you never know what we might see."

"We brought some wine with us, we should celebrate your find," I said.

"I had planned to do just that," he laughed. "It's chilling now."

We drank our wine looking out over the lake and talking about the find that Ian had made. He had, in his mind at least, already mapped out a paper that he would write and submit to *Man*. I think he was going to frame it all around the length of the femur and what that meant in terms of bipedalism and how erect the man walked.

"I may need some help with statistics," he said to me.

"Of course," I said. "What do you need to look at?"

"The distribution of femoral length in the skeletal remains that have been dug up around the world," he said. "That, and the relationship between femoral and tibial length and what that might suggest."

"Just give me the data and we'll see what we can do with it," I promised.

"I just wish there was a computer that we could access in Nairobi."

"Doesn't the university have one?" he asked.

"Yes, they've got an ICL machine at the campus in Chiromo, but getting time on is not always easy, railways has one, so does the power company and the police, I can buy time on the power company machine, but it's slow and the turnaround times are slow," I told him. "It's actually better for me to take stuff to London and use the Imperial machine."

"If you offered to teach a class at Chiromo, would the uni give you better access?" he asked.

"Possibly," I agreed. "I need to talk to the chancellor about that, if I could get decent time, then it would be easier than London, but the Imperial machine is still bigger and faster than the one here."

"How do you put stuff into the computer?" Ian asked.

"It's all keyboard entry, that's then stored on tape," I lamented. "So, I have to write the program, then enter that and make sure it runs, then I have to submit data and that means lots of typing. What really gets me is when I submit a job and it comes back with syntax errors, even telling me what they are, but the bloody machine doesn't fix them, I have to go back and edit the program and resubmit the job. It all takes time as jobs are usually run overnight and it is a teaching college, so there are student jobs as well as mine."

"What does a computer cost, could you buy your own?" he asked.

"Well, a couple of years ago I looked into that, and an IBM Model 75 rented for about $70,000 a month and the cheapest I could buy one for was $2.2 million, and then there's the room you have to have to install it, plus all the acolytes to run it," I told him. "But, IBM just announced a personal computer, the 5100, and there's also an Altair machine, a

Xerox unit and an Olivetti unit, they all retail for somewhere around $15,000 to $20,000, depending on the memory. I'm keeping an eye on those, because I think that will be a big market in the future and machines will really come down in cost."

"Do you really think there will be a market?" Ian asked.

"I do," I confirmed. "When big computers first came out in the late 1940's, Watson of IBM said he could see a worldwide demand of only five machines, now airlines have them, car companies, electricity companies, governments, banks, and on and on, I think the same thing will happen with these personal computers, people will soon find uses for them and then demand will be created, only limited by imagination."

"So, are you planning to invest in a computer company?" he asked.

"When the right one comes along and I think their product is worth it," I said. "Anyway, back to your femurs, get me some data and I'll see what I can make of them."

"Okay," he said. "Another glass of wine?"

"Love one," I said. "Then we should think about dinner."

"I've got that organised," he said. "It's *braai* time."

We went to bed that night happy that Ian had made a discovery that could bring fame if not fortune to his name. I was sure that part of Ian wanted to go back to his dig site and excavate more, but he also knew that that would take months, if not years, to properly explore what could be there and he had made a commitment to HMG to be the Third Secretary at the High Commission, so, unless he abandoned that career, he would have to live with his find and forego further digging. In the morning I was up first and made tea, which we took looking east towards the hill we proposed to climb. Isaac saw us and waved and came over to talk to us.

"Jambo," he said.

"Jambo," Ian replied.

"What are your plans today?" Isaac asked.

"We were thinking of climbing to the top of that mesa," Ian said, pointing to the hill.

"Ah," Isaac said. "Would you like a ride to near the base of the hill?"

"That would be nice," I said. Then we could spend more time at the top looking at the view.

"I could take you there half an hour from now," Isaac suggested.

"We'll be ready," Ian promised. Isaac then left to do whatever he was going to do and we grabbed some breakfast. We were ready to go when Isaac came back with his Land Rover. The drive to the bottom of the hill was rather circuitous, but it only took about twenty minutes. Isaac dropped us off and offered to come back and collect us, but we assured him that we would be happy walking back. The hill rose steeply out of the surrounds and it looked like it would be quite a climb up.

"How far do you think we have to go up?" I asked Ian.

"I'd guess about 250 ft," he thought. "Shouldn't take too long, ready?"

"Ready," I said. We started off and for the first few yards of the walk we actually went down a little until we crossed a dry watercourse, then we started up, then we climbed up quite steeply until we came to the flat top of the hill. Then I understood why Ian had called it a mesa. It was a flat-topped hill just like the western movies. To the south of us was a ridge that dipped then climbed even higher than we were, probably another 300 ft. To the north it was flattish as far as we could see, to the east there were more little hills and to the west was the lake. I calculated that our horizon distance would be about twenty miles, so we could not see the other side of the lake, only the hills that were beyond it, we would have to climb the higher ridge to do that. I asked Ian what he thought.

"Let's do it," he said. We left our mesa and climbed down a short way then started back up again, climbing steadily for about a mile until we came to the top, another nice flat mesa.

"There's the other side of the lake," I said, pointing out to the west. "It makes a really nice picture. Look, over there, there are some islands, the big one must be the Central Island where there are the volcanic craters."

"Coffee break," Ian suggested. "I brought coffee as well as water and something to eat. Make sure you drink enough water and only a little coffee, coffee tends to dehydrate, so be careful."

"I will," I promised. I drank down the water he gave me and then sipped on my coffee and munched on the sandwiches he had made, looking out over the lake.

"What a wonderful view," Ian said, as he sat down beside me. "Look, there's a herd of zebra down there."

"That's great," I said. "And, isn't that some oryx way off there in the distance?"

"Good spot," he said. "There must be twenty of them, not coming this way though. What else can we see?"

"Some gazelles over there, and what is that on the mesa we just left?" I asked.

"That's a bloody leopard," he said. "Just as well we came over here. What else? There's our cottage down there, and it looks like Isaac has company, there's another Land Rover there."

"How can you tell?" I asked. All I could see was a little dot reflecting the sunlight.

"It's a guess," he admitted. "But, Isaac's definitely got company, perhaps we should start back?"

"Okay, you first," I said, pointing down the steep slope. Ian scrambled down and I followed until we reached the flatter ground at the bottom, then we struck overland headed for the road. The road made for easy going and we were able to march quite quickly back to the guest house. Isaac did indeed have company, it was Barbara Green again, with two others in tow.

"Hello Ian," she said as we arrived. "I wanted to show David and Celia where you found your femur."

"If you're not certain where it is, Isaac knows," Ian suggested. Barbara took that as a hint and went with Isaac and the others for a brisk walk that would take them to the gully.

"You don't want to go with them?" I asked Ian.

"No, the experts are taking over now and they'll look on us as amateurs who have dabbled a little in archeology," he laughed. "No, the real reason is that I've no need to go along, Isaac can show them where we were digging, he's the one who told us roughly where to dig in the first place, and I'm sure they'll plan out a more thorough investigation of the area, and I don't want to get in their way."

"Are you happy with your find?" I asked him.

"I am," he said. "It's a brilliant find and I'm sure now that Farnsworth will be delighted and I'll be able to finish my doctorate."

"How long will it take you to write everything up?" I asked.

"That depends on how quickly I can get data on the femoral bones found at other sites," he said. "I might ask you to do some digging for me, not the shovel kind of digging, but the sifting through artifacts and documents kind of digging."

"I'd be happy to," I promised. I suppose that he was excited to get this done as he had been disappointed at his first try at a thesis and this would make up for that, and would not be a rehash of someone else's work, but original work done on a new discovery.

"Fancy a beer?" he asked.

"I don't think so," I said. "If we're flying back this afternoon, I want a clear head. You know I was thinking that Ekstrom down at Olduvai is going to be green with envy when he hears about your discovery."

"I hadn't thought about that," Ian laughed. "You're right, he'll be royally pissed if the Koobi folks make a big find here."

"But, isn't your femur a big find?" I asked.

"Yes, but what if they turn up a whole skeleton?" he asked. "Think about that, that would be truly amazing."

"Is that possible?" I asked.

"Maybe," he said. "The femur and tibia were lying in a way that didn't suggest that they'd been scavenged or washed there, so it's possible that a decent dig might turn up the rest. I suppose I could have dug more to see if the fibula was there or any of the foot bones, but I'm happy with what I have, if the Koobi folks turn up the whole thing, then good for them."

"You wouldn't want to be part of that?" I asked.

"Five years ago, I'd have given my eye teeth to be in on something like that, but I like what I'm doing now, so am happy to let them get on with it," he said.

Barbara and entourage came back and David and Celia wanted know what experience Ian had had in the field. He quickly went through his three years at Olduvai and they seemed somewhat mollified by that, I suspect they had been ready to deliver lectures about people digging who did not know procedures and methods. Well, Ian acquitted himself well and started interrogating them. That was fun to watch. Finally, Celia deigned to talk to me and asked if I was also a budding anthropologist. I explained that I was not, merely a mathematician who dabbled in the field of statistics. I was dismissed then as unimportant in the current scheme of things. I think what most interested them was how Ian was going to present this find. Ian explained that he planned to write a paper and submit it to *Man* and thereafter to his thesis advisor. That led to more questions, but it seemed that Farnsworth was heard of and approved of. Ian was asked about photographs and he turned to me for the answer. I promised to have copies made of all my pictures and to forward them to the Koobi Fora team, all I needed was a name and an address. I had taken some 250 pictures in all and had just about exhausted my supply of film. I had in fact one film left, and that I wanted to preserve for the flight that afternoon when we would fly over the Central Island. Ian offered the Koobi Fora team a beer and they took him up on the offer and drank all that we had left. We left the empty bottles with them, they could transport them out by land, whereas I was always concerned about weight as we had to fly. The landing strip might be lower in altitude, but it was hotter than in Nairobi, so the density altitude needed careful attention. Not that I thought we anything to worry about, the strip was long enough to give us a good take off roll.

Isaac was kind enough to give us a ride to the airstrip and I left Ian to remove all the tie-downs while I pre-flighted the plane. The first thing I did was remove the baffle from the wings, leaving it on would have probably led to an ignominious crash at the end of the runway. We packed everything into the plane, then I gave Ian my camera with instructions to photograph the Central Island when we flew over it. We had obviously consumed a fair bit since we landed because we were in the air far quicker than I had anticipated. I waggled our wings over the guest house in salute to Isaac, then set course for the island. We were there in no time, so I circled around it a few times so that Ian could get some good shots, then set course for Nairobi. Essentially, we retraced the route we had taken going north, so we flew back over Lake Baringo then Nakuru and on into Wilson Field. It had been a wonderful trip, made all the better by Ian's discovery, that was something to remember!

Drums of war

"So, that's how Ian got his doctorate?" James asked.

"Yes," I confirmed. "He wrote up a paper and sent it off to *Man* and it was published with great acclaim. Then I gathered up all the data I could find on femurs from other digs and helped with the statistics. Then he rewrote his doctoral thesis and it was accepted."

"There was no demur this time?" Portia asked.

"No, Farnsworth was quite happy with it, I think largely because Ian's paper had been published by *Man*, and was getting good reviews," I replied. "It's probably hard to turn someone down who is the talk of the town that month. He did make a flying visit to Oxford for orals and he told me that they went really well and he came back very happy."

"Very cynical," James commented.

"It probably is," I agreed. "But, apart from Ian's experiences, my own told me that a lot has to do with college politics, funding and personal biases."

"Did he credit you with any help?" James asked.

"He did give me a brief mention the forward and allowed as how I had contributed to his better understanding of the nature of the femur in early man," I laughed. "At least it was something like that. Why is it that theses supervisors seem to want long and complex sounding words and sentences, is it supposed to convey the idea that the writer is all so very erudite, why can't things be put in simple English?"

"I suppose the argument would be that simple English might not be adequate to describe what the thesis is about," James suggested.

"You're probably right, and why use one word when ten will do, like in a will when they talk about property situate, lying and being, why not just say the property at Number 34?" I asked.

"It has to do with legal definitions and descriptions," Portia, the lawyer, added. "That way that can be no argument later that you did not really understand where the property was."

"I'm sure Ian felt happy to be vindicated," Maman commented.

"He was," I said. "He was also happy that he didn't have to deal with Ambrose."

"I'm sorry I missed the ceremony when they handed out the diploma," Maman said. "That would have been nice."

"It was," I confirmed. "I got to see the college again, where they despair of me because I've strayed from pure mathematics into the grubby world of commerce. You know we almost missed the ceremony."

"Why?" Maman asked. "I don't remember anything happening then?"

"There was a problem with Somalia," I explained.

"I think there'll be problems with Somalia forever," James commented dryly.

"I think you're right," I said. "Ian had always said it was the powder keg of the region. But this was a quick issue that my guess indicates what will probably be a bigger problem in the future."

"Why what happened?" Portia asked.

"A bunch of Somalis came through Kenya to raid Ethiopia, but on the way, they shot up a Kenyan border post," I said.

"I remember something about that," James said. "So, what actually happened?"

"It was difficult to get too much information," I said. "The Kenyan government was trying to keep a lid on things and there was not too much getting out of the North East Province. But we did get dribs and drabs and Ian and the others put it all together."

Somalia

In June of 1977 I went back to Paris for a final meeting with my airline client. I had provided them with a fuel pricing model and with a statistical prediction model for part failures and now had the enterprise model ready. It encompassed all that I could think of in terms of running an airline, and I had been through a few iterations with my contacts and now had the final version. I had the program on a tape reel that I had with me, it was the only way to easily carry programs, the other was reams of paper, but that meant retyping everything in again. I had taken Ian's suggestion and talked to the people at the university, so was now a visiting professor and taught a couple of classes, and more importantly, could get free computer time. That helped a lot as I could access their machine at almost any time.

I flew BA to London, then took a short hop over to Paris. I stayed with Mémère at her flat and she wanted chapter and verse on our trip to Lake Turkana and the items that Ian had found. I think she was delighted that she had another doctoral candidate in the family, particularly as she had not finished high school, but had gone to work at sixteen as a cleaner at the French government offices in Tahiti. It had been while she was doing that that she had met my grandfather, and, I have to give him a lot of credit, he married her and took her back to France with him. I am sure that back then, that that would have been frowned upon by the hierarchy, take a local girl as a mistress, but marry one. For all Mémère had little formal education, she was one of the most intelligent people I knew, she had read widely and was a fount of information for me. Her time associating with the government officials that Pépère worked with had prepared her for any situation and people that she met all went away with the impression that she had been schooled at the best schools and university. Even at 76 she still had all her faculties and was as inquisitive as ever, ever ready to investigate the newest and latest, be it art, literature or technology. She had been sounding me out about personal computers and wanted to know when she could get one and, if she did, would I teach how to use it. I think she was really referring to the Apple Series II that had just gone on sale. I needed to get one for myself before I could teach Mémère how to use it. We also talked about family history. My aunt Claudette came on the scene a year after Pépère and Mémère returned to Paris, but sadly she was killed when she had been captured while she was operating as part of the Resistance, just prior to D-Day. Maman was only thirteen when Paris fell, so took no part in any action, later doing her part in a hospital, which is where she met Dad, after the liberation of Paris in 1944. Other French relatives I had came from the side of Pépère, who had a brother, Charles, who had had two sons, one Philippe had been killed in 1944 and the other, Henri, who lived on in Marseille as a ship's chandler. Henri has a daughter, Antoinette, a nurse, and a son, Dion, who is a chef. We stay in touch peripherally, and Mémère sees them perhaps once a year. Well, enough of my digression into family history.

I met with Pierre and Pascal and they took me to their computer centre. I loaded the tape and waited until it loaded, then did a test run.
"It looks as though it's running," I said. "No bugs, but you never know one may show up at some time. Now we just need to check the data input and the results."
"You used the data we gave you?" Pierre asked.
"I did," I assured him. "The outputs you see now are the projected financial results base on those data."
"That doesn't look as good as I'd like," Pierre commented. "What do we have to do to improve things?"
"I tried varying different data sets to see which had the most influence and if I change this, this is what happens," I told them, changing a few numbers.
"Ah," Pierre said. "I like the look of that, now, as I understand the model, we can change just about everything?"
"You can," I agreed. "But you may wish to change only a few things at once, so that you can keep track of what actually drives results, for instance if you change fare prices, don't change load factors, unless you are certain that load factors will go up or down depending in the price change. You'll want to see which has the greater impact, fare basis or load factor, or if there's an optimum combination."
"What about operational availability?" Pascal asked.
"Well, if we drop this number here, then this is what happens," I said, inputting a number and waiting for the result.

"Oh," Pascal said. "Not good, we have some work to do to keep the availability of equipment high."

"True, it doesn't matter what the fare is or the load factor if we can't fly," Pierre laughed. "We'll need to play with this for a while."

"I did some variability studies and these are the results," I told them, bringing out a set of charts.

"Ah," Pierre said. "That's very useful, it gives us a good start with what we might want to vary."

"Do you have any recommendations?" Pascal asked.

"I tried a lot of scenarios, and this set would seem to give you the best results," I replied, handing over another set of charts. "And if you get into a price war with Air France, this is what's likely to happen, depending on whether the war lasts one month or a year."

"Ugly," Pierre said.

"Ugly," I agreed. "No matter what people may think, unless your price war actually enables you to kill the competition completely, all it does it reduce earnings in the short term, with sometimes no ability to recover, and Air France will have the backing of the government, so I would find another way to attract customers if I could. Perhaps think about some kind of reward program that lets people earn points towards a free flight in the future if they fly so many times with you. There are balance sheet issues with that as the accumulated points imply a non-revenue fare that may be redeemed, lessening the revenue for that flight. But it may be worth it to get customer loyalty and better load factors if you have to compete."

"We'll get the marketing people to think about that," Pierre said. "It seems to me that that's a program that would take some thinking about the basis for earning and redeeming points."

"What about space available cargo, I didn't see much data on that?" I asked.

"We get some," Pascal said. "Perhaps we should take a look at the baggage holds and typically how full they are and where our weights come out."

"I agree," I said. "No point in trying to sell space available if you're weight restricted, and with your typical long hauls, you're going to be driven by weather, winds and fuel loads."

"You seem well acquainted with weight restrictions," Pascal said. "But then I was forgetting you have your own plane."

"I'm really aware of it now," I said. "We recently made a trip to Lake Turkana and I was weighing everything that went into the plane. There's no fuel there, so you have to have enough to get there and back, plus there's the altitude of the Nairobi airport and the temperatures. We left in the afternoon, so the density altitude was not the best."

"Nice to talk to a pilot who understands those issues," Pascal said. "I wish everyone in the company had a better appreciation of weights, weather, winds and fuel loads."

"Why don't we do some testing of our own?" Pierre suggested. "Then, why don't you come back in a month and we'll review what we've done and you can give us your perspective?"

"I can do that," I said. "Is there anything else I can do for now?"

"Come and work for us," Pierre laughed. "But maybe I should talk to Francis, I think you'd be a big asset on our board."

"Thank you," I said. Privately I doubted whether the existing board would countenance a woman in their midst, and to them one so young to boot. But, as the company was essentially privately held, anything was possible. I had been approached be three other companies about serving on their boards, but the equation of directors' fees versus potential liability just was not very attractive.

"Do you have time for lunch?" Pierre asked.

"Of course," I replied. I had planned nothing for the whole day until later that night when Mémère and I were going out to some event she wanted me to see.

"I thought we'd go to *Le train blue,*" Pierre said. "Have you ever been there?"

"No," I said.

"It's at the Gare de Lyon," Pierre explained. "I like it and the food is good." We left the office and Pascal hailed a taxi to take us to the Gare de Lyon. I had images of a railway station café, but could not quite reconcile that with any kind of fine dining. The restaurant turned out to be rather delightful. It had obviously once been the station restaurant in the days when travel was a little more genteel than it is today. Access was via the station, but once inside it was amazing. It had ornate ceilings, the sort of thing a mathematician loves, lots of little bits to count and compare. The seating upholstery was blue and looked like the kind of furniture one would find on a romanticised version of *Murder on the*

Orient Express. Pierre was obviously known and we were shown to a table and waiters hovered ready to do our every bidding. Pierre had been right, the food was very good, and he and Pascal kept up a running debate on the plusses and minuses of changing the seating pitch in the planes to give more seats. Pierre was all for adding seats, and therefore revenue per flight, but Pascal was arguing that too tight a seating pitch would be uncomfortable and cause passengers to seek out other carriers. That came down to the crux of it, what competition was there on the routes they flew, and was that competition likely to change. Without competition, they could, within reason, do just about anything, but with competition those decisions were more complex, trying to guess what the other might do and what impact that would have on the business. I thought it all came down to the market, and who would be flying and why. If the prices were cheap enough then the potential for people who wanted to take an exotic holiday was huge, but it all depending on the disposable income of the buyers. For business and government travel, the equation was a little easier. For each of their destinations they knew what related businesses were and how many trips those businesses would generate in a year, the same was true of government travel. Price was an issue, but did not have the same driving force that it did with people picking their holiday destinations. Pierre finally called all this to a halt and said that they had to get back to their offices to resume the work of managing the airline. I told them that I could get a taxi from the Gare de Lyon to go to my grandmother's flat. I promised to return after a month to see what they had done and then give my views on the results.

Mémère was waiting for me to return and almost propelled me into the shower with instructions to wash off the dirt and grime of business dealings. Scrubbed clean and perfumed, I wondered what next, then she handed me a sarong and told me to tie it about myself.
"And what underneath?" I asked her.
"Rien," she said. So, I suppose that was normal for her, a sarong wrapped around the body and knotted in the right places, and nothing else. I noted that and thought that Ian might like that. She also had on a sarong, and I would have guessed that that was it also.
"Where are we going?" I asked.
"There is an exhibit of paintings of Tahiti at the Musée d'Orsay," she explained. "We have been invited to a private party to open the exhibit."

"Do you know the painter?" I asked.

"There are several," she replied. "There are even a couple of Gauguin works borrowed for the exhibit. Come we shall take a taxi."

"What did you do today?" I asked her as we settled into the back of a taxi.

"I wanted to see this new Star Wars film, but it's not scheduled for release here until September, so I wrote to the studio to complain," she said tartly.

"I wonder if and when it will ever get to Nairobi?" I thought. "Did you see 2001?"

"I did," she said. "It was really interesting; I wonder if by 2001 we will be able to fly to the moon?"

"Well, the Americans landed on the moon in 1969," I said.

"Yes, but that was NASA with a budget which while not unlimited is big, far larger than anything you or I could afford," she countered. "Costs will have to come down a lot before anyone other than a select few governments can afford such a venture."

"Who will be at this opening?" I asked.

"We'll find out," she said. "I know the museum director and he asked me to come because he knows I am from Tahiti."

"Would you like to go back for a visit?" I asked.

"I would," she said. "Would you come with me?"

"Just me, or may I bring Ian with me?" I asked.

"I don't mind," she said. "I just want someone to go with me."

"What about Maman and Portia?" I asked.

"Yes, them too," she said. "I would just like someone to travel with, it's a long way and I would rather have someone with me. But that is for another day, we have arrived."

We were detained at the door by an official who wanted to see our invitations. We had none, so he wanted to turn us away, but Mémère told him to call the museum director and tell him that she had arrived. He did so, very reluctantly. We waited then another man came scurrying towards us.

"Madame Garnier," he said. "Thank you for coming, I am so sorry for the confusion."

"It is nothing," Mémère said, graciously. "This is my granddaughter, Dr Fiona Hartley."

"Enchanté," he said. "Please, Madame, this way." He led us off into the museum eventually to a gallery hung with paintings of Tahiti. Some, like those of Gauguin were impressionist, others were simple water colours, there were some realistic oils and some modern that I could not make head nor tail of. I thought that it was a pity that Ian could not be there, he at least could talk intelligently to people about paintings, all I really ever did was say whether or not I liked them. Mémère got us a couple of glasses of champagne and then we mixed and mingled. I am not sure most knew what to make of us, the rest were dolled up to the nines and there we were in simple sarongs. But, because the director was making a fuss over Mémère they all seemed to think we were something special, perhaps the token Tahitians?

There was a lull in the festivities and a group of dancers were ushered in. Mémère whispered to me that these girls were actually from Tahiti, in fact they were all cabin crew from UTA, Union de Transports Aériens, and regularly flew from Paris to Pape'ete. UTA was one of the exhibit sponsors and I supposed that among the crowd that there were executives from UTA. We were treated to a couple of dances, then the director nodded to Mémère and she kicked off her shoes and told me to do likewise, then she launched into a dance of her own. It was a dance that I knew, she had choreographed it after she had moved to Paris. So, this was a set up job and I knew why I had been dragged along. I just followed along and thankfully did not make a complete mess of things. It had been a year or two since I had done the same dance for Ian, but I still remembered it. When we were done there was applause, then the Tahitian girls came over to talk to us. For the most part they spoke French, but two of them spoke to Mémère in Tahitian, and I am gratified to say that I had picked up enough from my childhood that I was able to follow the conversation. They wanted to know where I lived and what I did, and to a one, they all extended invitations to come and stay with them in Tahiti. Perhaps, one day I would do that. We danced no more that evening, but the crowd now deigned to speak to us, as we had been one of the star attractions. I think Mémère disabused them of any notion that we were any kind of hired help, and made a point of introducing me as Dr Hartley, a renowned economist.

The balance of the evening was taken up by chit chat to the various dignitaries who were there, sipping champagne and trying to understand some of the modernist paintings that were supposed to be of Tahiti. Two older imitations of Charles Boyer tried to pick me up, but I flashed my wedding ring at them and politely told them that I had no interest at all in their advances. I was flagging before Mémère and eventually had to beg her to let us go home. She relented and we took a taxi back to her flat. It had been a pleasant enough evening, but I was happy that I would be going back to Nairobi, I missed Ian. Mémère understood, and she shooed me off to take a shower. I was happy to do so, and even happier to take myself off to bed and sleep, after I had called Ian for a few minutes, just to let him know I was still alive and coming back the following day. But when I went to bed, I had some apprehensions knowing that I would be stiff and achy in odd places is the morning from the dancing.

We spent the following morning reading the papers and drinking coffee until it was time for me to go off to the airport to begin my trek back to Nairobi. I took a taxi to Charles de Gaulle and found my BA flight to London. There it was the seemingly interminable transfer from Terminal 2 to Terminal 3, quite why they made it such a rigmarole I have no idea. The flight to Nairobi was full. I suppose June was a good time for people to take a holiday on safari, because it certainly looked as if most of the passengers were going to do just that, all with their guide books and cameras. I had a seat mate; he went by the name of George Martin and he was a coffee buyer. He said that he represented one of the big coffee shops chains and was going to visit some coffee farms and see if there was a way to inject life back into their business. I rather suspect that he worked for Joe Lyons, which was having financial difficulties that I saw as bad enough that it would take far more than some fancy coffee to turn things around. He had list of coffee farms that he was going to see and I noted that Robert's farm was among them. George knew little about the farming and processing of coffee, just that the company bought green beans and roasted them in huge commercial roasters. I commended him to Trevor at the High Commission who would help with anything he needed to make his trip successful, anything that improve the economy of Kenya and increased trade was bread and butter to Trevor.

In Nairobi I wished George well on his mission and went home, stopping briefly at the High Commission to let Ian know that I was back safely. But Ian was not there. He had left at five that morning with Edward, the military attaché to check out some activity in the northeast of the country. Trevor gave me a letter that Ian had written for me, I was disappointed, but thought that Ian probably felt that way too, when I was gone gallivanting around England and France in pursuit of my own interests. At home I unpacked and arranged my next projects on my desk. I had four on the go, five if I counted the airline. But that was a simple follow up to see how they were doing and give an opinion. The next one I thought I should spend some time on was an economic analysis of the publishing business. Were reading trends changing, was the hard back doomed to be cast aside for paperbacks, what was the impact of changing paper weight, what was the impact of changing inks, what was the minimum run to make it worthwhile setting presses, and what were the long term potential impacts of personal computers on books. All very weighty topics that required some thinking and some serious analysis of buying trends. Then I made myself some coffee and sat outside on the terrace to read Ian's letter. He apologised for the change in plans, but apparently a situation had arisen near Rhamu that required some attention. I consulted my map of Kenya and discovered that Rhamu was a good 640 miles from Nairobi, so it would either be a long day for them, or they would take two days to get there. That meant that the earliest that they would be back was Monday, so it was going to be a long and lonely weekend.

The next few days dragged. They really dragged because there were no telephone calls from Ian, because I suppose that there were limited, if any, telephones where he was. I kept myself busy, taught my classes at the university and tried to stay positive about things. The times I had been away from Ian lately had been when I was in London or Paris and I had been busy and had either my flat or Mémère's flat to go home to at night. Now, I was in our house alone and I missed having Ian there. I thought about what Ian must feel when I was away on business and he had to go home to an empty house, with no one to come home to, no one to share the day with, no one to share a sundowner with and no one to sleep with. I thought that I should make more of an effort to be sensitive to his feelings and not just breeze through life on my own little cloud of well-being. When I thought about it, I had few real friends in Nairobi. I had acquaintances by the score, but few real friends. Ian and I were friends as well as husband and wife and lovers, and I just enjoyed his company and most of the time felt no need for others in my life. Such family as we had between us were also many miles away, so it would have been easy to get maudlin, lonely and depressed. I countered that be keeping myself really busy, and I have to say, that I got a lot done in those few days.

On Monday afternoon there was a hoot at the gate and it was Ian. He was back from his trip, alive and well. I scurried out and let him in. He was driving a Land Rover that belonged to the High Commission and it had obviously seen some miles on dirt roads.

"Fi," he said. "God, it's good to be back."

"I'm glad you're back safe and sound," I said. "Did your trip go well?"

"I'll tell you all about it," he said. "Right now, I could do with a shower and a beer."

"One beer coming up," I promised. "I'll bring it to you in the shower." I got a beer and went to the bathroom where we had the shower and pulled aside the curtain and handed him the beer. I stood there looking at him and decided that I was going to join him in the shower. That led to the obvious conclusion. Later we sat out on the terrace and ate our light supper and I brought up the subject of his trip.

"So, what took you haring off to the northeast?" I asked.

"Somalia," he said. "It seems that Somalia has decided to go to war with Ethiopia over the Ogaden."

"What's the Ogaden?" I asked.

"It's a chunk of Ethiopia that borders Somalia and which Somalia claims saying that it is populated mostly by ethnic Somalis," he explained.

"Is it large, small, fertile?" I asked.

"It's a fairly large chunk of territory," he said. "It's good grazing land and sad to say our government pulled a fast one on the Somalis. After World War II, we gave control of the Ogaden to Ethiopia, despite treaties that had been in place since 1884 and 1886 with the Somalis. The decision to give the Ogaden to Ethiopia was in return for Emperor Menelik's help with raids by hostile clans."

"So, the classic political solution," I commented.

215

"Right," he said. "At the same time that we gave the Ogaden to Ethiopia we also gave the Northern Frontier District to Kenya, despite the fact that most of the people living there wanted to be part of Somalia."

"So, there was British Somaliland, Italian Somaliland, wasn't there also a French Somaliland as well?" I asked.

"There was," he confirmed. "They held a referendum in 1958 and voted to stay independent of Somalia, so they are now Djibouti, still part of France. Mind you there were stories about vote rigging and expulsions of Somalis prior to the referendum."

"So, what is Somalia doing now?" I asked.

"Well, they launched a raid into Kenya with the purpose of passing through to enter Ethiopia by the back door so to speak," he explained.

"What happened?" I asked.

"There was a gun fight and a lot of chaps from here were killed," he said.

"Are the Somalis still in Kenya?" I asked.

"No, they're in Ethiopia now," he replied. "Look for more action in the coming weeks."

"Will it affect us?" I asked.

"I doubt it," he said. "There have always been problems with the Somalis and their raids, but for the moment they're concentrating on trying to win back the Ogaden."

"Do you know how many Somalis crossed into Ethiopia?" I asked.

"By our estimation there were some 1500 of them and they left 30 Kenyan border guards and soldiers dead," he replied.

"Who else is involved?" I asked.

"Well, the Russians have been arming Somalia and the Americans have been arming Ethiopia, mainly because the Russians support Somalia. The Cubans are involved as well. The Russians and the Cubans have been trying to persuade both Ethiopia and Somalia to form a common Socialist Federation, along with Yemen, but that seems to be falling on deaf ears. So, now we've got two Marxist régimes getting ready to fight it out with Barre and Somalia on the one hand and Mengistu and Ethiopia on the other."

"And where do we stand?" I asked.

"I suppose that it will depend on where the US falls," he said. "I don't see us as taking the other side to the US, so we'll wait and see what happens, right now we're ostensible supporting Ethiopia, but why we all continue to arm these régimes is past me. I know it means weapons sales, but too often in history those weapons get turned back on us, so is it such a good idea?"

"I thought when we came here that this was going to be a quiet place with no wars," I said. "Since we've been here, we've had issues with Uganda, the border with Tanzania is closed and now we've got this Somali business to worry about."

"True," he agreed. "I thought there might be some minor issues, but I have to say I didn't expect all this. I suppose it all stems back to the colonial era and the allocation of territory to various countries."

"Well, one thing's for sure, we won't be flying out that way," I said. "We'll have to stick to the west and the north."

"Good idea," he agreed. "I think it's time for bed, it was a long drive today."

"Did you drive all the way?" I asked.

"We did," he confirmed. "We traded off every two hours, but it's still a long way."

For the next couple of weeks things were quiet, then we got the news that Somalia had invade Ethiopia. Ian came home from the commission one day and gave me all the details.

"Well, Fi, it's happened. The Somalis have made their move," he said.

"Is it serious?" I asked.

"Serious enough," he said. "Our information is that they've taken most of their armed forces and are making a serious push, our sources tell us that they've got some 70,000 troops, 250 tanks, 350 armoured personnel carriers, 600 artillery pieces and 40 fighter planes."

"That's a lot," I thought. "What does Ethiopia have?"

"That's not clear, but our estimation is that they're going to have a hard time repelling the Somalis," he replied. "The Russians have been trying to mediate, but it seems they got nowhere, so they've officially dumped Somalia and are now supporting Ethiopia, but it seems that now they're actually supplying both sides with arms."

"Who else is involved?" I asked.

"Well, with the Russians are the Cubans, and the word is that they're actually sending troops, some 15,000 according to intelligence reports, that's a lot of men and equipment to move in. Then there's the North Koreans and the East Germans, but the Chinese still support Somalia and so does Romania," he explained.

217

"How is it going for the Ethiopians?" I asked.

"Early days yet," he said. "But early reports are that the Somalis are doing well and are pushing far into the Ogaden. We'll have to see how this all comes out. The one bright spot for Ethiopia that we've heard of is that their air force is doing better than the Somali air force."

"What do they have?" I asked. Planes were something I now took an interest in, since I got my own.

"The Somalis have MiG-21's and the Ethiopians have Northrop F-5's from the US," he said. "By all accounts the Ethiopians are gaining air superiority, even though the Somalis have more planes."

"Does air superiority really help?" I asked.

"It does," he said. "But eventually the land war really decides things, so Ethiopia controlling the skies will help them, but it won't completely stop the Somalis, in Rhodesia we controlled the skies completely, but the war is still going to go to the insurgents."

"Is the war between Ethiopia and Somalia a bush war like the one you were in?" I asked.

"No, this is much more conventional, armoured brigades against other armoured brigades and infantry battles," he replied. "There may be some irregulars about the place, but for the most part it's such straight out land warfare."

"What will be left afterwards?" I asked.

"That all depends on how much artillery and tank warfare is used," he explained. "If you go to parts of France and Belgium you can still see the effects of the artillery from the First World War, so buildings can get damaged or destroyed, bridges blown up, airports wrecked, railways and roads mined, so the infrastructure damage can be huge, then there's the psychological effect on the people, no one comes out of a war well, even the victors."

"How long will it go on?" I asked.

"That's difficult to say," he thought. "I suppose now it will really depend on how much aid the Cubans and Russians provide to Ethiopia and can Ethiopia push back the Somalis."

"What's your opinion?" I asked.

"Without the Cubans and Russians, the Ethiopians are going to have a hard time, but with help they should be able to take back all the territory that the Somali have grabbed, it's just going to take a few months," he replied.

"Don't you need food, water and petrol for your army?" I asked. "Where does Somalia get all that from?"

"Food and water, they can supply from their own economy," he said. "But petrol they have to import and that all has to come in through Mogadishu. If I were the Ethiopians, I find a way to try and stop that, but they're a landlocked country with no navy and they have the same problem, all their petrol comes in through Djibouti."

"Would the Russians send boats to blockade Mogadishu?" I asked.

"No," he said. "That would be seen as too belligerent and I doubt that they would even contemplate that."

"Does Somalia have a navy?" I asked.

"Not really," he said. "They don't have anything that could cause problems at the port in Djibouti, but they do have pirates that grab ships of the coast."

"Is that a problem?" I asked.

"Not that big a problem, yet," he said. "But I look for it to be in the longer term."

"So, the big problem right now is just that the Somalis are disrupting the Ethiopian economy?" I asked.

"Yes," He agreed. "But I think the bigger problem is that there will be guns and ammunition by the ton left over after the war, however it ends, so look for increased raids by cattle thieves, increased terrorist activities and all-around unrest in Somalia, which will spill over into Kenya."

"Are we in any danger?" I asked.

"No," he said. "The action right now is all Ethiopia and that will take some time, depending on who wins there, we can make some guesses as to what will happen next."

Perhaps I was being paranoid, perhaps I imagined things to happen that would never happen, perhaps that essence of self-preservation was kicking in, but I decided that I should hone again my shooting skills, particularly my pistol shooting skills. I went to the range regularly and shot off hundreds of rounds until I was happy with my score, then I discovered a new sport, Combat Pistol Shooting. It was developed in the 1920's by some British policemen assigned to Shanghai to better train their officers to deal with the lawlessness that was Shanghai at that time. There were targets set up and one had to go through the course, shoot, or not shoot, depending on the silhouette that popped up, change

219

magazines, change hands, all while being timed. The Kenya police had a course set up and I talked my way into trying it out. My first time through was pretty hopeless, but I kept at it until I was fairly proficient. My pistol of choice was the Beretta 9mm which I had brought with me from England. Kenya had strict gun laws, so there were forms to fill out for registration and I had to demonstrate a basic level of competence with the pistol and answer a whole load of questions about firearm safety. I talked Ian into coming with me, and the first time I went through with him, he beat the pants off me. He was really good. Even the instructors were impressed. But then I suppose while he was in the Rhodesian Army and involved in the bush war, his very life might depend on his competence. With the instructors he was very vague about how he had acquired those skills, passing it off as just natural ability. The instructors knew we could both shoot, because we had been to their range before, but that was with regular targets and over sights, the trick to the combat shooting seemed to be more along the lines of what one would see in the western movies, just shoot and know where you were shooting, instinctual shooting if you like. That took a bit of practice as I was used to taking slow and deliberate aim to get the shot just where I wanted it on a small target. This was different, one had to be able to use reflexes and just shoot and know that what you shot at would be hit. In some ways it was like using a shotgun, with a shotgun, you do not really aim, you know where you want the shot to be and you lead the target. I got better in time with the pistol until I was nearly as good as Ian, but I could never quite match him. With targets and open sights, I could match him and, at times, beat him, but this was a little different and I had to concede that he was better at it that I was, much to my chagrin.

We did get some more welcome news in all this. I collected the mail one day and there was a very official looking letter for Ian from the college in Oxford. I was tempted to open it, but left that for Ian, it was after all addressed to him.
"It's official," Ian said when he opened the letter. "I've been awarded a doctor of philosophy degree and they would like me to be at the ceremony if possible," he added.
"When is it?" I asked.

"They've suggested Saturday the 13th of August," he said. "I'll need to check with the Commissioner and see if I can get a little time off then."

"If you can, get a week and we'll go to Oxford, then take a trip to the Scottish islands, how does that sound?" I suggested.

"I like that idea," he said. "I'll talk to him tomorrow morning and see what we can do."

"Do you feel vindicated?" I asked.

"A little," he said. "I'm just wondering if Ambrose will have the gall to show up at the ceremony or not."

"So, should I book us flights to London?" I asked.

"Why not?" he thought. "I'm sure that the commish will give me the time off, makes the legation look good if one of its members moves up in the academic world."

"Fine," I said. "I'll book us here to London on Friday night, arriving Saturday morning, I'll get us a hotel in Oxford where we can bath and nap before we need to be dolled up for the ceremony. On Sunday, I'll get us a plane and we can fly to Mull and spend a week doing nothing, then come back to Heathrow on Saturday morning in time to get the flight back on that evening, so that we have Sunday to recover before you go back to work."

"Sounds like fun," he said. "What if the weather's bad and we can't fly?"

"I'll have a plan B," I promised. "So, Doctor Hartley, what shall we do to celebrate?"

"A glass of wine, some bread and you," he laughed.

"I thought it was a jug of wine, a loaf of bread and thou?" I asked.

"I thought you weren't that well-versed in classic literature," he said. "But whichever sounds better, either way, wine and you definitely."

"So, here and now, on the terrace, in the bath, on the bed?" I asked.

"All of the above," he said.

"So, boasting, are we?" I laughed. I reached for him and pulled him close and reached down to unzip his trousers. I undid them, then undid his belt and let the trousers fall to the floor. Then I eased his pants down over his hips and let them fall to the floor. He pulled his shirt off and stood in front of me in all his splendour.

"So, Doctor Hartley, is this the *homo erectus* that your thesis was about?" I asked.

"I'm beginning to think it should have been," he laughed.

"So, I think we should put it to good use," I suggested. I stripped off the few clothes I had on and then instructed him to lift me up. He did as I asked, and we between us put everything in the right place. He moaned a little with pleasure and I hung on for dear life as he lifted me up and down. He swung us around and eased me onto the counter so that he did not have to support me, then he went to work. It was so good to feel him in me and feel him slide in and out. I spread my legs further so that he could get closer and pulled him into me.

"Oh God, Fi," he said. "I hope you're close because I can't hold things any longer."

"Let it go," I whispered in his ear. "Let it go."

"I am," he said, and then the spasms of his climax came and he thrust deeper into me.

"That's good," I said. "Oh, that is so good." And good it was. I was ready for more but he needed a few minutes to recover and be ready to go again. So, I reached to the side of me and got the wine bottle that was there and opened it and poured us a glass each. If you have ever tried to do that while sitting on a counter and entangled with another, let me tell you, it is quite the feat.

"Cheers," he said.

"Cheers," I echoed. "If I take both glasses can you carry me out to the terrace?"

"Oh, we are going to do that are we?" he laughed.

"You suggested it, so yes," I said. "We've done the here and now, next it's the terrace, then the bath then finally bed."

"I'll be worn out by then," he said.

He picked me up again and carried me out to the terrace, while I hung on the glasses and the wine bottle. We made love on the terrace, then we had dinner and after dinner made love in the bath and finally in bed. What a wonderful way to celebrate one's husband being awarded his doctorate.

It was about a month later when we got more news. Apparently, the Somalis had pushed far into the Ogaden and had even reached as far as Dire Dawa, a place I had to look up in my atlas to see where it was. It was located towards the frontier with Djibouti and it was where the second largest military airbase of the Ethiopians, and where the railway ran through to the Red Sea. Loss of Dire Dawa would have cut Ethiopia off from shipping goods either in or out, so it was really important. Ian reported that despite heavy fighting, the Ethiopians held onto Dire

Dawa, so preserved their lifeline to the sea. Also, by this time Cubans and the Russians had really stepped up their aid to the Ethiopians. To counter that the Americans had stepped up aid to Somalia. I thought that strange and asked Ian about it.

"It's been the same for a while," he said. "As soon as either Russia or the US supports someone, then the other supports their foes."

"Isn't that rather ridiculous?" I asked.

"It would seem so," he agreed. "But, it's all about power and projection of power and influence. Both sides would like to recruit as many countries as they could to their way of thinking and military aid is one of the ways."

"Why would either Russia or the US want to go all out to support either Somalia or Ethiopia, it's not as if either would make a good trading partner, they've got little enough to trade and even less in the way of foreign currency reserves?" I asked.

"It's all about influence and appearance," he replied. "Both superpowers want to be the one people turn to, if and when they do have something to trade, if either one of them had oil, then they would get all kinds of backing. At the moment it seems to be it's more of the if he supports you then I'm going to support your adversary, just because."

"Stupid," I said.

"Stupid, I agree," he said.

"And us, I mean HMG, where do we stand?" I asked.

"Ah, good question," he said. "It all depends, do you want my views of the official line?"

"Your views," I said.

"I'm with you," he said. "All the posturing generally leads to nothing good. The US has a history of backing dictators, like Batista and Pinochet, and they also have a history of losing to popular revolutions because the dictators get more and more brutal in order to stay in power. The same could be said for Russia, they back Kim in North Korea and he's not exactly the model of a nice chap. We as Brits tend to go along with the US because we've basically lost much of our standing in the world and we can no longer use gunboat diplomacy."

"Politics," I said.

"Politics," he agreed. "But through all the politics we try and survive."

"Well, I suppose you and I won't change it, so we'll have to just live with it," I thought. "There are times when I could go for a remote tropical island and ignore the rest of the world."

"Doesn't Tahiti have a small island or two?" he asked.

"We could always try Maupiti," I suggested. "It's one of the Leeward Islands and does have higher ground, so that in the event of tsunamis or hurricanes there is somewhere to retreat to. It even has an airstrip."

"How far is that from Tahiti?" he asked.

"I think from Maupiti to Pape'ete is about 190 miles," I said.

"How do you know all this?" he asked.

"Mémère would give me geography lessons when I was a child," I said. "She told me stories, legends, tales and myths about all the islands."

"Is it true that the women there all go bare-breasted?" he asked.

"Not anymore," I said. "When missionaries arrived, they were shocked at what they thought were loose morals and rampant promiscuity, so as they began to get sway over the rulers, dresses that looked like night gowns came in and promiscuity went underground."

"So, what about you?" he asked.

"Sadly, I've never been to Tahiti," I said. "Mémère was trying to get me to go with her, maybe we should, take a holiday there and then I'll undo my sarong and let it all hang out."

"What do you wear with the sarong?" he asked. I had been waiting for this, so was able to show him. I undid the sarong and there I was in all my splendour, naked as a newborn, well not quite, I had a little more hair than a newborn.

"Nothing," I told him.

"Wow, Fi," he said. "You are beautiful."

"You're just saying that because you're lusting after me," I commented.

"I am," he agreed. "But you are beautiful. So, if women wear sarongs and nothing else, what do men wear?"

"I'm not sure," I admitted. "I imagine before the missionaries, just a loin cloth, then it would be that plus trousers or a wraparound skirt."

"So, I could get away with just a wraparound skirt?" he asked.

"You could," I agreed. "Especially on Maupiti."

"You don't have much of a tan line," he commented.

"I've been sunbathing nude," I confessed. "I've been limiting myself to the morning hours when the sun isn't too bright and I've been using sunscreen, but I have been slowly tanning and getting rid of the lines."

"Looks nice," he said. "I daren't do that, I'd burn and get skin cancer late in life."

"Let's see your tan line," I commanded. He stood and shrugged off his shirt, then dropped his shorts and underpants and stood in front of me and slowly spun around. He did have tan lines, on his legs and arms and around his neck. The exposed bits were quite brown, but the rest was pale and I could see his point, any reasonable amount of sun would turn his into a lobster. The paleness did not in any way affect the muscular shape that he had, his flat stomach, well-defined legs and arms and firm buttocks. He was a joy to look at. I reached out and trailed my fingers down his chest and over his stomach until I found him already stiffening.

"What do you have in mind?" he asked.

"Oh, I don't know," I said. "Perhaps a little of you here and now."

"You'll get more than a little," he boasted.

"Ah, I see," I said, as I noted his growth, amazed as ever that the human body could make such a change from a flaccid thing to a rigid pole. "I could put that to good use. Come, let's go and lie on the grass and see what we can do with this." I led him out into the middle of the lawn and lay down and opened myself up to him in invitation. I guided him in and was rewarded by the sensations that that provided. I hooked my legs around his back and pulled him towards me, so that he was buried as deep into me as he could go. From there it was not long before we both reached climaxes and then clung to each other panting, and I have to say, panting for more. I rolled him onto his back and straddled him, gently working on him until I felt him stiffen again. Then I did all the work, rising and falling so that he slid out and in, sometimes almost all the way out, sometimes just quick movements that kept him deep inside me. It took longer than the first time, but the second time was as spectacular as the first, perhaps even more so. Spent, I lay down on his chest and just relaxed there, content, happy, revelling in the moment and feeling thoroughly pleased with myself. Making love to Ian never got old, it never got boring and it was never a chore. It was something that I enjoyed, I relished, I looked forward to and I remembered often. It did not matter if it was in bed, in the bath, on the grass, in the shower, on a chair, it was all good and I had come to really appreciate what a good lover Ian was. He was patient, sensitive to my needs, ever ready to try something new and not at all bashful about telling me what was good, what was better and what was best. I had discarded my own inhibitions and was quite ready to tell him what I wanted, where I wanted him to touch me and how I wanted him to make love to me. One day I had even given him a running commentary on our love making and he had had a hard time concentrating because he was laughing so much. Another time I did that it had been so stimulating for both of us that we had both come far quicker than we had expected, but it had been fun.

After a while, he looked at me and grinned and announced that he was hungry. I told him that I eat anything that he prepared.
"What is there to live on on Maupiti?" he asked.
"I imagine fish and other things from the sea, then there's pigs and chickens and for vegetables I'm sure they've got some sort of taro, maybe sugar, then you could grow avocados, mangos, bananas, melons, tomatoes, passion fruit, aubergines, radishes and who knows what else," I replied.
"So, we wouldn't starve?" he asked.
"Not likely," I laughed.
"So, what should I make now?" he asked. "Let's see, some fruit and cold meats?"
"That sounds good," I agreed. I disengaged myself from him and let him stand up and go off to the kitchen. I followed with our clothes in hand and stood watching him as he made dinner, standing there, no clothes, not at all bashful and quite relaxed. It was as well that our house was walled off and that the gates were solid and not just bars, our neighbours would have probably been horrified to see us parading around sans clothes and I am sure that quite a few of the local African traders would have sold tickets. I detached myself from my viewpoint and set the table. Ian brought our food over and I found and poured wine and cheers'd him, toasting this life we had together. I think that was the first time we had eaten in the nude, and I rather enjoyed it. I am not sure that I would go as far as visiting a nudist colony, but I certainly liked the idea of discarding clothes when the occasion presented itself.
"I was thinking," he said, as he opened up and ate some figs.
"That's dangerous," I laughed. "What were you thinking about?"
"I was thinking of Lady Chatterley's lover," he said.
"Why, do you see yourself as the gamekeeper?" I asked. "You can't be both Sir Clifford and Mellors."

"True," he agreed. "No, I was thinking that British society was really prudish and hypocritical. Just because Lawrence wrote what he actually meant to say instead of beating about the bush, the book was banned for years as obscene."

"Probably stemmed from the Victorian era," I said. "I'm sure that if you went back further in history that things were a little more basic."

"When did you read the book?" he asked.

"I think I was about twelve," I said. "There was an old first edition in the library at home. It was interesting enough, a lot of social commentary and then to spice it up the sexual goings on with Mellors, and you?"

"I didn't read it until I was at Oxford," he said. "I'm not even sure if you could buy it in Rhodesia, they were strange in many ways. I think they were afraid that if the blacks read it, it would show that whites had clay feet and weren't all paragons of virtue."

"Why think of it now?" I asked.

"I'm not sure," he said. "There must have been something in the back of my mind, maybe I was thinking just as well no one writes novels about British diplomats and their antics."

"I think you can bet that if you dig into history that there was plenty of antics," I said. "I doubt that all Brit diplomats were all totally without sin, sin is what makes us all interesting, it makes us all human with our foibles and weaknesses."

"Well, I have a weakness for you," he laughed.

"That's not a weakness," I said. "It's a strength you have, being able to recognise greatness when you see it."

"Ha," he said. "So now you're great?"

"Of course," I said. "I'll show you how great if you come to bed now."

227

Ethiopia prevails

"As I recall, Ethiopia won that one," Maman said.

"They did," I said. "It took long enough, the Somalis invaded in July 77 and they weren't completely pushed back until March 78."

"What happened to the Somali army?" Portia asked.

"The intelligence we received was that about a third of the invading army was killed and they lost about half their air force," I said. "That led to problems at home and it's a mess now that is probably going to go on for a while."

"How much help did the Russians and Cubans provide?" Maman asked.

"A lot," I said. "The reports were that there were some 15,000 Cubans in Ethiopia, with artillery, tanks and all the usual stuff that armies have. There were also Russian advisors. The biggest fight seemed to be around Harar, where some 40,000 Ethiopians, plus 11,000 Cubans and 1,500 Russians fought a pitched battle with the Somalis. The Russians used their big helicopters to move armour behind the Somali lines and the Somali defence collapsed and they were pushed back to their own border. There are still rebels who are fighting to gain control of Ogaden, but it's guerrilla war now, with hit-and-run tactics. Barre is probably living on borrowed time, there will be more from this failure in time."

"Why did the US support Somalia?" James asked.

"Probably because Russia supported Ethiopia," I said. "But Ian thought that they were also angling for bases in that part of the world to be closer to the Middle East."

"Were you really worried?" Maman asked.

"I was probably paranoid," I said. "But, if the Somalis had won in Ethiopia, then the next target would have been the northeast part of Kenya, which is mainly ethnic Somali. I know that if anything bad would have happened, that I would have been shipped out along with all the other mission dependents. How long Ian would have stayed is a matter of pure guesswork."

"So, is your shooting still good?" James asked.

"It is," I said. "I have kept up with the normal target shooting and I've become quite proficient in the combat pistol shooting."

"With all this shooting, did you have time to work?" James asked.

"Of course," I said. "I wasn't shooting all day every day, I would go out twice a week in the afternoons, so still had plenty of time for clients and their projects."

"So, when in all this did you find the time to go to Oxford and see Ian get his doctorate?" Portia asked.

"It wasn't long after the Somali invasion of Ethiopia," I replied. "Ian got the week off he had asked for and we went to Oxford, then rented a plane and went up to Scotland for a couple of days."

"A bit different to Kenya," Portia commented.

"It was," I agreed. "The flying was interesting because it was much busier than Kenya, and flying over the Irish Sea and the coastal waters of the Scottish islands was quite different. It was colder and the winds came from all over the place."

"Tell us about the trip," Portia suggested.

Ian Hartley DPhil

I went into town one day to the British Airways office and made us the bookings for the London flight, then while I was there asked them to send a telex to the Randolf Hotel in Oxford to make a booking there for a night, actually for three nights, the first two when we arrived in England and the second in our way back from Scotland. I asked for the same suite that I had booked when Ian and I first made love, and was delighted to hear back from them that it was available for both nights. I called Maman to tell her about Ian.

"Bonjour," she said, when she answered the telephone.

"Bonjour, Maman," I replied. *"Ça va?"*

"Trés bien, et tu?" she replied.

"Very well," I replied, switching into English for a while. "You remember me telling you that Ian had been notified that he's got his doctorate. What are you doing on the 13th of August?"

"I'll be in Tahiti with Maman," she said. So, Mémère Monique had got her to go to Tahiti with her. That was good.

"Is Portia going with you?" I asked.

"She is," Maman confirmed. "It will be fun; we'll visit the village where Maman was born and swim naked in the sea and frolic in the forest."

"Enjoy yourselves," I said. "Don't shock the tourists too much."

"We'll be well off the tourist path," Maman said.

"One day, I'd like to go to Tahiti," I said.

"You should," Maman said. "Perhaps when Ian gets his long leave, you'll think about it. If you do, and can stand the company, Portia and I would love to come with you. We won't get in your way, or put a damper on your activities. I'm assuming you'll want to screw Ian in any possible way while you're there?"

"Of course," I assured her. "I did last night, it was wonderful, we made love in the kitchen on the terrace, in the bath and in bed."

"Don't wear him away," Maman laughed.

"What about you and Portia?" I asked.

"She's still a tigress in bed," Maman boasted. "God, I love her. I'm so happy now."

"That's wonderful," I said. "I need to go Maman, there are things I need to do. *Je t'aime.*"

"Je t'aime," she replied.

Then I called Dad and asked him to find me a hotel on Mull or one of the other Inner Hebrides that had an airfield close by, and a plane to be picked up near Oxford. I specified the same Cessna that I had, so that I would not have to worry about being checked out on another type. Dad promised to reply by the end of the day, so I left him to it. Ian called me just before lunch and told me that his leave was set and approved. That was good, because I had already paid for the tickets. Now all we needed was to hear from Dad about a place to stay in Scotland. He called about five that afternoon.

"Fi, how are you?" he asked.

"Fine Dad, do you want to come to the award ceremony when Ian gets his doctorate?" I asked.

"When?" he asked.

"The 13th of August," I said.

"Sorry, can't do that," he said. "Felicity and I will be in California then."

"Business or pleasure?" I asked.

"Both," he said. "I've got a company I'm looking at, and while we're there we'll take a look around."

"Well, have fun," I told him.

"Okay Fi, I have a house for you, a client of mine has an estate on the island of Colonsay, and she told me that you can have the house for as long as you want, it's fully equipped and she says that the pantry, freezer and wine cellar will be well stocked and to help yourselves, apparently there is a housekeeper by the name of Kirsty who lives nearby, so you may see her," he said.

"How much?" I asked.

"Nothing," he said. "She has owed me a few favours for a while and this takes her down from five to four favours owed."

"Is there a field on Colonsay?" I asked.

"There is," he confirmed. "It's a grass strip, but you're probably used to them. Plus, there's car there at the field, apparently, she also flies in and out, so will leave the car there with the key under the right of the front bumper, car licence number ASB 615. I got you a Cessna 172, flying out of Oxford and returning there. You'll have to pay for that. Oh, and I laid on a car at Heathrow to pick you up when you arrive and take you into town to get clothes, then take you out to Oxford, my treat."

"Thanks Dad, who's the company in California?" I asked.

"It's an aerospace company, name of Torrance, believe it or not in the city of Torrance, they make mechanical bits for aircraft," he replied.

"How big?" I asked.

"Sales of about 250 million, dollars," he said. "Before tax earnings of 18 million."

"So, doing okay, but not wonderful," I commented.

"That's about it," he said. "I've looked at it a bit and concluded that with a bit of clean up and some new management that we could boost earnings."

"And cash?" I asked.

"Not too bad," he said. "Could be better, but what company couldn't. I might come to you for some analysis at some point, if I show you all the numbers you might even want to take a small share."

"I'll take a look at the numbers," I promised. "If, big if, I think they can be improved, I'll think about a position, what's the going price?"

"They've put it on the market at 200 million dollars, which I think is a little high," he replied. "That's more than ten times earnings, and the markets, although they look good in terms of dollars, if you factor out inflation, they're still not back up to the numbers of the late 60's."

"Well, let me know how things look to you," I said. "Thanks for the car and the house on Colonsay."

"Not at all," he said. "I have to go Fi, companies to buy, money to lend. Enjoy your trip to Scotland and tell Ian congratulations from me."

After he hung up, I thought about the situation and how lucky I was to have the wherewithal to be able to just buy tickets to London, rent an aeroplane while in England and not really worry about where the money was coming from. In Kenya so many people lived close to the poverty line or below, so, was I being incredibly selfish in not using the funds that I had for a better good?

When Ian came home that afternoon, I told him about the arrangements that I had made then I put my question to him about being selfish with my good fortune.

"Well, if you're really bothered by it, then set up a foundation to do good," he suggested. "You can always add to it as you want."

"That's a good idea," I said. "Any idea how I do that?"

"Not a clue," he said. "Maybe Portia can tell you how to do it."

232

"Of course," I said, kicking myself for not thinking of her. When she was active in the legal field she had to have dealt with trusts, foundations and the like, I would write to her and ask her what I needed to do. That actually was a load off my mine, I suppose I was feeling a little guilty about my good fortune, I am not sure why, it just seemed unfortunate that I had so much and so many others had so little. I was not becoming a socialist, I did not believe in just taking from those who had and giving to those who did not, that, at least to me, led to the diminution of effort and striving for a better life, after all why strive when the government will provide, at the expense of someone else. But there were times when a helping hand could be of great benefit.

"So, what do I need to take to London," Ian asked.

"Well, if we stop at the flat before going to Oxford, not much," I replied. "We know you'll have to wear a suit and you'll need the gown and hood from your undergraduate degree and the same for your doctorate."

"I can get those in Oxford," he said. "I'll send ahead and organise them, what about you?"

"I could just wear a dress," I suggested.

"Good idea," he said. "Do you have anything in mind?"

"I think the dress I wore to our wedding," I suggested.

"I like that dress, I often wondered why you didn't go for a traditional wedding dress," he said.

"I didn't want to get dressed up like a doll," I said. "What's the point of a dress that you wear once, the dress I got was much more practical, it's white, so good for the summer, the matching coat will come in handy if the weather turns cool, and it looks very elegant?"

"That it does," he agreed. "Are you sure you don't want to get dressed up in doctoral gown?"

"No, this is your day," I said. "And, besides which, I don't want to have to wear stockings or tights."

"I know, I know," he laughed. "Anything else we need for the trip?"

"When we get to the flat, we should pack a bag for Scotland," I said. "We may need a pullover and even a raincoat, but I'd put in bathing suits in case the weather is really nice."

"I suppose so," he said. "It is an island after all and there must be beaches somewhere."

The time before out trip to Oxford seemed to drag, but it did come and we packed our small bags and got Trevor to drop us at the airport.

"Dr Hartley," the British Airways lady manning the desk said. "So nice to see you again."

"There is another Dr Hartley, Jane," I said. "My husband has just been awarded his doctorate and we're off to the ceremony."

"Congratulations Sir," Jane said, playing it safe. Sir covered a multitude of possibilities and was always a safe bet. "Today, I can offer you seats two A and B or three A and B. which would you prefer?"

"I think two A and B," I replied. "Unless Ian you want three?"

"Two is fine," he said. "You do this more often than me, so you probably know the planes better and where best to sit."

"Jolly good," Jane said. "Here are your boarding cards, do you have any luggage?"

"Just these small bags," I said, holding up mine for her to see.

"Those will be fine in the cabin," she said. "Have a nice trip, I see we will see you back in about a week."

"This is just a short trip," I said. "England and back."

We walked over to the departure area and showed our diplomatic passports to the immigration agent there, the High Commission had stated that this was to be an official visit, so we could use them. Once on the plane I saw that the crew were some that I knew, so they were very chatty and wanted to know about our trip. They were not used to seeing me with someone, so I had to introduce Ian. I was able, for the first time to introduce him as Ian, Dr Ian Hartley, it sounded good! Technically Ian did not yet have his doctorate, that would only be official after the ceremony, where, from my recollection of similar ceremonies that I had participated in, there was a tense moment when the Proctor walked to the door and back to see if anyone objected to you getting your degree. I recall someone telling me that an objection had been voiced some 150 years ago, but the objection had not been on academic grounds, but the failure to clear all accounts, so money was owed. How that was resolved I never discovered. So, strictly speaking I should not be calling Ian doctor until the Vice Chancellor had made his proclamation, but that was a nicety that I was willing to risk.

Our flight to Heathrow was on time, both leaving and arriving. At Heathrow we breezed through immigration and customs and found a driver outside with a placard that said, Hartley.

"Dr Hartley?" he asked as we approached him.

"Yes," we both said in unison, and then laughed. This was new to us, both responding to the title doctor.

"My name is Gerald and I'm here to take you wherever you wish to go. Where to Sir, Madam?" he asked. I gave him the address on Cadogan Place and then we walked over to the car park and he escorted us to the car, a rather imposing black Rolls Royce. He whisked us into London in a surprisingly short time, it was a Friday, so traffic was the usual chaos of a week-day, but Gerald seemed to manage it well. At our flat, I told Gerald that we would be about half an hour as we had to pack bags for the coming week. He told us that he would go and get himself a coffee and be back to collect us. I am not sure who got their bag packed first, but it took us about twenty minutes to sort through our cupboards and pick out clothes for the ceremony and for the trip to Scotland. I had asked Dad to get some clothes out of the cupboard and see if they needed ironing. That had obviously been done, because my dress and Ian's suit were hanging in bags on the outside of the cupboard. I rather think it was not Dad who did this, but Gabriela, the live-in maid that Dad and Felicity employed. Gerald was waiting by the kerb when we went downstairs and Ian asked him to take us to the shop in Oxford where his academic gowns and hood were waiting. The drive out to Oxford was wet. It started to drizzle not long after we passed Hyde Park Corner, then it turned to actual rain. We worked our way out of London on the old A-40, past Northolt and Uxbridge until we picked up the M-40. From then on until well past Stokenchurch it was full speed ahead, or at least as fast as the rain and road conditions would permit.

"Gerald, is this forecast to continue?" I asked. If it did then the flight north would be dreary, I could do it, I could file an IFR, instrument flight rules, flight plan, but it would be much more pleasant if we could see the ground.

"No, Madame," he said. "The forecast is for sunshine throughout the country tomorrow, and the coming week."

"What time will we be in Oxford?" Ian asked.

"We'll there before noon, Sir," Gerald replied. "Not much farther, Sir."

Gerald was right, at noon, almost on the dot, we pulled up outside the shop and Ian darted in and was back out again in under five minutes, cap, gown and hood in hand, and the additional doctoral gown over his arm.

"Where to?" Gerald asked.

"The Randolf Hotel," I said.

"Very good, Madame," he said and he quickly threaded us through the streets until we arrived at the hotel. A porter came scurrying out to take our bags and Ian thanked Gerald and asked if he would be driving us back to London and Heathrow the following Saturday. Gerald, it seemed was the driver, and he understood that he was to meet us at the Randolf. That settled, we said our goodbyes and went in to register.

"Dr Barclay," one of the front desk staff, Agatha, said as we made our way to the front desk. "So nice to see you back. It has been a few years."

"It has," I agreed. "This is my husband Dr Ian Hartley." I got a real kick out of saying that, first my husband, and second Dr Ian Hartley.

"Nice to have you with us," Agatha said. "Just the two nights?"

"Just the two nights," I confirmed. "Sunday we're off to Scotland. But we will be back next Friday."

"Very good," Agatha said. "The account has already been settled, and that includes any other charges that may arise for meals, so enjoy your stay with us." She waved to the porter who came and took out bags for us to the suite.

"This place brings back memories," Ian said as he walked about the room and peered out the window at the rain.

"It does," I agreed. It had been here that we had first made love after a disaster of a college ball that had left me in tears. But it had all worked out well, and we had spent a delightful weekend.

"So, what do we have to do this afternoon?" he asked.

"I've nothing on, your ceremony is tomorrow morning, so, lunch, a nap, perhaps a walk later if the rain stops," I suggested.

"Lunch and a nap sound good," he agreed. We went downstairs to the dining room and consulted the menu for lunch.

"Do you remember when we were here before, those ladies thought that you were a French singer?" he asked.

"I remember," I said. "I've no idea why they thought so, I don't look anything like Françoise Hardy."

"So, what shall we do after lunch?" he asked.

"Nap time, and after a nap I'll see if you're worth making love to," I said.

"I'll make it worth your while," he promised, laughing.

"We'll see," I challenged. We ate our lunch, then we did actually take a nap before amorous adventures took over. That took us almost to dinner time.

"Bath time?" Ian suggested.

"I think so," I said. "But, no making love in the bath, we really do need to get dressed and go down for dinner."

"Why?" he asked. "We could get something sent up and I could eat it off you."

"As exciting as that sounds," I said, wistfully. "We won't be able to, unfortunately I invited Chris and Heather to come for dinner."

"Oh," he said. "Well, after dinner then, let's try the sofa again."

"You're on," I promised. Chris was an old friend of Ian's. They had met on the boat travelling from Cape Town to Southampton, and Chris ran the Trout Inn at Godstow, Heather had been one of his staff and they had married. Chris had been very nice to me when I went through some difficult times and I thought that Ian might like to see his old friend again.

Dinner was fun, we were able to regale Chris and Heather with our adventures and wanted to know how they were doing. Heather it seemed was expecting, so she was going to do less at the inn and focus more on the anticipated infant. Chris was delighted to know that Ian had earned his doctorate, but sadly we were not able to invite he and Heather to the ceremony, the university only provided two tickets for friends and family, so with me going there was only one left. Added to that, Chris said that they had a particularly busy weekend ahead and were sold out of rooms, and had a waiting list for lunch and dinner the following day. He had prevailed upon a friend of us to run things that night so that he and Heather could take the time off to see us. We were to bed late; Chris and Heather had stayed quite late just talking with us about our lives and theirs. When they finally left, they left in a taxi, which was wise as they had both had more than enough to drink. Ian and I had a quick bath, then we decided to forego the sofa and just make passionate love on the bed. That was something I loved about Ian, he was not only ever ready to make love with me, he was tender, considerate and caring as well, which made it all the more special.

Saturday morning, we were up, not with the birds, but early enough. We did treat ourselves to breakfast in our room, mainly so that we did not have to dress up until the last minute. The rules for the graduation required that *subfusc* be worn, which was just a very fancy way of saying that a dark suit was to be worn under the academic robes. I remember that from the various graduations I had gone to, my first two degrees and my doctorate, when I had worn a black skirt, white blouse with a black bow tie, black jacket, black shoes and worst of all black tights. Ian had a plain dark gray suit that he donned with a white shirt and white bow tie, failure to conform meant that you would not be permitted into the ceremony. The last item Ian donned was the hood he had that denoted his undergraduate degree, that and the robe would be exchanged part way through the ceremony for his much more colourful doctoral robe. Satisfied that Ian would pass muster, I quickly dressed, deciding to forego stockings or tights. I was under no proscription for dress as merely an onlooker and supporter, the final touch was the emerald earrings that I had that matched the engagement ring that Ian had given me.

"How do I look?" I asked Ian.

"Like a film star," he said. "Are those new sunglasses?"

"I got them on my last trip to Paris," I confessed. "They're Yves Saint Laurent, I think they're called, Lunetto Optique."

"Very elegant," he said. "They go with the dress, as I said, makes you look like a film star."

"Shall we go?" I asked.

"Let's," he said. I picked up the hat that I bought on my previous trip to London, it was white to match my dress and had a broad brim to keep off the sun, and we left.

Gerald had been right; the rain was gone and the sun shone gloriously. It was going to be a nice day. We made our way to the college where Ian sat through the briefing that told everyone what to expect and when, then we walked in a big procession to the Sheldonian Theatre for the ceremony. The Sheldonian is an older building, designed by Wren, and is used for ceremonies, the occasional lecture and other events. I left Ian so that he could go to the Divinity School and lay out his doctoral robes, and went and found myself a seat in the tier looking down onto the graduands. The place was filling up fast as more family and friend made their way in. Finally, the graduands streamed in and took their seats, followed by the various officials. There was the Vice Chancellor, who was to give a speech and actually confer the degrees, the Registrar who confirmed that those present had in fact earned their degrees, and the Proctor, who was a sort of disciplinarian and managed things. The ceremony went as it should and after the speech and a Latin declaration of the rights and privileges of the graduates, the various graduands were presented and Ian was among the first, because doctoral graduands came before masters and bachelors. Then they all filed out and after what seemed an interminable time, filed back in dressed in their new hoods and in the case of Ian his very colourful red and black doctoral robe. There was the actual conferring of the degrees, and then the lesser ranks filed out to salute the officials and the doctors as they left.

That was it, a ceremony that had not really changed much since the thirteenth century. I was thrilled to hear Ian's name read out and to see him make his appropriate obeisance to the officials, then heard his *do fidem* as he promised to adhere to the rights and privileges of a graduate, then shake the Vice Chancellor's hand. I recalled my own experiences of all this and the only thing that had changed was the speech. Ceremony done, we walked back to the college for a lunch and mix and mingle with the academic staff and all the graduates. Ian pointed out his thesis advisor. Professor Farnsworth, and other notables, most of whom I knew from my own days at the college.

"Have I got something on backwards?" I asked Ian.

"No, why?" he asked.

"Well, people keep staring at me," I explained.

"I'm not surprised," he said. "Look around, you've got parents of new graduates, and they must all be well into their forties, you've got the women graduates, who for the most part are in their twenties and all dressed up in *subfusc* and black, and there you are, dressed up in white looking like a film star in your hat and sunglasses. They're probably wondering who you are, the women are probably pricing out your outfit and jewels and are coming up with big numbers, that has them curious, and the men and simply looking at you with lust in their hearts. Here comes Farnsworth."

"Dr Hartley," he said, as he came up to us. "Congratulations Ian, well deserved."

"Thank you," Ian said. "I don't think you've met my wife, Fiona, this is Harold Farnsworth, Harold, this is Fiona."

"Nice to meet you Mrs Hartley, you're causing quite a stir here," he said.

"I am?" I said. "I can't see why, it's the graduates who are the important ones today, I remember my own graduations and how I was so pleased that they had finally come."

"Where did you graduate?" Farnsworth asked.

"From here," I replied. "I did my undergraduate and first doctorate here."

"Wait a minute," Farnsworth said. "You're not Fiona Barclay?"

"I am," I confessed.

"We were sorry to lose you to the business world," Farnsworth said. "The Master would love to have you back, but I suppose that's not possible as long as you're living in Nairobi. Is there any chance that you would come back?"

"As you said, as long as we're in Nairobi that would be difficult," I said. "I do do some teaching at the Nairobi University and at Imperial, mainly to get easy access to computer time."

"Come and meet my wife," he said. He led across the lawn to a group of women.

"Charlotte," he said to one of them. "This is one of my graduates, Dr Ian Hartley, and his wife, Fiona, also Dr Hartley."

"So nice to meet you both," she said. "We were just wondering; whose design is the dress?"

"It's a Rachel Adams," I said.

"It's so elegant," Charlotte said.

"I like it," I said. "Rachel did it for me a couple of years ago."

"You know Rachel Adams?" Charlotte asked.

"I do," I confirmed. "I've done some economic models for her."

"Oh, so you're an economist?" Charlotte asked.

"Well, my first doctorate was actually in mathematics, but then I focused more on economics," I explained.

"She also got a doctorate in economics from LSE and lately another in computer science from Imperial," Ian added. "It keeps her busy while I attend to consular affairs at our High Commission in Nairobi."

"Oh, so you're in the diplomatic service?" Charlotte asked.

"I am," Ian confirmed.

"But then how did you get your doctorate in anthropology?" Charlotte asked.

"I was an external student and we were fortunate to make a discovery near Lake Turkana," Ian explained.

"It was a truly important discovery," Harold interjected. "Quite changed some thinking. I'm still amazed that you found what you did."

"We were pointed in the right direction by one of the Kenya National Parks people who had seen something," Ian explained. "All Fiona and I did was dig up the bones."

"Yes, but the subsequent analysis of femoral lengths was quite inspired," Harold said.

"I had help there from Fiona," Ian said. "She helped me with all the statistics and mathematics."

"Here comes the Master," Charlotte said. "Master, you're coming to join us?"

"I am," he said. "Congratulations Dr Hartley and it is so nice to see you again Dr Barclay."

"It's Dr Hartley now," Harold interjected. "She and Ian are married."

"Oh, so you're now also a denizen of Nairobi," the Master said. "So, I suppose no chance of getting you back here?"

"Not while we live there," I said.

"But she does some teaching at Imperial," Harold said. "So, perhaps we could get her as a visiting professor."

"That would be splendid," the Master said. "I understand that you've been doing great things for the Chancellor."

"I'm not sure everyone would regard it as great," I commented. "It has a lot to do with tax policy and revenue streams."

"Still, better for one of ours to do it than Hopkins," the Master said. "If Harold has your address, expect to hear from me, must dash, more people to see, more hands to shake, enjoy the lunch."

We mixed, we mingled, we chatted and we ate lunch, all very civilised and very far from digging in the dirt by Lake Turkana. Each had its own attraction, but I think on balance I preferred Lake Turkana. When we finally got back to the Randolf I was quite glad to take off my shoes and just relax, no more small talk and no more being polite to people. Ian had managed well, and had even been gracious to Professor Emeritus Ambrose, the man who had thrown a spanner in the works when Ian had first written up his thesis, and who then had had the temerity to steal Ian's work and publish it as his own. The Lake Turkana find eclipsed anything Ambrose had done, so Ian could afford to be magnanimous. We had a late dinner and then bathed and went to bed, tired from the day, but not too tired to make love a couple of times. It was a perfect end to the day.

Sunday morning, we were up early and I went down to the front desk and asked if we could leave a bag in their care for the week. They were happy to oblige, so we packed our finery and left it with them. I checked the weather and it was still good for the next two days, then rain was forecast for Scotland, but sunshine was supposed to come again later in the week. We had breakfast then took a taxi to the Oxford airport and found the fixed base operator where we would get our plane. I went in and showed them my licence and log book, then went out with one of the people to check out the plane. I did a walk around and was satisfied that it was in good condition, so went back in and paid for the hire. We fuelled the plane and filed our flight plan, then loaded our bags. We had little enough, so weight was not an issue. Our flight would be first to Prestwick, which is on the west coast of Scotland, a little south of Glasgow. There I planned to take on more fuel to get us to Colonsay and back to Oxford. It was about two hours to Prestwick, so about 17 gallons of fuel, then another 45 minutes to Colonsay, about another 6.5 gallons, so, even with the long-range tanks, that gave one 54 gallons, not enough to go there and back and still have a 45-minute margin of safety. I went through with Ian the safety procedures, and because we would be flying over quite a bit of water made sure that we knew where the life jackets were. Once in the air, we droned along, past Birmingham, then Stafford then Blackpool and out over Morecambe Bay, skirting along the Cumberland coast to St. Bees Head then out over the Solway and across Kirkcudbright and on into Prestwick. Ian had the better view of the Lakes as we skirted the coast and used my camera to get some pictures. We stopped long enough at Prestwick to go to the loo and fill our tanks, then we took off again over the Firth of Clyde, the isle of Arran and then the Mull of Kintyre, starting our descent over Jura and on into Colonsay just before noon. On the ground we tied down the plane, and because we were on a Scottish island exposed to the Atlantic, I secured a baffle along the top of the wing, then we found the car, an older Land Rover that had seen better days, but it started and the petrol tank was full. Even though we had been assured that all supplies were on the house, we found our way to a shop so that when it opened we would know where we could stock up with essentials, and discovered that there was also a petrol pump there, so that we could fill up when we left.

We drove to the house, following the map and instructions left under the passenger seat of the Land Rover. The island is not that big but it took us a little while to navigate the twists and turns that the road took. We finally came to the house, if that was a good word for it, for it was not a house, it was a stone castle, a solid looking square building along the lines of Castle Stalker in Appin, only a little taller and with some outbuildings and all surrounded on three sides by a ditch and a large stone wall, the fourth side being the cliffs, that dropped a good hundred feet to the sea. We drove across a bridge over the ditch, that I saw to my delight was actually a drawbridge, and through a gate in the wall and parked by what looked like a garage. The castle was to the north of the island on the east coast, so sheltered from the worst of the Atlantic storms, but I imagined it could still get cold in the winter. The housekeeper, Kirsty, appeared and introduced herself and told us to call upon her if we needed anything, she said that she would be away for the rest of the afternoon visiting her friend who lived near the shop that we had found earlier. Kirsty was in her late thirties and she seemed to me to be a most efficient kind of person and someone good to have looking after a property that was often empty.

Ian and I dropped our bags in a room that looked like a guest room and decided to go out and explore a little. Not far from the castle was a beach, that must have stretched for about a quarter of a mile, there was no one on the beach, and even above the high-water mark, the only footprints were old. It was warm enough that I decided that a swim was in order. There were no people about, so just stripped off and waded into the sea. Ian came in soon after me and we actually swam for a little. I was floating when a face popped up near me, I nearly died of fright, but realised that it was a seal. He, or she, looked at me and I looked back, then he dove beneath the waves and was gone. Ian came over to me and pointed.

"Look," he said. "There's a whole group of them over there."

"What kind of seals are they?" I asked.

"Common, or harbour, seal," he said. "Apparently you can also see whales and other marine mammals here, and judging back the tracks I saw when we came down to the beach, even otters."

"I'm ready to go in now," I said. "Are you coming?"

"Race you there," he challenged. I swan as best I could, but could not beat him. There are times when sheer masculine strength just outweighs skill and technique. It was not far to the castle, so we slipped on shoes and just ran back carrying our clothes, goodness knows what the neighbours would have thought, if there had been neighbours. Once in the castle we found towels and dried ourselves off and went exploring in the castle.

"A sheepskin rug," I noted, pointing it out to Ian. "I've always wondered what it would be like to make love on a sheepskin rug."

"We should find out," he said. I went to him and slipped my arms around him and kissed him.

"You're all salty," I noted. "Does that make you a salty dog?"

"Maybe," he said. He picked me up and then laid me down on the rug which was soft and luxurious. He kissed me and then started down my body with his kisses. "You're salty too," he said. "But, not as much as when we were in Lake Turkana."

He moved further down and spread my legs and buried his face between them. God, I loved that. I let him just do what he liked and lay there enjoying every minute of it. I could feel myself getting close to a climax and started to move my hips in time with his ministrations. When it finally came, I thrust myself up into his face and revelled in the waves of sensation that seemed to come from my toes all the way up my body. He then moved and lay on top of me and we helped him in and he started to thrust slowly in and out. I hooked my legs around his back and welcomed every thrust. He moved slowly, then more rapidly, then slowly again, at times with just short movements, at times with longer movements when he almost withdrew, in fact once or twice he did, but was always able to come back in with no help from me.

"That's so good," I breathed. "I love you Ian Hartley."

"I love you Fiona," he replied. "I love you, I love your body, I love making love with you."

"I know," I said contentedly. "Now, I'm in the mood for love, I'm in the mood for a good shag, so, shag me Dr Hartley, shag me on this shaggy rug."

"Taking dirty again," he laughed. "Well, I can but oblige."

"Kiss me," I commanded. He did and we kissed and moved with each other until we both climaxed dramatically.

"God, that was good," he said, panting a little.

"It was, it was," I agreed. "I wonder, did the woolliness of the sheepskin rug make any difference?"

"Probably made things more primitive," he suggested.

"Well, my primitive man, we'll have to do that again," I said. "But, now, I'm starving, we've had nothing to eat since breakfast time. You know, you've studied *homo habilis*, *homo sapiens*, *homo erectus*, but I think the one I like best is *erectus*, *habilis* may be useful with his hands, which is nice in itself, *sapiens* may know what to do, but *erectus* can actually get it done."

"I never really thought about anthropology in those terms," he laughed. "Maybe I should write a paper for *Man* about it. Anyway, let's go and find something to eat."

We ate and drank, then took another walk along the beach, but this time did not go in the water. My seal friend looked as if he had taken up residence on the rocks at the south end of the beach and he had friends. I wondered about the makeup of seal colonies, how many males, how many females and were they all amicable until mating season. Ian admitted that he knew little about seals, I suppose that was reasonable, how many seal colonies are there in landlocked Rhodesia. There were birds by the hundred and Ian was able to identify most of them, but for some he had to consult a book he had brought with him. I would have to keep an eye on him, it seemed he was not above smuggling things aboard the plane, on this trip weight was not an issue, but there could be times when I needed to know exactly what we had aboard. The day stayed light well into the late hours, sunset did not come until nine that night, so we were out until late. The castle had been well equipped and the bedroom we had picked boasted a large bath with claw feet and, most useful of all, a hot water system that seemed to be endless. Still, with two people in the bath we actually did not need that much water.

We actually made it through bathing without descending into lust and, instead, made up for it in bed.

Monday morning, not too bright and early, we heard someone in the kitchen and could smell coffee. We dressed and went downstairs and found Kirsty preparing breakfast.

"Good morning Kirsty, you didn't have to do that," I told her.

"Nae bother," she said. "Did you enjoy your swim yesterday?"

"I did," I said, a little alarmed by the notion that she had seen us running around bare as babes, but decided to play along with her matter of fact manner. "But I did get a scare when the seal popped his head up to look at me."

"Aye," she said. "They'll do that. What's your plan for the day?"

"I thought we'd go to the south and watch the birds," Ian said.

"Well, there's plenty of them," she commented.

"I left my book upstairs," Ian said. "I'll just go up and grab it."

"You have a good man there," Kirsty said after Ian had left. "So nice to see people enjoying themselves and each other."

"He is nice," I agreed. "I'm sorry if we offended you yesterday."

"Don't be sorry, I tak no offence for that which is natural, many is the day when I was younger I would tak a dip in the sea wi' nae clothes, and the mistress here often goes about the house naked as a new bairn," Kirsty said. "If I had a body like yours I would want to bare it to the man I loved, and he's rather good to look at, and well-endowed too, don't let too many of the women on this island see him as I saw him, they would be beating down your door."

"He's taken," I said smugly.

"But, don't go doing that near the village," Kirsty warned. "There are those who are strait laced as ministers. If you're wanting the place to go outdoors, then take the field over there, follow the wall to the north and then follow the corrie down to the shore, there's a secluded beach there and no one to see, on the way there, look out for twitchers, there might be some around."

"Thank you," I said, not really sure what I was thankful for, the advice on where to go to make love in the open, or the fact that Kirsty was too old to be of interest to Ian.

"Would you be wanting some lunch to tak wi' ye?" she asked.

"That would be nice," I replied.

"Go and get your things and you can be off," she suggested. "I'll have a lunch basket for you when you come down."

As we drove south to look at the sea cliffs and the birds, I recounted my conversation with Kirsty to Ian and he laughed.

"Just as well she's broad minded," he said. "But we can't have been the first to have discovered that beach."

"Probably not," I agreed. "But I doubt that too many other visitors go running about dressed only in shoes."

"It's just as well that this island has a very small population," he said. "Not many people to see us *au naturel.*"

"So, birds, what do you expect to see today?" I asked.

"Mainly sea birds I think," he said. "So, petrels, shearwaters, divers, skuas, puffins, ducks of one type or another, geese and then some land birds."

"Have you seen them all before?" I asked.

"No," he said. "I've never been this far north before, so this is all new."

"I suppose no sea birds in Rhodesia," I commented.

"Only the occasional vagrant who got lost or blown in from the Mozambique Channel and landed up too far inland," he replied.

"How much farther?" I asked.

"Must be just about there," he said. "Just look at all those birds."

"So, what do you see?" I asked.

"Fulmars, kittiwakes, shearwaters, over there in the water, divers, up there on the cliff, puffins and auks, I've never seen so many birds in one place at one time," he said. "I wonder what it's like when all the deep ocean birds come in, must be noisy."

We watched birds, ate our lunch, watched more birds then went to the shop to see what they had. They had all the basics, plus a generous assortment of Scotch Whiskeys. Ian got himself a Scotch from a local, or nearly local, distillery and we made our way back to the castle. We had just arrived and the telephone rang. Kirsty answered it and then came to find us.

"I'm sorry if this ruins your holiday," she said. "But the mistress is back and asking if you will go to the airfield to collect her."

"How will we know who to collect?" I asked.

"She'll be the only one there," Kirsty assured us. "And, she'll know her own car."

We drove back the way we had come and went to the airfield. A woman was standing talking to a couple of other women and she looked familiar. She turned as we drove up.

"It's that woman from the plane," I told Ian. "Freya McIntosh."

"Fiona," Freya said as we got out of the Land Rover. "I didn't know it was you who would be coming, William didn't tell me who, just two flying up from Oxford."

"It's nice to see you again, Mrs McIntosh," I said. "This is my husband, Ian."

"You'd better keep him on a tight rein," she said, looking him up and down. "There's many a woman here would be looking for a roll in the hay with him. Marie, Elspeth, I will see you soon." That was her dismissal of the two she had been talking to, apparently, we did not warrant an introduction, or she just forgot. Ian took her bags and stowed them in the back of the Land Rover, I climbed into the back seat and he held the door for her. She thanked him graciously, climbed in, and we were off.

"So sorry to intrude on your visit," she said. "I just had a row with my publisher, so had felt the need to come home, get drunk, mope about the house and generally feel sorry for myself. But, perhaps between us we can liven things up a little, and, please, it's Freya, there never was a Mrs McIntosh, except my mother, I go by Freya McIntosh, I never took my husband's name."

"How were your researches in Kenya?" I asked.

"Very successful," she said. "Loved the place, even thinking of buying something."

"If we can help, please let us know," Ian said. "I'm with the British High Commission in Nairobi and may be able to point you in the right direction for whatever it is you want."

"I may do that," she said. "So, let's hope Kirsty has done something for dinner, I'm getting hungry."

At the castle Ian carried Freya's bags in for her and she directed him to her bedroom, which was the rather grand one we had taken a quick look at when we had first arrived, and had decided that it was the master bedroom and not for us. I went to the kitchen and told Kirsty that I had met Freya before, on the plane to Nairobi.

"Aye, she does flit about," Kirsty said. "Shall I bring you a drink on the main room?"

"Thank you," I said. "If there is a chardonnay, that would be super."

"And, for your man?" she asked.

"I think a Scotch, one of the smaller distilleries if you have it," I replied.

I went to the main room, the place where we had made love on the sheepskin rug by the fireplace and Freya came in dressed in a mini kilted skirt and black sweater.

"It's good to get out of those business clothes," Freya said. "It's good to shed a few things, clothes, worries, annoying editors."

"Is this an old castle?" I asked.

"Not really," she said. "My grandfather made a huge fortune in South Africa burrowing for gold and diamonds and he came back and wanted to buy a castle. No one would sell, so he made a deal with the laird who essentially owned the island to buy this piece of land and he built this, it meant that unlike the older buildings, he could install everything needed for running water, electricity, and telephone. He brought everything in by boat, the steel, the stone, the concrete, everything. My father then made improvements with the windows and the electrical system. We have water cisterns in the cellar and in the garage building outside we have a large generator and fuel tanks for about a year. We have storage for food and supplies for a few months, in case the gales are too bad and the ferry from Oban cannot get here."

"Do you get many visitors?" I asked.

"No, you are the first I've had," she said. "I value my privacy. When I was married, we spent nearly all of our time in London, he never actually came here, so it has been my sanctuary where I can wander around as I see fit, I keep the heat up, even in the winter, so even if there's snow outside, I can look at it and wonder what it feels like against my skin. The villagers don't come out here, I think they think I'm a witch, which I suppose to them I am, I'm not an adherent of the Christian faith, but tend more towards the ancient beliefs that held to the earth goddesses."

"If you'd rather we left, we'd be happy to try one of the B&B's in the village," I offered.

"No," she said. "I'd far rather you stayed, I like you and I really rather fancy that man of yours, don't worry, unlike my ex, I don't go chasing after someone else's spouse. It will be fun, and you can tell me all about William and what I can use against him when next we negotiate a deal."

"You've had business with him, I gather," I said.

"We've bought a few companies together," she said. "We're up to eight now and the money is pouring in, only to be taken by the bloody tax man, we can't get a new government quickly enough. Ah, Kirsty, a Scotch, thank you, what are we eating tonight?"

"Venison," Kirsty said. "It will be ready in about fifteen minutes, does that suit?"

"That suits well," Freya said. "So, Fiona, I'm sorry I talked your head off when we first met on the plane, I was annoyed and just needed someone to vent to."

"That's quite all right," I said sheepishly. "I admit I was terrified of you."

"Well, I will make amends," she promised. "Is that man of yours coming down soon?" She had no sooner asked when Ian came into the room.

"Freya, we don't want to intrude in you and your privacy, if it's more convenient we would be happy to take a B&B in the village," he said.

"I was just telling Fiona that no, I don't want you to go, I rather like the idea of you being here," she replied. "Ah, here's Kirsty with dinner."

Kirsty joined us and we dined on venison, we talked, we drank wine, and we thoroughly enjoyed ourselves. We got Freya's life history and learned that she too had been educated at Oxford a few years before either Ian or I were there, Freya had read classics and had decided early on to be a novelist, and particularly romance novels, something she noted that was very *à propos,* as Freya was the goddess of love. Her parents had died in a car crash on the mainland some ten years earlier. She had met and married her husband some five years earlier, and they had spent their time between London and Paris. The marriage ended when his lover's husband had come across them and killed them both. The cuckolded husband got off scot free under the *crime passionnel* laws of France. We also had a long discussion about books and what could be classed as literature as opposed to books for the masses. Freya wrote for the masses, as she said, there was just more money in it and the romance novels she wrote were all formula based, boy meets girl, one of who should have money, boy behaves badly but is eventually tamed, brought to heel or convinced to be a better person by the girl, everyone lives happily ever after. The only thing that really changed was the era and the place. Kenya was the start of a whole new series set in different parts of the world. When Ian and I went to bed that night we found one of Freya's books and read the parts that pertained to the bedroom and then reenacted them. It was fun, but the language was all a little too flowery for me, but I suppose it avoided using baser language that might offend the sensibilities.

In the morning the weather changed, gone was the sunshine, replaced with howling winds and driving rain. I looked out of the window and watch the rain streak by. Farther out I could see the sea and the waves were up and crashing onto the rocks by the beach we had been to. Not a day for outdoor excursions. Ian was already up and gone, so I dressed and went downstairs to the kitchen. He was not there, but Freya and Kirsty were chatting away in what I presumed must be Gaelic. When I came in, they switched to English.

"Good morning Fiona," Freya said. "Tea, coffee, whiskey?"

"Tea would be super, thanks," I said. "Have you seen Ian?"

"He's in the basement looking over our water cisterns and treatment plant," she replied. "Not the nicest of days."

"Indeed," I agreed. "Perhaps the day to stay in and read a book."

"I have some business to do, but perhaps first some breakfast, then a quick tour of the castle, then I'll leave you to your own devices for a while," she suggested. We breakfasted on porridge, bacon, eggs, tomatoes, mushroom and toast. I felt that I would need to eat again until the next day. Freya then took us on a tour of the castle, starting at the roof that had been designed to catch all the rain that fell on it. The we came down to the top floor, two bedrooms, then the next floor, the master bedroom plus what was obviously Freya's office, then down to the large living, dining, whatever room, then down to the kitchen, pantry, scullery, the down again to the cisterns and other storage. Freya told us that the design was such that each floor could be opened up to one large room if necessary. The construction had used a lot of large steel beams to support the outer walls and the next level up. Modern, or more modern, building materials had allowed a construction that would not have been possible when many of the older castles in Scotland had been built. The last part of the tour was to the outbuildings, that included a garage with two Land Rovers, a couple of motorbikes, a tractor, and next to it the generator room with two huge Caterpillar generating sets and beyond them the fuel tanks. After the tour we left Freya to her writing and went and sat in the main room, looking out at the sea. Kirsty brought coffee and sat and chatted to us. She had been in the employ of Freya since leaving art school, and it was she who provided the often lurid illustrations for the books. She laughed about that and said that it paid well, and in her own time she painted oils of the island, the birds, flowers, seals, anything in the natural world.

Lunch we ate at about one, all trooping down to the kitchen and finding something that suited us. Kirsty asked if we minded if she sketched us, I think with future book covers in mind. We agreed, but with the proviso that if she used our likenesses on a cover, they be modified enough to disguise who we actually were. I was surprised at how quickly Kirsty did her sketches and how good they were, she really was a talented artist. She then asked Ian if he minded if she did some life sketches of him. I am not sure that he knew what she meant at first, but she explained and he looked at me for guidance. I nodded yes, so he disrobed and stood where Kirsty indicated while she sketched away. She had him do about a dozen different poses and produced sketches that Leonardo de Vinci would have been proud of. Freya's turn was next, it was apparent that this was not the first time they had done this as she just dropped the robe she had been wearing and took up whatever pose Kirsty asked for. Freya had the most amazing musculature I had seen in a long time, she was tall and lean and all her muscles were well defined, not in the sense of body builders who look to accentuate the structure, but just very well defined, so that as she moved you could see the muscles take a new shape. I could see that in time it would be my turn and looked to Ian. He whispered to me that I should go ahead, he would ask for one of the sketches when we were done. My turn came and I followed instructions as Ian had and sat, stood, knelt, lay on the floor and generally exposed myself to the world, or at least the three others in the room. After that marathon session, Freya suggested a drink and Kirsty scuttled off and came back with couple of bottles of wine. They were from the winery that Charlize and James ran, so I knew them well.

"You look after yourselves well," Kirsty said. "I like the body structure you both have, which sketch would you like for yourselves?" Ian and I looked through them and picked out one of each, mine of Ian was a three-quarter frontal view that I could just see hanging in the bedroom. Not to be outdone, Ian selected a similar one of me, grinning like a Cheshire cat as he did so. I thought afterwards that it might be prudent to leave these sketches in our London flat, taking them back to Kenya might create some problems.

"You should visit Kirsty's studio at some time," Freya said. "She has the whole upper floor of the garage, so has her own flat there as well as the studio."

"You should also show them the armoury," Kirsty suggested.

"I should," Freya agreed. "Come, we'll take a look." We followed her downstairs to where the water cisterns were and in one corner was a steel cupboard. She opened the door and lifted a flap at the back and inserted a key and the whole back of the cupboard slid out of the way revealing a large room replete with gun racks and cabinets.

"Wow, I could have used this lot in Rhodesia," Ian said. "You've got everything here, are you worried about an invasion?"

"My grandfather started it," Freya explained. "He collected all kinds of guns, then my Dad added more after the War, and then he happened upon a shipment that we think was destined for Northern Ireland and he grabbed it. I don't think anyone ever worked out where it had gone, all they ever found was the wreckage of the boat. Do either of you shoot?"

"We both do," Ian said. "Fiona's pretty good, beats me at times and lately she's taken up combat pistol shooting."

"Does anyone have any idea what you have here?" I asked.

"No," she said. "I have a shotgun upstairs that is registered, but this lot, I'd probably have a lot of explaining to do. I'm trusting that this will remain between us?"

"It will, it will," Ian assured her. "This room would be hard to find."

"Grandad put it here on purpose," she said. "The concrete I think is three feet thick all around and the door is six inches of steel, there is a separate power supply for the room and there is even a bolt hole to a spot well away from here."

"You don't think anyone will find the other end of the bolt hole?" I asked.

"No," Freya said. "It's well hidden and even if you stumble upon the entrance there is a cunning door that looks like a rock face."

"How did he get it built without people remembering where it was?" I asked.

"I'm not sure," she said. "But I got the impression that he brought miners in from South Africa to do the work, then sent them back home. There was enough construction going on at the time with the castle and the wall, that no one apparently noticed this. Dad added the mechanism for the door and the separate power, water and air supplies. Okay, so while we're wandering about, Kirsty, would you show us your studio, the rain has slackened a little, so we won't get soaked?"

We toured Kirsty's studio and saw new book covers in work as well as her own paintings. As one who never exhibited much in the way of artistic talent, I was rather awed by it all. Tours over we went back to the main part of the castle and Kirsty promised us dinner. That night it was salmon, which was terrific. I was never sure whether Kirsty just had a talent for cooking or if she had taken classes. After dinner we talked about Kenya and what was happening there and in the surrounding countries. I think both Freya and Kirsty were a little surprised as to the amount of bellicosity that some of the neighbours were showing. Ian assured them that we would be safe, no matter what happened. Just before we all retired for the night, Freya looked out the window and announced, "The rain has stopped, looks like tomorrow will be a nice day"

She was right, when we got up in the morning the sun was shining again and the wind had dropped to almost calm.

"Who's for a swim?" Freya asked as we went into the kitchen.

"I'll go," I said. "Ian?"

"Count me in," he added. We all went down to the beach and Freya just shed her clothes and waded out. I quickly saw why she was in such good shape, she could swim like a fish, she had a wonderful style and seemed to effortless slip through the water. Well, if she could swim without clothes, so could I, so I stripped off my clothes and went out into the water. It was not as warm as it had been when we first arrived, the day had just dawned, so there had been no time for the sun to heat the water even a little. Ian came in after me, then Kirsty. We all swam seriously for about thirty minutes then breakfast called. I noted that the others did what Ian and I had done on our first day there, they just slipped on their shoes and trotted back to the castle. We followed and ran up the stairs to our room, to have a quick shower and then get dressed. Breakfast was scrambled eggs with toast, followed by a fruit medley that seemed to contain just about every type of fruit I could think of.

"Let me take you for a tour of the island," Freya offered. "It usually doesn't take that long, but we'll take our time and see what's out there today, then we'll stop in Scalasaig and see if the ferry brought what I want. We'll take lunch with us. Kirsty, are you coming?"

"Not today," she said. "I've got some good ideas for the new cover and I'd like to get them down on paper and canvas."

Freya took us for an extended guided tour of the island, down each lane, around each corner and into every nook and cranny. She knew each resident and could tell us their life story. She told about the sheep, the fresh water lochs, the historical monuments and areas, the history of the island, going back some 7,000 years, with intermittent habitation during the Neolithic, Bronze and Iron ages, then more recently with Viking raids, and finally Christianity, which led to the priory on Oronsay, the small island immediately to the south of Colonsay and often accessible by ford at low tide. Ian was fascinated by the early settlers and let it slip that he had just been awarded his doctorate and his subject was anthropology.

"I knew I was right to insist that you stay," she said. "Tell me what you know about the Neolithic age?"

While Freya and Ian talked about the Neolithics, I gazed out at the countryside that was Colonsay. It was grazing lands, heather and gorse covered hills, coppices of trees, surprising to me that they were still all essentially vertical, I would have thought that they would have all taken on a permanent list in the wind. There were occasional houses, barns and other buildings scattered about, and everything was neatly divided up, parcelled out and contained by miles and miles of drystone walls. For an island so small, there was a surprising amount of fresh water evident, in Loch Fada, Loch an Sgoltaire and Loch Cholla, plus a few other lesser bodies of water. There was even a golf course, but I doubt it came up to the standards of the Royal and Ancient in St. Andrews. The roads were for the most part single lane roads with passing places, but the traffic as light and there was nowhere to rush to, so waiting for a car coming the other way, which we did a few times, was not a huge inconvenience. The hills were unremarkable, rising to 456 ft at the highest point, which was not in the centre of the island, but on the cliffs of the west coast. The harbour and pier were located on what must be the generally leeward side of the island, facing Jura, and serviced by a MacBrayne's ferry from Oban, some two and a half hours away. Freya picked up the package she had been expecting and loaded it in the back of the Land Rover. What was noticeable was the quiet, there was no background traffic noise, no aircraft overhead. There were birds, in places so plentiful that they created a racket, but away from the coast, it was quiet, just sheep, birds of the meadow and the occasional car, but in the background the distant roar of the surf and the pounding of the waves on the cliffs and shore. I came back to reality when I realised that Ian had asked me a question.

"Sorry," I said. "I was day dreaming, what was that?"

"We were wondering where we should have lunch," he said. "Any ideas?"

"What about on a hill overlooking the sea towards Jura?" I suggested.

"I have the perfect place," Freya said. She stopped the car, turned around and we went haring off towards the south. Soon she turned off the main road and we took the road that led to Oronsay, just before the coast, she turned left and crossed a field and we climbed up a hill. Near the top we stopped and had to walk the rest of the way, but when we breasted the summit, there was Jura in the distance.

"This is Beinn Eibhne," she announced. "Over there is Oronsay, over there, Jura, and over there behind that hill is Scalasaig."

"Perfect," I said, and it was perfect. The weather was cooperating, there was a breeze, but not a howling gale and the skies were absolutely clear, the perfect place for a picnic lunch.

When we got back to the castle late that afternoon, Kirsty was waiting and it was clear that she had something to tell us.

"You may wish to change your plans," she said. "There is a storm coming that will hit tomorrow afternoon late and stay with us for the next four or five days."

"How bad?" I asked.

"Winds force eight to nine," she said. That did not sound good, winds of up to 47 knots were flyable, but why do it, particularly as there was likely to also be rain?

"Ian, is it okay if we leave tomorrow morning?" I asked.

"You're the pilot," he said. "What do you think?"

"Why fly in bad weather unless you absolutely have to, and it's only day earlier than we were going to leave anyway?" I said. "So sorry to leave you Freya, but it would be better if we did leave tomorrow morning early."

"Let me call Gerald and see if he can pick us up at Oxford, if we leave tomorrow early, when will we be in Oxford, Fi?" he asked.

"If we leave at eight, then ten thirty or so," I thought.

"Freya, is it all right if I use the phone?" he asked.

"Of course," she said. Ian left and went into the hall where the telephone was and came back after a few minutes.

"Gerald is set to pick us up at the Oxford airport when we get in and he'll take us straight to London, and then pick us up again when we need to go to Heathrow," he said. "I also called the Randolf and cancelled the one night we were going to stay there."

"I'll run you down to the airfield tomorrow morning," Freya promised.

"May we come back at some other time?" I asked Freya.

"I am expecting you," she said. "You must come back at any time you like and for as long as you like, just call and tell us whether you're flying in or coming on the ferry and we'll pick you up."

"Thank you," I said. I think that Freya really meant what she said, and that we would be welcome back.

Our flight back to Oxford the next day was pleasant enough, but as we flew over the Firth of Clyde and the Irish Sea, we could see clouds building to the west and could feel the wind picking up a little. Going straight back meant that we flew over quite a bit of the Irish Sea and I checked on the map for all the available landing fields close by in case there was any issue. I was happy to see Liverpool and know that our over water adventure was at an end. From there on it was dry land. When we landed at Oxford, Gerald was waiting and he whisked us into Oxford to collect our clothes from the Randolf, then he drove us into town to our flat. We made arrangements to be picked up on Saturday in time to get the flight back to Nairobi. I had enjoyed Colonsay, but I think the next time we went we would use the ferry, so that we were less likely to be affected by the weather. Of course, there might be times when even MacBrayne's did not run, but I saw that as rare.

"So, we have a day and a half to kill," I said to Ian. "What would you like to do?"

"Do you have to ask?" he said grinning from ear to ear.

"Apart from that," I laughed.

"You know," he said. "I've never been to the Science Museum; shall we do that tomorrow?"

"Good idea," I agreed. "What about this afternoon?"

"Lunch," he suggested. "Then we'll see."

We lunched, we walked, we talked, we held hands, we giggled like teenagers, we laughed at each other's poor jokes and finally went back to the flat to a bath and the pleasures of the bedroom. The next day, we walked to the Science Museum, I was surprised that Ian had never been. He told me that he had spent a lot of time at the British Museum, but that was in quite a different part of London. We lunched across the street in the Victoria and Albert Museum, a place I knew well and where I had met Charlize for lunch more than once. We also took a quick look at the Natural History Museum and the Geological Museum. None of this involved any great trekking as they were all essentially in the same area, on the corner of Cromwell Road and Exhibition Road. While we were out, I bought a cardboard tube long enough for our life studies and when we went back to the flat stored them away on top of the wardrobe. In time I would frame them and hang them somewhere in the flat. Our last night in London before going home we treated ourselves and went out to a fancy restaurant. It cost me a little, but it was worth it. It had been a week full of interest, excitement and new experiences, something to be remembered.

Two doctors

"I would have liked to have gone to Ian's graduation ceremony," Maman said. "But we were off in Tahiti. Nice to have another doctor in the family."

"It was interesting to sit in the audience for a change," I said. "I was so thrilled when Ian's name was called, he really deserved his degree and I think the college was delighted that he had been published in all the journals."

"Are you going to take up Freya's offer?" Portia asked.

"I may," I said. "I'll finish up in London, spend some time with you on the Riviera, then a week or so with Charlize and James, then I might just go and visit Colonsay again. I liked it there, it was quiet and Freya's castle is well off the beaten track."

"Don't become too much of a hermit," Maman cautioned.

"I won't," I promised.

"What did you do with the life sketches?" Maman asked. "I don't recall seeing them in your flat."

"They're still in the cardboard tube on top of the wardrobe," I confessed. "I haven't framed them yet; I might do it now and hang them."

"Have you read any of Freya's books?" Maman asked.

"Only the one that Ian and I read and re-enacted," I said. "I know the genre sells well, but not really my style. Freya told me that she writes them because they sell well and it's a hedge in case her other investments don't perform as well as she would like."

"Are she and Kirsty in a relationship?" Portia asked.

"Don't really know," I said. "They're close, but I'm sure if they're that close. They work well together and both seem content enough."

"Does Freya write anything other than romance novels?" Portia asked.

"She does," I said. "She uses another name, Edwina Campbell, and writes quite serious historical novels."

"I read a couple of those," James said. "They're really good, so Edwina Campbell is Mary Stuart is Freya McIntosh, who'd have thought it."

"Freya told me that whereas she can churn out the bodice rippers quite quickly, her historical novels take a year or two because of the research she does," I added. "I asked her if it was difficult to write two quite different genres and she told me that there were times when she found herself drifting between one and the other, but she said that she does have good editors, one for each and they help her to stay on track."

"That must be hard," Maman commented. "Almost like having two very different personalities, you're sure she's safe, not a little schizophrenic?"

"Seemed very sane to me," I assured her.

"And Kirsty?' Portia asked.

"Feet very firmly on the ground," I replied. "She does the covers for Freya because it pays well, but her other stuff is getting better known now and she commands high prices for her work at galleries."

"So, what was the next big event in your time here?" Charlize asked. "Apart from safaris and early man discoveries."

"I think when Mémère Monique and Kenyatta died last year," I said. "You all know about Mémère's funeral because you were all there, but the Kenyatta funeral was a big event and Ian was busy and I'd tried to just stay out of the way. There were all kinds of dignitaries, but fortunately meeting them all at the airport and looking after them was the Kenyans' problem, not ours."

"Tell us about that time," Charlize said. "I remember the day the Mémère Monique died, but not Kenyatta.

Deaths

We received an early telephone call one Monday in early August of 1978.

"Bonjour," I heard Maman say.

"Bonjour," I replied, it was far too early for a normal telephone call, so something must be wrong, so I asked. *"Qu'est-ce qu'il y a?"*

"Your grandmama has just died," Maman replied.

"How, why, when?" I asked.

"She was hit by a car at about six last night, they took her to hospital, but her injuries were too great and she died at about two this morning," Maman explained.

"Was anyone there with her?" I asked.

"Charlize and James," Maman said. "They were able to get there in time and have just called me, I will be travelling to Paris on the first plane this morning."

"I'll come to Paris," I said. "I'll look at flights and see if I can get a flight to London tonight."

"If you do, just go straight to Mémère's flat," Maman suggested.

"I will, say good morning to Portia for me, I will see you tomorrow or soon afterwards," I promised.

"What happened?" Ian asked.

"Mémère was hit by a car and died this morning," I explained.

"I'm so sorry Fi," he said. He sat up in bed and put his arms around me as I burst into tears. I sobbed my heart out thinking of what I would miss about her. She was such a beautiful person, full of curiosity and life and now she was gone. She had tried to stay abreast of all things and I had just bought her an Apple II and was getting ready to go to Paris to help her learn how to use it. She had lived a full and interesting life and I was really devastated that I would not see her again. Ian just held me until my sobs abated and then suggested that he get me something, tea, coffee, brandy, whatever.

"Just tea, please," I said. He got up and went to the kitchen and I heard him busy there. I got up and joined him and just put my arms around him and held him close. I was lucky to have someone to hold onto and be with. He poured tea and we sat at the kitchen table and looked at each other.

"She was lovely," I said. "I can't believe I won't see her again; I was looking forward to going with her to Tahiti."

"It's hard," he said. "When my folks were killed, it didn't seem possible."

"I know," I said. "It doesn't seem possible does it. Well, crying won't solve anything. I'll go into town as soon as the BA office opens and try and get a flight out tonight."

"What will happen to her flat and all her things?" he asked.

"Maman is her executor," I said. "She's also the sole heir, so my guess is that the flat will stay in the family. Her things, Maman and Portia can sort out all that."

"I suppose it's far too early to be asking about funeral arrangements," he said.

"Yes, and no," I said. "Mémère had a plan and it's all laid out, she showed me one day, told me that it would be easier on everyone if her wishes were clearly set down on paper. She wants a simple service, a cremation and her ashes to go back to Tahiti, and she clearly stated that she wanted a celebration of her life, not a whole lot of mournful dirges."

"When you get there, let me know when those will be and I'll join you," he promised.

"I will," I said. "I was getting ready to go and help her learn how to use her new Apple II, she was so eager to learn."

"What will you do with it?" he asked.

"Probably give it to James," I thought. "I'm sure we could find a way for him to use it for the vineyard. God, I can't believe she's dead, she was so alive the last time I saw her. I'm so glad I've been able to spend time with her on my trips to Paris. How long did it take you to get over the death of your parents?"

"Pretty quickly," he said. "But I had a mission, to find those who had ambushed them, so I wasn't so much in mourning as angry, I think the mourning came when the terrs were dead and my mission was to all intents and purposes over."

"You never knew your grandparents?" I asked.

"Not really," he said. "They were these mysterious people who lived in England that I think I met once or twice when I was growing up, but they all died fairly young, so we were pretty much on our own."

"I suppose I should get dressed and make some breakfast," I said.

"I'll do that," he said. "Go and get dressed and I'll have your breakfast ready."

I went into town as soon as the BA office opened and they could not help me for that day, but suggested that I try Kenya Airways, they had two flights a week that actually went to Paris. I did, and was delighted to be able to get a flight direct to Paris that night. It left Nairobi at eleven thirty and put me into Paris at seven thirty-five the following morning, with one stop in Rome. That was really good, all I had to do then was make my way from the Orly airport to the flat. The plane was smaller than the BA plane, a Boeing 707, but serviceable enough. With a ticket in hand I had the whole day to kill before my flight. I stopped by the commission and told Ian that I was flying out that night on Kenya and would call him when I got to Paris. I spent the day trying to work, but my mind kept drifting, drifting off to those times I spent in Paris as a child, to the more recent times when I had spent hours talking to Mémère about life, Ian, sex, politics, Tahiti, wine, computers and all manner of things. The more I thought about it, the more I realised how lucky I had been to have had those discussions, it had provided me with an outlook on life that was more complete, or if not complete, then broader. I was still sorry that she had gone, but my sorrow was for me and the fact that I would no longer have those talks, no longer be able to share a meal and a joke with her, except in my memories. By the time the time for the plane finally came, I was actually quite looking forward to going to Paris and visiting the flat again and reliving some of the memories. Oh, it would be difficult and heart rending to hear from James and Charlize what her last moments were like, but I would get over that and have the happier memories to fall back upon.

Ian took me to the airport and I checked in with the Kenya Airways desk. I had an option of seats, and picked 4E in First Class, that put me just behind a galley, in the aisle and with a clear view of the movie screen. Ian saw me off, coming out to plane to see me up the stairs. The airport authorities knew him quite well and were quite willing to have him see me off to the plane itself. On board I chatted to the hostess in Swahili and she made a couple of private remarks to me about some of the other passengers. Looking them over they were for the most part visitors from either Italy or France, with perhaps one other like me, a resident of Kenya. Because of the late hour, I was only mildly interested in dinner, so ate lightly then tried to compose myself to sleep. I must have fallen off, because I awoke as we were descending into Rome. Time on the ground in Rome was short and we were then off to Paris. We had lost quite few passengers in Rome and only a few joined us. There was enough time in the air to serve breakfast, which I did eat, with some enthusiasm. The service on Kenya Airways was excellent, quite on a par with BA, perhaps I would fly them more, particularly if I was going to Paris, the only drawback being that they only had two flights a week to Paris.

At Orly, I breezed through immigration and as I had no luggage to collect sailed on through customs and out. I had a choice, taxi or bus. I opted for taxi. It was still early enough that traffic was not yet at its usual standstill, and if it got really bad, I could always abandon the taxi and take the metro. The driver was quite chatty and wanted to talk about Roman Polanski and his flight to France. I had heard a little about it and was interested to hear his views. I sensed that he had daughters because he was quite opposed to Polanski hiding in France and felt that he should be summarily shipped back to the United States to face whatever fate there was there. At least his chatter was a distraction from the traffic now building and the dark and dismal morning. It was drizzling and the temperature had to be close to freezing, altogether an unpleasant day. I stayed with the taxi all the way to the flat and had brought enough Francs with me that I could pay the fare. I let myself into the flat and found the others of my family having breakfast.

"Fi, you're here already," Maman said. "We weren't expecting you until later."

"I came on Kenya and flew into Orly," I explained. "How are you Maman?"

"I'm fine," she said. "And you?"

"I cried a lot yesterday, but I'm fine," I said. "James, what happened?"

"A woman tried to grab a parking space before someone else and she really messed it up and jumped the kerb and hit Mémère," he explained. "They took her off to hospital and called us, we're on her call list, so we drove into Paris as fast as we could and we sat outside the surgery where they were trying to fix things, but I gather that the internal injuries were too great."

"So, what happened to the woman?" I asked.

"The police have her," James said. "She has lots of connections, the prosecutor is going to have a hard time there, all kinds of strings will be pulled, Daddy will probably bail her out, again."

"Should I pay her a visit?" I asked.

"Probably not," James said. "There would be a record of your visit and if she was in bad shape afterwards, they might have to come after you."

"I suppose so," I agreed grudgingly. "When and where are we going to do the funeral?"

"Well, we can't go next door to Saint-Nicolas-du-Chardonnet, there are issues there, so we've set things up for this Saturday at Saint-Étienne-du-Mont," Maman said.

"I should call Ian and let him know," I said. I called the operator and asked her to connect me with Kenya. That only took a few minutes.

"British High Commission," a voice said when the telephone was answered. "How may I help you?"

"Hello Janice," I said, recognising the voice. "It's Fiona Hartley, can you find Ian for me?"

"Of course," she said. There were a few clicks and then Ian came on the line.

"Fi, how are you, how's Paris?" he asked.

"I'm fine," I said. "Paris is cold and damp. I wanted to let you know that Mémère's funeral is on Saturday at, what time Maman, ten."

"Okay, I should be able to get there, I've been checking, there's a Kenya flight that gets me into Paris at eight ten on Saturday morning, that should give me plenty of time to get to the flat before the funeral, how far away is the church?"

"Maman, how far away is the church?" I asked.

"About a quarter of a mile," she said.

"Ian, a quarter of a mile, so five, ten minutes' walk," I said. "Bring a suit and tie."

"Yes, Dear," he said dutifully. "How about you, do you have what you need?"

"I don't, but I can go shopping and get something appropriate," I said.

"When were you planning to come back?" he asked.

"If we leave here on Monday and fly to Rome, we can pick up the southbound Kenya on Monday night, Tuesday morning and be back Tuesday," I suggested.

"That works," he said. "I'll book my ticket that way."

"Super, I'll see you on Saturday then, there's some Francs in the drawer by my side of the bed for the taxi. I'll call you again tonight," I promised. "Love you, bye."

"Good, so Ian will be able to come," Maman remarked.
"Yes, a flying visit, but he'll be here," I said. "Have you let Mémère's friends know?"
"We started doing that yesterday and we'll do the rest today," Maman said. "What we really need is another phone. I've put notices in Le Monde, Le Figaro and Le Parisien, I think that should be enough."
"What are you going to do with the flat?" I asked.
"I think I'll keep it," Maman said. "Then we can use it whenever we want, you have a key, James and Charlize do, and so do Portia and I. I'll take care of the bills for the flat and make sure that it's heated in the winter. Mémère's things I'll sort out this week, if there's anything you'd really like, tell me."
"It's strange to think that she's not going to be here anymore," I said. "I've spent a lot of time with her in the past couple of years."
"She enjoyed that," Maman said. "She was telling me only on Friday how much she enjoyed your visits and she was really looking forward to learning how to use the computer you bought her, what are you going to do with that?"
"I was thinking that perhaps James and Charlize could use it at the vineyard," I said. "I can show you how to program it and what kinds of things you can use it for."
"That would be great," Charlize said. "I've been thinking about how we can do some things better, and that could be a big help."
"We didn't ask, but did you have breakfast Fi?" Portia asked.
"I did, thanks," I said. "Kenya served a pretty good breakfast between Rome and here, they had to scurry a bit, but it was good."
"What about coffee now?" she asked.
"That would be super," I said. I had been thinking that a cup of coffee would go down well. Portia busied herself and soon produced coffee and a selection of pastries. We drank and ate and reminisced about Mémère, what she had meant to us all, the funny stories, the momentous times, the sad time when Pépère had died, how full of life she was, how she was curious about everything and how strong her opinions were about politicians and the government. I laughed a lot, wept a few tears, then

laughed more. It was really good to be with people I loved, and Ian would be joining me at the end of the week, and we could fly home together.

The rest of the week we spent sorting through Mémère's things. It was sad when you think about it, a whole life reduced to material items that were to be kept, donated or discarded according to their perceived value or utility. The photographs that were in the flat stayed in the flat, other items that were the links back to Tahiti also stayed, it was mainly the clothes and other accessories that went. The church where we were going to hold the funeral were happy to take everything and would make good use of them. I thought that it must be sadder still for those households where the home was also to be disposed of and the furniture and knick knacks would be fought over, argued about or just sold or discarded. On Saturday I was up early and I went to Orly to meet Ian's plane from Nairobi. He was there, grinning at me, happy to see me as I was him. Now I could face the funeral and the cremation with at least solid support by me. We took a taxi back to the flat and had time for coffee and a quick shower and change of clothes before the walk to the church. It was still cold, but no rain or snow, so the walk was brisk but not miserable.

The church was impressive, high vaulted ceilings and all the bits that mathematicians like to count. I did note that one of my heroes, Blaise Pascal, a mathematician of more than a little note was buried there. Unlike many British churches that I had been in, this one did not have pews, it had chairs set out in rows, so we picked the rows that were closest to the minister. I was surprised at the number of people there. Mémère must have had a wide circle of friends and acquaintances. Some I knew, most I did not. Maman knew quite a few, including many of the Tahitian community that lived in Paris. I saw some there that had been at the gallery event I had gone to with Mémère, including the director. The service was quite short and then the coffin was carried off to go to the crematorium. We had planned a wake after the funeral and many of those at the funeral came, at least for some time. I heard many stories about Mémère and realised how difficult it must have been for her when she first moved to Paris, but how she made a life and became a well-respected member of the community. I gave credit again to Pépère for having the courage to take her back to Paris in the days when I am sure that relationships between old family French officials and island girls were usually casual, or at least confined to the islands, not taken to the formal level of marriage and certainly not foisted upon Paris society. It must have said a lot for Pépère's worth as a civil servant that his marriage seemed in no way to hinder his career.

On Sunday, we just spent the day quietly and contemplating what life would bring us next. Ian told us that in Ethiopia the Somalis were in full retreat and that their army had been decimated in the Ogaden war. One side note that he made was that Kenya and Iran were at odds over remarks made by the Shah that Iran would not stand by if Kenya invaded Somalia. Kenya was concerned that Barre might try and save face over his Ogaden misadventure by turning to Kenya and the North Eastern Province, which was largely ethnic Somali. The war of words was still going on between Kenya and Iran and Britain and Belgium had both been asked to mediate. Ian was of the view that Iran was making trouble and should stay well out of African affairs, there were troubles enough without one of the Middle Eastern countries getting involved. It seemed that it was all go on the Kenyan front. Quite why the Shah should be actively supporting the socialist régime of Barre was a mystery to me.

We started for home on Monday, flying first to Rome on Air France and then picking up the Kenya Airways flight to Nairobi. Once home, life returned to normal again, but with the knowledge that when next I went to Paris on business and stayed at the flat, I would be there alone, there would be no Mémère to make me coffee and listen to my tales of the day, no Mémère to drag me off to art galleries and museums, or out of the way cafés where she knew the proprietors and we would be treated as long lost relatives. I wished I had been able to go with her to Tahiti, it would have been really exciting to see the islands through the eyes of a native and not just as a tourist. One day I would go, perhaps with Maman and Portia and try and get a sense of where part of my family came from.

It was a couple of months later when we got another early morning telephone call, this one was for Ian, from one of his contacts.

"Kenyatta just died," he said, when he hung up the telephone. "Heart attack."

"Now what?" I asked.

"Well, they are organising moving the body back to Nairobi, I think they're going to use a military transport to Eastleigh. Then, there'll be a funeral, mourning and then the fun will start when they talk about succession," he said. "Moi is the VP but, he's not Kikuyu and there's a faction that would rather have a Kikuyu in charge, so we'll see."

"I suppose that you'll have someone from the commission at the funeral," I said.

"My guess is that they'll send someone from London," he said. "Not sure who right now, but Kenyatta is a big deal, so neither the Kenyans or the FCO will be satisfied with just the commish."

"So, who from London was here at independence?" I asked.

"The Duke of Edinburgh," Ian said.

"So, will he come again?" I asked.

"My bet is that it'll be Charles, heir to the throne and all," Ian said. As it turned out, Ian was right. The British Government sent HRH Prince Charles to represent them at the funeral. Ian was given his marching orders and was on hand to assist. I felt sorry for the Kenyan security services, they had all these heads of state visiting, some of whom that did not have the best relations with Kenya.

So, I took myself off to the airport at times to watch the arrivals, I saw HRH arrive along with Foreign Secretary David Owen, Lord Carrington and the former Governor and High Commissioner to Kenya, Malcolm MacDonald, it was a weighty British contingent. I also saw Idi Amin for the first time, in person. I also saw Julius Nyerere from Tanzania, who had come despite the border being closed between Tanzania and Kenya. I also saw Dr Kenneth Kaunda of Zambia, he had been granted an Honorary Doctor of Laws from Fordham University, then there was Dr Hastings Banda of Malawi, he had earned his medical degree in Tennessee and then again in Edinburgh and had practised as a doctor in Scotland and in Malawi. Those were the first generation of leaders of African nations post-colonial rule, and to round out the funeral attendance by heads of state there were Morarji Desai of India and Muhammad Zia-ul-Haq of Pakistan, two other former British colonies, or at least one until India partitioned into India and West and East Pakistan, and then Pakistan further split into Bangladesh and Pakistan. Other countries had their ambassadors or High Commissioners there, or were represented in some way. There was another tiff with the Iranians who complained that the message of condolence sent by the Shah had not been properly acknowledged.

I was fascinated to see how the Kenyans would handle all the heads of state and if two arrived anywhere at the same time, who would they greet first and who would be offended. As far as I could tell they managed this very well and I saw no outraged egos because another got apparently preferential treatment. I was also intrigued to know, but never found out how the Kenyans dealt with the issue of all the protective details these heads of state would arrive with and whether or not they were armed and if the Kenyans would let them keep their arms. I could just see a gunfight erupting between competing details. It was as well that for the moment at least India and Pakistan were in a period of relative peace, so there was little likelihood of anything erupting between the two delegations. But there was always something simmering between the two countries, often driven by competing claims over Kashmir. Finding accommodation for all these dignitaries was also a challenge. The hotels in town only had a limited number of rooms, and not all of the same grade, so who got which room or suite. I suppose whoever booked first. We were asked to host some of the British entourage, which I suppose came with the territory of being part of the local legation. They were nice enough, essentially just needing bed, food and water, because they were gone most of the time.

The funeral itself was a grand affair, planned, according to Ian, some years earlier by Bruce McKenzie, who had been until recently the Minister of Agriculture, but who had been assassinated when flying his plane from Uganda back to Kenya. A bomb planted on the plane had brought it down and McKenzie had died along with Keith Savage and Gavin Whitelaw. McKenzie had sought help from the British back in 1968 with the funeral planning and it was to all intents and purposes organised well before it was needed. There was a gun carriage, towed by members of the Kenyan armed forces, there were dignitaries galore, including Ian and I suppose me. We were there in the flesh watching all that went on and comparing the pomp and circumstance with the simple funeral that had been held for Mémère. The *Times* reported an awkward moment when it looked as if Idi Amin was going to try and shake hands with HRH, a diplomatic no-no if you no longer had diplomatic relations. But the High Commissioner passed it off as pure fantasy. My viewpoint was such that I could neither confirm nor deny the report, but it would have been interesting if in fact, it had occurred. The EAD, the East Africa Department of the FCO, would have been beside themselves. I got to hear for the first time a 21-gun salute, and fell to musing about who had picked the number 21 for the salute and why only 21, why not 25. That was something I would have to look into when I had the time, perhaps Ian knew the history and the answer, but I could hardly ask for an explanation in the middle of the ceremony. After the ceremony I never got around to asking Ian about the salutes, so never discovered the whys and wherefores.

After the funeral and the departure of all the dignitaries, life again returned to the more humdrum. Politics in Kenya continued, with the Acting President Daniel Moi, then with his election as substantive president later in the year. Apparently, Kenyatta had made a change in the constitution that upon the death of the president then the vice president was the acting president for ninety days, until such time as elections were held. As far as I could see Moi had managed things well and his early election in October went off without a hitch, as he was returned unopposed. Given world history and the number of times that chaos followed the death of a strong leader, Kenya stayed calm and things appeared to be going well for Moi.

I had time to reflect on the two deaths. The death of Mémère was for me deeply personal and I would miss her. Her funeral had been simple, there had been no lying in state, there had been no national period of mourning, but I would miss her all the same, I would miss her wisdom, her humour, her stories about Tahiti and her deep intense interest in all that was happening. I wondered how I would deal with the deaths of

Maman or Dad, or even James, Charlize or Portia. Those would be more difficult. I suppose for the Kenyans the death of Jomo Kenyatta was in some ways similar to the death of Mémère. He had been the father of the new country. He had campaigned for independence from British rule, he had even been gaoled by the British for a while. He had led Kenya since 1963 and would be missed. I remembered the outpouring of emotions following the death of Winston Churchill, and Jomo Kenyatta was Kenya's Churchill. That was reflected in the funeral arrangements which mirrored those of Churchill's, both elder statesmen, beloved by their countrymen and both who had led their countries in time of need, one through a major war, and the other through the birth of a new independent country. There was sadness in the deaths, but there was also the legacy that both Mémère and Jomo Kenyatta had left for me and for the people of Kenya, a time to remember.

I miss Ian

"21-gun salutes come from a navy tradition of showing that your guns were empty when entering a foreign port and as a way of showing no hostile intent to a foreign vessel," James explained. "It started out as 7 guns, then I think it was Pepys as Secretary to the Navy who settled on 21 guns."

"Oh," I said. "Well, at any rate, it was impressive."

"I can't imagine the logistical and protocol nightmare it all was," Portia commented. "At least it was the Kenyan's problem."

"Yes, and it all went off without a hitch that I could see," I said. "But I suppose because it had already been planned, all they had to do was follow the plan as closely as they could."

"So, when I die, I want a gun carriage and a 25-gun salute," James joked.

"I don't think you deserve even a 3-gun salute," Charlize said, poking him in the ribs.

"Ah, but you do," he said, trying to mollify Charlize. "We should think about leaving soon, we do have a plane to catch."

"I know," she said. "Fi, when you're tired of the Med, come and spend some time with us at the vineyard, I could do with some more help writing programs for my Apple."

"I'll do that," I promised. "Thank you for coming, both of you and you look after yourself Charlize, James make sure she doesn't work too hard in the vineyard."

"I'll try," James said. "But she will insist."

"I'm fine," Charlize protested. "I'm not an invalid, I'm only pregnant and since time immemorial there have been women pregnant working in the fields, it's only the Western World that coddles its women."

"If you say so, Dear," he said. They had clearly had this discussion before, and he had always lost.

"There will come a time when you won't want to do too much," Maman assured her. "Then it's up to James to shoulder the burdens that you normally carry."

"I can do that," James promised. "And, if you won't listen, I'll get your Ma to come and stay with us, she'll take you in hand."

"Okay, okay," Charlize said. "Just don't impose my Ma on me too soon, or I'll be yelling at you both."

"Are you ready to go?" James asked.

"I'm ready," she said. "Maman, Portia, good to see you again, come and see us soon, and Fi, please come and spend a little time with us, I need your programming skills."

"I will," I promised. We all hugged and kissed and said our various goodbyes and Maman took my Land Rover and ran them to the airport.

"How are you, Fi?" Portia asked.

"I'm okay," I said. "It's still hard to think he's not coming back. I'm not sure what I'm going to do with my life now. I can work, in fact, I probably should work just to stay busy and not dwell on things, you remember how I was when I thought I'd lost Ian the first time, I don't want to sink that low again."

"If you need any help, any help at all, come and see me," Portia offered.

"I will," I promised. "I look at James and Charlie and you and Maman and it reminds me of what I'll be missing, so I know it will be hard. Leaving here will be good, because there's too much here that will remind me of Ian. I want to come back at some time, but too soon will be too difficult."

"When my husband went off with his paramour, I thought my life was over," Portia said. "But then I was lucky and met Brigitte and have been deliriously happy ever since."

"I know," I said. "I see it in both of you and am really happy for you. Are you going to stay with Charlie when the baby comes?"

"Brigitte will go, I think what I'll do is go afterwards, if Brigitte goes and Charlie's Ma go before, then having me there as well will just be too much, so I'll wait and go later," Portia said. "But, having said that, I don't like to be away from Brigitte for too long, you know how that is."

"I do," I said with a sigh. "It's funny when James first met you the first thing he asked me was whether or not, how did he put it, ah, I remember, he said, but do they, you know, Charlie and I weren't about to help him out, so he finally had to ask outright if you two had sex. Charlie told him that of course, you did and then went on to tell us about an aunt of hers."

"I know it's a difficult subject for many people, women as well as men, but thankfully your family is better than most," Portia said.

"I think that was Mémère," I said. "She was very open with Maman, and Maman was open with me, so when I met you and saw you together, I could see the love and affection and that made me happy. I know when I asked Maman about you, she gave me the usual description, then she grinned at me and said that you were a tigress in bed."

"Really?" Portia laughed. "If anything, I would have said it was the other way round, but, it's true we do enjoy each other."

"I think that's great," I said. "I had that with Ian, I'm not sure who was the more insatiable, him or me. I couldn't keep my hands off him and I know I only had to flirt with him a little to get a rise out of him, literally and figuratively. He had a lovely body and I revelled in it being close to mine."

"Was he a good lover?" Portia asked.

"I think so," I said. "But then he was the only lover I ever had, so have no standard to compare against."

"You were happy, that was obvious," Portia said. "I hope that you find that happiness again, I know I did, I know Brigitte did, and I know that Tom did after his wife died."

"Intellectually I understand that," I said. "But my heart is telling me at the moment that it's broken and will never mend."

"I know," Portia said, putting her arms around me. I cried into her shoulder, crying for the times that would never come because Ian was gone, crying for the loneliness that I knew would come and crying because I would never see him again. Maman came back from the airport and asked me to tell her the story behind Ian's travels to the west that had led to his death.

Uganda invades Tanzania

"Amin has really overstepped things this time," Ian announced when he came home one day in early October.

"Why, what's he done now?" I asked.

"Some of his troops raided into Tanzania and shot up some folks," he said.

"What the hell for?" I asked.

"Well, you know that things have been heating up between Amin and Tanzania," he said. "It seems that some Ugandan troops moved into Tanzania, shot up an observation post and set a couple of houses on fire. It's all pretty murky, with both sides telling different stories."

"So, what will happen now?" I asked.

"We'll have to wait and see," he said. "We've got our new defence attaché, chap by the name of David Wells."

"I'll talk to Valerie, we should do for him and, does he have a wife, what they did for us when we first came?" I said.

"There is a wife, Helen," Ian said. "They should be here in about a month. Have you anything on this weekend?"

"No, nothing planned," I said.

"Great, could we take a run out to Tsavo?" he suggested.

"Why not?" I said. "Tsavo West or East?"

"East," he said. "I got an invite from the warden there, how long would it take us to drive there?"

"Forever, could we fly? How do you know the warden?" I asked.

"It turns out that the warden is George Hartley, a cousin of sorts, I think his dad was a cousin of my dad, so what does that make him, second cousin, I think. As to flying or driving, we could fly," he said. "George said to let him know if we were going to fly and he'd pick us up at either the Manyani field or a strip in the park."

"Let's do that then," I said. "Let me get a map and work out distances and time, I presume there'd be no fuel at Manyani or the other strip?"

"No idea," he admitted. "But, agreed, unlikely."

"Where is the strip?" I asked.

"Two degrees, twenty-two minutes, thirty-five seconds south, thirty-eight degrees, forty-five minutes, ten seconds east," he read from a paper.

"Let's see," I said, as I consulted a map. "145 nautical miles to Manyani, so say an hour and fifteen minutes, if we left at what, three, we could be there before four-thirty at the latest, or 132 to the strip, we'd be there in just over an hour, so about four-fifteen."

"That would work," Ian said. "I'll tell him when we're coming and he said he'd meet us there if we flew. I think we'd better go into the park strip, it's in the park and Manyani is the strip for the high security prison, they used it during the Mau Mau days, and still do."

"Great, we'll stay away from there, what's the weather look like?" I wondered.

"Well, the short rains are not due until November, so should be good," he said.

"Agree," I said. "But I'll check anyway, don't want to run into an early storm."

"Okay, I'll talk to George and confirm that we're coming into the strip in the park," Ian said.

"Where are we going to sleep?" I asked.

"I gathered under the stars," Ian said. "Maybe under a mosquito net, but this is a definite mobile safari, we have to do everything ourselves, he did say he'll have all the camping gear, so we don't have to take any of that."

"Do we take food and water?" I asked.

"I'll check," he promised.

Ian checked with George and we needed to take food, beer and or wine, but he had plenty of water, so I started to put aside what we needed for the trip and do my weight calculations. This was not going to be like going to Lake Turkana, we could get to the strip and back on about 150 lbs of fuel, so there was plenty of capacity left for us, food, and gear. I put together food for three for Friday night, Saturday and Sunday morning, plus a few beers and a couple of bottles of wine. We only needed the minimal for changes of clothes, so not much there. I put aside binoculars and camera and wondered what Ian would smuggle aboard this time. I did my weight checks again, and we were well below the maximums recommended.

We flew to the bush strip, there was not much in the way of landmarks, but the strip was on the north side of a river, so should be easy to spot.

We crossed over the Athi River, then saw off to the left the community of Ikutha, then the scenery changed, no longer were there farms, now it was just bush, we had crossed into the park. We passed over the strip at Ithumba and I started to let us down, we had about fifteen minutes to landing. We saw the other river and the strip just to the north of it. I flew down low over the strip, looking for anything that might be on it, and also looking for clues as to wind direction. We put up a group of zebra and I noticed as they left that the wind was out of the north, so went around and came back in upwind and landed. I taxied to the very end and parked into the wind off the runway in the clearest area I could find. A Land Rover came over to us and it was the warden, George. Ian greeted him and introduced me, then started to unload the plane. I let him get on with that and busied myself tying the plane down. The winds were light and variable, but you never knew when they might pick up, so it was wise to be cautious.

"Good flight?" George asked.

"Good," I confirmed. "No weather to worry about, not much traffic and the runway was nice and clear."

"I saw a small herd of zebra," George said. "Which way did they go?"

"They took off to the west," I said. "But they put up enough dust that I could get the wind direction. Thank you for inviting us out here."

"No, my pleasure," he said. "I met Ian a while ago and have been meaning to get him out here. We've got a small Wildlife Service camp here, so we'll just stop by and pick up water and we can take a drive. Ever been to Tsavo before?"

"No," I said. "We've been to some of the other parks, but never here."

"Nice plane," he said. "Yours?"

"It is," I confirmed. "We had it delivered from Rheims a couple of years ago. I thought we were going to lose it once when the Tanzanians closed the border, but we were able to get off and in the air before the paras showed up at the airport."

We stopped at the camp and picked up water and some camping gear, then we were off. Tsavo was huge, George showed us on a map where we were and where he suggested we go. After about an hour we stopped, by a small kopje, and after he did a quick tour of it announced that it was safe for us to get out of the Land Rover, climb to the top, and set up camp. Camp was simply a groundsheet on the floor and a line strung for mosquito nets. George then detailed us off to gather fire wood while he cleared the space for a fire and collected stones to surround it. I stuck close to Ian, my bush skills were just not up to his and I relied upon his knowledge to keep me away from predatory animals, snakes or other hazards.

"So, what for dinner tonight?" George asked.

"We brought all kinds," I said. "So, take your pick, steak, chops, sausage, plus, I did actually bring vegetables."

"Maybe sausage tonight?" George suggested.

"Sounds good," Ian said. "I'll make a start."

"I didn't see any people as we flew over," I commented.

"We're trying hard to conserve what we have," George said. "So, Tsavo East has been designated as a conservation area and we are limiting visitors. Try as we might to keep places pristine, as soon as we have any quantity of visitors it cannot help but impact the ecosystem. Visitors in any number means lodges, camps, traffic, litter, you name it."

"Won't the government be looking to generate revenue from this as a resource?" I asked.

"In time," George admitted. "In time, we're just lucky that there aren't deposits of gold or copper under here, if there were then there'd be a big push to get revenue quickly in the form of royalties."

"Can parks be economic?" I asked.

"I think so," George said. "But, it's a long-term income stream, not a quick one-time boost. A park managed well will serve as an income stream for the grandchildren of the current generation."

"Can politicians look at it that way?" I asked.

"Now, there's the real question," George laughed. "Unfortunately, the recent change in where parks fits is going to lead to poaching both of elephants and of rhino. Corruption goes with politics."

"When you two have finished solving the future of the parks, dinner is ready," Ian interrupted. "Beer, wine?"

We dined, stamped out the fire, watered all the ashes down and then buried them, then we washed up and then slept under the stars with just a mosquito net above us. The skies were black, or as Ian would say, black black, but the blackness was punctured by myriads of stars. It was amazing what you could see away from the light pollution of even a small city like Nairobi. Ian started pointing out constellations, Tucana,

Hydrus, Phoenix, Musca, Pavo and on to include the Southern Cross, or Crux as it was named on the star charts, most of which I had never heard of. But, being raised in the northern hemisphere the ones that I knew well were the Plough and Orion. Sleep came with the night noises, the whoop of the hyæna, a distant roar of lions, the peculiar grunt of a tree hyrax and the shriek of a bushbaby, apart from the millions of insects that were all doing their part. When we awoke in the morning, it was to the sound of elephants. There were fairly close, busy ripping apart the forest as they ate. George was up first and made coffee, then breakfast. We sat, drank our coffee and ate and watched the elephants stream by in a seemingly never-ending parade. I had never seen so many, even on my trip before into Serengeti, there were not this many.

"What's here, apart from elephants?" I asked.

"Most things," George said. "Bats, monkeys, dogs, jackals, foxes, otters, civets, genets, mongoose, cheetah, leopards, lions, hyæna, caracal, lions, wild cats, zebra, giraffe, warthogs, duikers, kudu, buffalo, rhino and quite a few more, then there's birds, won't bore you to tears by naming them all, but there's a lot."

"Plus, I suppose, snakes, lizards and insects?" I asked.

"By the score," he said. "We've got your cobra, python, boomslang, puff adder, black mamba, green mamba, gaboon viper, plus a few others."

"How big is Tsavo?" I asked.

"West is 3,500 square miles and East is about 5,808 square miles," he replied.

"So, pretty big," I commented.

"Pretty big," he agreed.

"Have you flown the perimeter?" I asked.

"No," he said. "We don't have the funds for a plane."

"Maybe we could take a trip around tomorrow morning?" I suggested.

"Could we, that would be super?" he said.

"Let me just check on fuel numbers," I said. I did some calculations. "We could give you a two-hour flight over some of the park."

"That would be great," he said. "Why don't we camp tonight by your plane, then take off first thing in the morning and see what we can see?"

"Okay," I said. "Is that okay with you Ian?"

"Fine," he said. "We can get a guided aerial tour; I'll keep the camera handy."

We toured around parts of the park all that day and finished up back at the airstrip. I looked over the plane, and nothing had bothered it during the past nights and day. We camped by the plane and the following morning I was up first, doing my walk around while the others made breakfast. George was keen to take a ride, so we packed all our things away and then got aboard. I gave my safety briefing, how to get out if we had to, where the fire extinguisher was, essentially what to do if we down for some reason. I started up and we taxied down the strip, then took off. I stayed fairly low so that George could see the ground. He quickly started pointing out animals, landmarks, making notes is his book as we went. We saw a vehicle and circled back around and took another look.

"One of my people," he said. "Let me write him a note and I'll toss it down to him." He wrote a note while I circled back, then I told him how to open the window, and he dropped the note, secure in a tin to the man below. I suppose George must have brought the tin with him in his rucksack, because I knew I had none aboard the plane. Looking back, we saw that it had been seen and picked it up. We flew on and saw more animals, more scenery, more animals, more scenery, but no more people, until it was time to go back to the strip. When we landed there was the other vehicle there, fortunately off to one side of the strip.

"Henry," George said after he had got out of the plane. "Got my note, let me give you a rundown of what I saw today. Sorry, Henry this is Ian Hartley and Fiona Hartley."

"We'll leave you to it George," Ian suggested, sensing that George was keen to discuss whatever he had seen.

"You're sure you can't stay for a day to two longer, I could use another ride around the park?" George laughed.

"I'd need more fuel," I said. "Perhaps next time, I'll come with full tanks, and then we can do it bit more of the park."

"If, no, let's say when you come again, I'll get some fuel from somewhere and have it here in the back of a lorry," George promised. We thanked George for the opportunity to visit and left him and Henry poring over a map, obviously discussing what George had seen, and where.

In the air, Ian said, "George is going to have a challenge in days to come."

"Why?" was the obvious rejoinder.

"When the government reorganised the parks department and the game management people under the same head, conflicts arose. What was to be the Wildlife Conservation and Management Department is now ridden with corruption," he explained. "The joke is, is that it's the Wildlife Poaching and Mis-management Department. Look for the Somalis to be involved and look for poaching for ivory and rhino horn."

"Why?" I asked again.

"Politics and corruption go hand in hand," he said sadly. "There's money to be made and politicians here don't come into the position with lots of money, so make it while they can."

"That's very cynical," I commented.

"I'm afraid it is," he said. "But, sadly true."

"Do you think it's true of politicians in England?" I asked.

"To some extent, yes," he said. "Some are more subtle than others. But I don't think you go into politics and stay altruistic for very long. They all like the privileges and perks too much."

"I suppose that's not the kind of thing to be saying when you're at the commission," I commented.

"No," he laughed. "And lucky that this little plane doesn't have cockpit voice recorders."

"Just as well," I laughed. "So, what's going to happen in Tanzania?"

"God only knows," he said. "It's possible that Amin may invade just to distract from problems at home, but is he that desperate?"

"That's more your department than mine," I said. "Okay, time to talk to the folks at Wilson and get cleared to land."

We landed, nicely I am pleased to say, and, after securing the plane went home.

"So, what did you think of Tsavo East?" Ian asked.

"It's big," I said. "Big, and undeveloped. It must be like what most of Kenya looked like before people came on the scene."

"Probably does," he agreed. "It's a little different to Lake Turkana or the coast, amazing isn't it how much variety there is in this country."

"It is," I agreed. "I'm glad we've seen so much of it, I never thought to be much out of Nairobi."

"Having the plane makes that a lot easier," he said.

"So, Uganda, how is that going to end?"

"Not well," he thought. "I'm betting that the Tanzanians will prevail in the end. They may be a little slow to start, but if Amin invades, they will have to respond."

"I know I've said this before, but I thought we were coming to a nice quiet posting with not a lot happening," I said.

"Ironic, isn't it," he said. "First, we have troubles with Idi, then the Somalis and Ethiopians go at it, now it looks like Uganda and Tanzania. Who's next?"

"Mozambique?" I suggested.

"They've got their problems," Ian agreed. "Machel is a through and through socialist with support from Cuba and the Sovs, but he's got RENAMO being a thorn in his side. RENAMO gets support from Rhodesia, mainly to disrupt supply to the terrs coming in from Mozambique. That conflict will go on for a while. Rhodesia is about at its end and Mugabe will win there. Namibia will be next, leaving South Africa to the south to decide if it wants a long internal war, or a political solution. To the north, Sudan will have issues, the north and the south have been at odds for years, decades, even centuries. The Congo, Zaire, the Congo, take your pick, is still a mess and will continue to be so. And, finally for our near neighbours, Rwanda and Burundi are likely to see some internal issues driven by tribes."

"Quite a litany," I said.

"Quite," he agreed.

"Well, peace and love reign in this house," I said. "What can I get you to drink?"

"A glass of wine would be great," he said. We drank wine on the terrace, thanking our stars that we were well away from any war and fighting. A second glass of wine followed, then kissing followed that, then clothes were shed and love making on the grass ensued. I thought about it and decided that that was one of the things I was going to miss most when we were sent to our next posting. Being able to frolic outside without getting frozen to death, or spied on by all and sundry. Something told me that accommodations in Rome were not likely to be as luxurious or as private as those we were enjoying in Nairobi.

Amin did invade Tanzania. At the end of the month a large force from Uganda pushed over the border and occupied the northern part of the Kagera region of Tanzania. Amin argued that the river to the south of the region made a better border than that which had been negotiated between the British and the Germans. Again, so much for African Unity and the notion that the colonial borders would stay as per the OAU agreement. Nyerere of Tanzania responded by mobilising the Tanzania People's Defence Force and in the space of a few weeks the Tanzanian forces jumped from 40,000 to 150,000. They were joined by some dissident Ugandans who wanted to see the back of Amin.

"It's all go," Ian said, when he came home one day a bit after the Ugandan push into Tanzania. "The Tanzanians just got their hands on some Soviet weapons and apparently are using them to good effect against the Ugandans."

"So, what now?" I asked.

"My guess is that the Tanzanians will push the Ugandans back out of the country," he said.

"Is that all, or will they retaliate?" I asked.

"Retaliate," he said. "They'll want to make sure this doesn't happen again, so they'll push back into Uganda."

"Who else is involved?" I asked.

"We're not," he said. "Neither Kenya not HMG, we're both staying out of it. But I hear rumours that there are some forces from Mozambique fighting with the Tanzanians, and they're getting help from China, Algeria and Ethiopia."

"Anyone plumping for Idi?' I asked.

"Libya and the PLO," he said.

"So, how long will this go on?" I asked.

"Good question," he said. "A few months, I can't see it going on for years."

The war did indeed drag on for a few months, we kept track of things as they were reported in the newspaper, but then David Wells arrived and he started to dig into things. After that we started to get reports of Ugandan losses, and then reports of battles in Uganda. Ian came home one day with more information that David had gleaned.

"Libya has flown troops into Entebbe to support Amin," he told me. "The Libyans have tanks, artillery and fighter jets and are supposed to be supporting the Ugandans."

"But?" I asked.

"Our sources tell us that Ugandans are busy taking their loot away from the border and leaving the Libyans to fight the Tanzanians," he said.

"Will the war spill over into Kenya?" I asked.

"I doubt it," he said. "All the fighting is on the other side of Lake Victoria, so Entebbe and Kampala would have to fall before it would move this way."

"All the same, I am concerned about yet another war in the near neighbourhood," I said.

"It will be fine," he assured me. "We're keeping a weather eye on all that's happening, if it looks like anything is going to come closer to the border, I'm sure Kenya will more troops west."

"How can Uganda, and Tanzania for that matter, afford a war?" I asked. "I would have thought that they would have better things to spend their money on."

"You would, wouldn't you," he agreed. "Like most countries that get into wars, they'll go into debt, look what it cost the UK for World War II, I think the number is something like £21 billion, which they are still paying on, and would you believe that they're still paying on debts from World War I?"

"I remember that from my meetings with the Treasury people, when they were talking about where the money went, I remember they talked about certain payments on things called Perpetuals, and they told me that that harked back to 1917," I said. "I suppose if you're at war then you have to pay your soldiers, you have to pay for arms and ammunition and fuel, food, all those things, and because you're at war the economy shifts and therefore the tax base shifts and you don't have enough coming in. Would either Uganda or Tanzania be able to afford it without arms and ammunition from outside sources?"

"No, they don't produce things like tanks and aircraft themselves, so have to buy those anyway, and Russia and China might provide arms, but there's a cost, it might not be direct cash, but, there's a cost and they will call in the debts at some time," he said.

"So, with all this conflict going on around here, have you heard yet what your next posting will be?" I asked.

"Not yet," he said. "The commish hinted that I should get the word any day now."

"Hopefully somewhere with a little less local conflict," I commented.

"It's Italy," Ian announced when he came home day.

"Is that where we're going next?" I asked.

"It is," he said. "So, I suppose the tables are turned now and I'm not teaching you Swahili, but you'll be teaching me Italian."

"Italy, sounds nice," I thought. "We could learn to ski in the Italian Alps, plus, it's not that far to drive to the Riviera, even to Orléans."

"It will be a little while yet before we go," he said. "But, no harm in being prepared. How hard is Italian to learn?"

"Easier than French," I assured him. "You'll find pronunciation easier."

"So, when do we start?" he asked.

"Domani," I told him. *"Domani, parleremo solamente Italiano."*

"Okay," he said. "We would have to go back to London for a short while, then they'll ship us off to Italy, but I haven't been told yet whether its' to be the embassy in Rome or one of the consulates. It could be Milan, Venice, Florence, Palermo, or maybe even Cagliari."

"Milan would be nice," I thought. "Not so far to go if we wanted to learn how to ski. How soon before they tell you where?"

"Not sure," he admitted. "I would have thought they would know by now, so why not just tell us?"

"Bureaucracy," I told him. "Can't have everything sorted out ahead of time, that would be too organised. The appointment details probably have to go across six desks and get six signatures, all of which takes time. Are there any wars going on in Europe?"

"Not that I can think of," he said. "But there are the Red Brigades, a bunch of terrorists who really made themselves notorious when they killed Moro earlier this year."

"Would we be at any risk from them?" I asked.

"I wouldn't think so," he said. "But it never hurts to be alert, keep up your combat pistol shooting, and maybe we'll see how difficult it would be for us to get a permit for you to carry a gun."

"You think it might be that risky?" I asked.

"Honestly, no," he said. "But, being prepared is the best way to avoid problems."

"Is there nowhere in this world completely free from conflict?" I asked.

"Antarctica," he joked. "Maybe, Switzerland, Norway, Bhutan, Canada."

"I'm pretty sure they won't send us to Switzerland," I said. "I rather think that that's reserved for people with much longer service than us and with better connections."

"You're probably right," he admitted. "So, it's Italy, brush up on your karate and I'll get this chap I know at the SIS to give you a lesson in spotting tails."

"That sounds interesting," I said. "I can become a latter-day Mata Hari."

"No, I don't think so," he laughed. "The story is that Mata Hari traded sex for secrets and I'd rather you didn't do that, except with me."

"So, what secrets can I lure you into revealing?" I joked, baring one shoulder.

"I'm sure I could come up with something," he said. "But it's got to be worth my while, a shoulder doesn't get you much."

"Oh, so what about this?" I asked, stripping off my blouse and bra.

"Much more," he said.

"And this?" I asked, unzipping my skirt and letting it fall to the ground.

"Drop the panties and I'll tell you the combination of the commission safe," he said.

"You're on," I said. I slipped my panties down over my hips and let them drop to the floor. "Now, the number."

"Twelve right, six left, three right, eight left and ten right," he said. A combination that I am sure was pure invention, but it did provide to keep the moment. I sealed the transaction by undoing his trousers and freeing *homo erectus*, which I put to good use sitting in his lap.

"I love you Fi," he said, as he thrust deeply into me in the throes of his climax.

"Che chiavata meravigliosa," I whispered in his ear. *"Ti amo, ti voglio!"*

"What does that mean?" he asked.

"Tell you tomorrow when we start Italian lessons," I promised.

The war between Uganda and Tanzania took a turn for the worse for Amin. The Tanzanians pushed to Ugandans out of their country, but did not stop there. They pushed deeper into Uganda, enveloping Entebbe and threatening Kampala. Ian came home and told me that he and David were going to take a trip to Malaba to meet an agent there. Malaba was close to the Uganda border, not far from the town of Tororo, where elements of the Ugandan army were based. Ian said that they had information that people loyal to Obote were planning something there. The agent was well placed in the Ugandan army and was willing to cross the border and tell them what he knew.

"I thought we weren't involved?" I asked Ian.

"We're not, officially," he said. "But we need to know what's going on and how close to collapse the Amin régime really is. David's Swahili is adequate, but the commish wants me to go with him to make sure we get the whole story."

"Be careful," I pleaded. "Don't go too near the border."

"I won't," he promised. "There's no reason for us to cross, the agent will come to us."

"How long will you be gone?" I asked.

"About a week," he said. "We're going to drive up there, spend a day or so making sure that the meet is secure, then after we've met the chap, then we'll drive home."

"Is there a Kenya army presence there?" I asked.

"There is," he said. "Because of the proximity of the Tororo barracks, the Kenyans have stepped up patrols and increased the size of the local unit."

"When are you leaving?" I asked.

"The day after tomorrow," he said. "It'll take us a good day to get there, it's got to be about 300 miles from here. We'll take a commission vehicle with a driver and then get dropped at the meeting point a day early so that David and I can check it out carefully, then we'll get picked up the next day and drive home."

"Who's the driver?" I asked.

"Joseph," Ian said, naming one of the better drivers they had. I had met him a few times and he was not only a good driver; he was keenly aware of what was going on around him. I trusted Joseph and, as far as I knew, he was in the pay of the British not the Kenyans.

I sent Ian off with a smile on his face. I had awoken him early the day he departed and given him something to remember me by while he was off gallivanting in the western part of the country. I had taught him what the Italian meant and he was keen to learn more, so I promised him more lessons when he got home, he had apparently been studying, or he acquired a book of Italian slang, or he had talked to one of the people we knew at the Italian legation, because his parting words were, *ti vorrei fare un pompino*, I will leave you to research what that means. I watched them leave then went back to my economic models and mathematics. At least it would keep me busy while Ian was away. But all the same I sat and daydreamed for a while about Ian's return and what we might do together. The prospect of a posting in Italy was very exciting, it would, of course, be a huge change from Kenya, but there was a world of history there, history I had studied in school, but could now experience in the flesh so to speak. I was not sure which city I would prefer, perhaps Florence for the history, perhaps Milan, being closer to the Alps, perhaps Venice for the waterways, or even in a pinch, Rome. I had started to brush up my Italian and had had lunch a couple of times with two of the wives of men with the Italian legation. Chatting to them had been very helpful, and my fluency was returning quickly. Teaching Ian was going to be so much fun.

I followed the reports in the newspaper about events in Uganda and things were not going well for Amin. Kampala had fallen and the Ugandan army and its allies were in full retreat, actually I would have said full flight. So, it looked as if there was going to be a change in leadership in Uganda very soon. In fact, the very next paper I read said that Amin had fled the country and gone to Libya. So, perhaps Ian's trip had not been necessary. I looked for his return and counted the days. The evening when he should have been back there was a car hoot at the gate and I went out to open it, thinking it was Ian back, but it was a police car.

"Dr Hartley?" an officer said.

"Yes," I said, wondering what this visit portended.

"I am Superintendent Mwangi," he said, introducing himself. "This is Inspector Wambui, I am sorry to have to tell you that your husband has been involved in a traffic accident."

"Is he okay, where is he, can I go and see him?" I asked.

"I'm very sorry to have to tell you that he was killed in the accident," Mwangi said. That was like a stake being driven through the heart, killed, that meant he was not coming back, that meant that I was not going to see him again and enjoy his company, that meant Italy was out, no more Italian lessons, no more inventive ways to say I love you, just no more.

"Would you like to come in?" I asked, not knowing what else to say or do.

"Thank you, Doctor," he said. He and his driver both came in the house and I showed them to the kitchen, where I just sat and stared at nothing trying to take in the news.

"How?" I asked.

289

"The car he was in was hit by a lorry and the driver and your husband were both killed," he explained.

"And David?" I asked.

"Mr Wells sustained some injuries, but he is in stable condition in hospital," Mwangi said. "Is there someone we can call for you?"

"Valerie Whitmore," I said. "Her husband works at the commission." The superintendent nodded to Wambui who slipped out into the hall to use the telephone. I heard him in the background talking to people, but it was just background noise, the front of my mind was still trying to cope with the message that Ian was dead. Dead, how could he be dead, he was one of the most alive people I knew, he was careful in the bush, he was very aware of his surroundings, how could this have happened?

"May I make you some tea?" Mwangi asked.

"Please," I said. "Who was driving the lorry?"

"It was a Libyan fleeing from the war in Uganda, he drove straight through our border gate and kept going until he hit the car that your husband was in, some 80 miles from the border. We had been chasing him, but had not been able to stop him," Mwangi explained. Wambui came back and nodded to Mwangi. "Mrs Whitmore is on her way," Mwangi said. "I'm sorry to have to do this, but at some time we do need a formal identification, perhaps tomorrow you could manage that?"

"I'll stop at the morgue tomorrow," I promised. I did not hear her arrive, but Valerie was suddenly there in the kitchen.

"How are you Fiona?" she asked.

"Not good," I admitted. She put her arms around me and I just collapsed into tears. I had held it together for the police, but it finally really hit me, Ian was dead, he was not going to come back. At some point the police must have made a polite withdrawal because I noticed that they were no longer there.

"I'm so sorry, Fiona," Valerie said. "The police said it was a traffic accident, what about the others?"

"Joseph was also killed, but David is in hospital with injuries, but he's stable," I replied.

"Is there anything I can do?" she asked.

"Just stay with me for a while," I said. "I can't believe he's dead. I know he is, because they just told me, but, it's still hard to grasp. Why did this have to happen, why did he have to go off gallivanting near the Uganda border, why did the fucking Libyans get involved?"

"Why the Libyans?" Valerie asked.

"Some stupid fucking Libyan crashed through the border in a lorry and then hit the car that Ian was in," I explained. "The Kenyans had been trying to catch him for about 80 miles they said. I hope the bastard fries in hell."

"There's someone at the gate," Valerie said. "Let me just see who it is." She was back shortly with the High Commissioner.

"I'm so sorry, Fiona," he said. "Is there anything I, we, can do for you?"

"No, thank you, not just now," I said. "I need to go to the morgue and formally identify Ian, I said I'd do that tomorrow."

"I'll pick you up at nine," he said. "And I'll take you there."

"Thank you," I said. "I need to call his sister in London."

"If there is anything else we can do, please tell me," he said.

"I suppose there'll need to be funeral arrangements and then I'll need to go back to London," I said.

"There's time enough for that," he assured me. "Take your time, there's no rush to do anything. Are you all right here with Valerie?"

"I am, thank you," I said.

"I'll be here at nine tomorrow," he said. "Make sure she's all right Valerie."

"I will," Valerie promised.

After the Commissioner had gone, I steeled myself to make telephone calls. The first was to Irene, Ian's sister. I called her at her home, trying to formulate what I was going to say.

"Hello," she said when she answered the telephone.

"Irene, it's Fiona, I've got some really bad news, Ian's been killed in a traffic accident."

"Oh, I'm so sorry Fiona, how are you?" she asked.

"I'll survive," I said.

"I'll come to Nairobi," Irene said.

"That would be lovely," I said. "Oh, Irene, I miss him, I can't believe he's dead, I can't believe he's not going to walk in the door."

"I'll be there as soon as I can," she promised.

"I must tell my family," I said.

"Of course," she said. "I'll see you probably the day after tomorrow." I hung up the telephone and next called Maman.

"Allô," she said, when she answered the telephone.

"Maman, Ian, il est mort," I sobbed.

291

"Qu'est ce que tu as dit?" she asked.

"Ian est mort, il y avait un accident, et, Ian, il a été tué," I explained, through my tears.

"Ma pauvre," she said. "I will be there as soon as I can."

"Thank you Maman," I said. "Will you tell James and Dad for me?"

"Of course," she promised. "Is there anyone there with you?"

"Yes, Valerie from the commission," I said.

"Good," Maman said. "I will be there as soon as I can." I hung up and looked at Valerie.

"Would you stay here tonight?" I asked.

"Of course," she said. "Let me just get Trevor to bring me an overnight bag. Would you like a glass of wine, a brandy?"

"Brandy sounds good," I said. I probably bored Valerie to death, but I talked to her about Ian, about his researches, his humour, our trips to the bush, everything about him that I loved, until I could talk no more and went off to bed and slept.

The High Commissioner came the next day at nine and drove me to the morgue. Inspector Wambui met us there and I identified Ian formally, yes it was him. It was hard to see him so, laid out on a slab, lifeless, pale and covered so that I would not see the extent of his injuries. I cried again, how could this lifeless thing be the Ian that I knew, the Ian that would make me laugh, the Ian who could tell me all about the birds, the trees, the animals and about ancient hominids, the Ian that I would romp with in the garden. The Commissioner took me home and we sat and talked about Ian and his service at the commission. We then got around to the more mundane and set a date for the funeral and then he broached the subject of me leaving. I knew that with Ian gone that I would return to England, I was not the one appointed to the position, so without Ian, I had no claim to the house. The Commissioner was kind and made no immediate demands, but I knew I had to go, so we set a date and he told me that he would have someone from the legation help me with shipping my belongings back to England. The Commissioner also told me what I was entitled to economically with the death of Ian. It was pittance enough, but some minor recognition of Ian's service to his country. After the Commissioner left, Valerie and I had coffee outside on the terrace and just sat in companionable silence, looking at the trees, smelling the blossoms of the franji pani tree, listening to the birds and both wondering what next. What would I do, return to London and continue to work, take some time off and wallow in self-pity and grieve, go on a world tour, who knew what. It was one of those times in one's life that would stay with you forever, what had been shared with Ian, would be shared no more. He was gone, gone from my life, but not from my memories. I had so many memories, good and bad, but since we had been married, all good, the bad ones were from the time that we had been apart, but even that had a bright spot, when we had found one another again and had reconciled and vowed never to lose touch again.

Leaving

"Then you all arrived and you know the rest," I said.

"How are you now?" Maman asked.

"Surprisingly good," I said. "I know it would be easy to slip into depression, it nearly happened to me when I lost touch with Ian those years ago, but that was different, I thought I had lost him because he didn't love me. This time I know, knew, that he loved me and losing him was not because he didn't love me anymore, but because some stupid bloody Libyan couldn't stay where he belonged in Libya."

"What else do we have to do here?" Portia asked.

"I think it's all done," I said. "The church will collect the clothes I've donated, I think they're coming at about ten this morning, the shippers come tomorrow for the boxes, my Land Rover goes tomorrow as well, then we'll decamp to the Norfolk for a few days before flying back to London."

"Are there any social obligations that you need to attend to?" Maman asked.

"I think the commission is having a going away send off," I said. "That's tomorrow night, then I think we're done. Ian's temporary replacement comes in the day after tomorrow, and life goes on."

"Is there anything else you need to do before we leave?" Maman asked.

"Close my bank accounts, make some kind of arrangement with the university if they want me to continue to teach the odd class there," I thought. "Otherwise, I think I'm about as organised as I could be."

"So, boxes and car tomorrow, then the day after we'll do the bank stuff, then it'll be Friday and we fly out," Maman said, getting the timetable set in her mind.

"Would you come back?" Portia asked.

"I probably will," I said. "All my memories of our time here were good, except for those moments when I thought war might impact us, but our bush trips were so much fun that I'm sure I'll come back, maybe not to Kenya as often, but Tanzania, Zambia, Botswana, who knows?"

"There's a lot of Africa," Portia commented dryly.

"There is," I agreed. "What's the weather like in London?"

"Rain, showers, mist, the usual," Portia said. "But, on the Riviera the sun is shining."

"Okay, okay," I said. "I'll sort out what I need to finish in London, then I'll come and spend a couple of weeks with you."

The following day was busy. We had breakfast, then cleaned out the pantry and the refrigerator and added that to the donations we were giving the church. The shippers arrived at lunchtime and in no time at all the boxes and crates were gone. Then the Land Rover dealer came and my Land Rover was gone. I walked through the house one last time, partly to check to see that I had not left anything, and partly to say goodbye. I was sorry to leave, sorry to leave the garden with its trees and birds, sorry to leave behind the memories of what Ian and I had done in the house. If the walls could talk, what tales they would tell. I was reminded of a passage in the *Flame Trees of Thika*, when Elspeth is told to kiss each of the four walls in the living room and then she would sure to go back. I did not kiss the four walls, this was never to going to be my house again, but I touched the walls in each of the rooms, trying to draw from them what they remembered about our time there. Satisfied that I had left nothing, I locked up the house and joined Maman and Portia waiting for the taxi. He came and I asked him to go first to the British High Commission, where I dropped off the keys, and also surrendered my diplomatic passport, to which I no longer had entitlement, then to the Norfolk, our home for the next couple of days. The Norfolk had rooms ready for us and I dropped my bags onto the floor and looked out the window at the gardens, at the palm trees, the hadedas, the odd lawn decorations, like the old tractor and the horse drawn carriage. I would miss all this, particularly the palm trees and the hadedas. Some people do not like hadedas, but I do, I like the raucous call they have, they eat all manner of crawling things and when the sun hits their plumage just right, it has an iridescence about it.

Maman knocked on my door and we went down for afternoon tea that we took on the terrace.
"Ian and I sat here once," I said. "We were having coffee after lunch and he pointed out birds to me. I know he was an anthropologist, but he had an encyclopedic knowledge of birds, animals and trees."
"I suppose that was his upbringing," Maman commented. "So, how many projects do you have to wrap up?"

"Six," I said. "Two, one for a car company and one for a shipyard are all but done, two more are close, one for a large grocery chain and one for a shipping line need about another month, and then the last two, one for a computer company and the other for a printer company, they will take a little longer."

"Can you work on them at our house?" Maman asked.

"I could," I said. "I do need access to a computer, so would either have to find somewhere close to you that has the capability and capacity, or travel to London."

"Well, when we get to London, do what you have to do and then we'll go to France," Maman said. "When do you get your new plane?"

"I've no idea," I said. "I haven't heard from the factory yet, but probably a month or so."

"Could we go to Rheims and take delivery there?" Maman asked.

"I don't see why not," I thought. "When we get to London, I'll Telex them and see what they say."

"We could take the train up and fly back," Portia suggested.

"That would be fun," I agreed. "Ian really liked flitting around in our plane, we could decide to go somewhere and be off in an hour or so, as long as it took me to do the fuel calculations, fill up the tanks and do my walk arounds."

"He never got his licence did he?" Maman asked.

"No, he was close," I said. "He just needed a few more hours solo and he would have been fine."

"You know," Portia said. "If I were HMG, I would recruit you to either the Foreign Service or to MI5 or MI6."

"Why do say that?" I asked.

"You'd be perfect," Portia said. "You have a flair for languages, you see and remember things, you can shoot, fly a plane, a real Jane Bond."

"I don't see myself as a Mata Hari," I said.

"No, not Mata Hari, maybe a Georgina Smiley," Portia said.

"Given that it's the Government we're talking about I don't see the FCO as being particularly keen on the idea of a woman in the Service," I said. "I know there are a few, but I think it's still very much an old boys club."

"Well, I think you'd be terrific," Portia said. "What time do you want to go to the bank tomorrow?"

"I made an appointment for ten," I said. "They said they've got everything set to transfer the funds to London, give me some traveller's cheques and close the accounts. We also need to stop at the Post Office to clear the mail box and set things up for forwarding if anything comes in. I'm going to forward any last-minute stuff to the High Commission and they said they would send it to London for me."

"Sounds like a busy day, do want us to come with you?" Maman asked.

"If you would?" I said. "I'll be happier if you're both there."

"More tea?" Portia asked.

"No, thank you," I said. "Thank you both for coming, I'm not sure how I would have managed without you."

"It's the least we can do," Maman said.

We all trooped down to the bank the next day and I went through the process of closing out our accounts. The manager had everything ready and it was just a question of signing a few documents and my financial ties to Kenya were ended. We went through a similar process at the Post Office, I emptied the box, handed in the key and signed away my life again. That was the last link that tied me to the country, now I had no house, no car, no bank account and no mail delivery, I was truly back to being a visitor. We walked back to the Norfolk and had lunch, just three more tourists taking in the sights and sounds of Nairobi. I am not sure who saw them first, Maman or Portia, but we were joined by Julia and Henry.

"Fiona," Julia said. "I'm so sorry for you, how are you doing?"

"Sometimes fine, sometimes just awful," I replied.

"It seems it wasn't that long ago when we had dinner with you here, when you first came to Kenya," Henry commented. Indeed, we had had dinner with them, when I was on my expedition to discover why I had not heard from Ian, and we had taken a safari to Maasai Mara and the Serengeti and then on to Arusha and the dig offices.

"Thanks for coming," I said. "I'm sorry to be leaving, but without Ian, there is nothing here for me just now."

"Will you come back and see us?" Julia asked.

"I'd like to some time," I said.

"Please do," Julia said. "We'll take you out with us no matter who we have as guests."

"When do you leave?" Henry asked.

"Tomorrow night," I said. "We've got the BA flight to Heathrow. Then I have to go back to work for a while."

"Take some time off," Julia told me.

"I've told her the same thing," Maman interjected. "When she clears up some of her current projects, she's going to spend a few weeks with us on the Riviera."

"That sounds nicer than dreary old London," Julia said.

"It is," Maman assured her.

"We'll come to the airport tomorrow to see you off," Julia said. "We should leave you; we've got work to do, guests to greet, safaris to run."

That evening we had the going away affair at the High Commission. It was difficult for me. Everyone was very nice, but I got tired of hearing commiserations and other platitudes. David was there, out of hospital, but still with a cast on his leg. I was not sure what to say to him, and I am certain that he had no idea what to say to me. I was partly pleased that he had escaped with only some injuries, but I was also angry that he had survived and Ian had not. I suppose David would at some time have to deal with the survivor guilt that comes when one is spared from a catastrophe. The High Commissioner was fulsome in his praise of Ian, but I was sure that Ian would be replaced by someone else soon enough and then shunted off into the annals of the history of the legation. I was pleased by the number of people who had good things to say about Ian. I know I had him on a pedestal and to me he was as near perfect as another person can be, but it seemed he was as nice to everyone else. We stayed until the end, if would not do for the guest of honour to slink off part way through the proceedings, then we were dropped off back at the Norfolk by one of the drivers from the High Commission.

"I'm glad that's over," I commented to Maman and Portia.

"I can imagine," Maman said. "A nightcap?"

"I think so," I said. We went to the lounge and ordered a brandy each and then just sat and contemplated life.

"Will you come back?" Portia asked.

"After a while," I said. "I think too soon and it would be too hard, but, yes, I will come back one day, if only to put flowers on Ian's grave."

"You didn't want him to be buried in England?" Portia asked.

"No," I said. "He's an African, if there had been a way to do this in Mount Darwin, I would have done, but that's not a possibility, so he can stay here in Kenya, it's still Africa, even if it's not Rhodesia."

"Do you want us to stay with you in London for a while?" Maman asked.

"Please," I said. "I keep thinking I can manage, but then something comes along that reminds me of Ian and I can't help crying."

"I'm sure that will be true for a while," Maman said. "I remember when Claudette was killed, it was quite a while before I could even go into her room. But I finally did, and I remembered the times we had had and what fun she had been when we were growing up."

"What was she like?" I asked.

"My big sister," Maman said. "She was adventurous, she wanted to try everything, you are very like her, if she had lived through the War, she would probably be running for president now."

"Is France ready for a woman in the presidency?" I wondered.

"I don't think so," Maman said. "But that would not have stopped Claudette from running. She was fierce, when we were small, she would get into fights with the boys in the neighbourhood who would tease us, and most of the time she would win. She looked like you, you know that from the pictures Mémère had."

"What do we do tomorrow before the flight?" I asked.

"Is there anything you want to do?" Maman asked.

"I'd like to go and say goodbye to Ian," I said.

"We can do that," Maman agreed.

The following day we did go out to the cemetery and there was Ian's grave, not yet grown over, but still with freshly dug soil. We had put a simple marker there just to say who it was.

"Well, Ian," I said. "I'm leaving today, not sure when I might come back, but I know you'll be with me no matter where I am. You know I love you and I know that you loved me, I'll try not to get too maudlin, and to get on with my life. Do you have any advice for me?" I listened for a reply and heard the wind in the trees, a kite overhead and hadedas nearby. It was peaceful there at the cemetery and perhaps that was the message from Ian, be at peace. There was more, the hadedas were busy foraging for things to eat and busily going about their lives, oblivious to all else, even us. Thinking about it, that was the message from Ian, be like the hadedas, go on with life, and mix and mingle with the flock.

"Thank you, Maman," I said. "Ian told me to get on with my life and be at peace. He also told me to spend time with you and Portia and with James and Charlize."

"Good," Maman said. "Is there anything else?"

"No," I said. "I'm finished here, this part of my life has ended, it's time now to create a new life."

"Shall we go?" Maman asked. "When is your friend Julia picking us up?"

"About nine-thirty," I said. "That will give us plenty of time at the airport before the flight goes."

"So, we have time for afternoon tea?" Maman asked.

"We do," I confirmed.

We had a leisurely tea, then packed, bathed and had a light supper before Julia came to collect us.

"All ready?" Julia asked as she met us in the lobby of the hotel.

"All ready," I confirmed. Julia had brought a couple of her own staff and another Land Rover for the luggage, not that there was that much of it, she just wanted comfort. She had our luggage stowed then ushered us to her Land Rover. The drive to the airport was quite short and it seemed we were there in no time. Julia instructed her staff to take our luggage to the British Airways desk, where we joined them, tickets and passports in hand.

"You're leaving us Dr Hartley," Alison, the British Airways ground agent said.

"Sadly," I agreed. "But I'll be back one day."

"I hope so," Alison said. She came from behind her counter and gave me a big hug. "Stay well," she said.

"Thank you," was all I could think of saying. Alison had looked after me for a few years now and had seen me flit back and forth to London.

"I have your seats for you," she said. "And these are your luggage claims."

"Thank you for all your help over the years," I said.

"It had been my pleasure," she said. "I'll see you on the plane before you leave, enjoy the flight, and do come back one day."

"I will," I promised. We passed through immigration and there I was greeted by Mr Dett, he who had first greeted us when we had arrived.

"Dr Hartley," he said. "It has been my pleasure to know you and your husband while you were with us here. I hope you will come back and see us one day."

"Thank you, Mr Dett," I said. "This is my mother, Brigitte Barclay and our very close friend Portia Harding."

"A pleasure to meet you both," he said. "Please look after Dr Hartley for me, I will miss her, as I miss Ian."

"I will," Maman promised.

We waited, we boarded and made ourselves comfortable and we did see Alison one more time, when she came in board with the passenger manifest and the rest of the documents.

"*Kwa heri*, Fiona," she said.

"*Kwa heri*, Alison," I replied. She deplaned and the door was shut and the stairs pulled away and after what seemed an eternity the engines were started and we were on our way. Leaving at almost midnight meant that all I could see of Nairobi was lights, which I was quite disappointed in, I would have liked one more glimpse of Nairobi and Kenya as we wended our way north. So, this was it, I was leaving Kenya for good, if I came back it would be as a visitor, not as a resident. So much had happened in the few years we had lived in Nairobi, so this was a momentous day, to be leaving not knowing when I might be back, but a moment to recall and remember, almost as momentous as the day we landed in Nairobi for the first time.

www.ingramcontent.com/pod-product-compliance
Lightning Source LLC
Chambersburg PA
CBHW071111250626
47159CB00002B/697